THE
LAKE
HOUSE

BOOKS BY LORI FOSTER

The Guest Cottage
Too Much Temptation
Never Too Much
Unexpected
Say No to Joe?
The Secret Life of Bryan
When Bruce Met Cyn
Just a Hint—Clint
Jamie
Murphy's Law
Jude's Law

ANTHOLOGIES

In Bloom
The Two of Us
Love Comes in Small Packages
The Watson Brothers
Yule Be Mine
Give it Up

Published by Kensington Publishing Corp.`

THE LAKE HOUSE

LORI FOSTER

kensingtonbooks.com

KENSINGTON BOOKS are published by

Kensington Publishing Corp.
900 Third Ave.
New York, NY 10022

All Kensington titles, imprints, and distributed lines are available at special quantity discounts for bulk purchases for sales promotion, premiums, fund-raising, educational, or institutional use. Special book excerpts or customized printings can also be created to fit specific needs. For details, write or phone the office of the Kensington Special Sales Manager: Attn. Special Sales Department. Kensington Publishing Corp., 900 Third Ave., New York, NY 10022. Phone: 1-800-221-2647.

KENSINGTON and the K with book logo Reg. US Pat. & TM Off.

Library of Congress Control Number: On file

ISBN: 978-1-4967-5237-6
First Kensington Hardcover Edition: June 2026

ISBN: 978-1-4967-5238-3 (trade)

ISBN: 978-1-4967-5239-0 (ebook)

10 9 8 7 6 5 4 3 2 1

Printed in the United States of America

The authorized representative in the EU for product safety and compliance
is eucomply OU, Parnu mnt 139b-14, Apt 123
Tallinn, Berlin 11317, hello@eucompliancepartner.com

THE LAKE HOUSE

CHAPTER 1

Brogan Rafferty had a vague idea of how life should be. He hadn't ever lived it, but in his mind a picturesque image always formed: family, a small cozy home, people working together in love and loyalty . . . an ephemeral dream he'd never been able to grasp. He'd given up wanting it a long time ago.

But now, everything was different.

As he drove through Bramble, Kentucky, the old image materialized. Granted, the sun had just set and a rose hue bathed the houses, streets, and even the numerous trees, making everything prettier than it might otherwise be.

What really struck him was the quiet. There were no shouts, no sirens, nothing breaking—or blowing up. The few people he saw—walking together or sitting on porches—spoke quietly while smiling.

Driving slowly, he made note of the old-fashioned houses with vividly painted trim and bright front doors, lights shining from the windows. Unlike the settings familiar to him, no two houses were the same. The styles, sizes, and colors all varied.

Porch swings and window boxes filled with spring flowers were a popular theme. Birds and squirrels played in massive trees. Brogan came to a stop when a deer bolted out in front of him, froze, then leaped away to disappear into the foliage. Wildlife was always a good sign of peace and tranquility. "This is the right place for us, Sugar. I can feel it."

From the back seat, the baby made sucking noises as she feasted on her fist. Hopefully, he'd find the right address soon. She needed to be fed, and probably needed a fresh diaper, too.

Of all the things he'd survived in his lifetime—first as an emancipated youth living on his own, later getting through BUD/S and all the specialized training that followed, and then barely surviving an ambush and life-threatening injuries in northern Africa—caring for his tiny, precious cargo was the most challenging, and by far the most rewarding.

The mid-May weather was pleasantly warm, and spring rains had turned the grass and trees a lush green. Wildflowers grew in patches along the wooded side of the road, and occasionally on the other side, where he noted a few houses.

The farther he drove, the fewer houses he saw and the more natural the landscape became, until the road ended in a T and he had to choose left or right. Shortly after turning, he located the lake house.

The sight of the tiny place, set near the water and well-tended, immediately warmed him. The glow of the sunset reflected over the rippling surface of the lake. All around them, flickering fireflies began to appear. Only a few at first, then more and more.

Who knew something as simple as fireflies could envelop him in a sense of rightness? He wasn't a man to indulge indecision. He evaluated, planned, and then acted. The fact that he was now responsible for such a vulnerable little life had made everything different. These days, he constantly second-guessed himself, but this, the decision to come here, the plans he'd put into place, they were right. They had to be.

This was the perfect starting point for a new and better life.

He would not fail.

Gravel crunched as he pulled his black SUV into the driveway next to an older pale blue minivan. The baby was fussing in earnest now. Brogan would rather listen to his own bones breaking than hear that tiny baby girl cry. Nothing shredded his heart the way she did.

After hurriedly parking, he rushed to the back door, opened it, and reached for her. Getting her out of the car seat took him a moment, and then he had to grab up the diaper bag.

She was soaking wet, which meant his shirt was now soaked, too.

Fortunately, it was a warm evening, though he wasn't sure if it'd be too cool for a baby with a wet bottom.

"Shh, easy now, Sugar. I got ya." Thank God he had a bottle ready to go. One armed, he opened the back of the SUV, shook out a blanket, and settled her on her back. "Gotta get ya dry first."

"Excuse me," came a soft, quiet voice.

Brogan glanced up and spotted a slim blonde on the walkway. Keeping his palm on the baby's belly so she couldn't roll, he slowly straightened.

Pixie Nolan. Yes, he was here to see her—it was the main reason Bramble had seemed fated to be his new home. He'd thought to have a day or two, perhaps a week to figure out how he wanted to approach her.

Time to improvise.

Her gaze went over him, and when she looked up again, her blue eyes were comically wide. "You're Mr. Rafferty?"

"Yes, ma'am. Cort Easton is expecting me."

Though she continued to stare, her smile was shy and sweet. "Cort is also my landlord. His flight plans changed, and he and his wife had to leave a day early for a vacation. He asked me to give you the keys when you arrived."

Unexpected, but still, he could handle it. "Thank you."

"I, um . . ." She laughed at herself. "Sorry, I don't mean to gawk, but you're really tall."

True, enough. At six-foot-five, he stood above many people. "Might seem so with you being so . . ." Calling her short might be insulting, so he substituted, "Petite." She couldn't be more than a few inches over five feet, with a delicate build that made it difficult to believe she was a mother.

"I'm Pixie Nolan."

He knew that already because he'd seen a small black-and-white photo that hadn't done her justice. "Nice to meet you." When the baby gave a piercing cry, he said, "And this noisy bundle is Shayna Raye. If you'll excuse me, I need to tend to her before she wakes up the entire town."

Pixie stood there, illuminated by the moon and the golden glow of a porch light. Her nearness caused an unusual restriction in his chest that limited his airflow, as if he'd just taken a blast of artillery fire, feeling like that odd suspended moment in time before a man realized he'd been hit.

It was the anticipation, he decided.

So much hinged on building an association with her. It was what the baby deserved, what was expected, and yet it was something he'd never had.

Sucked that he knew almost nothing about blood families. All he knew was brotherhood. Hopefully, that would be enough.

Her brows came together in a puzzled frown. "You have a baby?"

A rhetorical question, obviously. "I've got my hands full here, so my attention is needed. I've got the hang of diaper changes, but not so much in the back of my SUV."

She inched closer and peeked around him. "Oh, yes." With a light laugh, she said, "I've been there, done that, so I understand. Here, let me help." She moved to the other side of him and retrieved a diaper from the bag, effortlessly opening it. "I'll hold the bottle if you want to handle the rest."

Damn, but he could smell her, a light scent of flowers and sunshine and possibly baby powder. The restriction in his chest increased. "You think it's too cool out here in the night air for me to swap out her clothes?"

"It's a warm night, so she'd be fine, but would you rather change her inside?" She nodded at his shirt. "You're already wet."

"True enough." As he spoke, Shayna decided to wail again. "It was a long drive and she's getting fussy."

"Long drives make me cranky, too," she said, and then, "I didn't realize you had a daughter. Cort only mentioned one person."

"Is it a problem?"

"No, of course not."

"I'm glad to hear it." Carefully, Brogan gathered up the baby, settling her against his chest and getting the bottle back in her mouth without her getting out a single additional wail. He felt triumphant.

"Good job," Pixie praised as she folded the wet blanket he'd used, wrapped up the sopping diaper, and grabbed the diaper bag. "Come on. I'll show you the house. You'll love it." As she led him to the front door, she said, "I lived here with my son until recently. Actually, I'd have been happy to stay here, but Andy is so active now, Cort insisted he needed more room. I'm in the guest cottage just up the street." She tipped her head to the left. "Over that way is where Cort and Marlow live. You'll like them. Everyone around here does."

A dozen questions came to Brogan, but he tamped down his curiosity. If he got too nosy, he might offend her. "You like to fish?"

She stepped into the house and moved aside. "No, but Cort does. Marlow and I just enjoy the sunrises and sunsets."

"Go boating or swimming?"

"Not much." As if confiding a secret, she said, "There are things in the water. Big fish. Occasionally, a snake. Snapping turtles."

He couldn't hold back his grin. "Nothing that would hurt you."

"Trust me, I've heard it all, but I still choose to stay out of the deeper water. My son and I sometimes sit in the shallow water at the sandy beach area, where he can play. I always put a life preserver on him, though of course I still can't take my eyes off him."

"Where's your son now?" For many reasons, Brogan was interested in meeting the boy. Pixie didn't know it, but it was because of her son that he was here.

"It's close to his bedtime, so he's with my friend Gloria." Again confiding in him, she said, "When I came here a year ago, everyone welcomed me. Even better, they all fell in love with Andy. I'm never short of babysitters when I need one, though I don't like to leave him very often."

Was that a hint? "Guess I'm holding you up." He should have realized. "If you want me to sign something, show some ID, we can take care of that real fast so you can get home."

"No, it's fine." She smiled at Shayna. "Babies first, right?" Walking again, she said, "This is the sitting room; down that hall is the single bedroom and a bathroom. Everything you need is already there. Blankets, pillows, towels. Even soap and shampoo, though you probably have your own."

He had a small overnight kit with a toothbrush and toothpaste, shaving gear, and soap. Toiletries were not, and never had been, his priority.

"I have the paperwork here in the kitchen."

Everything about the place was miniature. Small rooms, small furniture, and a kitchen that was no more than a single row of cabinets over a sink and stove, with a narrow pantry and apartment-sized refrigerator. Good thing he was used to living lean.

The chairs at the two-seater corner table didn't look sturdy enough to support a man of his size.

Pixie either didn't notice his scrutiny or assumed he'd love the place as much as she claimed to. And honestly, it didn't matter. He needed a safe, clean space for the baby. Nothing more.

She was his priority. Her comfort and security mattered more than anything else.

"There's a stack washer/dryer in the utility closet." She looked around as if seeing the tiny house again for the first time. "I know it's a tight space, but when I lived here, it just meant less to keep up with. Babies, as I'm sure you know, require the lion's share of your attention."

Brogan leaned back on the counter, set the empty bottle in the sink, and put Shayna to his shoulder so he could burp her. While he gently rubbed her back in a circular motion, he agreed with her assessment. "Logic doesn't apply, right? You'd think a tiny person with a smaller appetite, wearing only itty-bitty clothes and sleeping most of the time, would require less care, but somehow it's the opposite." His little angel belched, squirmed a moment, and then got comfortable in the crook of his neck.

Christ, he loved her, more than he'd known was possible.

"Around-the-clock care," Pixie said softly.

"Not that I'm complaining." Never. Having the baby's care entrusted to him was the greatest gift he'd ever received in his entire life. "It's fascinating, though."

When Pixie grinned, he didn't just see it, he felt it, clear down to his soul. Not even to himself did he want to sound corny, but she was like sunshine breaking through darkness. The magic of laughter after hearing so many broken cries.

She didn't know it, but she was an open door when every other exit was blocked.

He hoped she'd be okay with his plans. Everything he'd read about her made it seem possible.

"You might want to get her out of those wet clothes before she falls asleep again. You don't want to deal with diaper rash."

Of course, Pixie didn't know that she'd just stepped on a topic about as explosive as a land mine. He breathed a little harder, remembering things better left forgotten. He had Shayna now and he was determined she'd never suffer another ill.

Getting his mouth to smile wasn't easy, but he forced it, adding a lighthearted truth. "This girl sleeps like a champ. I've changed her, and once even bathed her, while she dozed through it."

"It's amazing how trusting babies can be."

It was especially incredible that this baby, after what she'd been through, could trust him—but she did. His voice emerged as a rasp. "When they're feeling secure. When they have reason to trust."

She tipped her head, studying him curiously. "As all babies should."

Glad that she shared that sentiment, he nodded. "Hundred percent."

"Do you have a crib for her in your car?"

"A Moses basket, though I'll probably need to get her a crib soon. She's started rolling over, and once she starts, she wants to keep going."

With a quiet laugh, Pixie asked, "Clean baby blankets? Another bottle ready?"

It amused him to see her shift into mom-mode. He could take exception to her question, which suggested he couldn't handle things, but obviously she loved kids and knew what she was doing. "Got all that," he said. "Though I'll prepare a few more bottles tonight." Worries caught up to him and he admitted in a low voice, "Sometimes she'll almost sleep through the night, like five hours or so, and it scares me. I almost preferred it when she was up every couple of hours." It gave him the chance to hold her, to know she was okay. To tell her over and over that he'd never let her down, would never leave her alone, that he'd protect her always.

Reaching out, Pixie brushed the back of one finger over Shayna's silky hair. "No other kids?"

He shook his head. "I wasn't here for her until she was nearly two months old." Remembering felt like having a part of his guts removed—without anesthesia. "I'm military and I was away . . ." *Dying.* Or at least that was what he'd wanted at the time.

To be left alone to quietly die. To join his brothers. To escape the gnawing guilt of surviving—when they hadn't.

Then he'd gotten the news about a half sister he barely knew, the niece he'd never met, and God, how it had invigorated him with purpose. He had a reason to go on. One hell of a reason.

"Cort was military, too," she shared. "A Marine recon sniper. He's considered a hometown hero around here."

"Once a Marine, always a Marine," Brogan replied. He felt the same way. The military was now in his blood, the better part of him, the survival instinct that kept him going—and thank God it had, since Shayna needed him now. "As a SEAL, I had the honor of working with a few of those guys."

"You're a SEAL?" Awe sounded in her voice.

Damn it, why had he said that? He *never* talked about his service. She'd taken him by surprise, just tossing out Cort's rank like that. She and Cort must be close for him to have shared it with her. Instead of answering her question, Brogan changed the subject. "What do you need me to sign?"

Pixie immediately got the hint. She took a seat at the table and turned the paper toward him. "Cort said you already sent the down payment and the prorated rent for the first month, so all I need is your ID, and then if you'll sign here, I'll give you the basic rundown and leave you with the keys."

Brogan knew he'd chased her off, but he'd tackle that issue another time. Right now, he needed to unload the car and get Shayna settled.

He held the baby close and withdrew his driver's license from his wallet.

Pixie was quick to confirm his ID. After he'd signed the paper and she'd put it in her purse, she sent a worried glance toward the baby. "Do you need help bringing a few things inside?"

"I've got it, thanks."

"You're sure? I wouldn't mind . . ."

She had her face turned up to his while she nervously twirled two fingers in her long pale hair. Damn, he wanted to spill his guts, to tell her the important role she could play in Shayna's life. Now was definitely not the time, though, not if he wanted full success. "I appreciate the offer, Pixie. Really, thank you. Right now, I think I just want to get my bearings."

Still, she hesitated.

He smiled. "I promise, we'll be fine for tonight. How about tomorrow you stop by and give me that rundown, maybe tell me a little about the town and where to find what?"

Nodding, she said, "Sure. Will noon work?" Without waiting for his agreement, she said, "Emergency numbers are on the fridge. I'm going to add my number real quick, just in case something comes up." Using the pen she'd given him to sign the four-month agreement, she jotted a number at the bottom of a long list that included police, fire department, hospital, and food delivery. As she hurriedly turned away to head for the door, she said, "Remote is with the TV. Outside lights are automatic, dusk to dawn. Hot water doesn't last too long, which is something I found out the hard way, so you might want to shower before doing any laundry. Oh, and Cort likes to make sure the basics are already in the kitchen cupboards, and some necessities are in the fridge. If you need anything else before noon tomorrow, just let me know."

After saying all that, she practically clamped her mouth shut and rushed off as if being chased.

In case he'd somehow made her uncomfortable, he trailed more slowly behind her. The last thing he wanted from her was wariness.

"See you tomorrow," he said as she all but jogged to her van.

With a careless wave, she got in the vehicle and left.

Brogan stood there with the baby in his arms and watched as her taillights went down the road, then turned into another driveway. She was nearby, yet there was some property between them. A nice arrangement.

Presumptuous as it might be, he already imagined Pixie in their future, his and Shayna's. She had a good heart; that much was clear. She wouldn't deny them.

The only problem might be Cort. Pixie was obviously close to the man. Because Cort had a military background, he was bound to be protective. That meant he wouldn't like Brogan's plans.

The baby stirred, rubbing her button nose against his shirt, stretching a bit, then settling in again. He decided he'd deal with the issue of Cort when it became necessary. He wouldn't let anything stand in his way.

"Now," Brogan said, his palm moving up and down the baby's narrow back. "It's time for you, Sugar—and our fresh start." He brushed his mouth over her downy crown, inhaled her sweet, comforting scent, and headed back inside.

It was time to get started.

Pixie kept remembering how bizarrely she'd acted last night. Chatty when she usually wasn't. Bossy about his baby, as if he hadn't already proven his competence. She'd been ridiculous.

A call from Cort saved her from further self-castigation. She set Andy in his playpen and answered the phone by saying, "Aren't you supposed to be off having fun?"

"We are," he countered. "Marlow told me to say hello."

"Hello to you both."

"I just wanted to check whether the renter showed up."

"Yes, he's all checked in. Did you know he has a baby?"

After the briefest pause, Cort said, "I wasn't aware, but it's not a problem."

Bull. Cort researched everyone who stayed at the lake house. More so, now that she and Marlow lived nearby. "Did you know he's a Navy SEAL?"

"Yes, it was in the background info he gave in his rental application. But how do you know?"

"He told me."

Another pause. "How exactly did that come up?"

She gave Cort a quick rerun of the conversation, then explained, "I think he wanted me to know why he hadn't met his daughter sooner. Does the military really keep fathers from being present for births?"

"Not deliberately, but being on active duty can make it tough to get away."

"So, like, you think he was on a mission or something?"

Cort exhaled. "Word of warning, hon, most military guys don't want to talk about their experiences—at least that's true of the Marines and SEALs I've known. It'd be best if you put a lid on your curiosity."

"Okay." Guilt flushed her face, and she fanned a hand at herself. "I didn't mean to pry."

"No accusations from me. I know you, remember? Just cluing you in, in case you see the guy again."

She bit her lip, then admitted, "I'll see him again shortly. He had some questions about the town. You know, where to eat and shop, touristy stuff, things like that."

The silence was damning.

And this time, it got to her. *"What?"*

"You're a smart woman, Pixie, and a good judge of character. I'll just say to tread carefully, okay?"

"You don't like the idea of me being alone with him?" Funny, but she hadn't even considered the risk. He was a renter. Like her, he obviously loved his child. Like Cort, he had a military background. "Andy and his daughter will be there, too."

"Right. Just keep alert, okay? With Marlow and me gone, you're there alone. In fact, I might ask Herman to keep an eye on things."

"You mean keep an eye on me." She rolled her eyes even as she smiled. It was nice to have people concerned about her and Andy. That hadn't always been the case. Now that she had such terrific people in her life, she would never take them for granted.

"That too," Cort said.

"I was going to suggest that Brogan try out his food anyway." Herman ran the Dry Frog Tavern, and his burgers, pizzas, and appetizers were, in her opinion, the very best. Plus, the tavern gave newcomers a great feel for the town, and Brogan could meet a lot of locals there. "But, Cort?"

"Yes?"

"Thank you for caring."

"It's what family does. Hey, Marlow wants to say hi. Hang on."

Marlow was nowhere near as quiet and contained as Cort. "Tell me everything."

Laughing, Pixie teased, "Everything about what?"

"Not what, *who*. The new guy. I could tell by Cort's posture that something's going on."

As she paced around the room, Pixie kept her eye on Andy. He sat in the playpen, stacking, unstacking, and rearranging his building blocks. The sight of him never failed to make her heart feel full.

Because this was Marlow, and Pixie could tell her anything, she whispered, "He's gorgeous, but also a dad, and I don't think he's married, but he hasn't actually said, so for now—really, I mean it, Marlow—I'm just being neighborly."

"Say that all you want, but I hear it in your voice. You're interested, and I'm cheering you on."

"Hello? Did you hear a word I said?"

"I heard every word, smart-ass, and I know exactly what you're thinking. But that whole debacle was a lifetime ago, and since then you haven't shown the slightest interest in men. They're not all bad, you know. They're not all him."

"Yes," Pixie quietly admitted. "I know." Cort was the perfect example. He was a dedicated husband to Marlow, a loyal friend to Pixie, and an amazing protector for Andy. "I guess . . . I am slightly interested?"

"You are."

She was. After the debacle, as Marlow had put it, Pixie had sworn off men forever. Lived the disaster, learned from it, never planned to repeat it again.

That she'd been involved with a married man, even if she hadn't known he was married, still shamed her. But good things had come out of that awful ordeal. She had Andy now, she'd met Marlow and Cort, and she'd found her independence. Good things. Wonderful things. Yet she never again wanted to be that naïve, or that gullible.

She'd met men she liked as friends, many of them in the small town where she now lived. But the very idea of risking her heart again . . . Well, it terrified her.

Somehow, with Brogan, she'd forgotten her fear.

"I think it's that he's so good with his daughter."

"Always a great sign," Marlow agreed. "So here's what you should do."

In the background, Cort said, "I already told her what to do. Caution, honey. We don't know the man yet."

Pixie grinned. "Tell Cort to enjoy his vacation instead of worrying about me. I promise, I won't give him any reason to worry."

In a whisper, Marlow said, "It's good for him to worry every now and then. Keeps his instincts sharp."

Cort said, "They're razor sharp, and you know it."

"He's still listening," Pixie informed Marlow, in case she hadn't figured that out.

"I'm overruling him. When you see Brogan again, ask him flat out if he's married. If he doesn't have a quick, ready answer, then you'll know not to trust him."

Cort's voice was louder now, indicating he'd moved close to the phone. "Liars always have their stories ready. Go with your gut, Pixie, but I can tell you, a military man won't appreciate being pinned down. As much as I love my wife, and as intelligent as she is, she's wrong about this."

"Men always think women are wrong."

"A truism? Really, Marlow."

Since Pixie was used to the way they worked things out, she took a seat near Andy and just listened in. It was awesome that Marlow never hesitated to speak her mind, and Cort always shared his perspective. She'd never seen them actually mad at each other. Irked a few times, sure. They had their disagreements. But there was never any doubt about their love.

If she ever did have another romantic relationship—and Pixie doubted she would—she'd want it to be as open and loving as what Marlow and Cort shared.

In his usual calm tone, which sometimes riled Marlow, Cort said, "I'll admit, with most people you're spot-on. But we're talking an elite military operator and that's a whole different breed."

"Hmm," Marlow said. "You could have a point."

Pixie heard the sound of a smooch, and then, "I do."

"Don't get cocky."

"Wouldn't think of it."

Laughing out loud, Pixie asked, "Are you two done debating my next move?"

"I guess so, but I want you to keep me posted, okay? I agree with Cort about using caution. The new guy will be around for the entire summer, so you have plenty of time to see how it goes."

"I approve that plan," Cort said. "Now come on, Marlow. We're running late."

Pixie glanced at the time on her phone. "Oops. Actually, I am, too. Thanks for calling, and have fun."

"Love you, sister."

She and Marlow weren't actually sisters, but hearing that endearment from a woman she admired so much never failed to affect Pixie. Meaning it from her heart, she whispered, "Love you, too. Both of you."

The second she disconnected, Andy reached out to show her a block. "Boo."

"Yes, blue. You're such a smart little guy." She picked up a red block shaped like a car, and asked, "What color is this?"

"Car." He grinned, showing off small white teeth.

Pixie lifted him out of the playpen for a hug. "Red car." Then she wrinkled her nose. "Let's get your diaper changed and then take a walk."

He jumped, smacking the top of his head into her chin. For her, it smarted. He barely noticed. "Wok, wok, wok!"

"You do love to be outside, don't you?" Pixie led him to the bedroom. This house, where Marlow had lived before marrying Cort, was bigger than the lake house, but still had only one bedroom. She could easily make the dining room into a bedroom, and Cort had suggested it, but she wasn't ready to have Andy on the other side of the house, where she couldn't hear his every move.

Honestly, he might need to be in his teens before she was ready for that. Glad that she didn't have to worry about it yet, she got what she needed from the closet, then lifted Andy to the changing table. After noticing that he'd gotten a little milk on his shirt, she decided to change his clothes, too.

She couldn't—wouldn't—primp over her own looks. Really, there was no point. But as a mother, she wanted her son to look his best.

While she hummed to Andy, her mind wandered to Brogan.

She guessed him to be thirty or so. With his bearing, the way he carried himself, she should have known right away he was military. Cort had the same presence about him, a calm confidence that drew people to him.

It was a remarkable sight to see a man so large and solid, with such a rock-hard physique, oh-so-gently cradling a tiny baby girl in his arms.

When she'd mentioned diaper rash, his gray eyes held a flash of strong emotion. On a lesser man, it might have looked like pain, but Brogan wasn't that easy to read. Pixie badly wanted to understand what he was thinking and feeling. Was it something about himself, the baby, or an experience they might have shared?

It would have been better if Cort had been here to get Brogan settled. Not that she wasn't happy to do it for him. She owed Cort and Marlow her life. Without them, she didn't know what she would have done.

It had taken her a year, but she could finally recall their first meeting without feeling smothering shame. She'd been at an all-time low, rock bottom with a baby to care for and nowhere to go, no way to survive.

They'd not only offered assistance, but they'd also accepted her, befriended her, and introduced her to a better way of life.

Because of them, she was able to be the type of mother Andy deserved. She could respect herself, and she was largely independent.

That meant she owed them everything.

For a year, she'd put her entire focus on being a mom, paying back her debts, and proving she could be more—more than the girl who had been duped, the girl who'd screwed up and ruined her life. Not once had she given any man a thought, at least not with any romantic interest.

Marlow had truly become a sister of her heart, and that made Cort a big brother. Family. Until they'd taken her in, that essential element had been absent from her life.

"Wok," Andy demanded, squirming to get up.

"Shoes," she told him, lifting him down to sit on the bed and quickly getting socks and sneakers on his pudgy feet. She managed, even though he draped himself over her, giggling and playing with her hair.

She playfully wrestled him down on the bed and blew raspberries on his tummy. Soon they were both laughing.

He wiggled away from her and took off, shouting, "Wok!"

Hoping he wouldn't bonk his head or run into anything, Pixie ran to catch up. Once she had him, she grabbed her keys and the diaper bag. With the stroller packed, they were on their way to the lake house only a few minutes later.

At fourteen months old now, Andy loved being outside and often kicked his legs the entire time he was in the stroller. He also enjoyed hearing her sing, so she did, softly when she was in public so no one else would hear.

In her opinion, he was an incredibly beautiful little boy. His blond hair often stuck up in adorable spikes around his head, like morning bedhead that could never be tamed. His light blue eyes were sweetly curious, and he was forever grinning about everything. Since learning to walk, he was always in a hurry, but he also enjoyed riding in the stroller.

And he dearly loved practicing new words, more so every day. She considered Andy extremely verbal for his age, but others reinforced that, too.

"Squir," he said, pointing to a squirrel that scampered across the yard and into a tree. "Bird. Bird."

"A lot of squirrels and birds," she agreed; then she peeked around the stroller canopy to make certain he was protected from the bright afternoon sunshine. Only his little sneakers-covered feet showed, but living near a lake meant diligence with sunscreen.

Because they were near the lake house, she stopped singing, worried that her new neighbor might hear her. The house looked quiet, but the big black SUV was still in the driveway, and she trusted Brogan would be there for their meeting.

"Sing, sing, sing," Andy demanded in his happy, high-pitched voice.

To distract him, she asked, "Do you want to meet a new friend?"

"Fend."

That sounded like agreement to her. Rather than struggle with the stroller over the gravel driveway, she cut through the lawn and went up to the front door. It opened as she was turning around to drag the stroller over the single step to the small porch.

Brogan stood there in the entry looking like a top-caliber male model—for a fitness gym. For a second, she went blank. The man made a plain gray T-shirt and worn, faded jeans look *really* good. Then she caught herself and smiled.

Chapter 2

"You heard us coming?" Pixie asked, already horrified by the idea that he might have heard her singing.

With a shake of his head, he said, "I tested the doorbell last night. It's loud."

He'd tested the doorbell?

"I didn't want it to wake Shayna—she's down for a nap—so I was watching for you."

Andy shouted, "Fend, fend, fend."

"Friend," she interpreted for Brogan. "I hope you don't mind that I brought my son."

"Of course not." He pushed the door open, bent, and lifted the stroller through the doorway as if it, with Andy inside, was no more cumbersome than a basket. "Come on in." As he spoke, he crouched down to smile at Andy. "Hello, friend."

Andy reached for him, but he was buckled in.

Brogan offered one finger to Andy's little hand, and asked, "Okay if I get him out?"

"Um . . . sure." She tucked her hair behind her ears, a little incredulous that this big, buff stranger would be so welcoming to her son. Andy sure liked him, though, and Pixie wondered if it was Brogan's composure. He was used to that calm assuredness from Cort and maybe felt the similarity.

"You can close the door," he said as he deftly opened the straps and then put his hands on Andy's middle. "Okay to lift you out, big guy?"

"Out." Andy leaned forward and fisted his hands in the shoulders of Brogan's shirt.

Smiling, Brogan stood with her son in his arms. Andy grinned and said, "Fend."

Okay, settle down, heart.

It didn't, of course. Nope, it just thundered even harder. It was one thing to see Brogan as an attractive male specimen.

It was another to see Andy smiling at him, accepting him as if he'd known him forever.

"He knows a lot of words for his age," Brogan remarked.

"He really does. I think it's because he has so many adults talking to him all the time. He gets a lot of attention."

"Nothing wrong with that." Brogan did the guy thing of lifting Andy high—and since he was so tall, it was really high—until Andy laughed; then he lowered him again and, still holding him, asked Pixie, "Want to sit in the kitchen? That is, if those spindly little chairs will hold me."

"They hold Cort, so you'll be fine." Still a little dazed by her new awareness of him, Pixie trailed Brogan to the kitchen. "Oh, you have Shayna in here, too."

The baby, dressed in a T-shirt, diaper, and little fuzzy socks, was in her basket. She looked cozy with her face smooshed to the side, a light cotton blanket clutched in one fist.

"I always keep her close," Brogan said. "Shouldn't I?"

"I guess . . . I mean . . . Why do you?"

"I wasn't sure I'd hear her if she was in the bedroom."

The smile snuck up on her. "Babies have a way of being heard."

A small, worried frown pinched his thick brows together. "Thing is, I don't want her to cry."

Yup, there went her heart again. Pounding hard, and then possibly melting.

It didn't even help that Brogan wasn't looking at her. His attention went back and forth between the children, and he noticed right off that Andy was staring fixedly at this other small person, his big blue eyes unblinking.

"That's a baby, bud. A younger baby, so I bet she looks itty-bitty to you. Want to see?"

Andy hugged Brogan's neck, but kept his gaze on Shayna.

"Andy?" Pixie said. "We have to be quiet, okay?"

Andy replied, "Shh," making Brogan grin again.

"You're an engaging little dude, you really are." He walked closer to Shayna, but once he knelt down, Andy turned and shyly hid against him. "No problem, my little friend. I get it. Infants can be intimidating, right?" He stood again and stepped away, all but ignoring Pixie.

Andy immediately peered over his shoulder, whispering with quiet awe, "Baby."

"That's right. You're a smart one, aren't you?" As if he suddenly remembered Pixie, he turned to her. "Hey, sorry."

She knew she probably had the oddest expression on her face, but she couldn't seem to get it together. She continued to stare at Brogan and her son, and suddenly she wanted to cry. Or laugh. It was a toss-up which emotion might win.

His brows pinched again. "You okay?"

Pixie cleared her throat. "Yes, just taking it in." *What did that even mean?* "You're a natural."

The right side of his mouth kicked up. "A natural what?"

She drew a blank. "I mean . . . with kids."

"That'd be one hell of a compliment, for sure. I'm trying."

Her eyes widened. "FYI, Andy repeats everything."

Lifting a brow in confusion, he said, "Yeah?"

"You said *h-e-l-l.*"

This time, he laughed outright. "Sorry."

"Shh," Andy said.

That made Brogan laugh again. "It's okay. My little Sugar is a sleeping champion. I got lucky there, right?" He glanced at the clock. "She should wake up soon. Until then, we could have an earthquake, and she might sleep through it."

"She must be a very secure little girl."

His humor faded until he looked solemn. "I hope so." Gesturing at a seat, he asked, "Can I get you something to drink?"

"Thank you. Anything is fine."

"Coke? Water?"

"Coke would be good." Pixie took the chair and set the diaper bag on the floor beside her. "Andy, do you want your drink?"

He moved so quickly, Brogan had to juggle him, but he got him to the floor safely. "Give a man a warning, bud, why don't you?"

"Sorry, I should have told you that he moves like lightning."

"It's all good."

Once Andy had his special spill-proof cup, he moved closer to Shayna and squatted down for a look. Pixie started to tell him not to touch the baby, but Brogan waved her off.

"He's curious. It's okay."

She nodded, then said, "Easy, Andy. Be very gentle." She explained to Brogan, "He understands to be careful with kittens and puppies, and occasionally Cort lets him pet a fish."

Brogan grinned as he got out two colas.

"He hasn't been around any babies, though."

Unconcerned, he asked, "Do you want a glass and ice?"

"Out of the can is fine by me."

He rinsed hers under the tap, dried it with a paper towel, and popped it open before setting it on the table before her.

His, he just opened and took a big drink.

"Are you going to sit?" she asked. She was getting a crick in her neck from looking up at him.

After eyeing the chair dubiously, he eased into the seat, waited, and when it didn't collapse under him, relaxed.

Just then, Shayna stirred and made a sound. It startled Andy so much, he fell on his bottom, scampered back with a cry, and dropped his cup. In a panic, he crawled to Pixie. She hurriedly left her seat to scoop him up.

Calmly, Brogan got to his feet and retrieved the fallen cup. "She spooked you, didn't she, bud? I used to react almost the same way." He knelt down by the baby and gently smoothed his hand over her. "See? She's okay."

Andy wasn't convinced. He squeezed Pixie, stared at the baby, and then squeezed her again.

"Come closer," Brogan said to her. "Let him know it's okay."

Andy was loosening up a little, so she took a step forward. "You want to see?" she asked him.

He tucked his face into her neck.

"Let's give him a minute." Pixie patted his back.

Standing again, Brogan walked over to them. "You okay, bud?"

To her surprise, Andy twisted away from her and reached for Brogan. That hurt, especially when Brogan just naturally gathered the little boy into his arms.

"Holding you is a lot different, my man. You're a sturdy little guy, aren't you? Almost as big as your mama, but then she's a little thing, too." He turned so Andy could see the baby. "Look. She's moving again. I think her nap is coming to an end."

From the safety of Brogan's arms, Andy watched in clear fascination as Shayna stretched out her arms and legs, scrunched up her face, and then blinked open her eyes.

"Baby girl," Brogan crooned softly, going to her with Andy in his arms. "Did you sleep well?"

She yawned, blinked a few times, and smiled.

"Yeah, there's my girl." He knelt down, and Andy didn't seem to mind at all, now that he was secure in the big man's arms. "You want to touch her, bud? Here, look at this tiny foot. Amazing, right?" He lifted her little foot, bared by a sock that had fallen off, and pressed a kiss to it.

Andy grinned, leaned forward, and loudly kissed the air.

Then he offered his own foot to Brogan.

Laughing, Brogan kissed the top of his sneaker.

Once again, Pixie felt invisible, but she didn't mind. Watching the three of them was something of a revelation. She was seeing a new side of her son, one she hadn't experienced before. Plus, she was seeing men in a whole new way. Jerks, she was used to. Friendly men from the town, sure. Cort with all his protectiveness, she'd grown accustomed to and now appreciated.

But this, with Brogan. What did she even call it? Admiration? Intrigue? Interest? It was unlike anything she'd felt before, which she supposed made sense. Before, when she'd been drawn to men, she'd been simply herself, insecure and shy Pixie Nolan. A girl without aspirations, intent only on getting by, day to day. In many ways, lost. And obviously easy prey to a smooth liar and manipulator.

It was why she'd so easily fallen under Dylan's charm. It shamed her to remember the gullible, needy girl she used to be.

Now she was Pixie the mother, a best friend, member of a close community, and respected businesswoman. She was a woman who paid her own way and planned for her and her son's future. She had her priorities in a tidy row, starting with her son and branching out from there. Now she had reason to be proud.

Her world was entirely different, so she reasoned that her reactions and perspectives would be different, too.

Brogan glanced up at her. "I guess this party is taking place on the floor. Care to join us?"

Absurdly thrilled to be included at last, she left her seat and joined them. Andy pointed and said, "Baby."

"Yes, she's an adorable baby, isn't she?" Funnily enough, Shayna and Andy shared nearly the exact same shade of blond hair. His was longer, but she still had plenty. Pixie brushed a finger over the fair silky strands. "Do you ever put bows in her hair?"

Brogan gave her an incredulous look. "How? She doesn't have enough of it for that."

"They make little bows that attach without clips."

He frowned. "Attach how?"

"Nothing painful, I promise." She couldn't keep her grin at bay. "I would never suggest you do anything that—"

"Right. Sorry. I just . . ." He gave a dubious glance at Shayna's wispy locks. "Bows, huh?"

Everything about Brogan was somehow refreshing. "A headband would be cute, too."

In a teasing tone, he said, "You telling me no one will know she's a girl if I don't give her ribbons?"

Pixie huffed a laugh. "Of course not. She's beautiful either way. I was just curious. Because Andy's eyelashes are long, some people thought he was a girl. It didn't matter what he wore." Carefully, she slipped the tiny sock back on Shayna's foot. "When I was pregnant, I used to daydream about the things I'd buy my baby if I had endless funds. At the time, I didn't know whether I'd have a boy or a girl, so I looked at cute overalls and soft dresses, lacy socks and ball caps. And yes, sometimes ribbons."

"Were you disappointed to have a boy?"

She smiled at Andy. "The second I held him, I knew he was perfect. I've never known anything like that."

Brogan went quiet; then he stood. "Let's move this to the living room and more comfortable seats." He offered his hand.

For a mere second, Pixie hesitated; then she slipped her hand into his. She felt rough calluses and the heat of his palm as his hand entirely engulfed hers.

Even after he released her, the awareness stayed as if all her nerve endings had centered in her fingers and were now hyper-aware. He, however, had already moved on to other matters.

"Which of these monkeys do you want?" He no sooner asked than he decided. "Tell you what, Andy already has a stranglehold on me, so how about you get Shayna? I'll get a quilt to put on the floor, along with a few toys, and then we can talk while we keep an eye on the kids." He strode off, her son in his arms, leaving her alone with Shayna.

Pixie would have been alarmed to let Andy out of her sight, except she knew the minuscule size of the house. From one end to the other, Andy couldn't really be far from her.

She took Shayna from the basket, amazed at her slight weight, now that she was used to the sturdy size of her son. Andy was big for his age and probably weighed fifteen pounds more than the tiny girl. "You're light as a feather, aren't you?"

When Shayna grabbed a hank of her hair, Pixie winced. "Oops. I'd forgotten all about grabby little fists. And damp, too." Carefully, she removed her hair from the baby's fingers, and then put it behind her shoulder.

In the living room, Brogan still held Andy as he flipped open a heavy quilt. "Does she need a diaper change?"

Pixie shrugged. "Doesn't seem to."

"Good. I fed and changed her right before her nap." He put Andy down to explore a bag of soft toys and came to get Shayna. "She's getting good at rolling over, but she doesn't usually go too far." He took the baby, gave her several soft smooches—on her head, her cheek, her hand, and her tummy—and then put her on the blanket with a soft rattle. "I have to fight myself not to hold her all the time," he said as he stepped into the kitchen to get their drinks. "The pediatrician said she needs plenty of tummy time to learn physical stuff, so I'm trying to remember that." He carried the colas to the living room, with napkins, placed them on the coffee table, and took the chair adjacent to the love seat.

"Thank you."

With a nod, he sat forward, his forearms on his knees. "I wanted to clear up some confusion."

Brogan couldn't possibly know her intimate thoughts about him, but still she felt her face go hot. There was no way he'd miss her blush, but fortunately he was watching the kids.

Andy picked up each toy, examined it, and then carefully placed it in front of Shayna. She now had a whole stack of colorful items to interest her. It was so cute that Pixie started to relax.

"She's not my daughter."

Surprise jerked her attention back to Brogan. "She's not?"

He shook his head. "She's my niece. My sister passed away, but she had me listed as Shayna's guardian." The flexing of his jaw showed his discomfort. "Half sister, actually. I didn't know her that well."

Words were impossible to find, so Pixie reached out and put her hand on his wrist. His gaze darted from the kids to where she touched him. Seconds ticked by, with neither of them moving. Abruptly, he patted her hand and then sat back—out of reach.

Awkwardness descended on them. "I'm sorry for your loss."

After a deep inhale and slow exhale, he further explained. "It's complicated, but the basics are that my father cheated with my mother and I was born. He was already married and had a two-year-old daughter with his wife. I wasn't a part of their lives. Overall, I imagine he wanted to forget I existed because my birth nearly caused his divorce."

Irritation hit Pixie. "His cheating nearly caused it."

Surprised at her outburst, Brogan lifted his brows, then shrugged. "Same result. I was born and there was strife."

"It's not the same at all." She realized she was overreacting and attempted to level her tone. She had personal experience with a cheater, and she thanked God every day that Andy hadn't been viewed in an unfavorable way by those involved. "Sorry, it's just . . . There's an important distinction between what a grown man does and the existence of an innocent child."

He lowered his head in agreement. "My point is that Brian, my father, wanted no part of me, and his wife despised me. My sister, though, found out about me when she was fifteen and secretly looked me up."

"That's enterprising for a girl so young. Did you live nearby?"

"Same state, but not at all close. She was two years older than me, and we talked online until she was seventeen. Then she got a bus ticket and came to see me." His gaze lowered, but a small smile touched his mouth. "Shocked the hell out of me. Connie had no business being in my neighborhood, but she was used to being safe and didn't feel at all threatened."

Used to being safe. Meaning Brogan hadn't been afforded the same sense of security? "It was a dangerous area?"

"Not so much for me, but for a pretty stranger? I practically shouted her back onto a bus, then rode with her to a diner. We talked until late that night."

He would have been thirteen, and even then, he'd been protective. "I bet that was nice."

"Would have been, but her phone was blowing up with texts and calls from our father and her mother. When they found out where she was . . ." He frowned, then changed the direction of the conversation. "Over the next few years, I only talked to her a few times."

Sadness squeezed Pixie's heart. She could guess what had happened without Brogan's explanation. "She was reaching out and you weren't reciprocating?"

That severe frown of his settled into confusion. "How do you figure that?"

"I don't know, but I'm right, aren't I?"

He rubbed his brow, then ran his fingers over his short hair. "I was working a lot, and I didn't have time for her."

She was willing to bet his father had warned him off, and God, how she wished she could kick the man for being so cruel. "Are you close to your father—"

"Hell no," he said, clearly forgetting about curse words. "Don't even want to be. That's the thing, though. When Connie died, no one could reach me. I was . . . out of touch. It took too long for me to find out about Shayna, and as soon as I did, I made plans to get to her."

Pixie noticed the deepening of his breathing. He stood, went to the baby, checked her diaper, moved some of the toys Andy had arranged around her so she could turn over, and smoothed his hand over Andy's head.

When he finished, he just stood there a minute, his back to Pixie, and she knew he was struggling with some strong emotion. She practically felt it.

"She hadn't been treated well," he said at last.

Shock left her floundering. Who mistreated an infant?

Because she couldn't sit still, Pixie left the seat to stand near Brogan. He'd made his preference clear, so she didn't touch him again, but she, too, felt compelled to look at Shayna.

Such a tiny little girl, innocent and so fragile. Pixie's thoughts churned over the idea that anyone would be less than attentive and caring to her. She'd known from the second Andy was born that she would take on the world for him, beg, borrow, or steal to see that he had the care he needed. To protect him, she'd have battled Satan himself.

As she watched Shayna reach for a soft toy, her tiny fingers awkwardly grasping, Pixie accepted that she felt the same about any child.

The baby rolled to her back and busily chewed on a yellow

terry cloth bear, babbling indistinguishable sounds and occasionally smiling at her own ingenuity.

"She looks happy now," Pixie said softly. "Safe and loved with you."

His inhale was audible, his shoulders tense. What a nightmare he must have lived through. Her instinct was to hug him tight, but of course she didn't. She couldn't.

He didn't want her to.

"I think my son is ready to doze off now." Andy was stretched out on his stomach, staring at Shayna, a toy clutched in each hand. His eyes were half closed and his mouth slightly open. "Maybe we should get out of your hair."

His gaze landed on her. "I'm sorry."

"I understand."

"No . . ." He gestured at the couch. "I'd rather you stay." His jaw clenched and he muttered an indistinguishable curse. "If you want to leave, I get it, but I didn't mean to go off track. I shouldn't have—I didn't mean to get into all that."

"Sometimes the details of our lives are so interwoven, it's impossible to share anything without sharing it all." She knew that better than anyone.

To let him know she'd be happy to stay, Pixie sat down and then was relieved when he did the same. "I don't mind if you want to talk about it. I can't even imagine what it must have been like."

"I'm still furious over it."

"At whoever hurt her?"

"And myself."

Every time he mentioned himself, he shifted uncomfortably.

"You didn't hurt her, Brogan." She felt certain of that. "And you said you were out of touch. I'm assuming with the military?"

"Mostly." The tension built again; then he said, "I should

have been more receptive to Connie. As it was, she barely knew how to reach me."

"Who had Shayna?"

Disgust showed on his face. "Connie's parents." With a shake of his head, he said, "Brian and Ruth—our father and her mother. They're a waste of space, to be truthful. All that time, I'd thought I was missing out on something, and then I realized Connie was the one who'd had the bad luck." He gave himself a moment before explaining. "I arrived in the middle of a party. It was so loud, no one heard me knocking, so I just went in. People were drunk or high, abrasive. I looked everywhere and couldn't find a baby. I thought maybe they'd left her with a sitter, but no one seemed to know what I was talking about."

How scary that had to have been.

"I was about to leave, but then I decided to check upstairs. I was halfway up the steps when I heard her wails."

This time, Pixie couldn't take it. She scooted to the edge of her seat and again rested her hand on his wrist. "She's here now and safe," she softly reminded him, aware of the tears gathering in her eyes.

His whispered voice sounded tortured. "She was a mess, Pixie. I don't think her diaper had been changed all day. The bedding was gross." He put his hand over hers and held on. "I swear, I wanted to kill someone, but the baby was my priority. Hell, I wasn't even sure she was Shayna, but it didn't matter. I grabbed a clean blanket and wrapped her up, then went into the bathroom and stripped her to get her clean."

Pixie squeezed her eyes shut, but her mind supplied a vision she didn't want to see, so she focused on Brogan instead. Big, strong, capable Brogan. Shayna's hero.

"I'd never handled a tiny baby before. She weighed next to nothing and seemed so breakable." His jaw worked. "The diaper rash . . . To this day, it destroys me to think how bad it was."

Heart aching, Pixie wondered who could allow such a thing. It was unthinkable—and beyond cruel.

"Soon as I got her cleaned up, I went back to the room to look for diapers, but couldn't find any. I ended up wrapping her in my shirt, and on my way back downstairs, I called the police. I also prayed that I'd find formula of some kind and a bottle. I did, but I had to knock out some drunk asshole who protested my going through the cabinets."

Imagining him doing that, while holding a crying infant, gave Pixie a slight smile. "Good for you."

"The cops got there fast, thankfully. A female cop was with them, and she saved me. She had kids of her own, all older, but she knew how to fix the formula. She cleaned the bottle first, telling me to keep doing what I was doing."

"Holding Shayna, talking softly to her?"

"Rocking a little, I guess, though I didn't realize it at the time. By then, my little Sugar wasn't wailing as hard, so I guess it was working."

"Just getting her clean had to help."

He dropped his head forward. "I didn't know jack-shit about giving a baby a bath, if the water was too warm or too cold, but I knew the mess had to go, even though she was raw." He clenched all over again.

Pixie sniffled, and that drew his attention.

"Aw, damn. I'm sorry. For God's sake, you barely know me and I'm dumping all this on you." Then he tipped his head back. "And I've been cursing again. I'm sorry about that, too."

"No, it's fine." She released him to dig in her purse for a tissue. "I'm just so glad you have her now."

"Yeah, me too." He glanced at the kids. "Look at that. Guess I got lucky with my verbal slipups, because Andy didn't hear me." He smiled. "They're both asleep."

Pixie gave a small laugh. "I hear that almost never happens. Moms in town have told me that two kids are impossible to get down for naps at the same time. I think we just lucked out."

He checked his watch. "Usually, she'd have been up for a while before nodding off again."

"I think they were soothed by each other."

Alert, he asked, "You really think so?"

"I hear that babies are fascinated by other babies. I don't really know that, though. Andy's my only child, and while he sees some kids around here, he's the only baby."

"I didn't ask, but maybe I should have."

There was something off in his tone, something Pixie couldn't quite name. "Ask me what?"

"If you have a husband."

"Oh." Though she didn't know whether he asked out of interest or mere curiosity, her heart did a weird little flutter. "No. That is, I never had a husband." For the longest time, she'd been ashamed of herself and her behavior, but not anymore. Yes, she'd been foolish, but she'd also been young, and she'd worked hard to make up for her mistakes. "Andy's father . . ." She shook her head. No way would she blurt out that he'd been married to another woman—the very woman who was now her best friend. At the time, Pixie hadn't known Dylan was married, and now Marlow had forgiven her. That was all that mattered. "I've never been married."

He took her confession in stride, saying, "Same." He nodded at the baby. "Shayna's father is gone. Passed away, I mean." He watched her closely. "Andy's dad?"

"Also passed away." It seemed incredibly odd that they'd have that in common. She started to ask how Shayna's father had died, but Brogan didn't give her a chance.

"So tell me about the town. Any good restaurants that wouldn't mind if I brought along a baby?"

"Since I rarely go anywhere without Andy, I can tell you that no one seems to mind at all. Most people fawn over him. He gets so much attention that I sometimes worry he'll become spoiled."

"You can't spoil a kid with too much love." No sooner did the words leave his mouth than he looked chagrined. "Not that I'm an expert or anything. Just seems to me you can dole out love, hand in hand with setting boundaries."

"That's my plan, at least it is when I'm thinking about it and not just reacting." In the moment, she knew she could be overly emotional and protective.

"Ah, I see some doubt."

"Best-laid plans and all that."

"Give me an example."

Sure, why not? It was nice to share with another parent who had, or would, face the same indecision and uncertainty. "I want Andy to be confident, but then I fall apart when he gets hurt. Like a few weeks ago. We were at the park, and he kept kicking off his shoes. I told him he had to wear them because of sharp sticks on the ground and bees everywhere, but he really wanted to feel the grass on his toes."

Brogan laughed. "I can see the lure of warm grass on bare feet."

"So could I," she said, "so I gave in. He was loving it until he stepped on a thorn." Even now, guilt filled her. "I tell you, the way he screamed, I didn't know what had happened. Instead of just taking care of it and telling him how careful we need to be when barefoot, I sat down and rocked him and kissed his foot a dozen times, and I swear, I was ready to cry with him."

Brogan's expression warmed. "See, to me that just sounds nice. You're a loving mom. You did what moms do."

She choked on her laugh. "Did your mother do that?"

His face seemed to freeze before he forced a curl to his mouth. "She wasn't around much, but she wouldn't have been the type anyway."

If his mother hadn't been around, and his father had wanted nothing to do with him, who had raised him?

"You did the right thing," he assured her. "Seems to me it's good for kids to have new experiences. I'm sure he wasn't badly hurt, but you let him know you're there for him when he needs you."

"Some of the other people at the park looked at me like I was bonkers. One dad came over to ask how badly my son was hurt. When I explained that he'd only stepped on a thorn, he very nicely checked Andy's foot. We could just barely see where he'd been poked." And she'd felt like a fool. "The guy was nice, but he suggested that if I was calmer, Andy would soon be calm, too. His wife brought me over an ice cube and together we held it on his little foot until he'd settled down."

"People can sometimes surprise us with their concern."

She had a strong suspicion that Brogan hadn't been surprised nearly often enough. "Around here, you get used to everyone being nice." The town was full of well-meaning, concerned, and sometimes nosy neighbors. "For three days, Andy wanted to show everyone his boo-boo—even though there was nothing to see. He insisted that Marlow and Cort should kiss it, then Herman and Robin, and even Bren Crawford."

"Okay, rewind." He spun a finger in the air and asked with comedic humor, "I recognize Cort's name as the guy renting out this place, but who are all the other foot kissers?"

The way he put things kept her amused. "Marlow is his wife and my best friend. Herman owns the Dry Frog Tavern—it's a place you'll love, I promise—and Bren is an adorably cranky older guy who refuses to retire. He still runs the boat launch and rental, but only Friday through Sunday. He's closed during the week."

"So . . . what happens if someone wants to take their boat in or out on a weekday?"

"Outsiders are turned away. Locals have to ask him nicely,

and that's not easy because he's hard of hearing. Believe me, if he doesn't want to hear you, he won't."

Under his breath, Brogan said, "Reminds me of a bull-headed commander I knew."

Pixie wondered at that, especially because he'd said it with an undertone of grit and possibly anger. Or disappointment? If she knew him better, she could probably interpret his mood, but he was still a mystery. He kept his emotions contained, much as Cort did, and yet he was ready with a smile, and he totally fawned over the babies.

"You mentioned someone named Robin?"

"Robin Merriman runs the Docker restaurant. It's a nice family place on the lake. People show up in both boats and cars. Seating inside and out. When you want more than a burger or pizza, you go to the Docker."

"Sounds great. I need to check it out. Anything else?"

She told him where to find the nearest grocery store, where to get gas and last-minute items, ice cream and pastries. "The beach area is quiet through the week if you like to jog. It gets busier on the weekend." Though with an infant, she didn't know how he'd manage much jogging. Grinning, she added, "And if you want to hang with a bunch of teenagers, Leo runs an arcade."

"Yeah, I might pass on the arcade. I was never much for games." He sipped his cola, then asked, "Do you work in the area?"

"Nearby, actually. Marlow opened her own small boutique, now named Marlow's Whimsy. It's just outside of Bramble, in Lankton, not that far away. I'm her manager." Her face warmed as she explained, "I also lucked into some design work. I do that freelance for various places."

"Wow, nice. What kind of designs?"

Yep, that was more heat flooding her face. At this point, with her fair complexion, she probably looked scalded.

Brogan's slow grin warned her before he asked, "Something risqué?"

"*What?* No. Of course not."

He held up a hand. "Sorry, but the way you blushed, I wasn't sure."

Gulping a drink of her cola gave her something to do, but also made her burp. She groaned, set the drink aside, and said, "Excuse me."

His expression sobered. "Hey, if you'd rather not tell me, that's fine."

"No, it's not that." Blowing out a breath, she got hold of herself. "I'm not used to having a reason to boast, and I'm not at all sure I'm comfortable with it. I mean, it's wonderful. I feel better about myself . . ."

That steely gaze of his, rife with curiosity, stayed intent on her face.

Right. Scratch that. She didn't want him delving too deeply into her scandalous past.

Determined to sound like a reasonable adult, Pixie started over. "When Marlow first came up with the idea for the boutique, she wanted to sell unique stuff that represented the area here. She loved seeing the fireflies that come out in the evening, so one day, when I finished organizing some stuff for her, I started to doodle. Somewhat by accident, I came up with a few stylized fireflies. Marlow loved them and insisted on paying me for my work. She uses the designs on a lot of stuff now."

"Wow. That sounds really great."

"It was. *Is.*" Remembering the numerous ways Marlow had helped to rebuild her—her spirit, her pride, her sense of belonging—filled Pixie's soul. "I thought she claimed to like the designs just to give me a boost. But then, other businesspeople around here asked me to come up with designs for them, and they insisted on paying me, too, and . . ." She shrugged. "It just sort of grew into a nice, easy part-time job that really helps my budget."

Brogan studied her face, her smile, and even the way she held her cola. "You're an impressive woman, Pixie Nolan. Not just as a mother, which I realized right off, but in every way, it seems."

"I . . ." Honestly, she had no idea what to say, so she settled on, "Thank you. But I'm just me—and I've had a lot of help."

"Maybe someday you'd like to tell me about that."

CHAPTER 3

The oddest thing happened. The more Pixie told him about the town, the more Brogan wanted to know, and somehow she ended up agreeing to show him around on her next day off.

And then she agreed to dinner, too.

Neither occasion would really count as a date, because they'd have the kids with them, and yet, it was the closest she'd come in a very long time and her anticipation was keen.

The following day, she and Andy had just gotten to the shop when her phone rang. She set Andy in the playpen behind the counter, kissed the top of his head, and dug out her phone. Seeing that it was Marlow, she swiped her thumb across the screen and put the call on speaker. "Good morning."

"Am I calling at a bad time?"

"Not possible," Pixie said as she placed the phone on the countertop. Marlow could call her in the middle of the night and she would make time for her. In many ways, she owed her life to her friend. More importantly, she loved her dearly. "We just got in. I can talk while I open up."

"Shoot. I was hoping to catch you on the road so you could talk on the drive. I know how busy your mornings are with breakfast and getting Andy ready, and then setting up the shop for the day. The drive is your only semi-free time."

"Andy and I both woke up spry this morning, so I figured I'd get an earlier start. I wanted to make sure those new shirts were front and center before shoppers stopped in." They were barely into May, but the inventory of pastel-colored summer wear had just arrived, and she was anxious to show it off.

In the past, Pixie was often unsure of her designs, but this one she thought would be popular. In stylized font was the saying: *Peace lights up the skies at Firefly Lake.* Sprinkled around it were little glowing fireflies. She thought the design looked especially sharp on the black shirts, but for summer she'd also chosen a rainbow hue of pastels with contrasting print.

She was in love with them.

"Any reason for feeling extra chipper today?" Marlow asked with a lot of innuendo.

Unable to suppress her grin, Pixie hugged a stack of shirts to her chest and twirled on her way to the front display window. "Yes! I had such a great time with Brogan. He's *so* good with Shayna—who, as it turns out, is not his daughter but his niece." She quickly explained the situation. "Isn't that amazing?"

"Thank God he got to her when he did."

"Agreed. She's the tiniest, sweetest little thing, Marlow. You'd love her."

"I look forward to meeting them both when Cort and I are back. So your time with Brogan—is that all there was to it?"

"Literally. We sat at the lake house, drinking Cokes and talking while the babies got familiar with each other. Andy didn't know what to make of Shayna at first. Next to her, he looks like a tank." She grinned as she said it. "Oh, but guess what? He fell asleep on the floor watching Shayna. Every little thing she did fascinated him. If she stretched, he got super alert. Whenever she made a sound, it startled him. He kept offering her toys, but didn't understand why she wouldn't play."

"Aww. That's so sweet."

"Then their naps synced up. Isn't that wild? I doubt it will ever happen again."

"And?"

"And what?" Pixie replied. "It was a nice, relaxing visit."

"And?"

She laughed. "Fine. He asked me to show him around the town, which I'll do on Thursday when I'm off. Then we'll have dinner on the weekend at the Docker."

"Dates! I love it."

"No," Pixie corrected. "Not dates. It's just that he's new and wants to get familiar with the people and places, since he'll be here through the summer."

"And he asked *you* to show him around."

"I'm probably the only one he's met so far." She wouldn't let herself make more of the invitation than that. It was bad enough that her heart seemed to beat faster anytime she thought of Brogan.

"Describe him to me," Marlow said.

Andy called out to her, so she said, "Just a second," and took the few feet necessary to check on him. The shop wasn't big by any stretch, but when Marlow had redesigned the interior, she'd set it up so every wall was filled with shelving and there were circular racks filling the central space, meaning Pixie had to dart and weave—and twirl a few times again—to reach him. Andy loved her antics.

Pixie lowered the phone. "Say hi to Marlow."

Andy immediately grinned and said, "Fend."

"Hello, sweetie." Marlow made several kissing sounds. "We miss you."

He made kissing sounds back and then repeated, "Fend."

"Yes," Pixie said, "Brogan is your friend," to help Marlow understand.

"Ah, yes, a new friend. And did you meet a baby?"

Babbling fast now, Andy told her all about it in his excited little squeaky voice. Though she was sure Marlow had only understood a few words, she was still suitably impressed.

Because Pixie never wanted to leave anyone trapped on a phone with a chatty toddler, she checked that Andy's diaper was dry, then found him a few colorful indestructible books to enjoy and settled him in his playpen. He stretched out on his stomach to "read," which meant playing with the book and enjoying the colors.

"I'm back," Pixie said, again putting the phone on the counter so she could return to work.

"Andy is sure taken with Brogan."

"It was wild, how quickly they bonded." She rearranged some shirts, trying to decide whether they should be hung by color or size. "I think it might be because Brogan has the same type of presence as Cort. You know, quiet and confident." Until the occasional memory disturbed him. "Brogan probably seemed familiar to Andy, since he and Cort are close."

"Mmm, now I'm doubly intrigued, so let's hear the description."

Closing her eyes, Pixie could almost see him again. "He's tall. Even taller than Cort. Dark blond hair—like almost brown with some sun highlights around his temples. Cut military short, but not too short. He has these intense gray eyes. Really direct. Big shoulders, big hands"—big everywhere, from what she could tell —"but he's gentle with the kids."

"Go on."

Pixie laughed. "Lecher. That's all I know. He seems to favor worn jeans and plain shirts."

"He sounds delicious, and I think you should go for it."

While straightening the shirts, Pixie said, "Go for what? I have a baby, remember. And he has an infant. The only thing we could go for, if he was even inclined, would be a quick kiss. *But*," she stressed, before Marlow could weigh in, "that's not on the agenda." Yes, Brogan made her think things, but she hadn't lost her senses. She was still working on herself, a never-ending process, now that she was a mother. She wanted to be the best parent possible for Andy. That left little time for entertainment of any sort, especially the big, hot male type of entertainment.

Priorities. Andy first, then his future, and of course her own continued improvement.

But for the first time in a long time, she was tempted.

"Anyway," Pixie said, getting her mind back on track, "aren't you supposed to be on vacation?"

"We're at the pool. I'm relaxing in the shade with a juicy novel while everyone else is eyeballing my husband."

"Everyone?"

"Women with interest, I'm sure, and guys with envy. Oh, Pixie, he looks so fine in his trunks. I'm just sitting here under an umbrella, taking it in and glowing. How did I get so lucky?"

"It's not luck, it's reciprocal awesomeness. You two deserve each other in all the best possible ways."

"Yes," Marlow said softly. "It's so ironic that Dylan's bad choices brought us all together. Do you ever think about the quirks of fate, or heavenly intervention, or whatever?"

"All the time," Pixie admittedly softly. If she hadn't made such a huge, awful mistake with Dylan, if her pregnancy hadn't been so problematic, if she hadn't hit rock bottom and come to Marlow for help—*if, if, if . . .*

She and Marlow had both gone silent, so when a tap sounded on the big window, Pixie jumped. Hand to her heart, she looked up, and there was Brogan smiling at her through the glass, with Shayna held in a carrier on his chest.

At first, she just stared at him; then Pixie rushed forward to unlock and open the door. "Hey, there."

"Am I too early?" He glanced at the sign on the door stating the shop hours. "I am. Sorry."

"No, it's fine. I open in just a few minutes."

"Pixie?" Marlow asked. "You there?"

Oh, good grief. She'd forgotten all about Marlow.

"Sorry, yes." She gave Brogan a "come on in" wave as she rushed back to the counter, picked up the phone, and said, "Brogan is here."

"At the store?" Before Pixie could answer, Marlow said, "Don't let him in yet. Let me say something to you first. I want you to have fun. You deserve that, Pixie, more than anyone I know. So go for it, okay?"

Horrified, because Brogan had followed her, she said, "Marlow—"

"But don't take any chances until you know him better. Don't be alone with him. Don't—"

In a horrified whisper, she choked out, "You're on speaker and he's standing right here."

With only a two-second pause, Marlow said, "Hello, Brogan."

Amusement put a crooked grin on his face. "Good morning, Marlow. I'm sorry to interrupt."

"No, no, it's fine. The store opens now anyway. There will be a crowd in no time at all."

Proving he wasn't the least bit fooled, he said, "Would you feel better if I stepped back out and Pixie relocked the door?"

"Of course not. Pixie is a great judge of character, and she's told me only nice things about you."

"Oh?" He propped a hip on the counter. "Such as?"

"You're military, like my husband; you're great with your niece; and you've bonded with Andy."

He glanced at Pixie. "All that, huh?"

Embarrassment burned her cheeks. "She's Cort's wife, and you're renting from him, so she was naturally curious . . ."

"I didn't mean to share so much," he said, his gaze still holding Pixie's.

"No, I get it," Marlow replied. "Cort doesn't talk about the military much, either, but Pixie is one of those warm people you just feel comfortable with."

"Marlow." Much more of this and she'd perish from embarrassment.

Andy saved her by shouting, "Fend, fend, fend!" from the playpen. He held the top rail and jumped up and down.

"I need to go. Andy just spotted Brogan, and I do have customers now." Two women had just come in, their interest in the new shirts obvious until they spotted Brogan. Now their attention was diverted. Pixie wasn't at all surprised. Big and built as he was, he looked very incongruous in the small-town setting of the shop. The cute infant on his chest was just added appeal.

"Go take care of the squirt, don't work too hard—and, Pixie, have fun!" Marlow disconnected without giving her a chance to protest that last order.

Brogan grinned at her. "I'll talk to Andy while you take care of your customers."

Unsure what else to do, Pixie nodded. "Okay, thanks." Her son was used to waving to people who came in, but usually she had a clerk in the shop, too. Since she'd opened a few minutes early, her help hadn't yet arrived.

The shoppers, who were in the area on vacation, ended up buying quite a bit. Shirts, hats, and a few souvenirs. Their plans were to see the small-town architecture and then go boating on the lake for the weekend.

They had just left when Renee arrived. The thirty-one-year-old part-time worker breezed in, saying, "You opened early!" She loudly slurped on a fountain drink as she headed to the counter, but came to a dead stop when she spotted Brogan. With the straw still in her mouth, she gawked.

At least I'm not the only one with that reaction. Pixie cleared her throat. "Renee, meet Brogan Rafferty. He's renting the lake house for a few months. Brogan, this is Renee Colson. She works with me here in the shop."

Brogan stepped forward with his hand extended. "Nice to meet you, Renee."

She put her limp hand in his—and suddenly came alive again. "Good heavens, you're a showstopper. What are you? Six and a half feet tall? And a baby? It's like the prettiest bow on a really nice package."

"Six-five," Brogan corrected. "And . . . thank you?"

Renee grinned. "I'm terrible, I know. My husband, who's the best, tells me so all the time. The good news is that I mostly manage to rein it in when I talk to my sons' teachers. At least I hope I do. I *try*." She laughed. "I have a runaway mouth. Thoughts turn into speech before I can properly censor. Bet you noticed right off, huh?"

What Pixie noticed was that Brogan looked more riveted by the speed-convo than insulted.

"And there's my guy!" Renee went to Andy and lifted him out for a huge hug.

Andy pointed and said, "Baby."

Being silly, Renee looked at the floor, the walls, and then the ceiling. "A baby? Where?"

Enjoying the antics, Andy laughed, bounced in her arms, and pointed again. "Baby, baby!"

"Ooooh, I see now."

Pixie stepped aside to watch, smiling at how quickly Renee and Brogan got to know each other. Renee laughed several times, as did Andy, and Shayna was busy cooing, occasionally twisting to look at Brogan. She'd smile at him often, and once she caught his hand to chew on his knuckle.

Pixie was pulled aside when another customer asked for help, and then another, and soon the flow of shoppers was steady. Being a mom, she still kept her eye on Andy and knew the very moment that Renee returned him to his playpen so she could ring up an order. Brogan helped to get Andy settled with a few toys, then strolled over to browse the shelves.

When she finished with her customer, Pixie approached him and asked, "Looking for anything specific?"

He lifted one shoulder. "I came into town to get a few things that the smaller shop in Bramble didn't have. Figured I'd stop in while I was here." He glanced around. "This isn't what I was expecting."

"How so?"

"Your artwork is amazing, for one thing." He lifted a tote bag. "I couldn't believe this was yours when I first saw it; then I noticed your signature."

"I created the original print." It was a simple design of the sunset over the water, with the name of the lake below it. "Sometimes I do stuff without thinking about merchandise, but then Marlow sees the potential."

"It's a busy shop."

"It is." Pixie tried to see it through his eyes, but it was tough to do because of all the pride she felt. She'd had a hand in creating it, and her designs were everywhere now. "Marlow had this amazing vision and made it come true."

"It's a dream life, right? Living on the lake, owning her own successful shop."

"Married to a Marine and loving her life." She grinned. "Yup, it's a dream come true for her. Not that she expected the Marine. Mostly, she wanted to downsize her life after a year of nasty divorce proceedings, only to have her husband—" Pixie drew to a hasty halt. Good God, she was running her mouth more than Renee did. She had absolutely no reason to tell Brogan any of that.

Instead of leaving her to flounder, he said, "I should get to my own shopping instead of monopolizing your time."

Relieved that he hadn't pressed her, she said, "You're fine."

He kissed Shayna's head. "She'll be ready for a bottle and a nap soon, and I'd rather be home for that, so can you make a recommendation on some clothes for the two of us?"

"Sure." After they picked out two cute outfits for Shayna, Pixie said, "And now something for you." Just to tease him, she led the way to a sunny yellow polo shirt with a stylized firefly stitched on the front breast pocket. "What do you think?"

Brogan's enigmatic gaze looked it over. "If you have that in a romper for Sugar, I'll take it."

Barely keeping her smile hidden, she asked, "You don't want one for yourself?"

He eyed her, then the shirt, and shook his head. "Got anything in black? Without a collar?"

The laughter escaped her, drawing the attention of other shoppers and Renee.

He flashed his own quick grin. "It's pretty, and I'm sure it'd look great on some guys, but it's not for me."

"No, it isn't." She turned to a shelf of T-shirts in gray, black, navy, and tan. "What do you think?"

"Much better." None of them were splashy, but on the front they said: *Lake Life is the Best*, with *Firefly Lake* in smaller print. He chose black with narrow white lettering.

He surprised her by taking a few more things—the tote he'd admired, to keep Shayna's things in, he said—and a little sun hat for her. Together, they headed to the register.

Once his purchases were bagged, he turned to Andy. "See you again soon, bud."

"My baby."

A silly laugh escaped Pixie. "He likes to claim his cup, his toys, things like that. Guess he's claiming Shayna now, too."

"My baby," Andy said again, in his cute little voice. They all understood only because of how he stared at Shayna while saying it.

"Oh, you think so, do you?" Brogan knelt down by the playpen while Pixie and Renee watched. "Laying claim, are you?"

Andy leaned forward, lips pursed, definitely wanting a kiss.

Brogan laughed and moved Shayna closer. "Head or foot?"

Stretching forward, Andy reached for . . . Brogan. He put a big wet kiss on his jaw, and then said, "My baby."

"You've almost convinced me." He used his shoulder to swipe his jaw before putting Shayna in range. She squealed as Andy put a loud smooch on her cheek.

"Kiss!" Andy demanded—and he was looking right at Brogan.

"Oh, um," Pixie said, unsure whether she should intervene.

Brogan cupped the back of Andy's head and brushed a barely-there peck on his forehead. "All good?"

Apparently, it wasn't, because although Andy beamed, he then wanted to kiss Renee and Pixie, too. She lifted him out for some cuddles, but her thoughts were on Brogan. He was so natural with Andy. She envied him that. Not that she wasn't comfortable with her son, but other people and other kids? She sometimes reverted to her old insecure self.

She supposed being a SEAL would give a man a huge dose of confidence in most situations. Brogan certainly had that, which was proven a moment later when Renee decided to be outrageous.

"Kiss?" she asked Brogan, and quickly said to Pixie, "My husband wouldn't mind. Look at him." She gestured at Brogan. "It's a once-in-a-lifetime opportunity."

Choking on her laugh, Pixie said, "I've met the man, and he would absolutely mind."

"Ugh, I guess you're right."

"Plus, you're indulging in sexual harassment, you know."

Without shame, she grinned at Brogan. "I was just joking, you know that, right?"

"I do."

"I mean, not that it isn't tempting. It totally is, but being real here, my guy is incredible—and also possessive and protective, lucky me. He likes that no other man's lips have touched me in the eight years we've been married."

Brogan winked. "He's a lucky guy."

"Darn right." She took Andy from Pixie. "Why don't you walk him out? I can handle things for a few minutes."

Why did everyone keep throwing her at Brogan? He'd clearly given more attention to her son than to her. Since Renee had already walked away, Pixie sighed. "Sorry about that. She's loads of fun, but she can be a bit much."

"No worries. I knew she wasn't serious."

Pixie wasn't sure about that. Every woman who'd seen Brogan today had probably wondered about kissing him—her included.

He lifted his bag as they headed for the door. "Thanks again for your help."

"Make sure you wash everything before you put it on her. Babies have sensitive skin."

"A nurse at the pediatrician's office told me that, too, when I was grilling her with a million questions. If you have any other advice, feel free to send it my way. I've read everything I can find, but I still feel like I'm learning as I go."

As they stepped outside, she asked, "You don't mind advice?"

He stopped to look down at her, but also held a hand over Shayna's head to keep the sun out of her face. "Is there something else you want to share?"

She could hear the sincerity in his tone. "Not at all. I'm in awe of how easily you handle everything. I know when I had Andy, Marlow and Cort were cautious about giving advice. Neither of them had kids. But some of the parents in town weren't the same. They tossed out advice all the time, a lot of it conflicting. I had a hard time sorting out what made sense to me and what I had no interest in."

"Give me an example."

He'd said that to her once before, but he asked again with genuine interest. "One mother told me it was good to let a baby cry it out."

He snorted.

"That's how I felt. I never could stand to hear Andy cry. Her kids were all happy and healthy, so whatever she did worked for her, I guess. But I couldn't do it." In case he thought she was judging, she added, "I only have one and she had four, so I'm sure that influenced her approach."

After smoothing Shayna's little tufts of hair, Brogan kissed her on the head again. "I want her to have siblings, but I don't see that on the horizon anytime soon. I need to get other things worked out first."

Pixie barely knew Brogan, and he'd given no indication that he was interested in anything beyond a friendly association. And yet his mention of siblings for Shayna caused a pinch in her heart.

Andy would never have siblings. After the difficulties of his birth, which had resulted in a hysterectomy, she'd accepted that he'd be an only child.

To her, Andy was enough. And yet, Brogan's casual comment stung.

He interrupted her thoughts by saying, "I should go. She'll probably be hungry before I get home, and then she'll get fussy. It bothers me a lot to hear her upset. If I could, I'd keep that from ever happening."

"Not possible," Pixie said softly. "But you're doing a great job."

He didn't look entirely convinced, but he nodded anyway. "Thanks. I'll see you soon."

Pixie watched him go to his SUV and carefully transfer the baby to her car seat before rushing to get behind the wheel and start the car. It took him a few more moments to settle in, and then he pulled away.

Strange, but she already missed him. With a sigh, she went back inside.

"Hubba, hubba," Renee said the second the door closed behind her. "You should warn a girl. I almost swallowed my tongue when I walked in and saw him."

Pixie nudged her with her shoulder. "I don't think you're the only one to react that way. He's just so . . . big."

"And gorgeous." Renee transferred Andy to her arms. "And hey, the way he dotes on his daughter is enough to steal all the hearts."

She didn't correct the assumption that the baby was his daughter. After being busted by Marlow, Pixie wasn't about to share with anyone else. If Brogan got around town enough, and it sounded like he would, he could tell people what he wanted them to know.

Then again, he was here for a limited time; by the end of summer, he'd go on about his life somewhere else, so none of that really mattered.

Andy laid his head on her shoulder and yawned. He was such an enormous blessing, she wouldn't regret the lack of other children. Softly to Renee, she said, "I want to spend a few minutes getting this little guy settled again, and then I'll finish the display up front."

Renee followed her. "Not like you need to. The shirts are already selling."

True, they were an instant hit. All but one customer this morning had purchased the new design. Brogan wasn't into pastels. She smiled and then put him from her mind to tend to her son and the shop. Those were her top priorities at this time, and Pixie wouldn't let herself backslide after making so much progress over the last year.

She vowed to stop thinking about Brogan and his adorable niece.

Unfortunately, that wasn't easy to do because everyone was

talking about him. During her workday, Pixie heard him mentioned over a dozen times.

Joann Dittmer, who ran the Dairy Bar ice cream shop, stopped in to ask Pixie what she knew about him. Sticking to her vow to keep Brogan's business private, she confessed only to knowing he was renting the lake house.

Butler, the mayor of Bramble, and the owner of the town's one—and only—inn, strolled into the shop for the first time that Pixie was aware of. He tried to pleasantly grill her about Brogan, but she shared the same information. The newcomer was a renter, that's all.

Later, when Pixie drove back to Bramble, she stopped at the grocery store to pick up something for dinner. Gloria and Bobbi, older sisters who liked to force their help on people in the nicest way, trapped her in the fresh vegetable aisle.

Bobbi immediately scooped Andy from the cart to hug him while Gloria fired off questions. It was almost laughable the amount of curiosity Brogan had inspired.

Even when she stopped to refill her gas tank, people approached her. By the time she got to her house, she was worn out from fending off the info seekers. She got that Bramble was a quiet town without a lot of excitement. Anyone new was deemed interesting. Someone like Brogan? He could probably make front-page news.

Now that she was home, she fell into her routine of playing with Andy, walking down to the lake with him for a bit so he could get some fresh air, and then fixing dinner.

It wasn't until she was giving him his bath that he put his little hands to her face and asked, "Fend?"

"I'm your mama."

He kissed her, said, "Mama," and then asked again, "Fend?" followed up by lifting his hands and looking around.

"Ah. No, he's not here, honey. He's at home getting the baby ready for bed."

"My baby."

She wrapped a big towel around him and lifted him from the tub for a hug. "She can be your baby for a little while, but not forever. Now, how would you like a story?"

"Bears!"

"Bears it is, but a diaper and pj's first."

Somehow, asking about Brogan and Shayna turned into a thing over the next couple of days. While at the shop, Andy kept watch for Brogan, and each night during his bath, he asked about the man. Pixie could distract her son with games, books, and sometimes just talking about something else, yet Andy didn't forget.

Twice, they ran into Brogan on walks, even though she walked Andy in the opposite direction. Apparently, Brogan did like to jog and he had a special stroller for Shayna. The motion seemed to rock her to sleep.

Andy spotted him again on the last night before her day off. They'd already had dinner, and the kitchen was clean. The days were getting longer, and with spring flowers everywhere, it was too beautiful to stay inside. Given how Andy kept looking out the window, he could use a little fresh air.

It was slightly later than she usually walked, so she doubted they'd run into Brogan this time. It would be interesting to see how Andy reacted to that. He always enjoyed walks, but even more so, now with Brogan and Shayna in the picture.

For a change in scenery, she went up the main street, pushing the stroller at an incline, which made her calves ache. They saw more wildlife, including a few chipmunks and a massive hawk that swooped down over a field, no doubt looking for mice.

After Andy spotted a bunny, too, she finally turned the stroller and headed back home. Though the evenings could still be cool, tonight it was mild. A fresh breeze came off the lake, rustling the leaves of the mature trees in the wooded areas. She had her head down, lost in the lyrics of a song she softly sang for Andy, and then suddenly he was squealing, "Fend! Fend!"

She looked up and there was Brogan, grinning as he smoothly jogged closer. Shirtless. In shorts and running shoes. Her heart was suddenly pounding against her ribs.

High on his right shoulder was a tattoo. At first, she couldn't make it out, but as he got closer, she recognized an eagle, an anchor, and a spear. It was similar to a tattoo that Cort had, and yet it was different, too.

As he neared, she also saw several scars, some small, many larger. The injuries were healed but not old, and in no way did they detract from his physical appeal. Still, she hurt for him. The wounds had to have been agonizing, especially the longest one that slashed across his ribs. Knowing he'd served made her immediately think of battle wounds.

Good God, she was staring at his body in the rudest way.

She was about to apologize when she saw that his attention was on Andy, not her.

They met at the intersection as Brogan pushed Shayna's spiffy three-wheel stroller alongside hers and knelt down to muss Andy's hair. "Hey, bud. Sorry, I can't hold you. I'm sweaty."

Beads of perspiration clung to his forehead and temples, and his upper chest and shoulders gleamed. He might be ignoring her, but Pixie couldn't take her eyes off him. Until she realized he was lavishing Andy with attention and she'd barely looked at Shayna.

Guilt had her turning quickly to the infant. Shayna was wide awake and grinning at her, showing off two shiny bottom teeth. She wore one of the new outfits Brogan had bought from the shop with a lightweight blanket over her. Surreptitiously, Pixie felt the material of her outfit and knew he'd washed it more than once for it to be so soft already.

"Hello to you, too, Shayna. Thank you for that beautiful smile." Unable to stop herself, she stroked the back of her finger along the baby's cheek. So soft. "You are such a cutie."

In answer, the little girl kicked her legs and cooed.

Andy announced, "My baby."

"Yes, sir," Brogan said in a crisp military tone, and dutifully pulled the stroller back enough that Andy could see Shayna.

Her son kissed the air and even blew a few kisses at Shayna, making both Pixie and Brogan laugh.

While he pulled a T-shirt from the back of the stroller, he asked, "Do you walk every night?"

"Most nights," she said, doing her best not to look at his chest or shoulders. "I want to make sure Andy gets some outside time on the days I work. If it's raining, we sit on the enclosed porch and listen to the storm." Pixie looked around the area. "It's so peaceful here, without much traffic, since there are only our homes on this stretch of road. Sometimes fishermen come by on the lake, and even when they whisper, I can hear them."

"It is nice," Brogan agreed. Acting as if he weren't covering battle scars, he pulled the shirt on over his head and tugged it down.

Pixie was mesmerized. The cotton stuck to him in some places and fell loose in others.

"Haven't seen a colorful sunset yet, but it's still pretty." He lifted the hem of the shirt to dry his face. "I should get going. I need to shower and then give Sugar her bath so we can both settle in. I read that keeping to a schedule makes it easier on the kid. What do you think?"

Without putting much thought into it, Pixie answered honestly. "I like a schedule because it makes it easier on *me*. I don't want to be too rigid, though. Life has a way of changing your plans, you know? Instead, I try to set up a routine. Snack, bath, clean his teeth, read, and then bedtime. That way, even if we're running late, I can get him back on track with all or part of his routine."

"Sounds like training," he said with a half smile.

"With flexibility," she agreed. "Like when you had to change Shayna's diaper in the car." She suspected a man of his ability could improvise at any time.

He nodded. "Gotta know how to make do with what you have on hand."

The conversation had run its course, and now both kids were chattering, but mostly at each other. It was so cute, as if they had their own language. Andy tried to show Shayna a bird, but she just continued to stare at him adoringly.

"You made a big splash in the town," Pixie thought to say.

Though he didn't actually move, it felt as if he took two big steps back—away from her. "What do you mean?"

Uh-oh. His frown isn't exactly encouraging. Pixie measured her words, finding the best possible way to describe the rabid interest he'd stirred. "Several people favorably mentioned seeing you."

The concerned frown didn't lift. "I don't know why. I mostly kept to myself while I ran my errands." He added, "I wasn't rude."

"Of course not."

"But I didn't go out of my way to chat with anyone, either. Well, except you, but that's because I already know you, and for as long as I'm here, you're my neighbor."

Unsure why the impression he'd made would bother him so much, Pixie asked, "Is it a problem that you were noticed?"

He ran a hand over his short hair, then realized that the sun was on Shayna. He adjusted the stroller to be sure she was shaded by the canopy, but could still see Andy. "I wasn't out to make friends," he finally said. "I'm here to help ease Shayna's adjustment."

"And your own?" He'd said Shayna was nearly two months

old before he'd found her. He hadn't had a lot of time yet to acclimate to being a caregiver to an infant.

The lifting of one hard shoulder was answer enough. "Honestly, I'd rather be ignored. I want my private life to stay private. How or why I have Shayna isn't anyone's business."

"No one questioned it. Everyone assumes you're her father." Mostly, people had been curious about his marital status. "Brogan, you have to realize that . . ." *What? You're incredibly delicious and everyone is going to notice?* No, she couldn't say that. "You're a big guy, and not an ogre, right? People, especially women, are going to take note of you." There, that sounded neutral enough, completely logical and not at all interested.

He shook his head. "I'd rather they ignore me. My focus is on her, you know?" He nodded at Shayna. "On getting this parenting gig figured out, getting her on a routine, like you said."

"And taking care of yourself, too." After all, he was out jogging—showing off all that awesomeness. Not on purpose maybe, but Pixie felt certain anyone else would have had the same difficulty keeping their gaze on his face.

"It's a win-win, if I can get in some exercise and she gets fresh air."

"Agreed." After all, that was Pixie's reason for being out and about, too. "I hope Andy and I aren't complicating things for you."

"No," he replied quickly. "That is, I don't want a lot of friends, though I plan to be friendly."

"Okay."

"Relationships complicate things."

"They do."

"But you have a baby, so I feel like I can learn from you."

That was great. Since she was a mom, he saw her as a teacher, not a woman. Pixie forced a smile. "I'm happy to help, however I can, no pressure at all." To salvage her pride, she added, "Like you, I'm busy enough already and don't need the hassle of a relationship."

The second the words left her mouth, she felt ridiculous. Here in Bramble, she didn't have to worry about hot dates because the aging population made that impossible. There were no young, handsome, sensitive, and caring bachelors around, except on the weekends and she wasn't into two-day flings.

Even if a suitable guy lived nearby, few men would want to get involved with the mother of an active toddler.

Determined to make her point, she forged on. "Between being a mom, working at the shop, and creating my freelance designs, I don't have enough free time for anything too involved."

"Perfect," Brogan said; then he backtracked. "Not that you're so busy—I didn't mean that. Sounds like you have your hands full."

She backtracked, too. "I'm not too busy to . . . have an acquaintance."

For some reason, that made him frown, but he looked more bemused than annoyed. "You're young and attractive. I was concerned that I'd be cutting into your date time."

"Ha!" Hearing that obnoxious sound leave her, Pixie slapped a hand over her mouth. Good grief, *she* shouldn't sound so incredulous. Brogan couldn't know that she'd ruined any chance for romantic socializing. "That is," she said, her tone now more moderate, "I don't really date." Going for a blasé attitude, she added, "No time, you know. Like I said, busy, busy."

His penetrating gaze moved over her face, those gray eyes seeming far too perceptive until he finally gave a nod. "Well, I should get Sugar home. The way the sun's setting, it's going to be tough to keep it out of her eyes."

She kept her smile pinned in place. "Same here." They

turned together to walk, and the mom in her fretted. "You put sunscreen on Shayna, of course."

Nodding, he said, "I found some made for babies."

"Good." They walked on, but Pixie had nothing else to say. Not that her silence mattered.

Andy kept up a steady stream of conversation with Brogan. They discussed animals, Shayna, and friendship. He spoke to Andy in a no-nonsense way. Not baby talk, but not complicated adult talk, either. He kept his sentences simple, like, "A bluebird," and "You saw deer?" along with, "Your baby, huh?"

Andy loved it and chattered back—until Shayna sneezed. That drew all his attention. He said, "Oh! My baby."

Brogan fought a laugh, which had his mouth twisting in a funny way. "Just a sneeze, bud. She's okay."

He kept pointing. "Baby . . . seez."

"Sneeze," Brogan enunciated slowly for him.

"Seez."

"Yeah, good job." He ruffled Andy's hair, then leaned around to check on Shayna, and said, "Oops, she's drooling." He used the edge of her blanket to clean her chin.

She was such a happy little baby, making noises and moving her legs and smiling with joy. Seeing her made Pixie happy, too. When it was time to go down their driveway, Andy insisted on hugs for Brogan, and kisses for Shayna.

Brogan was great, of course. Now that he wore his shirt, he took Andy from his stroller—with permission from her first—and held him close to Shayna so the little boy could kiss her head. Then he carried Andy against his shoulder while pushing Shayna's stroller one-handed until they reached her front door.

He didn't linger after putting Andy down. "Have a good night, you two."

"You as well," Pixie said.

"I'll see you tomorrow?"

Her day off was reserved for him. "Noon. We'll be there."

She kept hold of Andy's hand so he couldn't race after Brogan as he left. It was going to be a problem, how much he liked Brogan and Shayna.

Could she, in good conscience, let him get even more attached?

But at this point, did she really have it in her to deny him . . . or herself? Probably not.

It was a sad realization, but she was starved for male attention. Until Brogan had smiled at her, she hadn't even considered it. She'd been a shy girl in school, horribly backward and unfashionable. If a teacher called on her, she blushed. Getting her first job was an ordeal, but she'd made herself do it because there'd been no other option. Day to day, she'd gotten by—feeling awkward, mostly invisible.

Until Dylan.

Andy's father had opened the doors to a whole new world, and she'd gloried in every moment of the attention, the generous gestures . . . the joys of sex. She couldn't say if she'd really loved him, but she'd certainly loved the idea of him. Of them.

And then she'd gotten pregnant, found out he was married, and her entire world had crashed down around her.

Her perfect relationship had been one giant, earth-shattering, humiliating lie. He hadn't loved her. Probably hadn't even liked her. All he'd done was use her—and she'd allowed it, because she'd been a fool.

Pixie realized she had tensed up and her stomach felt twisted, as it always did when she recalled what a panicked, lost, humiliated person she'd been. Slowly, she inhaled, blew out her breath, and flexed her shoulders.

It wasn't fair to Andy to dwell on that ugly episode of her life. This was his time. Everything was for him.

After all, the payoff—her sweet baby boy—was more than worth the hell she'd gone through. Plus, she'd learned some valuable lessons. She was wiser now, better equipped for life both financially and emotionally, and she had Andy. He was her world.

How she'd gotten there really didn't matter in the grand scheme of things. She'd call her life today a win every time.

Where Brogan was concerned, she decided to get through the next few days, and then she'd reevaluate. With a plan in mind, she bathed Andy, cleaned his teeth, and then read to him until he nodded off. Gently, she placed him in his crib.

After a kiss on his head, she got into her own bed.

Alone, the same way she planned to do for the rest of her life.

With that dismal thought, she knew she wouldn't sleep yet, so instead she got out her sketch pad and a few pencils, then used her phone to search different fonts. She'd create for a while and hopefully she'd soon be able to get Brogan out of her thoughts.

CHAPTER 4

Shayna was fussier that night than usual, but he wasn't sure why. Brogan worried that she'd gotten too much sun, but her skin was as pale and soft as ever. She didn't feel feverish. Twice he checked that her diaper was comfortable, and he switched her clothes in case they were somehow bothering her.

She would settle for a moment, almost doze off, then fuss again.

While carrying her around the interior of the small house, he did quick research on his phone, trying to figure out the cause. When that didn't yield any results, he went outside to circle the property, hoping a change of scenery would soothe her.

It definitely helped to settle his own turbulent thoughts.

The chorus of chirping crickets, the soft sound of the water lapping the shoreline, and a truly stunning sunset gave him a sense of peace.

He looked down at Shayna, pleased to see that her expression was now relaxed and sleepy. He lightly kissed her forehead. "I can't bear it when you're unhappy, Sugar." Keeping his tone soft, Brogan continued to talk to her while he walked. "Good news is, you're not colicky or you'd be more upset. And since you're not chewing your little fist, I know you're not hungry again. I couldn't feel anything on your gums, so I don't think you're cutting a new tooth yet."

She blinked sleepily before giving in to a huge yawn.

"You're such a sweet little Sugar, aren't you?" At the back of the house, he paused by the door and just gently rocked her while he looked out over the water. "My guess is, you're more aware of your surroundings now, so we're going to try a little soft music while you sleep tonight. I have an app on my phone. What do you think of that?"

Gripping one of his fingers, she snuggled closer to his chest and closed her eyes.

Unfamiliar emotions left him feeling ungrounded. Voice low and gruff, he whispered, "Damn, Sugar, I love you so much. How did that happen so quickly? It's like you took my heart right out of my chest, and now you hold it in your tiny little fist."

This slight little girl owned him. *I wasn't there for you, Connie. I have to live with that, but I swear to you, I'll do right by Shayna.* The words didn't leave his tight throat, not with the baby now sleeping.

Brogan couldn't remember the last time he'd cried. He'd probably been no more than eight or nine when he'd learned that showing too much emotion drew unwanted attention of the negative kind. His mother had mostly lived in a fog of resentment against his father, life, and sometimes Brogan, too. When she focused on him, his life was hell. She rarely hit him, but her words could cut deep—especially because he'd known they were true. He had been unwanted—by Brian, by her, and by the men she'd paraded in and out of their lives.

He decided right then that as Shayna grew up, whenever she felt the need to cry, he'd let her do so; there was nothing wrong with her expressing emotion. The biggest difference was that he'd try to help however he could. He'd offer comfort, and he'd be there for her.

Never would he shame her, not for any reason.

To distract himself from the past he'd long since buried,

Brogan scrolled on his phone. He was still worried that visiting with Pixie and Andy had been a mistake. It wasn't what Shayna was used to. According to online suggestions, she could have been overstimulated by the visit and therefore needed more time to unwind. Not that he minded walking with her. Hell, he loved it, but he enjoyed it more when she was smiling at him instead of being disgruntled.

From the moment he'd known of her existence, he'd wanted to hold her, protect her. He'd have willingly faced another deadly ambush to give her whatever she needed.

He'd never really had anyone to take care of before. No, that wasn't true. He should have taken care of Connie, should have helped her when she needed it. But he hadn't known because he'd made assumptions. He'd accepted rejection, used pride as a shield, and had shut out the one person who'd really wanted to know him.

He'd failed Connie in the worst possible way, but he wouldn't fail her daughter.

And that was why he needed to maintain his growing friendship with Pixie. He immediately thought of Andy and knew he was making the right decision. Such a happy, curious little guy. Pixie was obviously an amazing mom, and that made him like her. The problem was that he was attracted to her, too. He hadn't expected that. How could he want her when his entire existence was focused on Shayna? He couldn't understand it, but he knew it was true.

Pixie was so small, she looked younger than she probably was; she could easily pass for seventeen. She even had the slim, willowy body to match. That should have been enough to turn his thoughts in a new direction, because he would never date anyone that young.

But the biggest lure was her kind heart. Everything about Pixie—even her name—screamed innocence. She was the light to his darkness, the calm to his storms.

She smiled, and he smiled, too. She held Andy, and in his heart, he felt the love she had for her son. She teased and his mood lifted.

That hadn't happened for years.

Those big blue eyes of hers held compassion and understanding. Her voice was gentle, her body tempting. And that long blond hair? He had the urge to stroke his fingers through the heavy locks.

He was a decade older than she, with a century of cynicism tangled up inside him. He had no business thinking about anything except his reasons for being here.

It'd be easier if Pixie wasn't so perfect, if she didn't seem so . . . pure.

An absurd thought in today's world, but with all the ugliness he'd seen in his lifetime, she was like a breath of fresh air after inhaling nothing but smog.

Looking down at Shayna again, he realized she was sound asleep, and here he was, still rocking her. He stilled, waited to see if she'd awaken, and was pleased when she didn't. He stepped to the side of the porch lights to better see the sunset pouring orange and vibrant pink ribbons over the ever-moving surface of the water. Stars began to dot the sky and fireflies soon followed.

On impulse, he lifted his phone and took a photo, then texted it to Pixie. He'd no sooner sent it than he worried about the time. What if she'd already gone to sleep?

Mere seconds passed before she sent back a smiley face with hearts in the eyes. He grinned, and after two seconds more, she clarified: **I love sunsets.**

As if he'd think the hearts were for him? His grin widened. He started to put his phone away, then changed his mind. Using only his thumb, he typed in: **I do too—now.** He hesitated, then sent it to her.

He'd seen plenty of sunsets over his lifetime, even some in Africa that were stunning. Rainbow hues that settled softly along the horizon.

None had been as nice as this, because here, there was true peace.

"Time to get you to bed, Sugar." He headed back in, making sure to relock the door securely and turning on the soothing musical sounds on his phone.

Shayna didn't stir when he lowered her into her basket and put a light blanket over her. He'd need an actual crib soon, and maybe a sound machine. Tonight he'd start a list.

And somehow, he'd keep his growing friendship with Pixie free of sexual thoughts, no matter how difficult it might be. He could do it.

Hadn't he blocked thoughts of the future when he was younger and didn't know where he'd end up? He'd concentrated on surviving the day. When on a mission, he didn't allow himself to think of a cold cola, a juicy hamburger, or a soft bed. Those thoughts were a distraction and made the time spent in a dangerous situation even worse.

If he could resist all that, surely he could resist the lure of Pixie's gentle touch.

Eventually, he'd tell her why he was really here, what she and her son meant to him and why. Pixie would understand because she'd already proven to have a huge but sensitive heart. The timing was critical, though.

Everyone else could just stay out of his business. He'd keep to himself, do his best to keep a low profile so he didn't draw attention from the locals, and when it was necessary to engage with them, he'd be merely polite. No smiling. No chitchat.

And no fantasizing about what it would be like to have a future with Pixie Nolan.

He knew how to survive without. He'd been doing it all his life.

* * *

The trip to show Brogan around town turned into a shopping expedition of monumental proportions. Pixie felt like a nag every time she explained that he didn't need something, but the man seriously wanted to overdo it. When he wanted to purchase an elaborately decorative crib, she'd reminded him that the lake house didn't have a lot of extra room and showed him how to accomplish the same look with pretty blankets and a mobile. When he took too long deciding on the blankets and a few more outfits for Shayna, she laughingly grabbed some and tossed them in his cart. He liked her choices.

He'd been involved in choosing toys—for both Andy and Shayna—when Shayna started to fuss. Without thinking about it, Pixie lifted the little girl into her arms and soothed her. Andy, who rode in the back of the cart, loved it and wanted her to stand close enough that he could snuggle the baby, too.

Shayna gave a wail, and Andy got ready to cry with her.

He said, "Baby cryin'!" in a panicked yell, clearly wanting Pixie to fix the situation.

"Yes, she is," Pixie soothed, followed by, "Shh, she might be sleepy."

"Shh!" Andy told her; then he turned to Brogan and loudly repeated, "*Shh.* Baby sleepy."

A sort of tingling awareness had Pixie looking up into Brogan's warm gaze. He had a look on his face that was . . . She couldn't define it. Full of tenderness, but yearning, too, and possibly a touch of fear. That didn't make any sense to her. She couldn't imagine Brogan being afraid of anything.

"Guess that's my cue to stop shopping," Brogan said quietly. He smiled down at Andy. "Want to play while we check out?"

Andy happily accepted the book with easy-to-push buttons on each page for animal sounds. Pixie leaned close to him. "Say thank you."

He gave Brogan a big grin complete with eyes squinted tight. "Tank you."

The registers were busy and it took another fifteen minutes to get through the line. By the time they were headed out to the car, she knew everyone had made note of the fact that Brogan held Andy and pushed a cart full of purchases, while she carried Shayna. She countered their assumptions by avoiding eye contact with the onlookers whenever she could, and when necessary, she introduced Brogan as a renter whom she was helping to get settled.

Brogan's quiet manner only spiked curiosity, and gossip spread like wildfire.

Even Marlow and Cort heard, which meant she got a call that night.

She'd just gotten Andy to sleep when her phone buzzed. To keep from waking him, she hurried from the room before she answered the call.

"Hey, Marlow."

Marlow huffed. "Don't play coy. Tell me everything."

"About . . . ?" Of course, Pixie had a good idea what she meant, but still, she wouldn't volunteer anything until she fully understood Marlow's interest.

"You, the hot new guy, gallivanting around town all cozy like . . ."

"Like what?"

"A little family." Quickly, Marlow rushed on. "That's what everyone is saying."

"I was worried about that."

"Is it true? Did you spend the day with him?"

"It's only a little true." Barefoot, in a big T-shirt and panties, Pixie paced through the living room and then out to the enclosed porch. She left the interior lights off so that if anyone was fishing on the lake, they couldn't see her. Dropping onto a padded seat, she curled her legs up and rested her chin on her knees. "I was just showing Brogan around town, but it turned into a shopping spree for his little girl. It's so sweet how he dotes on her. I swear if she makes a sound, he's on it, making sure she's comfortable, that her diaper is dry. The funny thing is, he gives almost as much attention to Andy."

"Well," Marlow said, as reasonable as could be, "Andy is a precious little guy. No one, not even big, badass SEALs, can resist his charm."

Pixie laughed. "I guess so, given all the attention he gets. And he sure knows how to ham it up, especially for Brogan. Did I tell you that he's decreed Shayna as *his* baby? Over and over again, he states: *My baby.* I'm starting to worry what will happen when Brogan leaves."

Marlow gave a very cryptic "Hmm," before saying, "Kids are amazingly adaptable. He'll have you to give him plenty of attention, and of course Cort and me. We miss you guys, by the way. I wish we could all take a vacation together."

Someday, Pixie thought. "We miss you, too, but I'm so glad you're getting some downtime. No one deserves it more."

"Have I told you lately how proud I am of you?"

"All the time," Pixie whispered with emotion. Marlow had been her biggest supporter in her journey to improve her life. "I wouldn't be here without you."

"Baloney. I've never seen a more determined young woman in my entire life. It takes a lot of courage to do what you did, and I think you're amazing. I hope Mr. Hot Stuff realizes it, too."

"Marlow," she cautioned. "The man is only here for a vacation. He'll leave at the end of his lease."

"Maybe, but I hope he gives you some sizzling memories before he goes."

Groaning, Pixie wondered how to derail her friend. She couldn't talk about this, not even with Marlow . . . because in truth, she wouldn't mind a few sizzling memories.

"Hey," Marlow said, "I need to go. Cort is ready to make our own sizzling memories."

Pixie laughed, especially when she heard Marlow squeal, which meant Cort was right there, doing something outrageous. "Good night," she said. "Have fun, and give Cort a hug from Andy and me."

After they'd ended the call, she still sat there for the longest time, watching the fireflies, thinking things she shouldn't, and wanting things she hadn't thought about in a very long time.

Pixie wanted to meet Brogan at the Docker restaurant, thinking that might help quash speculation, and it would be easier than either of them moving car seats from one car to another, but he wanted them to ride together. He thought it'd be fun for the kids to sit together in the back seat—and it was. Andy kept up a steady stream of talking while Shayna entertained him with various sounds and squeals and gurgles.

They were highly amused by each other.

She and Brogan didn't do much talking because they were both so enthralled listening to the kids. She spent much of her time looking into the back seat. He couldn't do that, but she did catch his small smiles when Andy said something cute or when Shayna gave an extra enthusiastic coo.

As they got closer to the restaurant, though, Pixie felt honor bound to remind him of their shared intent. "You know this dinner is going to ramp up rumors. We've been seen together too much."

Though reflective sunglasses hid his gaze, she saw his brows tweak down. "I guess that's one of the drawbacks of a small town. People notice everything?"

"For me, it wasn't a problem. I mean, at first I thought it was, but everyone was so helpful." She didn't want him to think badly of the friends she appreciated, so she explained, "When I first got here, I was"—there was no way to sugarcoat it—"a disaster." Healthwise, financially, socially, and morally. "Andy's dad had died in a car accident, and everything I had was suddenly gone."

"You counted on him a lot?"

The sad truth was also embarrassing. "For everything, really. He'd wanted me to quit my job so we could be together more. He got us an apartment." One he used only occasionally. "He bought my car." She could feel her face heating at her own gullibility. God, she'd been a fool. "I'd say it was bad planning on my part, except I didn't have a plan."

"Sounds like your plan was to be with him. That doesn't seem so bad to me."

Feeling a little sick at what she was about to admit, Pixie shook her head. "I didn't know it when we started dating, but he was married."

After a beat of silence, Brogan merely said, "Oh?" without a hint of condemnation.

Not even with surprise. That single word encouraged her to share more, and so she did.

"I had a really difficult pregnancy. I didn't realize until later just how bad it was, but I was supposed to stay in bed—only I couldn't. I didn't have anyone to do anything for me, and after Dylan was gone, I had no way to pay the rent or buy groceries, or . . . anything."

"You said it was bad?"

With a small shrug, she admitted, "I almost died."

He went still, his expression stark. "Thank God you didn't."

For once not noticing the scenery, Pixie stared straight ahead. "Even after I had Andy, I was still sick and without a job, but then I had a newborn to take care of."

She felt his hand close over hers and looked down in surprise. The sensation of warmth and strength was a revelation. It brought her out of her dismal memories and put her firmly back in the here and now. In the small space of the car with Brogan and both kids, the air seemed to thin so that she had to breathe faster.

His thumb brushed over her knuckles. "It proves how strong you are, to recover from all that and still be so nice."

A sweet ache of yearning and awareness came over her. "I, um, I didn't feel nice. I felt like the scum of the earth."

"No, not ever. Don't say that, okay?" He gave her hand a gentle squeeze before releasing her. "It's not true."

He didn't know her well enough to draw that conclusion. "You don't understand. I didn't have any family." None that mattered. "There was no one close for me to turn to. I would have done anything for Andy, but the only person I could think to go to . . ." Even now, the words stuck in her throat. The feelings of inadequacy, utter failure, almost smothered her at times.

I'm a better person now. Marlow is proud of me. Cort is a dear friend. The townspeople respect me. She gave herself the necessary pep talk far too often.

"Who?" Brogan softly asked, again encouraging her.

She closed her eyes against her own shame and whispered, "I went to Marlow." It still astounded Pixie, the way things had transpired. Yes, she'd prayed, and she'd been so hopeful, but never in her wildest dreams had she expected her life to turn out as it had. "It was an awful thing to do. This is private," she explained, "so please don't ever repeat it. But you see . . ." She bit her lip, then blurted out the truth. "Marlow was married to the man who fathered Andy."

Still, he showed no surprise, just simply nodded. "Did she give you the help you needed?"

No way. Pixie's eyes rounded. He couldn't accept the awful things she'd done so easily. Where was his shock? His disbelief?

At the very least, she'd expected him to be disgusted at her audacity. They'd be at the restaurant any minute now, so Pixie wanted to wrap it up. "Marlow went above and beyond." So many times, she'd wanted to brag about Marlow, but the sordid story of her husband's infidelity wasn't one that should be bandied around town, so Pixie had never been able to share.

Now here was Brogan, giving her the perfect opportunity to explain the magic of her very best friend.

The words seemed to rush from her. "I'd never had a close female friend—any friend, really—so I had no idea a woman could be that bighearted, that understanding or supportive. Marlow has such an enormous capacity for love, and she just wrapped us up in it. She didn't blame me. Instead, she helped me. She was still getting over her own devastation—the trauma of divorce proceedings, then the death of her husband, all on the heels of finding out that he was an awful cheater. But she never blamed me. Isn't that incredible?"

"I think it just sounds smart. How could she blame you if you hadn't known he was married?"

Marlow had said that often enough. Pixie shrugged. "Okay, fine. For that, I could be forgiven. But showing up on her doorstep with literally nothing but a baby and a single diaper? Brogan, that's how dire things were for me—and yet she took me in."

"Of course she did."

"No, there's no 'of course' to it. She could have pawned me off on someone else. Could have told me to go to a shelter or something. Instead, she let me in, took me to a doctor, and she and Cort, together, made sure I got healthy. Then she taught me how to survive. I wouldn't be who I am now without her. She was like a big sister, a best friend, an instructor, and a tutor." Her excitement gained momentum, until Pixie was smiling again. "She helped with Andy and she even gave me a job!"

Brogan smiled. "Nice."

"Beyond nice. Incredible, even. Brogan, she accepted me. She and Cort both. Other than an aunt who took me in when . . ." Pixie stumbled over her words. She was dumping enough on him already, without going into the failings of her parents. "She raised me when my parents couldn't. But other than Aunt Mary, I never had family. Definitely not close family. Now I do because they're it." They were *everything*. "There's not much I wouldn't do for either of them."

Thoughtfully silent, Brogan pulled into the lot and parked the SUV a good distance away from the entrance in the only open spot he could find. After a few seconds while Pixie fairly held her breath, unsure how he would react, he pulled off his sunglasses and gave her a smile.

His gray-eyed gaze held her. "Sometimes, when we run out of options and we have no idea what to do, the most unlikely answer turns out to be the right one."

Before she could sort that out, he continued.

"I'm glad Marlow was there for you. It's like a lesson, right? Good people really do exist, and fate helps us find them when we need them the most."

The sincerity of his words made Pixie wonder if he was talking about himself now. Had he run out of options, too? She thought of the scars she'd seen, the occasional look of yearning in his stormy eyes.

Maybe he meant that Shayna had come into his life when he'd needed her most. She wondered what experiences he'd had in the military, and if he might have faced a lack of options. As a child, he had been shut off from his father. He hadn't yet said much about his mother.

This time, she reached for his hand. "You were there for Shayna when she needed you. I'd say that so far, fate hasn't let her down."

He glanced into the back seat. "They've gotten quiet. Do you think they're falling asleep?"

Far too often, Brogan changed the subject on her; but then, they weren't really even friends. They were acquaintances. She had no right to expect confidences from him just because he'd let her share part of her past. "Andy?" she said, checking whether he was getting sleepy.

"My baby."

Pixie laughed at his reply.

"You should laugh more often." With that cryptic comment, Brogan got out and opened the back door. "I'll get the tank if you want to get the lightweight."

"Sure." She enjoyed holding Shayna. "You realize people are going to do more talking."

"I have a plan for that," he said. "I've been keeping a low profile, so with luck they've forgotten all about me. And if not, we'll ignore them. Other than a quick nod if I'm spoken to, I won't engage with anyone. Soon they'll decide I'm not worth gossiping about."

Pixie snorted. "You don't have to engage. You don't have to do anything. It won't matter. You're just . . . you, and that's enough." She straightened with Shayna in her arms, gently kissed the baby's forehead, and got the blanket from her car seat.

He stared at her over the roof. "And you're just you," he said with conviction. "More than enough."

"What—ouch!" The question was interrupted when Shayna grabbed a hank of her hair. "Little girl, I'm going to have to wear a bun around you."

"Now that would be a shame." Brogan grinned as he circled the car to assist her. "Your hair is fascinating, so I can't blame Sugar for wanting to get a handful." He held Andy in one arm as if he weighed nothing, and deftly loosened Shayna's damp fingers.

Pixie quickly pulled her hair to one side, then went still when Brogan helped, smoothing it down over her shoulder and away from his niece. When she remembered to inhale, her breath shuddered.

He smiled and stepped away. "I hope they have high chairs."

"They do, for toddlers and younger babies. If Shayna isn't comfortable in the infant seat, we can bring in the stroller."

He paused, undecided, then said, "I'm going to bring it just in case. I need her diaper bag anyway."

"If you don't mind, I could put one of Andy's diapers in there, too. Then we won't need both diaper bags."

Since he was agreeable, they ended up combining their supplies. Bibs and sanitizer wipes, bottles and a sippy cup, extra blankets and sunscreen. A few toys to keep the kids occupied, as well as books.

Pixie had to laugh. "Well, this won't confuse anyone."

Very seriously, Brogan said, "We're not going to worry about that, okay?"

Right. Sure. Clearly, this man doesn't know how small towns work.

It was a few minutes more before they entered the restaurant and were greeted by a waiter—and a lot of curious stares. Brogan kept his attention on the young man offering them an option of indoor or outdoor seating, but Pixie smiled at the people she knew.

Since the deck offered a view of the lake, Pixie suggested they sit outside. It was a mild, sunny day, but the table was shaded. She knew the kids would enjoy seeing the birds that swooped over the water, along with the occasional sailboat floating by.

Andy was already in his high chair and Brogan had just finished getting Shayna settled by padding her seat with a thin cotton blanket rolled up, when they heard the roar of a boat engine.

"What in the world?" Pixie said, pushing back her chair and standing for a better view. The cove in front of the restaurant was a no-wake zone, meaning boats were prohibited from going fast enough to cause a wake.

Brogan muttered, "Shit" as he pulled his wallet and phone from his pocket and kicked off his shoes.

"What are you . . . ?" Pixie didn't understand, not until a fast-moving pontoon rammed right into a dock holding several people, including some young kids. The dock shuddered, wood cracked, and people screamed as the kids fell in. The motor continued to churn the water. "Watch the babies," Brogan ordered, and then he was vaulting down the stairs, three at a time. He hit the grass at a full run.

"Dear God," Pixie said, her heart in her throat as she took in the chaos.

As the driver frantically tried to reverse the boat away from the dock, she heard Brogan shout, "No!"

There were people in the water behind him! With the front of the boat wedged half up on the dock, the propeller churned, spraying water with a horrible grinding sound.

Everyone started yelling at once, but no one was doing anything.

Except Brogan. He was a man in motion as he pounded onto the dock.

In smooth succession, he grabbed the driver out of the boat, switched off the motor, and pocketed the keys. "Everyone okay?"

"My son!" a woman screamed hysterically. "I can't find him."

Another said, "Oh, my God, there's blood in the water."

Brogan didn't hesitate to dive in. People hung at the edge of the dock, watching, waiting.

The inebriated man staggered to the shore and collapsed onto a bench.

For what felt like the longest time, Brogan didn't come back up.

Pixie glanced at Andy and Shayna. As if they sensed the tension, they stared back at her, their eyes big and watchful, but they were okay. They weren't fretting, thank God.

To ensure they wouldn't see anything too awful, she half-turned their chairs. They no longer had a view of the lake, but they could still see the hill beyond, the birds and trees, as well as a part of the restaurant.

Trembling all over, she moved closer to the deck rail, her gaze searching the surface of the lake. Where was Brogan?

He emerged to a collective gasp from the crowd. In his arms, he held a limp boy whose head was covered in blood. Pixie covered her mouth, fear gripping her.

Seemingly without effort, Brogan climbed the ladder, carrying the boy. Water dripped off him, forming a puddle as he carefully laid the child on the rough wooden dock. To Pixie, the boy appeared to be only seven or eight, and he was frighteningly lifeless and pale. The crowd surged around him.

Pixie heard Brogan loudly instruct, "Call 911," and then, "Back up, damn it!"

With obvious expectation that his orders would be carried out, he started CPR.

Tense silence gripped the onlookers as everyone anxiously waited, not moving, barely breathing, until the boy abruptly gave a harsh, sputtering gurgle that turned into a fit of coughing. Brogan turned him to his side and held him steady. Pixie couldn't hear what he was saying, but she knew he was offering soothing words as he supported the boy.

The poor mother sank to her knees, sobbing uncontrollably. Brogan put one hand on her shoulder and leaned close to speak near her ear. Whatever he said, she nodded agreement. He removed his shirt, wrung it out, and wrapped it around the boy's head. Fresh blood was already seeping through. Lifting the child in his arms, Brogan stood and took long, sure strides up the grassy incline. The boy hugged his neck so that blood now covered Brogan, too. His mother ran frantically behind them.

When Brogan got closer, she heard him say to the woman, "Try to calm down or you're going to scare him."

The poor mother instantly mopped her eyes and gave her son a wan smile.

Brogan issued calm instructions as he reached the deck. “I need dry towels, plenty of them, a first aid kit, and ice.”

Two women ran off to find the necessary items.

Using his foot, Brogan pulled a chair away from a table and then carefully lowered the boy into it. “Hold his hand,” he told the mother, but he also kept a hand on the boy’s shoulder as he turned to a young waiter. “I need a dry shirt for him. Can you find something?”

Another man stepped up and asked, “What can I do?”

“Make sure everyone else on the dock is okay.”

“The driver of the boat?”

Brogan dug in the pocket of his wet jeans, pulled out the keys, and handed them to the man. “Don’t let him go anywhere.”

“I won’t.” The man started down the hill.

Pixie stood between the two high chairs, one hand stroking Andy’s hair, the other on Shayna, as she watched Brogan efficiently care for the boy.

He was magnificent.

Confident and in control as he tended the awful gash on the boy’s head, as well as another on his forearm. His hands were sure, his words comforting, and soon he had the bleeding somewhat under control. Pixie knew the boy would still need stitches, and she worried about the bruising already showing up on his face.

Others watched in awe—and no wonder. They, too, could see Brogan’s scars, as well as the tattoo that proclaimed him part of the elite Navy SEALs. Yes, she’d looked up the design. The eagle, anchor, trident, and flintlock pistol were specific to SEALs.

Brogan was a larger-than-life hero, right here in Bramble, Kentucky, and he’d just handled a devastating situation with ease.

She was so proud of him.

At the same time, she felt completely useless.

The injured boy looked far too pale to Pixie, especially with blood still staining his face and neck, and even his chest, but he was alive thanks to Brogan.

"What's your name, son?" Brogan asked.

"Benny." He wiped at his eye, saw the blood on his fingers, and started to panic.

Brogan cleaned his hand as if it was nothing. "What a strong kid you are, Benny. Not too many people can brag about tackling a propeller. I wouldn't recommend it, though." New towels arrived, so he switched out the wrap on Benny's head. "You've got a cut on your noggin, and noggins bleed a lot, but it's not too serious. I want you to know that, okay?"

With a weak smile, the boy tried to look at his arm, but Brogan carefully tilted his face back up. "You're going to be fine. You can take my word for it, okay?"

"Okay." Still worried, the kid asked, "Will I need stitches?"

"Yes, but you won't feel a thing, and just think how many stories you'll be able to tell your friends. In a town this size, you're bound to be a local legend. For years to come, they'll be talking about Benny, the boy who blocked a boat propeller with his head."

Benny grinned. "I didn't mean to."

"You still did it. No one else got hurt, so I say you're a hero."

His mother stroked his wet hair. "He has so many friends. They'll want to hear all about it, I'm sure."

Brogan smiled at her. "Of course they will." When the mother's lips trembled, Brogan nudged the boy. "Tell your mama you're fine so she doesn't start crying again." Lower, as if in confidence, he said, "Mothers worry a lot, and if you're like me, you'll do anything to keep her from crying."

The boy grinned, and with blood staining the side of his

face, the expression was especially endearing. “Don’t cry, Mom. I promise, I’m okay.”

“Good job,” Brogan praised as he painstakingly cleaned the wound on Benny’s arm.

His mother nodded. “Totally convincing, honey.” She took her son’s hand when he winced. “Thank you, sir.”

“You can call me Brogan.”

“I’m Ellen.”

The man who had gone down the hill returned, cleared his throat, and said, “Everyone else is fine. Lot of damage to the dock and boat, but everyone is accounted for.”

“Great. Thank you.”

Straightening, the man said, “No, thank *you.*” He glanced back, then at Brogan again. “From all of us.”

Brogan merely nodded.

Finally, EMTs showed up. As soon as they were on the scene, Brogan explained what had happened.

Tears filled Pixie’s eyes.

The boy’s mother cried, too, as she whispered to the EMT, “I thought I’d lost him, but this wonderful man brought him back to me.”

The EMT bent to check the boy’s arm. “Nice job.” He asked Brogan, “Where’d you learn to treat a wound?”

“I served.”

Brows up, the EMT glanced at the tattoo on Brogan’s upper arm, then gave his attention back to the boy. “Thank you for your service.” He smiled to the boy. “What do you say, kiddo? Want a ride in an ambulance just for kicks?”

Frantically, the boy turned to his mom.

She asked, “Am I allowed to ride with him?”

“Yes, ma’am.”

“What about my car? Both of my friends already left.”

Pixie cleared her throat. “Brogan and I could follow with one of us driving your car.”

All eyes moved to Pixie, and it suddenly felt as if the entire restaurant was watching her.

Brogan didn't get a chance to weigh in on her plan before the woman rushed to Pixie to embrace her. "Thank you so much. I . . . Nothing like this has ever happened before." She touched her forehead. "I never even considered . . . He loves the lake. I thought it would be a fun day."

"I'm sure it was, until he got hurt." Pixie took her hands. "I can't imagine how you must be feeling. Is there someone you can call so you won't be alone tonight?"

"I'll be with Benny." She smiled back at her son. "He's all I need."

For Pixie, it was like seeing her own future laid out before her, except she had Marlow and Cort; and whenever necessary, she knew they'd be there for her. Still, the situation felt eerily similar to what her own life would be.

The EMTs were ready to go, so she said to Ellen, "If you want to give me your number, I'll call you once we get to the hospital so I can give you back your keys."

They exchanged numbers quickly, and Ellen described her car and where it was parked. Pixie was aware of Brogan watching, his laser focus on her as if he wanted to figure her out. She'd volunteered him without a qualm, when maybe she shouldn't have. He was soaked, shirtless, and he'd just been through his own trauma.

Or at least she assumed fishing a boy from the lake and bringing him back to life had been traumatic for him. It had certainly rattled her. Still, she had to believe he'd be amenable to assisting the woman just a little bit more.

When the mother and her son started out, Brogan moved to Pixie's side. He glanced at the kids, then asked her very quietly, "You got this for another minute?"

She nodded.

"I'll be right back." He paused to touch her cheek, looked as if he wanted to say something, but then strode after the EMTs.

Shakily, Pixie sank into her seat. Everyone was looking around as if unsure what to do, now that Brogan wasn't on the scene. She felt the same. Fortunately, the babies were enthralled with all the chaos, rather than afraid. Since she'd turned their chairs, they hadn't seen Benny or all the blood.

It was on the decking, the chair—she'd never seen so much blood.

Pulling her chair from the table, she scooted it over so she could sit directly in front of the kids. She knew they had to be getting hungry, so she got out Andy's cup for him, along with a cookie, and then found one of Shayna's bottles. The infant would likely need a diaper change soon, too.

Some people still watched her, but she concentrated on feeding the kids, talking softly to them while waiting for Brogan to return. Andy noticed a bird. Shayna took her bottle with greed.

She really needed three hands, but for now, she was making do.

"Who is he?"

"I've never seen him before."

"He sure took charge."

"Did you see how he ripped the guy out of his boat? It was like he weighed nothing."

"He looks like he's been through war, and that was definitely a SEAL tattoo."

"Thank God he was here."

The whispers swirled around Pixie, but she did her best to tune them out. When a waiter stopped by the table with a cola, she looked up in surprise.

"He asked me to bring this to you. He, um, said the caffeine and sugar would help."

"He who?"

"The big guy."

"Oh." Yes, her throat was parched and she was shaky, but she hadn't thought about it until that icy drink was placed before her. "Thank you."

He nodded. "Robin said your meals are on the house. Whatever you want."

Robin Merriman ran the restaurant, but Pixie hadn't seen her yet today. "She's here?"

The young man nodded. "She's got her hands full with all the excitement."

"I can imagine. Give her my thanks, but I don't think we'll have time to eat now." As soon as Brogan returned, they'd be heading to the hospital.

The waiter left, but Robin returned a few minutes later with a big bag and two more drinks in carryout cups. "I know you're in a hurry, so I chose meals for you. Take them with you."

"You didn't need to—"

Robin put a hand on her shoulder. "I want to." Lower, she said, "About bowled me over when I first got a look at him."

In her mid-forties, with stylishly short dark hair and pretty green eyes, Robin was an attractive woman. Never before had Pixie heard her mention a man in such a way.

"He's renting the lake house."

"And saving customers." She turned to smile at Andy, and then Shayna. "What a guy, right? He'll be the talk of the town for a year. A real live action hero. I don't know what would have happened if he hadn't been here."

Pixie silently agreed. Without Brogan, would Benny even be alive now? The thought was chilling.

Just then, Brogan returned. He wore a new shirt that advertised the Docker restaurant. His jeans had been replaced with loose shorts. She assumed his wet clothes were in the bag he carried.

Before Pixie could ask, he explained, "One of the workers had the clothes with him."

"The shirt is a little small," Robin noted. "I think you needed an XL."

"It's dry, so no complaints from me." He tried to pay her for the food, but she shook her head and took a step back. "It's on the house. And I'm going to get you that XL, too, next time you come in."

As he pushed his feet into his shoes and put his wallet and phone in a pocket of the shorts, he said, "You don't need to—"

"This town owes you, Brogan. A few meals and a shirt are the very least I can do. I know Ellen. She and her girlfriends visit often." Robin closed her eyes, drew a quick breath, and tried to find her composure. When she opened them again, she said, "I'm short on words, but thank you."

With a nod, he relented and put away his money.

"Um." A nearby waiter shifted his stance. "Cops will be here soon."

"Robin has my number. They can call." He lifted Andy from his seat, half-chewed cookie mess and all, quickly settled him in the stroller, put the bag of food in behind him, along with the bag of his clothes, and then lifted out Shayna. He was careful to make sure she could finish her bottle. To Pixie, he asked, "You ready?"

She sensed his haste, knew Robin's gratitude had made him uneasy; they really did need to go. "Yes, of course." She collected the diaper bag and her purse. "I can push the stroller."

"Great. Let's go." Ignoring all the curious gazes, he kept his attention straight ahead.

That didn't stop anyone from looking, of course.

A chair slid back, and someone clapped.

Then more chairs were pushed from tables, followed by more clapping.

Pixie fought a smile, especially when she noticed Brogan's disconcerted expression.

So much for keeping a low profile.

The commotion swelled until it seemed everyone at the restaurant, inside and out, was on their feet applauding him.

Brogan's jaw locked.

She leaned into his shoulder and said, "They're only thanking you."

Pausing, his shoulders rigid, Brogan turned to face the crowd. Once everyone had quieted down, he gave a nod and said, "Have a nice night, everyone." Then he turned again and ushered Pixie to the lot.

She couldn't stop grinning, especially when Andy clapped his hands and yelled, "G'night!"

CHAPTER 5

As they reached the car, Brogan floundered. He owed Pixie an apology, but maybe here, in the restaurant lot, wasn't the right time, especially since he wasn't sure what to say. He'd asked her out, told her they'd talk, and then he'd more or less abandoned her without a thought.

He ran a hand over his face. Instincts were all well and good; he'd survived more than once because he'd listened to that internal call to act instead of think. Now, however, he had more than himself to think about. More than other trained team members. He had Shayna, and if things went right, he'd have Andy and Pixie, too.

After giving him a worried glance, she pushed the stroller to the back of his SUV. She was loaded down with everything while he let Shayna finish her bottle.

"Pixie . . ."

"I'm sorry." In a rush, she turned and put a hand to his chest. "I should have asked before volunteering you to do even more. I just . . . I looked at Benny's mom and I felt so bad for her, I wanted to do something, too. It was thoughtless. I'm sure you'd rather go home and—"

"It's not a problem," he interrupted, bemused that she would be apologizing when it should be him. "I'm glad you offered.

With so many other people around, I didn't even think about how she'd get her car. I just assumed someone would help."

"Someone probably would have."

After all that turmoil, he found a smile. "Someone did. You." Because that's the type of woman she was. While the others had stood around, unsure what to do, Pixie had stepped up.

"But you have to be . . ."

"What?"

"I don't know. Upset?" She shook her head as if to discount the word as soon as she said it.

"No, I'm not upset." His mouth twitched.

Granted, his adrenaline was still pumping, but that would subside soon. Mostly, he was ready to move on, but it made sense to make sure a single mother had what she needed first.

Pixie frowned at him. "After what you went through, I'm sure you're ready to change into your own clothes. And you must be hungry."

He covered her hand with his own. "The same is true for you."

"Except I didn't do anything."

That made him frown. "Of course you did."

With a puff of exasperation, she said, "I did nothing, except panic a little."

"You watched the kids."

"Ha! They were fine, more interested in the confusion, a new setting, and the birds than anything else." Lowering her gaze, she admitted, "I wish I was more like you, but overall, I was useless. I had no idea how to help."

The way her words tumbled out, rushed and defensive, bothered Brogan a lot. "Listen to me, okay? No one there was qualified to help that kid."

"Except you, and that's my point! Without you, he'd be . . ." She shook her head, refusing to say the word.

"He's alive because of *you*, too. I wouldn't have left Shayna with anyone else, and that means I couldn't have saved the boy."

"No, I—"

"Pixie." He tilted up her face, much as he'd done with Benny, in a gesture meant to calm, reassure, and connect. "No one but you."

After a second of uncertainty, she drew an uneven breath. "You mean that?"

"I never would have trusted Shayna's care with anyone else, definitely not a stranger. On my way down that hill, I knew someone was going to be hurt, maybe killed. I felt it in my guts. A drunk asshole with a big boat, a churning propeller, kids everywhere—that scenario equals disaster." Okay, so maybe he *was* a little upset. Even now, he felt a killing rage at how badly things could have ended. He understood and accepted accidents, but he had zero tolerance for gross negligence, which was exactly what that driver had exhibited. "No one else was trained to react, and I kept thinking, 'Thank God Pixie is with me.'"

She stared up at him with her big, solemn blue eyes, and finally nodded. "Thank you for trusting me."

I want you to trust me, too. Damn, he wanted that. Instead of saying it out loud, he searched her face and realized how the near tragedy had affected her. "You're shaking. Are you sure you're okay to drive?"

"Yes. I'm positive. I'm rattled, I won't deny that, but like you, I wouldn't risk Andy if I wasn't sure it was safe."

Brogan accepted that. "All right. I'll be right behind you, okay? Any problems, just pull over."

With a half smile, she handed him Ellen's keys. Together, they got the kids in their car seats, with everything else stowed in back. Shayna was already yawning, ready for a nap, and Andy looked a little tuckered out, too.

Brogan pressed a kiss to each baby's head, then had to resist doing the same with Pixie. Wasn't easy, but he got into Ellen's car, moved the seat way back to accommodate his long legs, and waited to follow Pixie.

Thankfully, the hospital wasn't too far away, because he just knew Shayna needed a diaper change. He'd probably have to handle it in the hospital parking lot.

He'd had big plans for that dinner, damn it. He'd wanted to ease Pixie into the idea of a closer relationship. Instead, she was shaky, upset, and still going out of her way to help others.

The night wasn't half over, either. He knew that, even if she didn't.

Trailing behind her, he had to smile at what an overly cautious driver she was. She didn't go one mile over the speed limit, used her blinker early, and was courteous to other drivers, too.

He thought of how she'd looked when she'd taken Ellen's hands, the compassion in her eyes. It didn't take a mind reader to know that Pixie, also a single mom, had felt a kinship to the other woman. It helped that Pixie had such close friends. From what she'd said, they were better than any family he knew.

Brogan had no real concept of family. Sure, he'd thought of his team as brothers. He'd have given his life for any one of them.

Instead, they'd died, and he'd been left behind. To miss them. To live alone. To wonder over and over again what he might have done differently to change the outcome.

Every time those memories resurfaced in his mind, his heart raced and his throat tried to close up. He gripped the steering wheel harder, aware of sweat breaking out on the back of his neck as he fought to stay focused, to push the smothering sense of failure away so he could do what had to be done here and now.

Yes, he'd wanted to die, too. Being the only survivor had felt like a kick in the face. Worse than death in so many ways.

Until he'd been told about Shayna.

His sister would never know the gift she'd given him. If he could have Connie back, if he could redo his past with her, he would. Instead, she'd thrown him a lifeline. Not just by entrusting him to care for Shayna, but because she'd left so many letters, too. He knew what Connie wanted—for her daughter and for the brother who'd let her down.

God, the ways that he'd failed the only family who'd cared for him was an unbearable reality.

Now, whenever he thought of Connie, he thanked God that he was alive, able to care for Shayna, to show her what he thought love should be. His life had meaning again.

It wasn't what he'd thought it would be. It was better.

Gradually, the awful anxiety faded and he felt more like himself, like a man in control. His muscles relaxed. The sweat on his neck dried. He was able to draw an even breath.

Pixie turned on her signal to give him plenty of notice when they neared the small hospital. Thankfully, the lot wasn't too crowded, and they were able to park near each other.

He walked up to the SUV to open her door.

She got out quietly, saying, "Andy's asleep, but I think Shayna needs her diaper changed. She just started to fuss."

Nodding, he opened the back door and unbuckled his little Sugar. She was working herself up to a real fit. He lifted her out, carefully cradled her close, and crooned to her. "Shh, baby girl, it's okay. I'll have you dry in no time."

"I'm sorry," Pixie said. "I should have checked her diaper before we left the restaurant."

No way would he let Pixie take that blame. "It was my job to check, but we both wanted to get here. She's fine, I'm sure." Already, Shayna had settled down and now she was busy snuggling into his neck, one small hand fisted in his shirt as she rubbed her face against him. God, he loved it, and he loved her. He kissed her forehead, then kissed her again. And once more. He'd never tire of her sweet scent and softness, or the way she clung to him.

When he looked up, Pixie was giving him one of those "aww" smiles.

To fend off whatever she might say, he asked, "Are you familiar with this place?"

"Yes." She stroked the baby's back, her expression tender. "I had a few appointments here. I mean, back when I first came to Bramble." Mouth lifting to the side, she admitted, "Marlow insisted. She was like a general giving orders, but they were all for my own good."

"Because you were sick, and you did need care?" He'd love to know details, the extent of her illness, just how much help she'd had. Hell, he wanted to know everything about Pixie, every tiny detail.

"Yes." Letting the subject go, she went to the back of the vehicle and opened it, spread out a blanket for him, and got out a diaper and wipes. "How do you want to do this? Do you want to stay here with the kids while I run in Ellen's keys, or vice versa?"

Brogan indicated his mismatched clothes. "If it doesn't matter to you, I'll wait here."

"That's fine." She handed him the key fob to the SUV and got out her phone to call Ellen. "You have my number if Andy wakes up and needs me."

"Yes, I do."

Knowing she'd ask Ellen how she was and if she needed anything, he said, "Don't rush, Pixie. Take whatever time you need, but let me know if you're going to be gone awhile." If so, he'd find something else for the kids to eat. They had to be getting hungry.

He was more than ready to eat, but his own comfort was a

secondary concern. Taking care of the kids, and then getting Pixie home where she could relax; those were his priorities.

"I will." She hesitated a moment more, then put in Ellen's number as she headed to the hospital's emergency entrance.

Watching her go, he realized that Pixie did trust him. She wouldn't have left Andy with him otherwise. Talk about a boost to the ego.

Every time he was with her, she did or said something that confirmed he'd made the right decision. Coming here to meet her, to get to know Andy, was the right move.

Now he just had to explain it all to Pixie—hopefully, in a way that got her on board and didn't offend her.

He rarely avoided an unpleasant task. His MO was to get it done and out of the way.

But given what they'd just gone through and the fact that Pixie was still shaken, maybe he needed to hold off. It wouldn't be a smart move to overwhelm her.

The last thing he wanted was for her to find him creepy or stalkerish.

After he changed Shayna, he got behind the wheel, holding her in his arms, and started the car again so he could keep the air-conditioning on. The weather wasn't too warm, but with the sun on the windshield, it wouldn't take the car long to get uncomfortable.

Andy slept on, but Brogan figured if the little boy woke, then he'd just get in the back seat between the two kids to keep them entertained.

For now, he quietly played with Shayna, earning not only a grin, but a giggling laugh.

"I love you, little girl. I hope you know that."

She grinned again, kicked her chubby legs, and said, "Haaa."

His brows shot up. "Wanna try *Da* instead?"

She reached for his nose and repeated, "Haaa," followed by a raspberry.

Never had Brogan grinned so much prior to getting Shayna. To him, she was endlessly amusing, precious beyond words, and utterly brilliant. They were still playing that nose game when Pixie returned fifteen minutes later.

Like a very attuned mom, she peeked in the car, saw Andy was still sleeping, and walked around to the driver's side.

Brogan opened the door. "All done?"

"Yes." Her eyes were red with unshed tears. "Would you like me to put Shayna in her car seat now?"

She looked as if she needed a moment, so he nodded. "Sure." Carefully, he passed the baby to her.

She must have needed a hug, because Pixie drew the baby in close and nuzzled her little neck. Of course, Shayna got two fists full of hair. Pixie didn't seem to mind.

Silently, Brogan got out of the car. "Hey," he whispered. He could hear Pixie's strained breathing and it shattered him. Putting a hand on her back, he gently stroked. "It's okay." Praying he was right, he asked, "The kid?"

Her swallow was audible. "Benny's fine."

What a relief. Head wounds were tricky. There was always the chance he'd missed something, especially since the boy had needed CPR. "How about I get this grabby little girl out of your hair—literally?"

With a broken laugh, Pixie reached for one fist while Brogan got the other. In only a few seconds, they had her free. "I really will have to start braiding it." Instead of handing Shayna to him, she opened the door and leaned inside to finish the task. This time, she avoided little fingers and got the baby strapped in, then gave her a lightweight blanket to cuddle. Lastly, holding her hair away, Pixie kissed Shayna's forehead.

He was ashamed to say his attention had gone to her backside.

How long had he been celibate? Too damn long, for sure. There'd been the assignment in northern Africa, the ambush that had left him stranded as the only survivor, finally his recovery, and then the grueling weeks spent in the hospital.

Sex, women, had been the furthest thing on his mind once he'd gotten back on his feet. He'd wanted only to get to Shayna, to figure out the best path forward for her. She deserved better than the kind of childhood he'd had, and he was determined to see that she got it.

When Pixie straightened, he led her around to her side of the car. "Let's get you home."

Her smile flickered into place. "I'm more concerned about the kids. Right now, I'd rather Andy stay asleep, because when he wakes up, he's going to be a bear. But if he sleeps too long, I'll never get him back to bed tonight."

Brogan waited until she was seated and was fastening her seat belt before he circled back to the driver's seat to reply. "This is one of those times when a contingency plan is needed, right? Everything will be happening late. His dinner, his bath."

"My dinner, my shower." She dug a tissue from her purse and dabbed away her tears. "He'll go to sleep later, but he'll probably wake up just as early. Oh, well." She sent him a look. "We parents have to be adaptable."

We parents. That sentiment sank into his heart, his bones—his very soul. "I like this conversation." Especially with her.

Pixie laughed quietly. "Most people don't want to talk about kids."

"Guess I'm not most people." He backed out of the parking space and turned back onto the road. She was so quiet, it bothered him. "Do you want to talk about it?"

"What do you mean?"

"You were a little . . . emotional. After you saw, Ellen, I mean."

"Oh, yes." She sighed. "If someone cries, I cry. It's ridiculous. She's okay, just overwrought. Benny is tired and scared, and cleaning the wounds hurt."

"Yeah, that's often worse than the stitches."

She gave him a curious look.

"In general, I mean." That explanation didn't quite cut it, so he added, "My training included basic medical." Yet she'd no doubt noticed his wounds, so she knew he had personal experience, too. Twice now, she'd seen him without his shirt. Hell, the whole restaurant had seen him today.

He didn't hide his wounds, but he didn't showcase them, either, and whenever possible he'd rather avoid questions. In the hospital, that hadn't been possible. Here in Bramble? He didn't yet know.

Pixie seemed to understand his aversion, because she said, "Ellen started out thanking me; then suddenly she was sobbing." Again, she dabbed at her eyes. "She's trying so hard to hold it together for Benny, but, Brogan, she literally almost lost him." With a sniffle, she added, "It breaks my heart, imagining how she must feel."

He could hear in Pixie's voice that she was close to crying again. "Believe me, I know." He hesitated, but she was being so open with him, he found himself opening up, too. "When I first found Benny underwater, I didn't know if I'd gotten to him in time."

"Oh, God." She put her hand on his forearm. "That must have been horrible."

"Finding someone in lake water is always iffy. It's dark, and the currents keep everything moving. Where a body goes in isn't necessarily where it'll be a minute later." Frustration bit into him. "She's clearly a good mom who loves her son, but . . ."

"But?"

"Benny should have been wearing a life preserver. All of the kids should have. The restaurant should have a rule or something," he ended on a grumble.

Pixie blinked at him, then nodded. "That's a great suggestion. I think I'll mention it to Robin. Anyone under a certain age should be required to wear some kind of safety device, even if just floaties."

"Floaties?"

"You know, those inflatable things that go on kids' arms."

He shook his head. "No good. A life vest would be better."

She smiled. "I'll pass along the suggestion."

"That ought to make me popular," he said, his tone deadpan.

She gave his shoulder a little push. "I'll act like it's my idea, if you want."

"Yeah, let's do that."

Her soft laugh went a long way toward taking off his edge. "I like hearing you laugh more than seeing you cry." Of course, it took mere seconds to rethink that. "Not that you can't cry with me. You can." He meant it. "You're empathetic. It's nice that you feel for other people. I don't mean to discourage that."

This time, her hand smoothed over his shoulder. "You don't need to worry about offending me. I know I'm often too weepy, but you're right, I do feel for other people. I know when I was at my worst, how awful it was. I don't want anyone else to feel that way."

She was such a good person—and he hadn't been 100 percent honest with her. He hoped her empathy would extend to his situation, once he gave her all the details.

Since he probably wouldn't do that tonight, he decided to shift the conversation. "Do you think Ellen will be okay to drive home?"

"One of her friends is coming to the hospital to bring her some clothes. The doctor said Benny is fine, and he's fully alert, but since he was resuscitated, they want to keep him overnight."

"Not a bad idea. Ellen's staying with him?"

Smiling, Pixie said, "They'd have one heck of a time telling her she couldn't. Thankfully, they're bringing in a lounge chair that she can use, along with a pillow and blanket." She slanted him a teasing look. "According to Ellen, Benny's bragging to everyone that you said he was a hero."

"Not a lie. He was a brave kid. That could have gone either way, you know? He could have been screaming and hysterical, but instead he kept it together."

"Well, *I* felt a little hysterical. I've never seen so much blood."

"You were on your toes the whole time. I noticed how you turned the kids' chairs. That was smart thinking. We didn't need them seeing all that blood and getting scared." He had no idea if Shayna was old enough to understand the significance of blood, but Andy might have been. "You gave them snacks, too." His brows drew together as the truth dawned on him. "You were a partner, Pixie." *There when I needed you*—though he doubted she'd see it that way.

To him, the realization was huge. "I appreciate that a lot."

She smiled a moment, then quietly asked, "What do we do now?"

What he wanted to do and what he needed to do were two very separate things. "What do you mean?"

"You and I have food to share, but we're in two different houses." She faltered only a moment before asking, "Do you think you'd want to come in? We could have dinner and give the kids a little time to unwind before we start our separate bedtime routines."

Damn, he wanted that a lot. Sitting down in her house, spending a quiet, private evening with her. It sounded great to him.

He was about to answer her when her phone buzzed.

She had been watching him expectantly, but he said, "Get that if you want."

Blowing out a short breath, she said, "Thanks," and took her purse from the floor to retrieve her phone.

Seeing her disappointment bothered him, so before she answered, he said, "Pixie?"

"Yes?"

"I'd love to come in. Thank you."

There was a lot of confusion once they got to the house. Andy woke up cranky; Brogan was supposed to call back the police, who had a few questions about the boating incident; Shayna was hungry; and their food was now cold.

Still, Pixie was unreasonably excited. Nervous too.

Of course, she understood that Brogan's visit was only friendly. Not at all romantic. Undoubtedly, he wasn't even interested in friendship if it came with any type of restriction. She got it. Before Brogan, she'd felt the same.

Andy's father had burned her so badly, disrupting her life in ways she never could have anticipated, that the idea of getting close to a man, any man, turned her stomach. Trust another guy? No, never.

Except . . . she trusted Cort, mainly because he was like a big brother, showing only the concern of a natural-born protector. It hadn't taken Pixie any time at all to see that Cort loved Marlow, and vice versa. They were perfect for each other.

Brogan, however, was not in the same category.

For one thing, he was completely unattached. For another, she'd never met a man so physically imposing, or so appealing. What she felt for him was in no way sisterly.

She hadn't even felt this way about Dylan. With Andy's dad, she'd mostly been delighted to be noticed, flattered to be included, and thrilled by the numerous gifts he'd given her. She hadn't looked at Dylan and gotten tongue-tied or felt warmth swirling in her stomach. She hadn't fantasized over him when she should have been sleeping.

The sex had been great. Eye-opening even. But already she anticipated dinner with Brogan far more than she'd ever wanted sex with Dylan.

Such a startling realization.

As they went through the house, she flipped on lights, aware of Brogan's curious gaze taking in everything. The foyer led straight into the kitchen, with a dining room on the left and the living room just beyond that. Along the entire left side of the house was a long, narrow porch that had been enclosed and turned into a summer room. It was her favorite spot in the house.

He spotted the playpen in the living room and asked, "Okay if I put Shayna in there for a minute?"

"Sure." She had her hands full with Andy as he woke up. He clung to her, grumpy and no doubt hungry. She kissed her son, then said, "Our food is still in the car."

"I'll get it. I was going to grab the stroller, too. If you don't mind, I can use it like a high chair, assuming you only have the one." He nodded to Andy's chair in the kitchen.

"Good idea. I'll keep an eye on Shayna while I change Andy's diaper." She paused when she caught his smile. "What?"

"Sorry, nothing. It's just . . . fun." He gestured around the house, at Shayna and Andy fussing, and their diaper bags on the floor. "Sorting this out with you, I mean."

Now that he mentioned it, she agreed. Hoping it wouldn't be too much, she said, "Better than doing it alone."

He hesitated, then gave a nod. "Definitely better."

The second he turned to leave, Andy started crying. "Shh, Andy. None of that now. Brogan is coming back."

"Fend," he said in a pitiful little voice, and Pixie couldn't help but smile. “Yes, sweetie, he’s our friend and he’ll be right back. First, you need a clean diaper.” His shorts were wet through, so she put his changing pad on the floor next to the playpen and knelt down with him. “You’re soaked, little man.”

His face lit up at seeing Shayna. “Baby!”

“See? Brogan wouldn’t leave her behind.” She quickly stripped off his shorts and put on a dry diaper, all the while knowing that Andy was already far too attached to a man who’d only be around for a temporary time. “We’re going to share dinner—just this once. Are you hungry?”

“Baby.”

“The baby will eat with us.” She was sorting through the diaper bag, looking for clean socks, when Brogan reentered. Andy was off like a shot, wearing only his little T-shirt and snowy diaper, his bare feet slapping the hardwood floor as he ran.

Laughing, Brogan quickly set the food on an entry table and caught Andy up in his free arm. The folded stroller was held in his other hand. Immediately, his gaze went to Shayna. The baby was on her tummy, head and shoulders up so she could look around with wide-eyed interest.

“I’ve got her,” Pixie said as she lifted Shayna out of the playpen. “Her diaper is still dry.”

Brogan was careful not to ding the walls as he carried the stroller into the kitchen.

Pixie carried Shayna and the bag of food. “Do you want to eat first or make your call?”

Grumbling, Brogan said, “I should return the call, I guess. Officer Jansen Flynn said it wasn’t urgent, but he had a few questions.” Clearly, making the call wasn’t his preference.

“Let’s get the kids in their seats and then I’ll reheat our food while you talk to him.”

“More teamwork. I like it.” He lowered Andy to the floor

again, but caught him when he would have taken off. "Hang on there, speed racer."

Somehow he managed to open the stroller and restrain Andy at the same time. Pixie figured it was his long reach and strength that made it easier for him. As soon as he finished, they switched kids. She got Andy into his high chair and Brogan got Shayna into the stroller.

The kitchen had once felt large, but now, with Brogan here, the space felt wonderfully crowded.

Obviously, she was worse off than her son. When Brogan's lease ended and he went away, she'd probably miss him even more than Andy would.

As she turned, they collided. Brogan caught her upper arms and laughed. "Hey, sorry. You okay?"

Um . . . no. Absurd for a twenty-one-year-old mother to blush clean down to her toes, but she did. She could feel the warmth in her skin and knew her face had turned red. "Sorry." She tried a laugh, too, but it sounded a little strangled. "Go make your call. I'll have the food ready in no time."

Slowly, his hands fell away from her. "I'll just step into the other room. If you need help, give a yell."

"I won't," she promised him.

He already had his phone to his ear as he walked away. With the kitchen open to the living room, Pixie saw him pace toward the porch to look out. His deep voice was pitched low, and he kept his broad shoulders and back to her, giving her a chance to look him over without his knowing.

He really was large, towering over most people, with the physique to match. He kept his dark blond hair military short. It made her fingers twitch with the need to stroke the back of his head, to feel that rough velvety texture.

As if he felt her stare, he turned, which had Pixie scrambling to do something—anything—else. Her face quickly got hot again.

Andy helped her by saying, "Cookie."

"Not just yet, sweetie. Very soon." She gave him water in his cup instead, then watched as he tried to pour some on Shayna. "No, you don't," she said in a rush, scooting his chair a little farther from the infant. Then she worried that he might throw the cup anyway, something he'd done before, so she let him take a drink or two and then reclaimed it.

"Cup!"

"In a second." She had no idea what Robin had sent them to eat, so she quickly emptied the bag, hoping it wasn't steak, which would be tough when reheated. She inhaled the aroma of pork loin wrapped in smoked bacon. The glazed apples were packed separately, as were the asparagus and onion straws. "Bless you, Robin."

She wrapped the pork to reheat it in the air fryer, with the onion straws left unwrapped to keep them crisp. She'd microwave the asparagus. After she had the food ready to heat, she peeked into the living room. Brogan was still talking, but looked up when he saw her. She lifted the choice of bottled water or cola, and then whispered, "Or tea?"

Covering the phone, he said, "Tea, thanks," before getting back to his call.

Pixie held up two fingers as a question.

He returned four.

Nodding, she set the table and started heating the food. In the diaper bag, she found a bottle of water for Shayna, with a travel dispenser of formula. She set both on the counter and then prepared finger food for Andy, including soft chunks of cheese, a couple of his favorite crackers, steamed carrots and broccoli, and just a bit of diced chicken. She put it all in his divided bowl just as the microwave dinged. The air fryer finished next. She'd just finished putting the apples on her pork when Brogan reentered.

"Man, that smells good."

"Mam," Andy said, using the same enthusiasm Brogan had.

"He calls me Mam," Pixie said, "and he's ready to eat, too." She put bibs on both of the kids. "I have Shayna's stuff there on the counter, but I wasn't sure of your process with her bottles."

"Thanks." Brogan set her plate and drink on the table for her. "Why don't you sit. I'll finish my plate and put Shayna's bottle together."

He did so quickly and efficiently, proving he was now a pro.

"The apples are great," she said, in case he didn't want to include them. Cort usually didn't, but she and Marlow loved the combination of tastes.

Brogan took her suggestion while she fastened the suction cups of Andy's bowl to the tray on his high chair.

"Officer Flynn said that Benny wants to talk to me." He took his own seat at the table. "I think I'll go see him."

"That would be terrific. I know Benny would love it. Ellen too." And it wouldn't hurt Brogan, either, to get a little more appreciation.

Fifteen minutes into the meal, she had to tell Brogan how impressed she was. He cut up his food first, then fed himself while also holding Shayna's bottle. The man was a master, never missing a beat.

"You're really good at that." She'd only eaten half of her portion and Brogan was almost done. She got up to give him the rest, smiling when he gladly accepted. A man his size probably needed a lot of fuel.

"When I first got Shayna, everything was scary." He reached out and wiped broccoli off Andy's nose. "I had no idea what I was doing, so I spent half the time carrying her around and worrying while I researched everything I could. I held her in one arm and read on my phone at the same time. It was hard, I won't lie."

Pixie often thought it was still hard. There were days when

exhaustion caught up to her, but she was the only mother Andy had. The only parent. So she put on a happy face and did her best. Sometimes that meant the laundry wasn't done and the house wasn't anywhere near tidy.

Other times, she managed it all, and when that happened, she honestly felt like a superwoman. But when she fell short, she tried to cut herself some slack with a reminder of how far she'd come.

"Now," he said, "it's a little easier. Never been this easy, though." He nodded at the food. "Thanks for getting everything together. This is really nice."

"The Docker makes great food."

"Agree, but I meant all of it. Getting the food ready for me and the kids. Setting the table. Watching them while I made my call. Usually, I'm trying to do all that at the same time. I can multitask when necessary, but it was nice that I didn't have to."

She was about to reply when a chunk of food came flying across the table. Somehow Brogan dropped his fork and caught it. Then he stared at her, and after two seconds, his incredulous gaze slowly swiveled toward Andy.

Andy grinned at him. Still speechless, Brogan opened his hand and saw that he'd caught a mishmash of vegetables and meat.

It took everything Pixie had not to laugh out loud. She pinched her lips together and got to her feet, going to the sink to wet a paper towel while saying, "Andy Nolan, that's a no-no. We do not throw food."

"No-no," Andy said in his most serious voice, his face scrunched while he wagged a finger at Brogan. "No-no-no."

Brogan made a choked sound that was halfway between a growl and a laugh. He took the wet towel from Pixie and cleaned the slimy food off his fingers. "Kid has one heck of an arm."

"I'm sorry," she said, still struggling with her own laughter.

"That started when we were having dinner with Cort and Marlow. Cort teased Marlow, she threw a pea at him; and from then on, Andy has thought it's a game."

Brogan cleared his throat. Loudly. When he looked up, he'd managed to remove most of the humor from his expression.

Then Andy said, "Fend."

And Brogan's mouth lost the battle. Grinning, he said, "Your friend doesn't want to wear your food, buddy."

Andy offered another squished morsel from his pudgy little hand.

Brogan eyed it dubiously.

Pixie tried to help, saying, "Hey, Mama wants a bite."

"Fend!"

Brogan gestured at her. "Ladies first."

Frowning, Andy gave in and offered it to her. She bent to his hand—and without touching the food—made ridiculous "nom-nom" noises while pretending to chew.

Andy laughed.

"Ah," Brogan said, catching on. He leaned forward. "Okay, then, let's do this."

Unfortunately, he got too close and Andy smashed the food against his mouth and chin.

The stunned look on Brogan's face was so priceless, Pixie lost it. She laughed so hard that she couldn't sit up straight. Bending over, her head on her knees, she tried to keep Andy from seeing her, but he surely heard her. Tears came to her eyes, and every time she tried to catch her breath, she ended up cackling with hilarity.

Soon Brogan was chuckling, too, but he managed to get out a "Mm-mmm," just to appease Andy.

That made her roar. "Ohmigod," she said between gasps. "You even . . ." Another snort of laughter interrupted her. Even Shayna kicked her legs and giggled.

"I'm glad everyone's having such a good time," Brogan said,

deadpan. He reached over to rub Pixie's back. "Breathe before you fall out of the chair."

She tried, but one look at his face set her off again. It took her well over a minute to wind down—and Brogan was still touching her.

While she struggled to get it together, Brogan said to Andy, "No more throwing, dude, okay? It's not cool." Then he seemed to have an idea. "Although, we could divert you with a ball, maybe at the park. Or even in the yard."

He helped Pixie to straighten, but she couldn't do anything about her watering eyes and the giant smile still on her face.

Brogan's smile turned tender as he smoothed down her hair. "What do you think? Could you impress on him that a ball—outside—is the only thing he should throw?"

It felt as if her heart floated. "He's still so young, but we can certainly try."

After that, everything seemed more relaxed. They talked easily, joking and sharing stories, remaining at the table long after the food was gone. Even then, they didn't say goodbye.

The kids were cleaned up and the playpen was moved closer. Shayna went into it and Andy was given toys beside her. That worked out well while the adults put the kitchen in order, but then Andy tried to drop one of his toys in for Shayna, and it almost landed on her head.

Nothing heavy, just his soft vinyl book, but it put both Pixie and Brogan on alert. They spent a good five minutes explaining to Andy how dropped toys could hurt Shayna, and then he wanted to kiss her head. He kept telling Shayna, "No boo-boo."

"He's a terrific kid," Brogan said. "Smart and considerate, especially for his age."

Drying her hands, Pixie stepped up beside him and watched her son squat down to peer at Shayna through the mesh netting on the playpen. "So you've recovered from the food incident?"

He nudged her with his shoulder. "I'll have you know I've handled worse things being thrown at me than a little mushy food."

"Still." Pixie smiled up at him. "I'm sorry it happened, and sorry I found it so hilarious."

"No." He shook his head, firm in his denial. "No apologies, okay? I enjoyed the whole thing. It was a perfect way to top off a day that could have been tragic."

"Yeah." Thinking of Ellen and Benny, and what a close call they'd had, she turned back to Andy. She was so thankful to have him in her life, even when he occasionally misbehaved.

Andy jabbered to Shayna, but whatever he said was indecipherable. Shayna cooed back.

Seeing the two of them so close to each other, practically nose to nose, was eye-opening. "Wow. It just struck me that they could almost be siblings."

Beside her, Brogan went as still as stone.

"Their hair is almost the exact same color, and of course they both have blue eyes." She felt Brogan's wariness and glanced at him. "Many babies have blue eyes, at least until six months or so. Then they might start to change."

"Andy's will stay blue," he predicted softly. "They're almost as blue as yours."

She knew the truth. "Blue, yes, but darker like his father's."

Brogan stepped away to lean a hip on the counter. "So he had blue eyes, too?"

"Yes. What about your sister?"

"Connie's eyes were like mine." He twisted his mouth. "Gray, like our father's."

"Do you know anything about Shayna's father?"

His inhale was slow and deep. He didn't look at her. "Enough."

"Oops." Pixie was instantly distracted when she realized Andy was falling asleep. "I need to clean his teeth and get him into his pajamas."

Brogan checked the time. "Will you go through your whole routine?"

"Probably not. A *b-a-t-h* right now might give him a second wind—then we'd be up all night." She spelled the word so Andy wouldn't start demanding. He did love to splash in his bath, and that would definitely wake him up again.

"I assume you're tired, though?"

Because he said it like a question, she answered honestly. "Not particularly. I think I enjoyed the evening too much." She grinned. "Guess I got my own second wind."

Brogan's jaw worked as he looked at Andy with his head on her shoulder, his eyes heavy. "I don't want to push my luck, but do you think you'd want to . . ."

When he didn't finish, Pixie's heart started racing. "Would I want to what?"

He glanced at Shayna, back at Andy, then at Pixie. "Would you want to let the kids sleep so we can talk a little longer?" He went on, "I totally get it if you want me to hit the road. I can't stay much longer anyway. Definitely not more than an hour. I just thought—"

"I'd love to," Pixie said before he could retract the offer. She thought of how the day had gone, how easily Brogan had taken charge at the restaurant, how he'd run to the rescue of a boy he didn't know, then willingly agreed to meet Ellen at the hospital.

She thought of how he'd played with Andy, how he'd cared for Shayna.

And she thought of those awful scars on his body.

He'd gone above and beyond, not just today, but apparently for most of his life. If tonight he needed to talk, she'd happily listen.

They stared at each other a moment; then she let out a shaky breath. "Make yourself at home. I should be back in fifteen minutes or so."

"Long enough to read him a story?"

She trailed her fingers over her son's spiky pale hair, then kissed his forehead. "Always. Every night." Smiling at Brogan, she admitted, "I enjoy it as much as he does." She started to turn away; then it occurred to her. "Oh, there's only one bathroom—it's through the bedroom. I need to brush his teeth, but if you'd like to go first?"

"Okay, thanks. I'll make it quick." He went past her . . . through the kitchen and into her bedroom.

Pixie stared after him. He didn't rush, and she saw him glance around the bedroom as he entered. She had the panicked thought that she might have left something out of place. *A bra? Panties? Please don't let it be either.* Jeans, shoes, or a top—she could handle that.

She was tidy, but not fanatical about it, especially when she also had to get Andy ready to go out.

Less than a minute later, she heard the toilet flush, heard water run, and assumed Brogan was using her scented soft soap to wash his hands.

It struck her as funny.

She, Pixie Nolan, had a man in her house. Not just any man, but Brogan Rafferty. All six feet five inches of him.

And he wasn't just *in* her house, but he'd walked through her bedroom, too.

The very moment he reappeared in the doorway, Pixie rushed past him. "I won't be long," she said quietly, and she slipped into the room, her gaze searching every surface. *Whew!* Fortunately, the only things out of place were a few of Andy's toys and her sleep shirt.

Without thinking about it, she kissed Andy's sleepy little face. "Today is a day of monumental proportions."

When Andy cuddled closer and yawned, she knew she had to get his teeth cleaned now or it wasn't going to happen.

"Do you want a book, Andy?" she asked as she carried him into the bathroom.

"Book," he agreed sleepily.

Pixie was grateful that he didn't ask about the baby—or his friend.

CHAPTER 6

Brogan could hear her quiet voice reading to Andy as he changed Shayna's diaper and put her into a clean gown. His little Sugar was out, and he didn't expect her to wake for at least a few hours. To help keep her asleep, he needed to turn on some soft music, but he also wanted to hear Pixie.

What a surprise she was.

When she'd mentioned the resemblance between the kids, it had shocked the hell out of him. Babies just looked like babies, right? But not these two. They definitely shared some features, which meant he needed to get to the heart of the matter. Now . . . tonight.

The timing couldn't have been worse. The day had been full of turmoil—at least until Pixie turned it nice with a warm meal and her laughter. His mouth twitched again, just remembering her out-of-control amusement. She was a beautiful woman, elfin in appearance with her big eyes, slim nose, and narrow chin. At least until she laughed. Then those blue eyes sparkled and her cheeks flushed and dimples showed in her cheeks.

He'd just gotten Shayna back into the playpen when Pixie spoke behind him.

"Andy's asleep."

He straightened. "Shayna too." Was it his imagination, or

did Pixie suddenly look shy? Brogan hoped she didn't expect him to make a move; that wasn't why he'd wanted to stay.

Whatever she was thinking, it set his own thoughts on a racing course down the wrong path. Babies, he reminded himself. If he could just keep focusing on the kids, then he could put aside the fact that he was here, virtually alone with Pixie in the quiet of the evening.

For starters, he appeased his curiosity by asking, "Is Pixie your given name? It's pretty, but unusual."

A smile teased over her lips seconds before she turned and headed to the couch. "My legal name is Joanna." She sat in the corner, one leg tucked beneath her, and hugged a throw pillow to her chest. "My father used to call me Jo, but when I went to live with Aunt Mary, she called me Pixie because I'm small." With a lift of one shoulder, she added, "Guess it stuck. Aunt Mary passed on when I was seventeen, and for all that time, I'd been Pixie. Now it's how I think of myself."

"Do you mind if I ask why you were living with her?"

Her smile twitched again. "It's funny because no one had ever asked me about it. Then I met Marlow, and she wanted to know everything. Now there's you."

Now there's me. Maybe he should retract his interest—but he didn't want to. "You don't mind talking about it, then?"

"Not really. It's all so far in my past, it doesn't hurt me or anything. See, my mother lost custody because she was an addict. I don't know if she tried to kick the habit, but she never did. So when I was five, my dad had me. But he had a drinking problem. Most of the time, it wasn't too bad. I mean, he could still work, and he usually stayed out of trouble. Then when I was ten, he was at a bar and got into a knife fight."

Though it seemed Pixie took her past in stride, Brogan was appalled and infuriated on her behalf.

"After that, he had a few . . . mishaps." She slid her fingers beneath her hair at the side of her head. "Everything changed when he threw his keys and accidentally hit me when I was ten.

He didn't mean to, but since he was drunk, his aim was off. I think they were supposed to hit the wall."

His heart lurched. Before he thought better of it, his fingers had gently tunneled into her hair until he felt the ridge of the scar left behind. Carefully, he traced the two-inch length. That had to have been one hell of a gash for a ten-year-old.

The idea of her as a little girl, being put through something like that, made his lungs burn. He drew back, but only far enough to curve his large hand around the side of her face. His thumb brushed over her jaw, her skin soft and warm. "That had to hurt."

"It wasn't that bad," she rushed to tell him. "If he could have treated it at home, he would have. Unfortunately, I needed stitches, and everyone at the hospital could tell he was drunk. One thing led to another, and my aunt Mary stepped in to take emergency custody."

How scary would that have been?

"For the longest time after Aunt Mary took me home, I thought my dad would come for me."

"But he never did?"

"No. At first, it worried me. But after a while, I liked Aunt Mary so much, and life was so calm, that I started to worry he would come."

"Did you ever see him after that?"

She shook her head. "When Aunt Mary got permanent custody, Mom and Dad just disappeared from my life. My aunt was wonderful, though, so all in all, I didn't miss them."

They had that in common. He knew he'd never let Brian or Ruth be a part of Shayna's life, not unless something drastically changed. Not unless the old man mellowed or Ruth located her heart.

Pixie watched him warily before saying, "Sorry. I know it's not a fun story, but to me it wasn't all that tragic, either. It was just life."

The only life she'd known. "You need to stop apologizing

when it isn't necessary. I'm glad you shared with me. It's hard to think of such a young girl being bounced around like that, but you're clearly healthy and happy now. I guess it bothers me even more than it should because I think of Shayna, what her life should be, what I want for her, and . . ."

"She has you," Pixie said with conviction. "She'll be loved and cared for."

Time to move the spotlight off him. "So because you were Pixie during those happier times, you've kept the name."

"I hadn't thought of it like that. To me, it was just what I was called. Like if you name a kid Theodore and call him Teddy. I got teased in school occasionally, but nothing especially mean. I knew I was short—"

"And petite."

She grinned. "I wasn't offended by most of the jokes."

Her cavalier attitude took the edge off his anger, but he couldn't dismiss the fact that her parents had abandoned her. Unlike him, she wasn't a big strong kid, tough inside and out. Pixie was something else. Soft, gentle, and caring. Strong, yes, but also vulnerable.

And yet she'd survived, clearly with a better frame of mind than he had. "You don't resent them?"

"No." Settling deeper into the couch, her posture relaxed, she explained why. "I've tried to look at things from a different viewpoint. If my parents hadn't flaked out, I wouldn't have been with Aunt Mary, and those were some of the best times of my life. In the same way, I don't resent Andy's father, because if Dylan hadn't lied to me, I wouldn't have Andy now—and I wouldn't have Marlow as a best friend."

"A nice way to look at it." Would she feel the same after he fessed up?

"What is it?" she asked.

"It just occurred to me that I don't know your exact age. You look . . . young."

"I'm twenty-one."

His eyes widened. "But . . . that would mean you were only nineteen when you got pregnant with Andy."

"Yes." Lifting her chin, she said, "Obviously, old enough."

Physically, sure. He'd seen girls even younger with children on their hips, and sometimes with another on the way. It was the emotional toll that concerned him, the fact that she'd been alone.

Yet here she was, her gentleness and caring still intact. "I wasn't judging," he said. "It just took me by surprise."

Her eyes, so full of challenge, held his. "It was tough at times, but I know your life hasn't been easy, either—"

"Shit." He didn't want her sympathy. "Don't—"

"But," she persisted, "if it had been different, you wouldn't have been here today and Benny likely wouldn't have made it."

Okay, he could handle that logic. "So I've been moved around like a chess piece, huh?"

"No, I'm just saying there's always more than one way to see things. Dylan badly hurt Marlow, but if he hadn't, she'd probably still be with him, going through the motions of life without really living. She wouldn't have come here to recuperate and she wouldn't have met Cort. You'd have to see them together to know how perfect they are as a couple."

Playing along, Brogan said, "If Dylan hadn't already been married, he might have married you. Your life would be different, too."

"Believe me, I've told myself that many times." With her lips tilting up in a tiny smile, she shifted closer. "I never knew I could be this happy. I look around at my life, at what I've accomplished and the friends I've made, and I feel successful. I love being Andy's mom, my job at the shop is great, and I have respect. That's a heady thing, and I never would have known it if my life hadn't gone through a drastic change."

Brogan wanted to relax, but she was closer now, so close he

could breathe in the scent of her shampoo and lotion. He'd known cravings before, but nothing like the way he craved her. He wanted to hold her close, kiss her, yes—and more—but he also wanted moments like this, every day, every night.

His image of family, of what it should be, was somehow all wrapped up in Pixie—her pretty blue eyes and her optimistic way of viewing the injustices in the world.

He sat back on the couch, but then she did the same and now they were only a few feet apart, their gazes lingering. Every natural instinct he possessed told him to make a move. Lean forward, touch her, kiss her. Drag her closer and hold her . . . His muscles flinched at the restraint. Fighting an enemy was a lot easier than fighting himself.

When Pixie looked at his mouth, he worried that she might be the one to make the move. He'd totally cave if she did, so he turned away. "If it wasn't for Shayna . . ." He started to say that he'd still be in the military, but that wasn't true. His injuries had been enough to necessitate a medical discharge. Sure, there were wounds people could see, but there were also hidden wounds. A few on his hip that would keep him from peak performance. One on his right foot. He was finally able to jog again, but he wouldn't be able to handle any major jumps.

Thinking of his physical limitations always soured his mood. For a man who'd pushed himself to dominate whenever possible, it was a bitter reality.

"Brogan?"

Regret was the damnedest thing, sneaking up on him when he least expected it. At least it had worked to tamp down his need for Pixie. "I started to say I left the military for Shayna, but that'd be a lie. You saw my wounds. I'm fine now," he added, in case she thought to fuss. "But I'm not up to snuff for what the military needs."

She touched his arm. "You're still more than most men could ever be."

He flattened his automatic grin. "Not how I'd look at it, but thanks. The point is, I don't know what I would have done if I'd still been active duty when I found out about Connie and the baby. I hope I'd have done the right thing." Somehow, regardless of how complicated it might have been. "I was still in the hospital, though."

Pixie scooted closer. "Because the injuries were so severe?"

And because he'd given up—but that was a shame he'd keep to himself. "I was going through rehabilitation. Finding out about Shayna really kicked me into gear. It was Connie's friend who found me."

"They were close?"

"Erin Benning is a powerhouse. A family law attorney, but after meeting her, I think she'd outtalk and outmaneuver anyone in any setting. The military could have used her to develop strategy." He shared a quick grin. "Connie was a paralegal, but also worked as her personal assistant for added income. They were good friends. Thankfully, Erin had all of Connie's legal papers, as well as instructions and other details that Connie wanted shared." Feeling the tension seep in, Brogan ran a hand over the back of his neck. "I wasn't easy to find, but Erin managed because it was important." Unfortunately, it had taken her a little too long. Brogan's fault, not hers.

"So you've met her?"

"Soon as I found out about Connie, I called Erin. She flew out to see me two days later and brought all of Erin's paperwork. A will, life insurance policy, and guardianship papers." The tension tightened, squeezing his neck, twisting until he felt as if he couldn't sit still.

Then Pixie touched him. Her soft voice brushed over him.

Brogan looked at her, unsure of what she'd said.

"It's still difficult," she repeated. "I understand."

God, he hoped she'd continue to understand. Bracing himself with a deep breath, he said, "Everything Connie owned became mine, but at the time, that didn't matter much to me. Erin shared a photo of Shayna, and that little girl just grabbed my heart." He realized then that Pixie's small, cool hand was still on his upper arm. He didn't just feel it there, though. He felt it everywhere, both calming his angst and igniting heat within him.

"Sorry." Brogan got to his feet and paced away to a safer distance. "I can't seem to sit still when I talk about this stuff."

Pixie shifted to face forward, hugging that throw pillow a little tighter. "I understand."

He rounded on her. "You keep saying that." Voice a low rasp, he explained, "You don't know, though." Sometimes, most times, the truth tortured him. "Connie died alone because I was a bastard, not just in reality, but in personality, too."

"No."

"Yes." Brogan turned away. "She had to do everything alone. Shayna's father wasn't there for her, and neither was I. That's how she got killed."

Several beats of silence passed before Pixie whispered, "Killed?"

Another reality he hated to face. "She was a single mother, like you. Her elderly neighbor watched Shayna for her when she worked at the office, though she did a lot of work at home, too. She was heading back from the office on a Friday evening when there was a fender bender that turned to road rage."

"I don't understand. If it was road rage, then how . . . ?"

"Shouting first, then a fight, and that turned into shooting. A witness said Connie was trying to get around the stopped cars when a shot went wide. It came in through her passenger window." Swallowing heavily, Brogan rasped, "She died on the scene."

After a few beats of silence, Pixie let out a low breath. "How awful."

"The babysitter had the number of the office for emergencies. She called, and everything got pieced together." That had led to his father picking up the baby. "I was named as the guardian, but Shayna went through hell because I wasn't accessible. I didn't get to her right away."

"You didn't even know your sister had a baby."

That didn't make it easier. Just the opposite. "She would have told me if I'd shown the least interest." He strode to the end of the room, then started back, glancing down at Shayna as he passed. Her cheeks puffed out as she pursed her lips, maybe dreaming of her bottle, and his heart turned over. She had her arms out at her sides, her tiny hands open in a trusting pose of slumber. "Erin said Connie thought about telling me, but she was in the middle of making her will, assigning a legal guardian for Shayna, and she worried that if I knew, I'd deny her."

"You wouldn't have."

Her faith was killing him. "I don't know that. Seeing Shayna now, you're right. I would never have rejected her. But some unknown baby?" He scrubbed both hands over his face.

Without making a sound, Pixie moved to stand before him. Though she couldn't wrap her fingers all the way around his wrists, she still caught them and pulled down his hands. "You wouldn't have," she insisted.

He wanted to be the man she saw. "Erin had Connie's hefty life insurance policy, and she also had long letters explaining what Connie wanted."

"For Shayna's future?"

He nodded. "I assumed it would only be about education and stuff like that. Instead, Connie wanted her protected from our father and her mother. She wanted Shayna insulated from that ugliness." His throat tightened and he had to look away. "She wanted her to be loved."

"Brogan." Before he could stop her, Pixie had her arms around his waist. When he stiffened, she held him tighter, using all her meager strength.

He didn't know what to do. Arms out at his sides, body

rigid, he tried to sort out the bombardment of feelings. This was not an embrace of sexual intent. She didn't stroke him, didn't rub against him. She simply held him.

Comfort. It was comfort and it *wrecked* him.

Breathing faster, he allowed his arms to close carefully around her. She was such a delicate little thing, so much smaller than he. He didn't know what to do with this, with her.

It wasn't until he returned her hug that she looked up at him with a smile. "I think Connie made an excellent choice."

"She didn't even know me. Not really."

Putting her cheek back to his chest, Pixie gave a quiet laugh. "She disagreed. And I disagree."

"Tell me why, Pixie." He desperately wanted to believe her.

She finally released him, but took his hand and led him back to the couch, saying, "We don't want to wake up Shayna."

He knew his little Sugar. She wouldn't wake up until she was good and ready, but he didn't mind sitting now. All the turmoil he'd felt minutes ago had dissipated beneath confusion. And hope. Such desperate hope.

"Now," Pixie said. She sat well away from him, both legs curled up on the couch and that lucky throw pillow once again held close to her chest. "When Connie visited you that first time, your immediate thought was protecting her."

Doubt brought his brows together. "It was a dangerous area."

"Right. Not to you, but for her—that's what you told me, even though she was older. And so your first instinct was to get her to safety."

That didn't make him trustworthy. Or capable of raising an infant.

It made him a realist.

"Then you not only joined the military, but you became a SEAL. That proves a lot."

"Like?"

"So many things! Special operations forces aren't for average people. That service requires dedication and intelligence, not just strength." Smug, she added, "I read up on it after you told me you were a SEAL."

She was interested enough to do a little research on me? "I shouldn't have mentioned it."

"And see, you're humble, too."

"No," he corrected with a sound that should have been a laugh, but didn't quite make the cut. "I'm not humble."

"Your denying it just proves you are."

"What kind of twisted logic is that?"

"It's the logic of someone who is getting to know you. You're an in-command, take-charge kind of guy—and before you ask, I know that after seeing how you handled things with Benny."

"Connie wouldn't have known that."

"Of course she would. She saw how you reacted after her parents freaked out over you, just because she'd visited you. They were complete jerks. To spare her, you cut all ties."

"How do you figure that?" His motivation had been to spare himself—right? He'd cut ties in a childish snit.

"Geez, Brogan, give me a little credit. And give some credit to your sister. I'm beyond certain that she looked you up. She met you, knew you, found out what she could about your service, and then she made the very intelligent decision—as a mother who loved her daughter—to name you guardian of her baby if anything happened to her."

He wanted to grab her conviction like a lifeline. "So you don't think it was a mistake?"

"No." She gave him a "come on" look, as if to sway him. "Remember, I've seen you with Shayna. No one could love and care for that little girl more than you do."

"I do love her."

Softly, Pixie said, "It's obvious."

"But, Pixie, I'm not the sterling person you seem to think I am."

Another challenging and exasperating look landed on him. "Puh-leeze."

He hated to disillusion her. "There are things about me you don't know."

For a split second, wariness appeared in her eyes; then she shook it off. "So? There are things about me that you don't know, either."

That put him on edge. "Like what?"

"You'll be here through the summer, right? That'll give us time to get to know each other. I'm sure I'll still feel the same way."

Suffering his own dose of wariness, Brogan eyed her. "What way is that?"

"That Connie was a loving mother who ensured her daughter's happiness by making a great choice of guardian. You."

Her opinion would definitely change when she knew the truth. She had a right to know, so he decided to get to it. "There are some things I should tell you. See, Connie left . . . well, not a journal, really, but a notebook full of explanations. Things she wanted me to know."

Pixie said nothing.

"A lot of it was stuff about her parents. Her mother, our father."

"Really awful stuff?"

God, he was botching this. "They didn't beat her or anything, but physical abuse isn't the only kind."

"I agree."

"She wanted me to understand why they weren't named as guardians, I guess, in case I balked at the responsibility."

"Get real. Never for a second did she believe that."

No, Connie hadn't, but how could Pixie know so soon? "She didn't want me to use them as even occasional babysitters, either. She left a nice life insurance policy, plus a house, car, bank account—stuff that she said should help if I needed to hire a sitter." Not that he had access to the house. That was going to take a while, because Ruth and Brian had moved in.

"Hmm, I haven't thought of any of that yet, but I probably should."

Did she think he was pointing fingers? "You have Marlow and Cort, right? You know they'd take care of Andy."

"True, and Andy's grandparents are wealthy. It's a struggle to keep them from taking over."

The casual mention threw him off for a moment. "Are they involved in Andy's life?"

"They are now, at least somewhat."

"Somewhat?"

"At first, they resented me. It's a long story, but right now, we're talking about you."

Brogan pressed on anyway. "You've worked out your differences?"

Appearing confused at his curiosity, she shrugged. "They idolized their son and saw me as a stain on his reputation."

Protective instincts reared up. "What the hell?"

"It's fine. They came around, and now they consider Andy a link to their son. We don't see them often, mostly because I still won't do things their way—and no, I'm not going into that right now. I'll just say that the animosity is over. Now they're distant, but doting, grandparents."

"Distant and doting can't coexist."

She grinned. "I guess not, but I meant that when they see him, it's all adoration. That happens a few times a year. They send gifts, have a trust fund set up for him, and generally invite us to travel with them during holidays."

"Do you?"

"No. I want Andy to have a simpler life, at least for now. When he's older, he can expand the relationship if he wants. In the meantime, they're affectionate with him, but they lead busy lives."

"You like them, though?"

"Let's say I don't dislike them. As long as they're good to my son, that's all I need."

Brogan tried to tiptoe around the topic. "So they're involved, but Andy doesn't have his father's last name?"

Her brows arched. "How do you know that?"

"When he threw that clump of wet food at my head, you called him Andy Nolan."

Her lips eased into a smile. "Right. Sorry again."

"You don't ever have to apologize for your kid being a kid. Besides, it was worth it to hear you laugh."

"Thank you for being a good sport." She sighed. "There are a lot of reasons why Andy doesn't have his father's last name. For one thing, I was never married to him—but Marlow was. She's Marlow Easton, now that she and Cort are married, but everyone knew her differently when I first arrived. Plus, there were those initial problems with his grandparents. Legally, too, it was just easier to use my surname. He's always been Andy Nolan to me, and that's been enough."

"I see your point. The grandparents are okay with that?"

"They have a recognizable name. It likely saves them the embarrassment of having to explain that their son wasn't perfect after all."

Even knowing he was pushing his luck, Brogan asked, "Recognizable in what way?"

Pixie gave him a pointed look. "Back to you. What other information did Connie leave you?"

This conversation got trickier by the second. He really wanted to know more about the grandparents, but he couldn't risk offending her. "She identified Shayna's father." He couldn't quite look at her when he said that. "She shared things about him. Details that . . . You see . . ." Damn it, he couldn't do it. "Sorry, but it's complicated."

"And you're struggling with the memory." She abruptly stood, tossed the pillow on the couch, and faced him. "Here I am practically grilling you, when I can see that you'd rather not talk about it."

Actually, it'd be better if he just got it said. The problem was that he liked her, more so every minute he spent with her. She deserved better than the disruption he planned to cause in her life. She and Andy had a nice pattern going. They were happy—what right did he have to intrude?

If it was just him, he wouldn't hesitate to let it go. He'd leave them in peace, wish them well, and probably miss them like crazy.

This concerned Shayna, though, and that meant he couldn't walk away. "I should explain."

"No, it's fine. Let's save some conversation for another day, okay? That is, if you don't mind doing this again." She rushed to explain, "I mean chatting, letting the kids play, sharing experiences."

He gave her the truth. "I've loved every minute." It was by far the best evening he'd ever had.

Her smile was a beautiful thing. "Me too." She looked as if she wanted to say more, but then she shook her head. "It's getting late, I still need to shower, and we'll both have full days tomorrow."

Maybe it made him a coward, but he was glad of the reprieve. "Let me carry out Shayna's things; then I'll come back in for her."

"Good plan." Her smile remained, accompanying the tenderness in her big blue eyes.

Now that he was off the hook, Brogan didn't want to linger. He gathered up Shayna's belongings, went out into the cool spring air, and stowed them in the front passenger seat. He started the car and turned on the headlights, then went back in to gather up his sleeping bundle and wrap her in a warm blanket. She stirred, stretched, but didn't awaken, even when he put her in the car seat.

Pixie stood in the open doorway, watching him. The golden glow of the porch light created a halo around her fair hair.

Leaving proved difficult. They needed a better way to say good night, but again, most of the options familiar to him couldn't happen. "I really did have a great time."

"Me too." She shifted, looked out at the night, then back at him. "Would you like to come to dinner next Saturday? I don't yet know my schedule, but I could text you tomorrow."

A tidal wave of relief washed over him. She wasn't inviting him back for tomorrow, but he could bide his time while she figured out what worked for her. "I'd like that a lot."

As if she'd thought he might refuse, her expression relaxed at his agreement. "Great. I'll let you know."

Having that promise made everything easier. "Lock your door behind you."

"I always do."

He nodded, appeased and yet reluctant for the magic to end. Then a firefly landed on his car door near the spot where he rested his hand on the top of the frame. It twinkled, then took flight again. He watched it move out to the yard and spotted dozens more, everywhere, on every shrub and tree. Pixie's laughter drifted out to him.

It was the perfect ending to the day. Feeling more at peace than he had in years, he smiled at her. "Good night, Pixie."

In a sassy tone, she said, "See you soon, Brogan." Quickly ducking inside, she closed the door.

The warmth stayed with him on his short drive up to the lake house. He thought about how she'd been. Wonderful in ways he'd never experienced before. Real, but gentle. Funny, yet sincere.

Once she found out that Andy and Shayna had the same father, everything was bound to change. Still, he was glad he hadn't pushed the issue.

Not tonight.

Next time would be soon enough.

Pixie thought about Brogan a lot over the next few days. Instincts urged her to offer him comfort, but those same instincts warned that he was wary of kindness. The kids were a sort of buffer for him. She sensed he often focused on Shayna, and even Andy, when emotion got the better of him.

It wasn't anything she could pinpoint. Brogan Rafferty had long ago learned to hide his thoughts behind an enigmatic expression. Other than a few rare occasions, he showed only what he wanted her to see.

And yet, despite his neutral expression and careful words, she often picked up on feelings of unease, hope, and expectation.

His father had clearly been a severe disappointment, and from what he'd said, his stepmother was even worse. Though he hadn't said too much about his mother, she certainly hadn't sheltered him or his feelings. His sister had tried to get closer to him, but like many things—family, love, and understanding—he'd missed out with her. Brogan believed he carried the blame for that, but Pixie knew better.

A person could only be rejected so many times before they were no longer receptive.

Was that why he'd made the military his family? A noble decision when he could have chosen many other paths.

Again and again, her thoughts churned over the facets of Brogan's personality. In some ways, she felt she knew him; in other ways, he was still a stranger.

They had arranged to meet for dinner at her house next Saturday. That felt like a lifetime away, but Pixie firmly reminded herself that she was off the market, that she'd been burned and now she had her sights on a bigger purpose: her son, her self-respect, her responsibilities.

She was building a new life, not just for herself, but for her son. Yes, she'd made great progress, but she wasn't there yet.

The problem, at least when it came to getting her mind off Brogan, was that she kept running into him everywhere.

On Monday, she saw him at the grocery store. "Fend!" Andy shouted loudly, almost leaping out of the cart seat. Pixie dropped her loaf of bread and caught him. "Andy Nolan, that's dangerous."

"Fend," he explained, pointing, then bouncing in her arms as Brogan pushed a grocery cart toward them.

When Andy squealed, Brogan said, "Shh, the baby's sleeping." Then to Pixie, "And I'll be better able to finish up my shopping if she stays asleep."

New energy flowed through Pixie, and she suddenly wondered if the wind had messed her hair and if her clothes were wrinkled after working all day.

She stopped caring when Brogan lifted Andy into his arms for a big hug, all the while smiling. There in the aisle, with townspeople openly speculating, they'd talked for fifteen minutes or so. She felt certain everyone had seen Andy give Shayna a very gentle kiss on the forehead—with Brogan's help.

On Tuesday, she was just getting Andy out of the car in the bank parking lot when Brogan stepped out with Shayna in his arms.

"Hey, you two."

Smiling from the inside out, Pixie said, "We have to stop meeting like this."

He laughed. "I kind of like it." Again, they lingered for a lengthy chat. Andy was thrilled that Shayna was awake this time and babbled to her in an excited way about who knew what.

"He really likes her, doesn't he?"

"You have no idea," Pixie admitted. "Last night, in the middle of his bedtime book, he yawned and asked about her."

"Oh? How exactly did he articulate that?"

Funny, since many of Andy's words were indecipherable. "One word," Pixie explained. "*Baby.* But he lifts his shoulders and holds up his hands, making it clear he's asking about her."

"Ah, yeah, that's cute. Next time, let me know and I'll text a pic of her. He'd probably like that, right?"

"Genius idea, thank you."

On Thursday, he stopped into the shop and bought a few more outfits for Shayna. Andy was napping that time, and she was busy with a new business owner who wanted to commission a design from her. It would go on T-shirts for his employees. That took precedence, so she wasn't able to chat with Brogan long, but he and Renee drew every eye with their laughter.

Nearly every evening, he sent her a photo of the sunset, and a few times she sent him pics of the sunrise. There was one she especially loved that showed Andy standing very still in the yard, silhouetted by the dawn as he stared at two deer near the waterline. That image had earned a lot of praise from Brogan.

Andy had even helped to inspire a new design when he'd looked at the pic with her, then lifted his hands and asked, "Baby?" as he so often did.

"I agree," she said, loving the idea that popped into her head. "We need Shayna in the pic." That night, after Andy had fallen asleep, she'd stayed up late to fashion the image into a T-shirt design showing both kids as dark silhouettes—Andy sitting, Shayna on her tummy—staring out at beautiful Firefly Lake as a colorful background. It was perfect and she couldn't wait to show Brogan.

And Marlow, of course. She liked the design enough that she'd save it for the shop, assuming Marlow was interested, and Pixie knew she would be.

On Friday, he sent a pic of Shayna blowing spit bubbles—presumably for Andy—and they both loved it, so she texted back one of Andy with an enormous grin.

On Saturday, which should have been her day off, Pixie ended up opening the shop. It was Renee's turn to open, but her mother had come down with a bad cold, so Renee needed to make alternate plans for her kids. Her husband had gone off to fish, but he was coming back. That would take a few hours. By noon, Pixie and Andy would be heading home. She'd have more than enough time to fix a wonderful meal.

Never before had she anticipated seeing anyone this much. She was in deep and she knew it.

She just didn't know what to do about it.

CHAPTER 7

Saturdays were always busy, but this day seemed more so. Thankfully, Andy was in an extra good mood and didn't seem to mind that it took her a little longer than usual to get him new toys and answer his questions. Some of the people who came through were friends, and they took turns giving him attention.

She had just finished ringing up the last person in line. Finally, she had a free moment, but she knew it wouldn't last. She desperately needed a bathroom break, and she'd love to grab a cold bottle of water, but she went to Andy instead to see if his diaper needed to be changed or if he needed anything.

There were still several people in the shop browsing, so she kept an eye on them, too, as she gave Andy some animal crackers and a cup of juice.

"Is he yours?" someone asked from behind her.

Pixie straightened and nearly bumped into the woman who loomed close to peer at Andy. She wasn't unattractive, yet she had a hard edge to her, visible in her stare and the pinch of her mouth. Probably late fifties, with short, mussed light brown hair highlighted with gray. She was a thin woman, her shoulders rigid, the flesh of her throat tight with antagonism, as if she barely restrained herself.

Cautiously, Pixie moved away from Andy. "May I help you?"

"I'm looking for Pixie Nolan." Heavy frown lines showed between her brows as she sent an insulting glance over Pixie. "Was told she'd be here with her kid."

The words were innocuous enough, yet Pixie had a very bad vibe from her. "Who told you I was here?"

"Don't know. Doesn't matter." Impatience leeched into her tone. "Someone in town."

"You were asking around about me?"

The woman leaned against the counter, blocking another customer who appeared ready to get in line. "Settle down, honey." Her smirk was far from a smile. "I don't know you, but I was told you were renting to Brogan."

Pixie held herself absolutely still. She said nothing, merely stared back at the woman. Usually, her protective nature was roused only for Andy, but now it came out in full force for Brogan.

"Well?" the woman snapped.

"I don't own any rental property, ma'am." Pixie kept her tone annoyingly polite. "Excuse me. You're blocking a customer."

The woman behind her gratefully stepped forward and put several things on the counter.

"Hey. I wasn't done." The stranger aggressively shoved things aside before planting both palms on the counter and leaning in. "I'm looking for Brogan Rafferty, and I think you know where he is."

"If you're looking for him, I assume you know him?"

"I know the bastard better than I want to."

The casually slung insult hit Pixie like a slap. "You will not use that language in this shop."

"Fine," the woman said. "Tell me where he is, and I'll get out of your hair."

"If you want to know where he is, give him a call and ask him." Pixie gathered up the items on the counter and prepared to ring up the customer. "Thank you for your patience. Did you find everything you needed?"

"I did," she said, after giving the rude stranger the side-eye. "Thank you. Everything is so cute. I was here once before, but now you have so many new items."

Pixie knew her hands were shaking as she scanned prices and folded each purchase into a bag. For the very first time since she'd started working at the shop, she wished she hadn't brought Andy along. Alarm bells were going off in her system—her head, her heart. She *knew* this confrontation was about to escalate, she felt the tension in the air, but she wasn't sure what to do about it.

Making small talk with a happy customer wasn't easy—not with the other woman fuming beside her, her nicotine-stained fingernails tapping on the counter. "We change our inventory often, except for the most popular items. Each season, we have new designs."

"How long's this going to take?" the intruder asked. "I'm not hanging around here all day."

Without meaning to, Pixie crumpled the cute hat the customer had chosen. "Good. I have no information for you. There's no reason for you to stay." Annoyance deepened her breathing so that she had to dig deep for a calm façade. Again, she turned to the paying customer. "I'm sorry." Carefully, she smoothed out the hat.

The customer gave her an understanding smile. "It's fine." Leaning closer, she asked, "Would you like me to call someone?"

Before Pixie could reply, the obnoxious woman snorted. "What? You think she needs the cavalry?" Eyes narrowing, she asked, "Do I look that threatening?"

Pixie's calm nature spiraled away. She'd never snapped before, but now she was dangerously close.

With propitious timing, Renee breezed in at that exact moment.

All eyes turned to her. She was halfway across the shop when she realized something was wrong. Taking in the scene in one sweeping glance, Renee rushed forward.

"Hey, girl," she said, coming around the counter and giving Pixie a hip bump. "Sorry, I'm late. Looks like you've got your hands full."

Relief nearly took out Pixie's knees. Not that she couldn't deal with the situation, but at every moment she was aware of Andy's attention focused on them. He'd never heard such rudeness before, and she knew he'd be unsettled. One glance and she saw his widened, watchful eyes.

This was no time to be divided, and Andy always came first. "It's fine. While I finish with this customer, would you take Andy to the breakroom?"

"Nope." Smile firmly pinned on her face, Renee moved to stand directly in front of the troublemaking woman. "I'll wait while you finish up. Then you can take him to the breakroom while I handle . . . *things*."

The way she enunciated "things" made it clear what she thought of the woman before her.

With alacrity, Pixie gave the shopper her total, and then accepted her credit card. She put the receipt in the bag. "Thank you so much—for shopping with us, and for being so patient."

Nodding, the shopper cast one last look at the rude woman. "Take care now."

When Pixie turned, she found Renee and the other woman in a staring contest. Renee appeared amused; the stranger, not so much.

"Now," Pixie said firmly, hoping to take control of the situation. "It's time for you to go—"

"Not until you tell me where to find him."

"No, ma'am, I will not."

"Him who?" Renee asked.

"Brogan Rafferty, my stepson."

That bombshell squeezed all the oxygen from Pixie's lungs, leaving her lightheaded. *No.* This horrible woman couldn't possibly be . . . but, of course, she was. She was the right age and Pixie could certainly picture her treating a young boy so callously.

Then it struck her that this woman had also had Shayna for a time. She'd been guardian to that beautiful, innocent infant.

Thank God Brogan has her now.

"You look like a nice enough girl," the woman said. "Don't let the bastard cause you any problems. Just tell me—"

Hearing that word a second time shattered Pixie's composure. Rage sent her around the counter to growl, *"Get out."* She stepped into the woman's space, her voice low and mean. "Get out *right now*!"

"Whoa. Don't tell me he has you bamboozled already?" She chortled, and the sound turned into a cough. Impervious to Pixie's fury, she bent forward to hack and wheeze until she finally caught her breath, only to cackle once again. "Look at you, all riled up on his behalf." Her lip curled. "As if he needs the likes of you defending him."

Renee had already picked up Andy and disappeared. Pixie knew she'd catch hell about that later, because Renee had wanted to deal with this particular ugliness. And it was ugly, extremely so. The woman was so foul, Pixie had to assume her husband—Brogan's father—was no better.

And yet *he* was wonderful. Truly amazing. It crushed her to think of what he must have survived.

Two other customers now stood silent on the other side of the shop, watching as if afraid to move.

Pixie said, "I pity you." She would never truly know Brogan, her daughter was gone, and she'd lost her granddaughter. Sometimes evil had a way of consuming itself. "You will leave now, and you will not come back."

"The hell I won't."

"My employee is even now calling the police," Pixie explained. "I intend to tell them all about you."

"Brogan stole my granddaughter and I want her back!"

"Then perhaps you should call the police." Pixie pointed at the door in silent demand.

"He robs his family, spits on his own father." She hefted a purse strap up on her shoulder. "You tell him, girl. You tell him Ruthie said he better call. He'll be damned sorry if he doesn't."

Finally, she turned and took her own sweet time moseying out, flitting her fingers over items as she went, stopping once to glare at the other shoppers, who hurriedly turned away. Then, at last, she was out the door.

The urge to race forward and lock it behind her left Pixie frazzled. She'd dealt with vile people before. Of course she had.

But she'd never met anyone like Ruthie.

She wanted to collapse. To sit down and hug herself and block images of what Connie's childhood had likely been. Her throat burned with the need to cry. Her entire body quaked with a dump of emotions too painful to bear.

By sheer force of will, she got her feet to move. Going back behind the counter—mostly so she could lean on it—she tried to act as if everything was fine. It wasn't. Far from it.

Though the shop wasn't in Bramble, it was near enough that if Ruthie continued to ask around, she'd find out where Brogan was staying. Given the temperament she'd displayed here today, there was no question that she'd go after him aggressively. What the woman wanted, Pixie didn't know.

But she did know she wanted to protect Brogan. She had to warn him.

He might choose to go away, to relocate. An awful possibility because she already cared about him. He'd come to town, bonded with Andy, and melted the ice around Pixie's heart. In a very short time, he'd gotten her to care.

Should she call him? Devastating news was never good over the phone.

The two other shoppers cautiously approached her. One asked, "Are you all right?"

Pixie nodded. "Yes, thank you." She wasn't. "I'm so sorry you had to witness that. I have no idea who that person was, and I regret that she disrupted your shopping experience."

"We started to leave," the other one said, "but we were worried for you."

Pixie thanked her with a smile.

"Do you know who she was looking for?"

Absently, Pixie shook her head in denial. Not even to these strangers would she confess Brogan's whereabouts.

Renee poked her head out of the break room and glanced around. "All clear?"

"Yes." Rushing to her, Pixie brought a now-sleeping Andy to her own shoulder, hugging him close. "Thank you. Your timing was impeccable."

"Eh, maybe a few minutes late, I'm thinking."

Choking on her gratitude, Pixie rocked Andy, kissed his head, and cherished the weight of him in her arms. What if he'd lived and she hadn't? Never before had she considered that, but thinking of someone like Ruthie having her baby . . . Well, she thought about it now.

Renee touched her arm a few minutes later. "Hey, customers are gone for now. Why don't you and Andy head home? Enjoy the rest of your day off."

Shaking her head, Pixie said, "I can't leave you here alone. What if she comes back?"

"I'll handle her if she does, *but,*" she stressed, when Pixie started to insist, "I already called in reinforcements. My husband and kids are coming."

Pixie groaned. "I'm so sorry for all the trouble."

"The kids are psyched. They like coming into Lankton. New things to see and do. Martin will get them ice cream after they stop by here; then when they're done with that, they'll visit a few shops."

"But he'll be close?"

"With his phone handy. He said he plans to stroll by inconspicuously a few times."

A smile came despite her worries. "He really is a great guy, Renee."

"Right? 'Course I wouldn't keep him otherwise." She grinned. "So come on. Let me help you get things in your car before more customers come in."

"I guess I should." Chewing her lip in indecision, Pixie looked down at Andy. His hair stood up in an adorable way, his little mouth open in slumber, cheeks flushed.

"He's precious," Renee said, attempting to smooth down one wayward lock. It popped right back up again.

Pixie kissed his nose, then smiled when he wrinkled it. If he slept on the way home, he'd be ready to visit with Brogan and Shayna. "You haven't asked," she said quietly.

"I don't think I need to. She said she's Brogan's stepmom, and if so, I pity him, but it's his business. When she called him names, she just made herself look . . . well, worse, because she already looked bad. Disgustingly so. Like the epitome of the evil stepmom, you know? The stuff they stick in movies."

"She wanted to make *him* look bad."

"Yeah, right. I met the man, remember? I've seen him with that little angel. He loves Shayna. Old Ruthie might've tried to get things started, but you didn't let her." Renee rolled a shoulder. "You know, though, she could be out there right now, spreading her venom."

"I know." Her stomach twisted at the thought. "I need to tell Brogan."

"Sooner rather than later." Renee picked up the diaper bag and led the way out to Pixie's car, which was fortunately parked near enough that they could keep an eye on the shop's front door.

Despite the mild spring weather, the minivan felt like an oven when Renee slid the side door open. A belch of heat rolled out.

"Keys," Renee said.

"In my purse. Front zippered pocket."

It was another minute before the van was cooling down and Andy was safely buckled in his car seat. She gave Renee a hug, then cautioned, "Be careful, okay?"

"You betcha. Drive safely and give that big guy a kiss from me."

"Renee," Pixie said on a laugh, but her friend was already darting back to the shop. Yup, Pixie knew she was putting off the inevitable. She'd have to tell Brogan about Ruthie, and delaying wouldn't make it any easier.

Dread made the trip shorter than usual. She was so preoccupied trying to come up with the right words that she was nearly home before she realized another car was following her. Fresh anger washed over her.

Ruthie.

How dare the woman do this?

Panic and indecision tried to take over, until she heard Andy talking to his stuffed dog. He was awake. That made it easier. Never would she risk her son in a confrontation.

Right before she was about to pull down the main road to her home—and the lake house where Brogan was staying—Pixie took a side street. From there, she backtracked, returning to the more congested area of town that was mostly commercial. The grocery store, the bank, the only hotel—and then she saw the Dry Frog Tavern. Marlow worked there, and Herman, the proprietor, was a friend.

With more haste than necessary, Pixie pulled into the lot. She stayed behind the wheel, watching in the rearview mirror until the unfamiliar car approached, then drove past slowly. Yes, that was Ruthie's frowning face staring through the window, checking out the tavern and Pixie's car. When the car drove on past and went around the bend, Pixie inhaled a bracing breath, backed out, and headed home yet again.

At this point, she had no idea how dangerous the woman might be. Certainly, she was ruthless, crass, and out to start trouble. But was she an actual threat? There was no way for Pixie to know.

Her hope was to get Andy inside before Ruthie had time to turn around and follow again. Heart hammering with dread, she continually glanced in the rearview mirror, but all she saw behind her was an empty stretch of road.

A deer leaped out in front of her, making her hit the brake. It jostled Andy and he started to cry.

"I'm sorry, baby. I'm sorry." Her voice shook. What she wouldn't give to have Cort and Marlow nearby. If they were home, she'd call them to meet her at the house and they'd take care of things.

The second she had the thought, it angered her.

I'm a grown woman, damn it. I can handle my own issues.

Andy said, "Mam," on a sniffle.

"It was a deer, sweetie. Just a deer. Mama didn't want to hit it."

"Der?"

"Yes, but the deer is fine. We'll be home in just a minute."

"Cup."

"Yes, I'll get your cup as soon as we're inside."

She should call Brogan—but she didn't want to look away from the road while driving.

Finally, the house was in view. She started to pull in, but then up the road, she saw Brogan jogging out of his driveway and she made a split-second decision. Instead of pulling in at her house, she drove a little faster to his.

Seeing her, he paused to smile—until she went right past him and parked at the side of the house, out of view. Frowning, he glanced toward her car. She got out and shouted, "Brogan, I need you up here. Could you hurry, please?"

If Ruthie turned the corner and saw him, she'd lose the opportunity to warn him.

Alarm showed on his face and in his posture. Pushing the stroller, he sprinted toward her while she rushed to get Andy out of his seat.

He reached her in seconds and asked, "What is it? What's wrong?"

She hefted Andy into her arms, then reached in for his diaper bag. "We have to go inside. Please hurry."

"Honey, you're scaring me." He glanced at Andy. "And you're scaring him."

She didn't have time to explain. "*Inside*, Brogan. *Now.*"

Her urgency became his. With a nod, he pushed the stroller to the front door, unlocked it, and lifted the whole thing inside. Winded as if she'd run a mile, Pixie crowded in behind him and shut the door, then went to the window to look out, but she didn't see Ruthie's car.

"Hey." Brogan took Andy from her, looking him over to assure himself that the little boy wasn't hurt. "Take a breath, okay? Then tell me what's happened."

Anxiety had a death grip on her. Now that she'd reached him, she knew it would be all right—somehow. "Today, at the shop, your stepmother showed up."

His head jerked back as if she'd struck him. "Ruth is in Bramble?"

She shook her head, but then nodded.

"Yes, no?" His sharp tone showed his confusion.

"The shop is in Lankton, remember, not far from Bramble, but Brogan"—Pixie braced herself—"she followed me. She's looking for you." Pixie stepped past him and knelt down by Shayna, who was still in the stroller. The baby grinned, pumped her legs in excitement, and cooed. "She said you stole her granddaughter." She glanced up to see anger and hurt in his eyes. "Brogan . . . she says she wants her back."

Rage boiled up, and with it a flash fire of disappointment. Did Pixie believe those lies?

"Fend?" Andy spoke in a small, confused voice. His palm open against Brogan's jaw turned his face so Andy could see him.

Knowing the child felt his sudden tension, Brogan immediately removed his frown, then kissed Andy's temple. "All is well, little man."

Pixie let out a long breath. "Ruthie was horrible," she said as she lifted Shayna from the stroller and protectively cradled the baby against her shoulder. "She was rude at the shop, and she caused a scene. I'm sure it upset Andy."

"I thought you were off today."

"Renee was delayed, so I filled in until she could get there." Holding the baby, she went to the couch and sat down. "I'm sorry if I startled you, but after she tried to follow me, all I could think to do was to protect Andy—and to warn you."

"Warn me?" He set Andy down when he started to wiggle, assuming he wanted to see Shayna. Instead, Andy tried to climb into her stroller. Troubled by other thoughts, Brogan helped him.

Then Andy said, "Wok."

"What?"

"Wok." Andy rocked, trying to get the stroller to move.

On autopilot, Brogan pushed him around the room while his thoughts churned. He stopped in front of Pixie. "My sister made me legal guardian."

"I know." Absently, Pixie checked Shayna's diaper, then cuddled her some more. "I don't think that awful woman cares, though. She said you'd better call her."

His heart was still lodged in his ribs. "You know?" *So Pixie isn't doubting my guardianship?*

She gave a shudder. "I kept thinking about Ruthie having Shayna, about the hideous way you found her." Her eyes closed a moment, then opened again so she could pin him in place. "I'm so glad she has you now."

"Wok!"

This was a new emotion for Brogan, some disturbing mix of relief, gratitude, and optimism that made his skin feel too hot and tight. He'd love nothing more than to have a moment to himself to come to grips with it, but he had a fourteen-month-old boy wanting to walk, a four-month-old girl who needed his care, and a bighearted blue-eyed woman waiting for his reaction.

Brogan turned to look at the front window. "How far did she follow you?"

"Far enough to know I live in this vicinity—and there aren't many houses near this part of the lake." She described everything from the time she realized she was being followed, until she backtracked, lost Ruthie, and then returned.

Pushing the stroller, he went to the window and looked out. The road was empty as far as he could see, but he couldn't dodge Ruth forever. And if she was going to harangue someone, it needed to be him.

Several decisions were made in a single instant. He had to tell Pixie everything.

And he could not leave her alone.

"I know it's early, but would you mind if I stuck close? I don't trust Ruth not to suddenly show up, and I don't want you to have to deal with her."

She hugged Shayna. "I'd be relieved if you did."

His heart was now pounding hard enough to break something. "Would you want to head to your place now? With me, I mean." The lake house was tiny, and he was basically wheeling Andy in small circles around the furniture.

As she nodded, Pixie whispered, "Brogan, is she dangerous?"

"Probably not the way you're thinking. She's unfeeling and mean as a rattlesnake, but nothing that Connie wrote to me included physical attacks. Neglect, yes. She stole from Connie every chance she got. And she has a nasty way of insulting people."

"She stole from her own daughter?"

"Several times. Connie said Ruth would visit, and after she'd leave, things were missing. Jewelry, cash, a coin collection." He ran a hand over his face. "Let's go to your house. There are other things I need to tell you."

"Okay." Pixie stood, one hand absently patting Shayna's back. "I'll need to get dinner prep started anyway, and Andy is probably ready for a snack." She stopped in front of him, her bottom lip caught in her teeth. "I'm worried."

There wasn't enough control in his arsenal to keep him from reaching for her. He cupped her face, rewarded when she turned her cheek into his palm. Looking at her, seeing all the softness she couldn't hide, Brogan started to believe it'd be okay. "I won't let anything happen to you."

He felt her smile before she tipped up her face and showed him the sweet curve of her lips. "I'm most worried for you. But yes, also for Shayna, and Andy and me. I considered calling the town police, but I thought that might draw unnecessary attention your way."

Talk about a kick in the teeth. "Listen to me, Pixie. Do not ever hesitate to call for backup if you feel threatened. Call the cops. Call me. Whatever is easiest. I can handle any blowback, and I can handle Ruth. What I can't handle is having my problems spill over onto you."

She agreed with a small nod. "When she said you stole Shayna, I told her to call the police. She just smirked."

"Because she's been in trouble with the law. I have not." He thought of Officer Flynn, the cop who'd interviewed him about Benny's near drowning. Maybe he'd give the officer a call, just in case. Now that he had Shayna, he had to start thinking differently—not just of his own capability, but of what was best for her.

Best for Pixie and Andy.

It mattered a lot that Pixie trusted him. Starting tonight, he had to tell her everything or he knew he risked losing that trust.

"I have some things to show you. Important things."

She tipped her head. "I don't know what you mean."

"Paperwork. From Connie." *Please don't hate me.* "It concerns Shayna, and I think you should know—even if it pisses you off."

For a few seconds, she considered his words. He waited for the questions to begin, but instead she nodded. "Okay."

Not about to give her time to rethink that decision, he stepped away. "I'll grab it all real quick—then I'll get Shayna's stuff together and we can head out." He looked down at Andy. "Ready for another walk?"

"Wok!"

"Through the house we go, bud." He wheeled the stroller down the hall in a weaving pattern until Andy laughed, then took a sharp turn into the cramped bedroom, wheeled him around so he again faced the hall, and told him to hang tight.

Darting to the closet, Brogan snagged the handle of the black canvas portfolio case that held copies of all his important papers. Erin, Connie's best friend, kept the originals.

At the small dresser, he opened the bottom drawer and got out a change of clothes for Shayna, as well as her footed pajamas and a few of her small flannel blankets.

Andy was just leaning out of the stroller to see what was keeping Brogan when he took the three big steps needed to join him. "You want to get out, or do you want to walk again?"

"Wok!"

Andy's shout was enough to lighten his current dire mood. "Okay, my man, hold on tight."

Andy grinned in anticipation and Brogan fast-wheeled him back up the hall with a little jostling thrown in. Andy's peals of laughter had everyone else laughing, too, even Shayna, who squealed.

Pixie held her close, watching them, and it was such a sweet picture.

It was what he wanted, what he couldn't help hoping for. Shared love of the kids. Mutual caring.

Family.

A lump the size of the Atlas Mountains lodged in his throat.

"I've never tried that before," Pixie said, "but he loves it, so now I'll need to."

For a second, he'd worried that he was too rowdy, but

Andy's demands of "Wok, wok, wok!" proved otherwise. Brogan cleared his throat, mussed Andy's silky hair, and did his best to get himself together.

Now was not the time to wish for things still out of reach. He had to earn that reward—and he would. Starting with complete honesty.

To Pixie, he said, "Let me grab some bottles and I'm ready to go." He kept the diaper bag prepped with powdered formula, plenty of diapers and wipes, bibs, a change of clothes—everything he thought he might need. He even had an empty bottle in the bottom of the bag, but it was for emergencies. He took it out to reclean it every so often, but he always packed fresh bottles.

"How will we do this?" Pixie asked, still holding Shayna and pushing the stroller one-handed. "Are we walking up, driving up, or what?" She glanced at Andy, then added, "Ruthie will recognize my van now, but I don't like the idea of leaving it here, either."

Brogan had hoped to put this conversation off until they were comfortable in her house, but it looked as if she needed answers now. He didn't blame her. In her shoes, he'd want them, too.

He turned to face her. "Ruth will show up, no doubt about it. I'll be with you when she does, though, and I'll handle it."

Wide blue eyes searched his. "Handle it . . . how?"

His mouth screwed to the side. "I don't plan to maim her or anything." He despised Ruth, but never in his life had he lifted a hand against a woman. Men who hurt women or kids were at the bottom of the scum pile, and not even Ruth would ever bring him that low. "I've dealt with her already, at least on some issues. Let's get to your place—you drive, and I'll push the stroller." Since he didn't plan on coming back home tonight, he didn't need his car. "We'll get comfortable and I can explain everything."

She chewed her lip again, then gave a firm nod. "Andy goes in his car seat, though."

So her trust didn't extend quite that far. He got it. "Okay. Shayna and I will be right behind you."

"You've made me curious," she said.

"Good." He just hoped she'd stay that way long enough to hear it all. If she kicked him out too soon, he knew he'd have a hell of a time ever working his way back in.

CHAPTER 8

Never before had Pixie realized she was such an impatient person. Every minute or two, she glanced toward the living room and that large canvas portfolio that Brogan had carried in and deposited in the foyer.

Though he tried to hide it, he was tense. Whatever he had to tell her, it couldn't be that bad. Could it?

"That was the best fried chicken I've ever had."

Pixie was pleased with how well the dinner had turned out, even though the day had been so wild. "I'm still a fairly new cook, but I'm learning."

"Marlow is teaching you?"

"Ha! She doesn't cook. Honestly, Marlow can do anything she sets her mind to—and yes, that's hero worship. Wait until you meet her, and then you'll see. But mostly it's Cort who's been teaching me, as well as Gloria and Bobbi. They're siblings, and they crack me up, especially when they start bickering with their brother, Wade. They're all older now, but still carry on like they're kids."

"I was never around any siblings. Do they . . . What did you call it? Bicker?"

She grinned as she dried the last dish Brogan handed to her. "I wasn't around siblings, either, but Gloria, Bobbi, and Wade swear they went at each other daily. Wade claims it was mostly the *girls* ganging up on him."

Brogan smiled. "Might have been fun, don't you think?"

"What?" He gave all his attention to arranging the dishrag over the middle of the sink. "Having a brother or sister."

"Maybe. I have Marlow now, and she's like a big sister. As an adult woman, I think it's pretty awesome to have someone that close."

"Imagine if you'd grown up with her." His pale gaze settled on her. "Don't you think it would have been . . . less lonely?"

Pixie put the dish into the cabinet. "I can't have any more children." There, she'd said it—even though it hurt. She felt Brogan freeze beside her. "I told you, when I had Andy, there were complications. Well, they led to a hysterectomy."

"I didn't know that."

She shook her head. "It's fine. I've accepted it." For the most part. Crossing her arms and looking up at him, she stated, "Any man hoping to have a kid of his own should steer clear of me."

The intensity of his gaze ramped up, and then his mouth softened. He reached her in one big step, but only to take her wrists and bring her arms down to her sides. "Don't be defensive, Pixie. Men will want to be with you because you're beautiful, not because you're a baby maker—even though you did make a damn perfect kid."

They both glanced toward Andy. He was on his stomach showing toys to Shayna again and jabbering away. She'd rolled to her back and was busy playing with her toes.

"He really is perfect," she agreed. "Even with his silly hair that won't lie down."

Brogan grinned. "Cowlicks, I think they're called. Shayna has one at her crown that makes her hair swirl in that spot."

"Dylan had one," she said, before she thought better of it.

"He hated it and paid a fortune at salons to have his hair styled in a way so it wouldn't show."

"You're joking."

"Every time he passed a mirror, he checked it."

Stepping away and again rubbing the back of his neck, a sure sign of frustration, Brogan asked, "How's your schedule looking?"

"What do you mean?"

"Now, the rest of the evening. I know you have your bedtime routine."

"If you want to talk, this is a good time. The kitchen is done, the kids are playing." And she was desperate to know what was so important, what he thought might piss her off.

"You want to sit on the couch? We can keep the kids in sight that way."

"Sure." Anxious, Pixie led the way. Brogan got the portfolio and dug out several packets of paper, which he set on the coffee table.

"That's a lot of documents."

He picked up one. "This is the guardianship paperwork. Or rather a copy of it. I left all the original paperwork with Connie's friend Erin. It's at her law office, under lock and key."

"Because you knew Ruthie would be a problem?"

"I didn't have a doubt." He gave Pixie time to scan the document before exchanging it with another. "That's the life insurance policy."

She whistled. "That's a lot of money."

"Connie wanted to make sure Shayna would have the care she needed. It's why Ruth is dogging me. She wants Shayna, but not because she loves her as a grandmother should. It's because the guardian gets a payout."

Anger rushed through her bloodstream. "It's made out to the baby's guardian. And that's you."

He nodded. "And if not me, Erin was next in line. Nowhere

is Ruth listed. Connie makes it clear in her instructions that Ruth and Brian should have nothing."

"But convincing Ruthie of that won't be easy."

He held on to a stack of typed notes. "She and Brian moved into Connie's house shortly after Connie died. They claimed it was to keep from uprooting Shayna, but an infant so young wouldn't have noticed. Missing her mother, missing love and attention—that was the big issue."

The reminder sent her gaze back to the baby. Andy was looming over her, dimples in his cheeks as he grinned down at her. "Andy, be very gentle."

"My baby."

She tried to smile, but her heart hurt. "Yes, she can be your baby."

He sat back with a laugh when Shayna flailed her arms.

"It crushes me," Pixie whispered, losing the battle to keep her emotions in check. "I think of that baby crying all alone . . ." Her lips trembled. "I don't know how you can bear it."

"Sometimes I can't." Suddenly, Brogan hugged her, up against him.

Glad of the comfort, Pixie tucked her face to his chest, warm and firm beneath his cotton T-shirt. She breathed in his scent, but ignored the stirring it caused. "It's not my place, really. But I'm so grateful for you. Too many children don't get the care they need, but I know Shayna will—because of you."

Held so close to Brogan, she couldn't see his face, but she felt the brief kiss he brushed over her temple. Honestly, she never wanted to move.

"Unfortunately," he murmured, "I have more to tell you."

"That's right. I'm supposed to be po'd, right?"

"Po'd," he repeated with a grin. "Is that your reminder that I shouldn't curse?"

"Well, you shouldn't."

"I'll try my best to curb the tendency." His smile dimmed as he released her and sat back. "Now the hard part."

It seemed to Pixie that all of it had been hard, Brogan's entire life, from being an unwanted child, to becoming a Navy SEAL, and now the role of single parent that he'd taken on while having to battle his stepmother. "I've yet to see the easy part."

"Loving Shayna. That's been easy."

See? He always had the right answer. How could she be indifferent to him? She couldn't, and she should probably admit that to herself, because every moment with him made her think of moments that hadn't yet happened. Tomorrows that weren't guaranteed. Weeks and months that she wanted.

"I'm sure it has." Again, Pixie looked at the kids. Andy was trying to sit a stuffed lamb on Shayna's belly, but it kept falling off, and each time he'd say, "Oh, oh, oh." And try again. Shayna gurgled a laugh, followed by a coo, and that kept Andy trying. Out of the blue, he leaned down and kissed her.

This time, Andy spoke quietly, saying, "My baby," in a near whisper.

A giant swell of emotion threatened to consume her. Desperately needing a diversion, she turned to Brogan and confirmed that he'd seen it, too.

"It felt like I was the only one who loved her." He kept his gaze on the kids. "Erin cares, but she's a busy lawyer and not real in tune with kids."

"Plus, she was still grieving over losing Connie. You said they were close."

Nodding, Brogan drew a strained breath. "I want you to read this." Again, he tapped the papers. "But first I have to tell you something."

She covered his hand with her own. "Whatever it is, it'll be fine." Pixie believed that with all her heart.

He huffed out a rueful laugh. "Pixie . . ." His jaw worked, and finally he said, "Andy and Shayna are related."

Her lungs seized up, making her gasp, and her heart missed a few beats. Pixie didn't move. "I don't know what you mean." She heard the words, but they didn't make sense. Slowly, she pulled her hand away.

Those stormy gray eyes, now filled with anguish, stared at her.

She got the sense that he was facing this moment just as he'd had to face everything else in life. With resolve and a determination to handle whatever consequences came his way.

"The kids share a father."

The urge to comfort him was there, but certain truths couldn't be denied. "Andy's father is dead."

He didn't look away. Didn't even blink. "Shayna's too."

Now her heart raced, so fast that it made her lightheaded. "But . . ." Math was not her strong suit. "Dylan died last year."

"Not long after he'd gotten Connie pregnant."

Dylan had cheated on Marlow with her. Had he also cheated on her with Connie? Or had their relationship begun after she'd discovered he was married and broke things off? Either way, she felt more annoyed than hurt. She'd long ago given up the idea that Dylan had been "hers" in any way. That particular fantasy had been nothing more than an immature illusion.

Brogan valiantly held her gaze. "I wanted to tell you sooner, Pixie, but—"

"You didn't!" and *that* hurt. The realization that Brogan had kept something so important from her proved that she'd done it again. She'd built up absurd expectations, with no basis in reality, about a man. "You never really trusted me, did you?"

He didn't avoid her anger. Of course he wouldn't.

Damn it, she didn't want him to be stoic right now because that robbed her of the opportunity to unleash her annoyance.

Probably a good thing, really, with the kids right there.

"I wanted you to get to know Shayna, and I wanted to get to know you. Everything I found out about you told me that you were a good person, a terrific mother."

He spoke so fast, Pixie could barely take it in. She didn't *want* to take it in. Feeling childish, she covered her ears.

Brogan dropped the papers on the table and caught her wrists. "Shayna deserves more than me. She deserves a family—and her brother."

Rearing back, Pixie breathed, "How dare you? You expect me to raise her for you?"

His eyes flared, then narrowed to silver flames. "No." Coming to his feet, he reiterated, "Hell no. No one will take her from me."

Oh. Well, that was better. His reaction went a long way toward soothing her dismay. "Then . . . what?"

At their angry voices, Andy had gone alert, and now he ran to Pixie in fear. "Mam!"

She scooped him up and squeezed him tight. "Oh, honey. I'm sorry. Everything is okay." Patting his back, she said, "We didn't mean to startle you."

Andy peeked up at Brogan.

Immediately, he crouched down before him, which also put him at eye level with Pixie. "I'm sorry, buddy. It's all good." He stroked a hand over Andy's hair, smiling when those wayward tufts sprang back up. "Were you showing Shayna your lamb?"

"My baby."

"Right." He flicked a glance at Pixie. "I was hoping you'd feel that way, too. She could use *more* family. Besides me, I mean."

"Brogan . . ."

"I sprang it on you. I get it." He stood. "Connie had no one, not even her brother. I don't want that to happen to Shayna."

When the baby gave a sudden wail, Andy jumped. "Oh, oh!" He scrambled down and ran back to her. "Baby cryin'!"

Pixie called after him, saying, "Andy, slow down." She half-stood. "You have to go easy!"

"I've got it." Brogan took two big steps and scooped Andy up before he landed on Shayna. "She screams really loud, doesn't she, bud?" He seated himself on the floor, situated Andy beside him, and scooped up Shayna to comfort her.

Shayna's little bottom lip stuck out, and she gave another cry, followed by a shuddering breath, making Andy fret. He looked ready to cry, too, until Brogan reached out to him.

Pixie sat there on the couch trying to mesh the new info with the image of Brogan and the kids. In no time, he had them both settled down, entertaining them with the stuffed lamb.

Shayna is Andy's half sister.

No, she immediately told herself. She would never differentiate like that. Siblings shouldn't be divided by halves or steps. They should just be siblings. Did she have it in her to keep them together? How could she not?

If it was true, and she had no reason to doubt it, then Brogan's hesitation in leveling with her made sense. Of course, he'd want to get to know her first. All of his life he'd been shortchanged, even abused, by the "family" who should have loved him. Being related didn't guarantee that someone was a good person who would treat others fairly, with respect and affection.

Where did that leave them all, though?

He was only supposed to be here until the end of summer. Already, the thought of his leaving left her aching. And to take Shayna away when she should have the right to know Andy?

Brogan started a silly story, which included the lamb talking and dancing. Andy scrambled for his own spot on Brogan's lap.

"Ah, I see you have this all figured out, huh?" Effortlessly, Brogan arranged Shayna into one arm, giving Andy room; then he scooted around so he could rest his back against the wall. Holding the lamb in one hand, he said, "Now we're all comfortable, right?"

"My baby."

"You're like a broken record, bud." He glanced at Pixie, and despite the guarded smile on his mouth, she detected a wealth of sadness in his eyes.

Pixie knew what he was doing: He was giving her time to get pissed off, and get over it, or at least come to grips with his stunning revelation.

All this time, he'd known the truth. Shayna wasn't related to her, but as Andy's half sister, it was almost the same.

Except . . . Ruthie hadn't felt that way at all. She'd deliberately ostracized Brogan, not only from his father, but his sister, too. It was easy to understand why the children's connection mattered to Brogan. After knowing so many awful people, he wanted Shayna's life to include more.

More family.

More support.

More love.

To reassure Brogan, she said, "While you three play, I'll look over these papers. But, Brogan?"

His gaze met hers again.

"Let me know if you need any help."

After watching her a moment or two longer, he released a tight breath. "No worries. We're fine." He got back to his silly story, even including a funny voice for the lamb. Andy loved it. Shayna kept busy blowing spit bubbles.

Pixie arranged the papers over the table, then picked up a few to skim them. Much of it was Connie explaining that she understood why Brogan had stayed away. Her parents had told her some of the things they'd said to him, heartbreaking things that no son should ever hear. Things that ripped at Pixie's heart as she read them:

You're not a part of this family, so don't try to be.
All you'll do is complicate things.
You're your mother's problem, not ours.

They were awful, awful people.

When she imagined Brogan as a youth, and how hurtful those words would have been, tears welled in her eyes . . . and Pixie didn't care. She was a crier. So what? If Brogan planned to hang around, or to know her and Andy long-term, he'd have to get used to it.

Curiosity had her skimming the papers until she saw Connie's address. Just as Marlow had, Connie had lived near Chicago. She found a few notes explaining how Connie had randomly met Dylan.

She didn't read anything in detail, not until she saw her own name. Settling back against the couch, she took in Connie's account of how Dylan had cried over Pixie's "betrayal," the way she'd kicked him out of her life, even though she knew he couldn't divorce Marlow. He claimed to have genuinely cared for Pixie, but understood that his parents would never accept her.

Connie, he'd claimed, was someone his parents would love. *Ha! More of Dylan's lies.* His parents, Andy's grandparents, didn't fully approve of anyone. Lately, however, they had tried to be more accepting of Pixie because in their own way, they loved their grandson.

As she read more and more, the kicker for Pixie was that her first inclination was to call Marlow. She always dumped her problems at Marlow's feet, because Marlow helped her to think things through, to work them out rationally.

But this? How would Marlow feel?

It was almost unbelievable that Marlow had accepted Pixie into her life, that she loved her as a friend and a sister.

Yet another woman? Marlow wouldn't resent Shayna; she didn't have it in her to feel animosity, or even indifference, toward a child. But this second betrayal would surely anger her.

Pixie hadn't been married to the man, and she was irate—at least a little. Dylan hadn't missed her, hadn't even gone that long grieving the loss of their relationship before he'd turned to Connie. Or maybe he'd been with Connie long before Pixie had ended things.

Possibly, during the entire time he'd been with Pixie.

In personality and behavior, he was the bastard, not Brogan.

Since Connie had been so thorough in her notes, it was no surprise that Brogan had so much info on Pixie. Dylan must have given her most of the details, but Connie had gone a few steps further and found Pixie's location.

She even stated why:

You and I were alone, Brogan. Shayna doesn't have to be. If Ms. Nolan is at all as Dylan described her, she might allow her son to know Shayna. She might help provide the family <u>you and I</u> needed—or at least that I needed. You, little brother, were always stronger than me. So strong. Yes, I admired you a lot. You were my hero and my inspiration.

Pixie dashed away more tears. How painful it must have been for Brogan to read that, to know how much his sister had needed him. No wonder he seemed to hate Ruthie.

I used to pray that eventually we could reconcile, that you'd accept me, but please, please know that I never blamed you. I knew who kept us apart, and I understood. I loved you then, and I loved you every single day.

Never, ever have I doubted that you would accept Shayna if something happened to me.

Brogan, if you're reading this, then she needs you, even more than we needed each other. Without you, Mom and Dad will have her. I know you won't let that happen, so thank you. Love her like she should be loved. That's all she really needs.

However, if you want my input (I know, I'm that pushy older sister!), then here's what I'd like to see happen. Only if it's possible. Again, the most important thing is that you love her—and I know you will.

Pixie's chest ached, her heart held in a vise. Oh, God, she could feel Connie's pain, knew that the poor woman had been imagining her daughter growing up without her, and she'd been doing the absolute best she could to make sure—even after her death—that Shayna would be cared for.

"Hey." Suddenly, Brogan was there, sitting down beside her. He took the papers from her hands and put them back on the table. "You okay?"

"Yes." Pixie nodded jerkily, gave an audible swallow, and again wiped her eyes. When she tried to speak, her voice broke. "No mother should ever have to make these plans. Not for an infant."

"I know."

Pixie saw that Andy was now jabbering away with the lamb, emulating Brogan's storytelling to entertain Shayna. It warmed her soul to see them together, especially with her new understanding of why it was so important—not just to Brogan, but to Connie, too.

On impulse, she turned to Brogan and hugged him fiercely.

Awkwardly, he patted her shoulder, saying again, "Hey."

That made her laugh, but it was a shaky laugh. He was such an enormous, buff, competent man—his awkwardness amused her.

Straightening away, she smiled up at him, then sniffed. "Well, Mr. Rafferty, you may as well understand that I'm overly emotional about many things, especially children. My own, and apparently anyone else's. For that reason, I get tearful a lot." She brushed the fresh batch of tears away from her cheeks. "I know, it's a hideous look. I'm so fair-skinned that I turn blotchy with the first tear, and it only gets worse after that."

Worry kept his brows together. "Mr. Rafferty?"

"Formality is important when making agreements, or so Marlow has always told me. She's the dealmaker, you know. Anyway, if we're going to know each other for more than a few months, then you should know that I'm a crier." Lifting a shoulder, she made it clear that she wasn't going to fight it. "I cry when I'm happy, and when I'm sad—"

"You're sad?" he quickly asked.

"For Connie, yes. For you and the unnecessary regrets I know you have. For what Shayna has lost." Saying it out loud brought more tears into her eyes. It really was absurd how easily she cried for a woman she'd never known, and a baby she'd only recently met. "What an incredible man you are to come here for your sister. And for Shayna."

"I don't feel incredible." He looked away. "It doesn't matter that Connie let me off the hook. I should have been there for her."

Pixie thought, at the time, he'd had to be there for himself first. She couldn't imagine tackling the obstacles he had, especially without any backup. "When did you last hear from her?"

"A few Christmases ago. She sent me a card. She'd randomly do that. Reach out in some way, and she always included a note as if we'd been in touch all along. As if years hadn't passed." His chest expanded on a strained breath. "She was like that."

Those had probably been the times when Connie had missed him the most. Brogan must realize it, too.

On the couch between them, his large hand curled into a loose fist. Pixie covered it with her own.

Startled, Brogan looked down, then into her eyes. "Sorry."

"For reacting to a bad memory? Don't be."

Looking as if he didn't understand her, he said, "I want you to know, I don't lose my temper. Even if I get tense, I swear to you, I would never hurt you."

Gently, Pixie said, "That thought never even crossed my mind." Mostly, she just wanted to offer comfort—and receive it. *We're friends only,* she reminded herself. Brogan had made his intentions clear enough, and now she understood why.

She wanted to ask him about his time in the military; when he'd joined; what his mother had thought about it; if he still saw his mother; what he planned to do about Ruthie.

She was sorting through all her questions, trying to decide the easiest way to start, when she heard a buzzing in the kitchen. "Oops, that's my phone."

Grabbing the opportunity, Brogan sat forward. "Go ahead and answer. I'll keep an eye on the kids."

As his tall, fit body unfolded from the couch, she pressed a hand over her heart. This one could rob her of all reason so easily.

"Thank you," Pixie said to his back, but she was smiling. Yes, there would be problems to face, but now she could assume Brogan would be in her future.

Difficulties and convictions aside, her heart was happy.

For the fifth time, Brogan reminded himself to stop eavesdropping on Pixie's conversation. From what he'd heard, Marlow-the-paragon had called. He half-smiled. Did Pixie realize that she glowed when she spoke of her friend? To hear her tell it, Marlow was an angel walking among mere mortals, a larger-than-life hero who could do anything.

It was nice that she'd found someone special, someone who

could fit the role of family, since she'd had no one of her own. That was how Brogan had felt about his teammates. They'd been a quirky lot. Badasses, all of them.

God, he missed them. He missed the life he'd built for himself in the military. He'd expected to be there still.

Shayna made a sound, and he looked up with a smile already on his mouth.

He'd have died for any one of his brothers, but he was grateful to be here now with Shayna.

He heard Pixie say, "It's not like that." Then in a mere whisper, "He made it clear, Marlow."

What had he made clear? Wondering if he'd ever meet Marlow, Brogan got the diaper bag to change Shayna's diaper and again resolved to stop listening.

Andy wanted to help him, and that stymied Brogan for a moment. Then he handed Andy a diaper. "Will you hold that for me?"

With great seriousness, Andy clutched the diaper in both hands as he crouched down, staring intently as Brogan got out the wipes and a changing pad.

"Can you say 'Shayna'?"

"Shen."

"Hey, good job!" He offered Andy a high five, then had to show him how to do it. High, low, Brogan even got him to attempt to bump fists. It was amusing, seeing Andy's pudgy, pale paw against his own rough, massive fist.

That made him think of Pixie covering his hand as they'd sat on the couch. He hadn't even realized that he'd tensed so much. Guilt was a terrible thing, an acid that burned his conscience around the clock. He could endlessly torment himself with *why*.

Why had he let his father and Ruth chase him away?

Why had he been so pigheaded about accepting Connie?

Why the hell had he let pride rule his life?

In many ways, he'd been no better than Brian, and worse than Ruth. They'd cut him out, but he hadn't really needed them.

He'd cut out Connie, and now he knew she'd needed him badly. That definitely made his sins far greater than theirs.

While he changed Shayna, he heard Pixie say, "Tonight? But you weren't due home yet!"

Hmm. Apparently, Marlow and Cort were cutting their trip short. Was it because of the trouble Ruth had caused? Judging by what he'd been told, Marlow was protective—not only of Andy, but of Pixie, too. She wanted to make sure they were all right, but the change in plans dumped even more remorse on his head.

He hadn't meant to bring trouble to these people. They didn't deserve the ugliness Ruth could dish out.

That made him wonder: How had Ruth known where to find him? There was no way Erin would have told her, but somehow Ruth had found out.

Pixie said, "Really, Marlow. I'm fine. I am! This is exactly why I didn't call to tell you." She laughed. "Fine. I should have anyway."

How nice that they had such a close friendship.

Now that Shayna was nice and dry, Brogan realized that Andy was immersed in her diaper bag, checking out everything. He had one of Shayna's colorful little hats sitting atop his head, and when he found her socks, he immediately wanted to try them on.

Brogan grinned. "Pretty sure those won't fit you, Andy."

Undeterred, Andy did his best to get his much chunkier foot into the delicate little lace sock. Such an amusing kid.

"Let's put them on Shayna, okay?"

Intrigued by that idea, Andy scrambled around toward the infant's feet.

Brogan swung him up and seated him carefully, so he didn't

bump her with his knees. "We have to be really, really careful, okay?" Brogan pulled off the sock she currently wore, sniffed it, and said to Andy, "Pee-yew."

Laughing, Andy smelled the sock, too, and pretended to keel over.

"You little actor," Brogan praised; then he sniffed Andy's foot and decreed it worse.

They were still laughing when Pixie joined them again. "What's going on in here?"

"Foot sniffing," Brogan explained.

Andy immediately jumped up to smell her feet.

"What in the world?" Pixie tried to back up.

Andy chased her, saying, "Whew!" as if her feet were the smelliest of all.

"You rodent! My feet are fine."

"Whew, whew," Andy insisted, his face all scrunched up in disgust.

Snickering, Pixie scooped him into her arms, pretended to chew on his belly until he giggled uproariously, and then came to sit by Brogan.

It felt nice, playing like this. Taking care of the kids. Sharing grins and hearing the sound of Andy's happiness.

Being with her. Being with *them*.

It was the kind of thing a guy could get used to.

Pixie's shoulder touched his arm, and she didn't move away. "That was Marlow."

"Everything okay?" he asked, accepting Andy when the toddler reached for him, as always, making sure he didn't accidentally kick Shayna.

Pixie went one further and lifted the baby girl into her arms. "It's fine. Marlow called the shop to check in with Renee and found out about Ruthie."

Something twisted inside him. Dread, disappointment. Embarrassment too, because he knew he was responsible for her being here. "And now she's headed home?" he guessed.

"She and Cort both. I probably should have told her, but I didn't want her to worry."

Brogan put Andy on the blanket and handed him a toy. "I'm sorry. I never meant to bring so much chaos into your life."

She shoulder bumped him. "Well, as to that, I'm glad you're here." She trailed a finger down Shayna's button nose, then tapped her chin and smiled. "Both of you. It'll take a little adjustment, but I rather like the idea of Andy having a sibling. I didn't want him to be an only child, but since I couldn't—"

Headlights hit the front window, drawing their attention. Dread crawled up Brogan's spine.

"I think someone just pulled in."

"Yeah." His mouth flattened. "Stay here with the kids." He started to stand.

Pixie stayed him with a hand on his wrist. "Something you should understand, Brogan. I don't take orders well."

"I didn't mean it as an order." His gaze went to Shayna in her arms, and then to Andy, who'd just found the infant's soft hairbrush. "I can't be two places at once."

A sudden loud pounding on the door caused Andy to drop the brush and made Shayna wail. Just as Pixie was consoling Shayna, Andy launched himself against her, scrambling to get as close as he could.

Brogan barely bit back his curse. He was a man divided, desperately wanting to soothe Shayna, while at the same time knowing he had to deal with Ruth.

Pixie adjusted, holding Shayna in one arm and gathering Andy close with the other. To Brogan, she said, "Help me up."

Right. She had her hands full. Though he couldn't seem to strangle out a single word, Brogan assisted her to her feet, then stared helplessly at her while she lightly jostled Shayna and hugged Andy close to her leg.

"Go," she said. "We'll be fine. But Brogan?"

He waited.

"Please be careful. That woman is dangerous. I don't trust her."

Not what he'd expected. He'd thought . . . Well, he wasn't sure.

Pixie gave him a small smile. "However," she said, "I do trust you."

Those words were like a suit of armor and a shot of adrenaline. On impulse, he leaned down and kissed her forehead. "Thank you." And with that, he headed to the door. "Lock this behind me."

CHAPTER 9

Pixie followed him to the door, but didn't scoff until he'd stepped out. *Lock him out? Not likely.*

Andy clung to her leg, but at least Shayna had quieted. Cuddling the little girl was something she could grow used to doing.

Sniffling, Andy said, "Fend," with his bottom lip stuck out and big tears welling in his eyes.

"Shh, sweetheart, he'll be right back." Pixie heard Brogan's calm, quiet voice ordering Ruthie to leave, and then she heard the woman's snarled demands. Every word dripped hate.

Shayna yawned and turned her face against Pixie's shoulder.

Smiling down at Andy, she asked, "Will you get Shayna's blanket? I bet she'd like that."

Given a purpose, he pivoted and ran to get it, but also grabbed the small stuffed animal. "My baby."

"Yes, your baby cried, didn't she? Babies do that sometimes."

As he ran back, the argument outside grew more heated—at least on Ruthie's side.

"Thank you, Andy." Pixie tucked the lightweight blanket around the baby and used one corner to partially cover her eyes. "You're such a good helper."

He made grabby gestures with his hands.

"You want me to hold you?" She wasn't sure how she'd manage that.

"My baby."

"Oh." Despite the nasty scene happening outside her door, her mouth twitched. "How about I hold the baby for now, and you can hold her in a little bit?" Without a thought, she kissed the baby's smooth, sweet-smelling forehead. "Shayna is falling asleep. Do you think you can whisper?"

Putting a finger to his mouth, Andy said, "Shh."

"Yes, perfect. Thank you, sweetheart. We're going to be very, very quiet, okay?"

From outside, she heard, "Goddamn it, you will listen to me!"

Pixie cracked the door open and saw that Brogan had moved away from the entrance, probably in an attempt to shield the kids from the shouting. Arms crossed and feet braced apart, he looked every bit the warrior protecting his ground.

Ruthie stood several feet in front of him on the gravel driveway.

Still in a controlled tone, Brogan said, "I imagine all of Bramble has heard you."

Ruthie took a step forward, but when Brogan didn't so much as flinch, she stopped again. "You don't even care, do you? You're such a coldhearted bastard, nothing touches you."

Brogan didn't reply.

To call him a bastard was an awful insult. Pixie badly wanted to go to him, to show Ruthie that she was on his side, but she didn't dare.

He was no longer a little boy. He was a man, and Pixie had full confidence that he could handle even Ruthie's obnoxious taunts.

Fortunately, Andy had wandered back to the blanket that Shayna had been on, crouched down, and was going through the diaper bag again.

Seeing that as her only chance, Pixie opened the door a little more so she could better witness what was happening. There was no way Andy could slip out past her, and neither Brogan nor Ruthie noticed her.

Jutting up her chin, Ruthie said, "Your father is sick."

"He drinks too much. Nothing I can do about it."

Infuriated by that reply, Ruthie kicked gravel in his direction. "Do you even care if he dies?"

"Is he dying?" Brogan asked with mild curiosity.

"Yes!"

Pixie froze.

Brogan didn't. "What hospital is he in?"

"Like I'd tell you."

"You're here—so if he's dying, who's with him now?"

Impotent fury balled Ruthie's hands and she glared. "He needs a safe place to recover, but you want to kick him out on the street. I had to come to try to reason with you."

"I haven't spoken to him in years. Wherever he is, it has nothing to do with me."

"It does! You know he's comfortable in that house. It's the only roof he's got right now. He's too sick to work. So if he leaves there, where is he supposed to go?"

"Again, not my problem—but you're saying you've been told to get out of Connie's house?"

It was clear to Pixie that he knew nothing about it.

"Bills have to be paid." Ruthie sounded petulant now.

"You were supposed to forward all of Connie's mail to Erin. She hasn't sent me anything, so I'm guessing you didn't do that?"

"I don't deal with that uppity bitch. Besides, it's the tax bill and more. Are you saying you'd pay them?"

Brogan considered her. "How much more?"

"We have to be out in a week."

"Wait." Brogan unfolded his arms, his tone incredulous as he asked, "You're being evicted?" A short disbelieving laugh huffed out of him. "More than the taxes. So, what else? Gas, electric, insurance?"

Ruthie stiffened.

With a snort, he asked, "Garbage pickup?"

"It's not our house! It's yours."

He ran a hand over his face. "You and Brian are living there."

"We were taking care of the baby. We should have been paid and we weren't."

"Taking care of her?" Anger propelled him forward. "You neglected her."

"It didn't hurt her to cry a little! Connie spoiled her."

From the front porch, Pixie saw the cords in Brogan's neck tighten. His shoulders stiffened, his biceps bunched. Through his teeth, he said, "You can't spoil an infant—" He broke off with a shake of his head. "I'm not discussing Shayna with you. There's no point to it. I have her and you're never getting her back."

"Court might see it otherwise," she said with shrewd manipulation.

"Give it up, Ruth. I'm not playing your game."

That really seemed to set her off. "I go by Ruthie, and you damn well know it!"

"Call yourself whatever you want. Make any threat you want. It won't change the outcome. No one is paying you a dime."

"You owe me!"

"If you get kicked out, it's not my doing. Not yet anyway. I'd planned to settle that mess later, after the summer. Sounds like bill collectors will take care of it for me."

"Then you'll lose out, too!"

He lifted one shoulder, as if he really didn't care.

Pixie thought about everything she'd just heard. Brogan had sidestepped other issues to put Connie's wishes first. He'd brought Shayna to introduce her to Andy in the hope that she could form a bond with her brother. Dealing with the legalities—and Brogan's absentee father and detestable stepmother—had taken a back seat to doing what was right for his sister and niece.

To Pixie, even without his military service, Brogan was a hero through and through.

Ruthie dug in. "You want to hang out in this hick town and pretend to be a father? Have at it. But you could make it easier on yourself if you'll just do what it takes to keep your father right where he is. Then I'll leave you be."

For the first time, Brogan lost his detachment. "You aren't listening, Ruth. You'll get nothing from me. Ever."

No man should have to tolerate Ruthie's nonsense after her abuse—that she expected money from Brogan was outrageous.

"You bastard," Ruthie whispered. "If your daddy dies, you don't even care, do you? That's what you're telling me?"

The rigidity in Brogan's back and neck proved he *did* care, but caring had never done him any good. Not with them. With Pixie and Andy, he'd find total acceptance. She'd see to it.

"He washed his hands of me long ago," Brogan said, his tone carefully neutral. "What he does, how he chooses to waste his life, is his business. It has nothing to do with me. Now leave and don't come back."

Just then, Andy almost got past her. Pixie caught him at the last second and held on. "Andy," she whispered. "We have to stay right here."

"Fend?" Andy called out.

Brogan looked up and spotted them. His frown deepened.

Ruthie used his moment of distraction to grab up a handful of rough gravel from the driveway. Mouth twisted and eyes mean, she hurled it at Brogan. The rocks hit his shoulder and back. One struck the side of his head.

Pixie gasped, taking a step back with Andy and Shayna, an instinctive reaction to danger.

Brogan didn't flinch, but he did move to block her and the babies. "Inside, Pixie."

A kaleidoscope of impotent rage whirled through her. If it weren't for the children, Pixie would gladly put herself in front of Brogan. By God, he deserved protection, too. Instead, he stood there, stoic as Ruthie found a larger chunk of gravel, and then an actual rock.

Without looking back at her, Brogan said, "I need you to go inside *now*."

What Brogan would do, she couldn't imagine, but Andy definitely didn't need to see it, and she wouldn't risk Shayna's getting hurt.

She said to Ruthie, "You're evil," before urging Andy into the house. He didn't want to go. In a rare defiant mood, her son struggled against her hold.

"Andy Nolan, stop it right now."

He might not have heard her over Ruthie's shouting, ugly words about Brogan getting his whole team killed. She threw more rocks, doing her best to egg him on.

Then another car, this one familiar, screeched to a stop on the street right in front of her house. The passenger door of the silver Lexus SUV opened, and as Marlow came barreling around the hood, the headlights highlighted her wrath.

Cort jumped out of the driver's seat, shouting, "Damn it, Marlow!" as he jogged after her.

Marlow stormed forward, right up to Ruthie to demand, "*What* do you think you're doing?"

Immediately, Cort was there beside her, strong and steady, ready to intercede if necessary, but as usual, giving Marlow her space.

Pixie stopped struggling with Andy and instead stood her ground. She maintained her hold on him, but she no longer felt threatened.

Cort and Marlow were here.

Brogan stared at them both, his confounded expression almost funny.

Drawing her first easy breath since Ruthie's arrival, Pixie called out, "Hello, you two." Squealing in excitement, Andy almost got away from her again. She held on, quietly reassuring him.

If anything, Ruthie got even more obnoxious—and she still had a rock in her hand. "Who the hell are you?"

Uh-oh. Pixie's eyes widened.

With one big step, Marlow was in Ruthie's space, backing her up with a glare and a quietly stated, "I am Marlow Easton. You are a vile trespasser, and I strongly, very strongly, suggest you get in your car and leave the premises immediately."

Ruthie frowned and opened her mouth.

"Immediately."

Bumping into her car door, Ruthie muttered, "You have no right to run me off."

"I have every right to have you arrested for assault. I saw what you did. The only reason I haven't already *put* you in your car is that my husband wouldn't want me to dirty my hands."

Cort took a step closer to her, but still didn't say a word.

God love him for being the quiet type who could easily back up any threat.

"However," Marlow continued silkily, further crowding Ruthie, "I don't mind displeasing him every now and then when necessary. Removing you is necessary—like taking out the trash."

"This is between me and Brogan."

"Not when my sister and nephew are watching. Not on my property. Not when you assault someone in their presence. *And not when you could have injured one of them.*"

Uncertainty turned Ruthie's face pale. "Wasn't anyone hurt."

Pixie disagreed. The entire ugly scene had hurt her, and she knew it was one more injury to Brogan's heart—not that he'd ever admit it.

"I'll give you until the count of three to be in your vehicle and backing out, and then you will drive away, and you will not, under any circumstances, return to *any* of my properties. If you do, I'll ruin you."

"You can't do that."

"Actually, I can. I have the means and connections to do it. I'm not normally a vindictive person, but I'll make an exception for you. I might even enjoy it. The count of three. Now, is that clear?"

Ruthie blustered. "No, it's—"

"One."

Eyes widening, Ruthie gasped, "How dare you—"

"Two."

She shot a glare at Brogan. "This isn't over!" Then she jumped into her car, locked the door, gunned the engine, and peeled out with a lot of noisy fanfare, spitting more gravel everywhere.

Marlow watched with satisfaction until Ruthie's taillights could no longer be seen.

Cort immediately got on his phone while attempting to usher his wife inside.

Marlow allowed that, at least until she came alongside Brogan. Then she stopped and smiled up at him. "Hello there."

Brogan still looked poleaxed.

"You're Brogan Rafferty, I take it?"

"Yes?" he said, eyeing Cort with uncertainty.

"It's a pleasure to finally meet you."

Never had a big, gorgeous, totally ripped man looked so discomfited. "Yeah, it's, um, nice to meet you, too."

"I apologize for the display. I'm not usually so . . . blunt with people."

"I'd say forceful," Brogan said.

"Maybe even ferocious." Cort gave her a brief smile, spoke a few more words into his phone, then returned it to his pocket.

"Herman will watch to make sure that woman actually leaves town. If necessary, we'll call in the cops." He offered Brogan his hand. "Cort Easton. Nice to meet you, Brogan."

Brogan seemed marginally more at ease with another man. "I'm sorry about all this."

"From what Pixie told Marlow, I assume it wasn't your fault." He gestured toward the door. "You'll come in so we can talk." It wasn't asked as a question, but spoken as a statement.

Nodding, Brogan replied, "Of course."

Marlow turned and knelt down. "Let him loose, Pixie."

Andy cheered and raced into the yard, chanting, "Lo! Lo!" as his short legs pumped, propelling him at Mach speed.

"Lo" was his version of "Marlow."

Arms open, Marlow scooped him up and kissed his face a dozen times, making Andy laugh.

Cort stood smiling beside her, his hand on Marlow's back.

Pixie's gaze met Brogan's, and she smiled to help soothe his confusion as she walked out and handed him Shayna. "I'm going to park Marlow's car, and then I'll join you all."

Cort said, "Thanks, hon." He took Andy from Marlow and got his own share of hugs and little-boy kisses on his jaw.

Clearly, though she'd told Brogan how these two amazing people had accepted her and Andy, he hadn't quite realized just how close they'd all become.

Very soon, he would find out.

Seated with Marlow on the couch, Pixie couldn't stop smiling. Shayna was now asleep on the floor, and Andy was dozing off in Marlow's arms. She rocked him, petting him often, and repeatedly kissing his head.

At first, there had been pandemonium with Andy so excited and Shayna ready for a bottle. She knew Brogan would have liked to escape, but no one gave him that option.

Explanations had been put off while he'd fed Shayna, cleaned her face and hands, put on a fresh diaper, and then changed her into a gown. Shortly after, she'd fallen asleep with Cort holding her.

Marlow had gone with Pixie to the bedroom, where she'd given Andy a super-quick bath, cleaned his teeth, and dressed him in his favorite pajamas. Afterward, with a blanket and a soft toy, he, too, had wound down in Marlow's arms.

"I should probably get him into bed now." There was still so much for them all to discuss, and it was getting late.

"I missed him so much," Marlow whispered. Her gaze lifted to Pixie's. "And you. My day felt very incomplete without seeing you."

"We've gotten into that habit, haven't we?" A day never went by without them at least speaking, and usually visiting each other.

"Do you mind?"

Pixie reached out to put her hand on Marlow's shoulder. "I'm sure I missed you even more." Having Brogan around had brought home several realizations. She was a little choked up when she said, "You and Cort are the only family Andy and I have. We both love you so much."

Marlow swallowed heavily, blinked fast, and said, "Blast. If I start getting weepy, your guy will think it's his fault, and Cort will come loom over me." Her mouth tilted in a smile. "He does that, you know. Looms. Especially if he's worried. Even if I cry over a silly movie, it worries him."

"Because he loves you."

They shared a smile, but Pixie couldn't keep her attention away from Brogan. He stood in the kitchen with Cort, looking like a soldier cloaked in pride and determination. "He's been through so much."

"You're in love with him," Marlow whispered.

Never would she lie to her friend, so she admitted, "If I'm not, I'm well on my way. How could I not be? When you get to know him, you'll see what I mean. He's . . . remarkable. In so many ways. He's gentle with Shayna, and natural with Andy." She told her about Benny and how she'd felt seeing Brogan in rescue mode. "It was awe-inspiring. Everywhere he goes, he makes an impression."

"He certainly did with Renee," Marlow quipped with a grin. "After all she said, I wasn't sure what to expect."

"Renee is outrageous," Pixie said with a grin. "You know that."

"I think she's half in love with him, too."

"Unfortunately, that's not what he wants, at least not from me."

Marlow gave her a long look; then she got to her feet with Andy slumbering in her arms. "Let's put him into bed, and then we can get into the nitty-gritty of this fascinating story."

"There's a lot I have to tell you, actually, and I'm not sure you'll like it."

Tipping her head, Marlow studied her. "Has he hurt you?"

"No! He wouldn't, not ever." He hadn't even said harsh words to Ruthie. Brogan's character was too honorable for that.

"Then whatever it is, it'll be fine."

With every quiet step they took together toward the bedroom, Pixie's anxiety deepened. The last thing she'd ever want to do was cause Marlow more upset, yet it was inevitable. Her friend had a right to know and Pixie felt certain that, after the shock wore off, Marlow would accept Shayna as Andy's sister.

"Look at him," Marlow whispered, smiling down at Andy with pure love. "I hope you know what an excellent mother you are."

"I hope I am."

Marlow shot her a look, then carefully lowered Andy into his crib, covered him, and pulled up the side rail. "There's no question about it."

"I think with children, there's always a question. You do

your best and adjust where necessary, but you don't know the result until they're grown."

"Probably true. I'm not sure Dylan was what his parents expected."

Pixie often wondered about that. To the outside world, they gave the impression that their son could do no wrong. But in quiet moments, were they disappointed that he'd treated Marlow so badly, that he'd lied to Pixie?

How would they feel when they found out about Shayna?

With Andy settled, Marlow led the way back out of the room. Pixie wanted to go back to the couch, but Marlow stopped in the kitchen—in front of the two men waiting there.

"He's asleep?" Cort and Brogan asked at almost the same time.

Everyone smiled.

"He is," Pixie assured them. The two men definitely had similarities, maybe because of their military backgrounds. "And so is Shayna."

Brogan nodded. "I checked on her right after you left."

Of course he had.

"So," Marlow said. She sat in a chair that Cort pulled out for her. "Let's talk."

"Marlow . . ."

"Take a seat, Pixie, and try not to worry so much."

Out of deference to Marlow and all she'd done for her, Pixie normally would have complied. This time, however, she had reason to worry. "I should talk with you privately."

"We've talked. It's his turn."

Brogan braced himself. "Right, this is on me." Never had a man looked so uncomfortable. "First, I'd like to apologize."

"You did already," Marlow said.

"For Ruth, but there's more."

Pixie couldn't stand it. Ignoring the seat, she went to stand beside him.

Lifting a brow, Cort put a hand on Marlow's shoulder. "I think we're all as ready as we can be."

Though he nodded, Brogan still hesitated.

Pixie didn't. "You know Dylan wasn't faithful."

"Obviously not," Marlow said.

Brogan didn't give her a chance to say more. "He fathered another child."

Marlow blinked.

Rushing out her words, Pixie said, "Shayna is Andy's half sister. I know, it's such a close thing on the timing, but I worked out all the math—and honestly, you can see it when you look at them. It's even more than that, though. Maybe Andy would have been taken with any baby, but, Marlow, he's over the moon with *this* baby. With Shayna."

Again, Brogan took over. "I wanted her to know her family, good family, I mean."

Expression a little dazed, Marlow said quietly, "Pixie and Andy are certainly wonderful."

Cort was often quiet, but this time Pixie had no idea of his mood. "Cort?"

"Sorry. I was doing my own math."

"I wanted children, you know. Dylan always said he wasn't ready." Marlow smiled up at Cort. "He's willing."

Cort held her gaze. "Whatever you want."

"But I'm so happy now, and everything is . . . was . . . so perfect." Marlow looked at each of them. "I don't mean that Shayna isn't perfect. I just . . ."

Pixie realized her hands were shaking. She clasped them together and leaned into Brogan.

With a glance of surprise, he put his arm around her waist and pulled her a little closer. "Pixie only just found out," he explained. "I know it's a lot for all of you to take in. You need time, and instead you pulled up and found Ruth raging in your driveway. Again, I'm damned sorry."

Marlow waved off his apology. "I wondered why you were here and why it seemed you were focusing on Pixie. Not that I don't think she's amazing and deserves every bit of attention any man would give her."

Both Brogan and Pixie remained silent.

After a long look, Marlow continued speaking. "But your attention felt deliberate, and at first that concerned me."

"It was very deliberate, actually." Brogan cleared his throat. "My sister, Connie, left a lot of paperwork when she died. It was as if she'd been writing out thoughts and instructions for herself, things she considered important, but also things she hoped to do for Shayna. Sometimes she included me in the notes, saying that if anything ever happened to her, she wanted me to know what to do."

"The notes were helpful?"

A fleeting smile touched Brogan's mouth. "You have no idea. Before Shayna, I'd barely held a baby. One of my brothers . . ." He glanced up at Cort, then at Marlow. "A teammate."

"Cort is military. I understand."

He nodded. "Anyway, he had kids, so he was great with them. During a raid, a father needed help with his baby. The kid was older than Andy, but not much bigger. I had him under the arms, wondering what to do, when Detroit stepped in."

"Detroit?" Pixie asked.

"A brother—from Detroit," Brogan said. "It was the damnedest thing. While the others were helping the family, I gave the kid a bottle. He stared up at me with the darkest, most intent eyes." He shook his head. "Anyway, that was the extent of my experience with babies."

"Until you found out about Shayna?" Marlow asked.

"Yes, ma'am. Believe me, I learned fast. I'm still learning." He stepped away from Pixie.

To her, it felt like a deliberate move.

"I'm doing the best I can, but I figured it couldn't hurt for Shayna to know other family." He looked at each of them. "Connie knew about Pixie because Dylan had told her. It's complicated, and I was a lousy brother, but Connie knew what it was to be alone, so she'd done her own research. I think, had she lived, she'd be the one reaching out instead of me."

Everyone was quiet. A wall clock in the kitchen ticked away the seconds.

"I suspected," Cort admitted, breaking the silence. "Like Marlow, I had suspicions, and I did my own research on you."

Brogan slowly inhaled—and held the breath.

"You know what really struck me?" Cort asked. "How a man with so few redeeming qualities . . ."

As if expecting a personal insult, Brogan waited.

". . . could father two such adorable kids."

Brogan's breath left him in an audible exhale.

Pixie wanted to throw herself against Cort and squeeze him tight. "They are adorable, aren't they?"

"You're not upset?" Disbelief kept Brogan's brows together. "After everything I just said?"

Cort squeezed Marlow's shoulder. "Losses are devastating. Expanding this family won't be a hardship."

Marlow beamed at him. "I agree."

Taking a firm step forward, Brogan regained their attention. "Pixie misunderstood at first, so I want to make myself perfectly clear. I'm not handing off responsibility. Shayna is mine, and that won't change. Ever. I won't keep imposing on you, either."

"You have a lease," Cort reminded him. "A rental agreement."

"I meant . . ." Brogan's gaze shifted to Pixie, then away. "I'm not relocating here. You won't have to contend with me—or Ruth—indefinitely. My goal was just to connect, for Shayna's sake, because it was important to Connie."

"And important to you," Pixie insisted.

He frowned, then gave a reluctant nod. "Yes. It matters to me, too."

Marlow stood as if in challenge. "How can she have family if you're not around?"

"I had hoped to make a connection. To . . . I don't know. Include Pixie and Andy in birthday parties and stuff." He looked off in the distance as he admitted, "I wanted her to have backup, people she could turn to, so she'd never feel alone the way Connie did."

The way he had. Pixie couldn't stop herself from leaning into him again. "It's a wonderful gesture, and I'm glad to count her as family. After all, she's Andy's sister. We won't ever forget that."

Chapter 10

When Cort's phone buzzed, everyone waited expectantly.

He spoke only a few words, thanking Herman and telling him to continue to keep an eye out. "There's only one road out of Bramble. It goes past the tavern, but Herman hasn't seen her." Putting the phone away, Cort faced Brogan with a speculative gaze. "That means she's still somewhere in the area."

"Is there a cheap place she might be staying? A motel or B and B?"

"Right outside of town, sure, but if she's still in Bramble, there's only the Inn. Butler wouldn't have given her a room without a reservation. He owns the Inn, but he's also the mayor and he's a stickler about things like that. The thing is, there are plenty of wooded areas and natural trails. Bramble prides itself on staying small, with as few commercial buildings as possible. There are even limits on housing. Doesn't mean Ruthie couldn't find a place to lie low—the woods or one of the parks, if you think she's that determined."

"Honestly, I can't say." Brogan didn't know her that well. "She's a hateful, unhappy woman and she indulges in too much alcohol. From what Connie said, she's into drugs, too. Pills mostly, I think. But until I took Shayna, I hadn't had contact with her since I was a kid, and that was only a couple of times."

Cort's brows went up. "For a woman who doesn't know you, she sure seems to hate you."

No kidding. To throw rocks at me? What pissed Brogan off the most was that she could have hit Shayna, Andy, or Pixie. Of course, Ruth hadn't concerned herself with that.

Is my father really ill?

He didn't know, and he shouldn't care. Brian had never showed even a hint of interest in him. If the man had denied being his father, Brogan would have believed him. Unfortunately, he hadn't denied it. He'd just said it didn't matter, that Brogan didn't matter, and that he had no room in his life for an accident.

Pixie stroked his arm. "Miserable people hate everyone, themselves most of all."

"I have a few more questions," Marlow announced. "But they're only for Pixie, so you boys can go on and get acquainted. We won't be long." She hooked her arm through Pixie's and ushered her out of the room.

The second Pixie's hand slipped away from his skin, Brogan missed her touch. There was something about her that made him feel more grounded, as if he wasn't a bastard who had no place in the world.

While he watched the women head quietly to the living room, Cort said, "SEALs, huh?"

Brogan gave up his scrutiny of Pixie's petite body, her slim legs, proud shoulders, and that long, fair hair, to turn back to Cort. Though he only looked a few years older than Brogan, Cort's assessing gaze made Brogan feel as if he was being dissected by a woman's father. "Joined up early and had planned to stay the course." He rolled a shoulder. "Shit during a deployment went sideways, I found out about Shayna, and here I am instead."

"Let me guess. They call you Hightower? Everest?"

That got a reluctant half smile out of him. "Sequoia, actually."

Cort nodded. "Makes sense. I like it."

"How about you?"

"Earnest—because I was always serious or some dumb shit like that." Cort glanced toward the living room. "That was before I met Marlow, of course."

"Happier now, huh?"

"Hell of a lot more content." Cort leaned back on the counter, crossed his arms, and said, "This is going to be a problem, you know."

Damn. Yeah, he'd known that was coming; Cort was too protective not to see the danger in the situation. "I have no idea how Ruth knew I was here, but I plan to find out."

"How? I doubt asking her will do the trick."

"Connie's friend Erin might know. I'll call her tomorrow."

"The point is," Cort said, "she does know, and now that she's tracked you down, I don't see her letting up anytime soon."

All Brogan could do was nod. In the region around his heart, a vast emptiness opened up, a place that had only recently begun to overflow with new, gentler emotions. A lot of emotions that he hadn't expected.

All thanks to Pixie.

Knowing he had no choice, Brogan said, "I can pack up and leave tonight if that's what you want. If not, I'll take off in the morning."

Cort eyed him. "That's the wrong move, and not what I was saying."

Not outright, no, but the suggestion was there. "It's necessary. Ruth will be like a tsunami coming through this quiet little town. She'll leave destruction in her wake. I assume when I leave, she'll follow."

"What does she want?"

"Money. Or maybe permission to stay in the house that Connie left to me." With a rough laugh, he said, "Possibly both. She and my father are in the house now. I haven't made any moves to kick them out, but I guess she knows it's coming."

"You had other priorities."

So many of them. "Connie's friend Erin—a lawyer—is keeping track of everything for me. She'll handle the legal end of things when it comes to the house." A headache started rapping at his temples, maybe from the coiling tension in his neck muscles. He rolled a shoulder, trying to loosen up, but it didn't help.

"Good idea. After seeing Ruth firsthand, I'd say the less you deal with her, the better."

But would kicking her out gain him any peace? "The thing is, even if I signed the house over to them, I have a feeling Ruth would keep coming back." It was almost funny that they had never wanted anything to do with him, yet now they saw him as financial aid, a quick way to gain a leg up. "Money only goes so far, and it's not like Connie left behind millions. But to Ruth, anything I have should be hers instead." Because he was a bastard. Because Brian had fathered him.

If he'd died in Africa with his brothers, would Ruth have rejoiced? Would his father have?

Their reactions didn't matter when compared to what would have happened to Shayna, so he blocked the questions from his thoughts.

"First it will be the house, then cash. And always, she'll threaten to come after me for Shayna."

Cort snorted. "Did you see Marlow with that baby?"

Hell yeah, he'd seen her. She'd looked at the baby with undiluted love. What the hell was that? What kind of person greeted such a messed-up situation with so much gentleness? With acceptance? He frowned at Cort. "Gotta admit, it confuses me."

"Used to confuse me, too. I remember standing back, taking it in." He shook his head. "Pixie showed up here with Andy, so sick she could barely stay on her feet—no money, no resources, no one to call for help."

Brogan hated the image that formed in his mind. "She's so small."

"True, even more so then because she'd been ill awhile. I still don't know how she made it here—maybe with sheer grit and a mother's determination to keep her baby safe."

Again, Brogan's gaze was drawn to the women. Pixie looked healthy now. Vital, energetic, and so damn sweet . . .

"Marlow and Pixie are two of the strongest women you'll ever meet. They've both overcome stuff that could have leveled them, yet there they are." He nodded at the women. "Still beautiful, both inside and out."

Yeah, Pixie was that, all right. Hearing Cort, seeing the women's closeness, left Brogan feeling like an intruder. Like the fraud Ruth had accused him of being. "I should be going."

"Like I said, that's the wrong move. I agree, Ruth is going to dog your heels, and there's no doubt it'll get ugly."

With every word, Brogan felt a little more lost. "Which is why I should go." He couldn't expect others to put up with the mayhem.

Cort shook his head. "It's why you have to stay, but not in the lake house. You need to be with someone."

Pride clawed up his spine, cinching the muscles in his neck and locking his jaw. Cort was tall, but at six five, Brogan topped him. Firm and irrefutable, he stated, "I can take care of myself."

Judging by the smirk on Cort's mouth, Brogan knew the other man was amused.

"Never doubted it, and in your shoes, I'd react the same way. Except that you're forgetting something," Cort pointed out.

Against his will, Brogan's gaze darted to Pixie. He saw her tip up her water bottle for a drink just as Marlow leaned close and said something. Whatever it was, Pixie nearly spit out the water with a quick laugh. She covered her mouth and leaned into Marlow, the two women grinning conspiratorially.

"No, not her," Cort said. "Though I wouldn't want to see her hurt."

"I wouldn't want that, either."

"There are still times when Pixie—very unnecessarily—wants to prove her worth. Marlow and I do what we can to show her how proud we are, but after being used by Dylan, then having to come to Marlow for help, she suffered a blow to her dignity."

Everyone around Pixie could see that she was a fantastic mother, a dedicated friend, a hard worker, and talented on top of it all. But the hurt remained as it always did and made self-respect difficult. He understood that.

Behind him, Cort spoke quietly. "I think in many ways, you and Pixie are the same."

"How do you figure that?"

Cort studied him a moment. "You don't want to accept help, either. It makes you think you're slacking, when you're not. Think of it like the military. There are few things you couldn't do, but others are sometimes better qualified, or your time is better allocated on different tasks."

Brogan shook his head, unwilling to mix his two worlds. "If you weren't worried about me hurting Pixie—"

"I'm talking about that tiny baby, who's now counting on you to shield her from ugliness."

Ruth was definitely ugly. Not on the outside. In appearance, she was still an attractive older woman. Slim, her gaze sharp, her hair only a little frazzled. But on the inside? As far as Brogan could tell, she was as callous and cold as a tombstone. "You think I won't protect Shayna?"

"I imagine you'd die for her, but dying isn't always an option, is it?"

The way Cort said it, Brogan guessed that he already knew.

Cort clapped him on the shoulder. Voice low and respectful, he said, "I lost men, too. I came home and they didn't. I can't say it gets easier, because it doesn't."

Renewed pain twisted in his guts. "I didn't think it would."

"Being with Marlow, having Pixie and Andy in our lives, that helps to balance the memories. I don't relive them as often as I used to. The pain is still there, always will be, but I know they'd be happy for me now. They would love Marlow as much as I do." Cort smiled. "And if they were here, they'd all be after Pixie. You'd have your work cut out for you."

Brogan found himself smiling back. "No doubt." Giving Cort one small admission, he said, "I didn't expect her to be so pretty, but that's not even the biggest part." If Pixie was only pretty, if it was merely a matter of avoiding her big blue eyes and shy smiles, he could handle that. "It's seeing her with Andy, hearing her talk about you and Marlow. Her laughs." *Everything, really.* "It's how she is . . . with me."

Cort was quiet a moment; then he straightened away from the counter. This time, when he spoke, his voice was loud enough for both women to hear. "Which is why you need to stay here with Pixie, or with Marlow and me. If Ruth comes back, there's no way you can deal with her and take care of Shayna, too."

Seeing Pixie stand, followed quickly by Marlow, Brogan wanted to groan. "If I leave, she'll have to find me first."

"And she will. Look at you and look at her. You think she's above crying that you mishandled her, that you bullied her? What will the cops say if she calls them?"

"She wouldn't . . ." *Or would she?* Ruth surely had her own reasons for wanting to avoid the law, but would she risk it to hurt Brogan? He couldn't rule out the possibility.

Pixie silently joined them.

Beside her, Marlow gave a quiet "Ha." She frowned up at Brogan. "From what I saw, that woman would dare anything."

"She would," Pixie agreed.

Cort held out his hand and Marlow went to him. "If that happens, you need a witness."

"Brilliant," Marlow agreed. "I would make an excellent witness, but so would Cort."

"Me too," Pixie said.

They all three stared at her.

Brogan shook his head. "I don't want you anywhere near her, Pixie."

Propping her hands on her hips, she glared at him. "I dealt with her in the store and handled myself just fine."

"That's not the point." He didn't remind her how shaken she'd been by the confrontation. As Cort had said, Pixie was strong, at least in spirit. But in other ways, she was incredibly soft and delicate. The idea of Ruth badgering her, or God forbid, putting hands on her, was more than he could take. "I agree with Cort that my first consideration has to be Shayna. The same is true for you with Andy."

Pixie gave him a brilliant smile. "Perfect. Then you won't even consider running from her—"

His back stiffened again.

"—and you'll stay put so that, if necessary, Cort can be your backup."

"And I can be a witness to anything that happens." Marlow nodded. "Done and done."

Locking his hands behind his neck, Brogan paced away from them, but that wouldn't do. Confused as he was, he knew he had to face them. "I don't understand this." He dropped his arms. "I don't understand any of you."

Marlow stepped away from Cort and hooked her arm through Pixie's. "I trust Pixie, and she said you're a very nice person."

Cort said, "And the little one is now family—of a sort."

Brogan shook his head, not in denial, but in disbelief.

"See," Pixie said. "Told you they were wonderful."

"So, what's it to be?" Cort stood behind the women, waiting.

Brogan swallowed heavily. "Pixie, could I talk to you a moment?"

She practically launched herself away from Marlow, her head held high and her shoulders back as if ready to challenge him. "We'll go to the porch."

Things were suddenly happening, good things, she thought, but would Brogan agree? He looked tortured at the moment. She wanted to hug him; she wanted to promise him that everything would be okay.

Thinking back to how wary she'd been when she'd first come to Bramble, lost and afraid and so uncertain, she knew her assurances wouldn't mean anything—yet.

Telling someone something was far different from showing them.

Her first month in Bramble, she'd discovered a lot about herself. She'd found her heart and her dreams. Her sense of self-respect. A core of emotional strength.

She doubted Brogan suffered any of her weaknesses, but he had a store of his own. With any luck, he'd stay long enough to find his inner strengths, too.

Quietly, she went past Shayna so she wouldn't wake her, pausing only long enough to smile down at the sleeping infant. That sweet little face was extra precious to her, now that Pixie knew just how unfeeling and harsh Ruthie could be. She knew

Brogan would safeguard the baby, but now Pixie felt driven to offer her own protection.

She could just imagine what a big, badass, heroic Navy SEAL would think of that.

Smiling to herself, she went out to the porch, striding to the far end so they wouldn't be heard. Windows bracketed the corner and gave a view of fireflies twinkling off and on over the lawn and down the slight slope to the lake.

Dim light filtered in from the moon and the security lamps outside. The couch was right there, but she didn't sit. Instead, she turned her back to the field of fireflies, folded her hands together, and faced Brogan in the heavy shadows of the unlit interior.

He approached slowly, stepping up beside her to look outside. "They remind me of twinkle lights at Christmas."

Forcing herself to stay still wasn't easy. Pixie had to fight her natural inclination to move closer to him. "Last December, with Andy, Marlow, and Cort, was the first time I'd helped to decorate a Christmas tree since my aunt died. When it was just me, it didn't seem worth the effort."

"I see them in commercials and movies, and whenever I was off duty in the winter, they were in shop windows." He shifted restlessly. "I don't want to talk about holidays, though."

Ignoring that, she said, "You'd like the holidays here. The Dry Frog Tavern, where Marlow waitresses, has a lot of parties for the locals. It's fun."

That got his attention. "I thought Marlow owned the boutique in Lankton."

"She does. And she also waits tables at the tavern. She had that job first, before she settled on a site for Marlow's Whimsy. By then, Herman was already a friend, and she loves waiting tables and chatting with everyone, so she does both."

"And Cort rents out property?"

"Plus, he's a handyman, and the local hero." Cort would deny that last part if he could. "Herman has a photo of him in his uniform hanging at the tavern. Cort's mother gave it to him before she passed away, and Herman hung it with pride." That was a long story, though, so she summarized. "People in Bramble can be sentimental. They loved Cort's mother, so they love him by extension. That's how it works here sometimes."

Somehow, while they spoke, they drifted closer together. Pixie didn't know if she'd moved, or he'd moved, but only a few inches separated them now.

She looked up at Brogan, seeing the glimmer of his eyes beneath the level line of his eyebrows. So serious, so resolute.

So alone.

Lifting a hand, she touched his jaw, highlighted by moonlight, and whispered, "Stay."

His fingers curled around hers . . . then lowered her hand to his chest, cradling it protectively. "I'll put a cramp in your routine."

Even through his shirt, she could feel his heat. Breathing became more difficult, especially when every inhale filled her head with the scent of him. "I promise it won't."

His thumb moved over her knuckles.

And sent a shiver through her. She cleared her throat. "There's, um, only the one bedroom and bathroom." Looking around as if she hadn't seen the house before, she tried to sort out the logistics. "Andy sleeps in the room with me—you and Shayna could sleep anywhere else." This close to him, she felt tiny. "You're a big man." When amusement caused a slight shift in his lips, she quickly clarified. "I mean, you're bigger than the couch."

"This enclosed porch is nice. Far enough away from the bedroom that if Shayna wakes up, it shouldn't disturb Andy."

"If you want to shower, you could—"

"Tomorrow I'll get hold of Ruth, but for tonight, it would worry me to leave you alone. Even before Cort suggested I stay here, I was dreading leaving you."

She hoped that was true. It'd be easier if they weren't coercing him, if he actually wanted to stay. "It worries me, too."

"A woman and child alone would be bait to Ruth."

Now that she'd seen her in action, that didn't seem at all farfetched. "You really wouldn't mind staying?"

His smile went crooked. "Thank you for letting me. I have a strong need to know that you and Andy are okay until I can get Ruth out of my hair."

Relieved to have that issue settled, Pixie stopped fighting herself and hugged him.

He said against her hair, "It's getting late. Do you think Marlow and Cort could hang out fifteen minutes while I run up to the house to get a few more things?"

"Knowing them, they'll insist on waiting until you're done."

His hand moved up and down her back. "Is it okay for me to leave Shayna here?"

"There's no reason to wake her."

"Good. Soon as I get back, we should both try to get some sleep."

She nodded, but didn't release him. She'd spent so much time celebrating her newfound independence and applauding herself for being on a better, more financially stable track for Andy's future, she hadn't really considered anything else.

Like meeting an appealing man.

Maybe wanting . . . more?

She was thinking about it now. Sleep? Not likely, not with him in the same house, so close but still out of reach.

She reminded herself that Brogan had made his position about involvement crystal clear. He was big and handsome, capable, and she was . . . in many ways, a failure.

Past failure, she corrected. To the best of her ability, she'd atoned for her bad decisions and the blunders she'd made. The sad truth was, even without the mistakes in her past, she wasn't all that appealing. She was too short and thin, and the thought of intimacy made her want to hide. The toll a baby took on a woman's body couldn't be denied. Her hips were a little wider now, her stomach not as flat, and she had a few faint stretch marks on her breasts.

The glaring truth couldn't be denied. If Brogan *was* interested in more—and he most emphatically was not, even if his hold now felt possessive, even if she felt his lips move against her hair and the gentle way he clasped her fingers—she still wasn't sure she had the courage to get naked with anyone.

When her body had been unmarred in her prepregnancy days, she hadn't been "enough." How could she risk being told she wasn't enough now?

After finally slipping out of Brogan's arms, she took his hand and led him back to the kitchen. Cort and Marlow agreed to wait while he went to the lake house. Once he was gone, Marlow insisted that she take her shower and change into her sleep clothes.

Pixie took the fastest shower in history. She was thrilled that Brogan trusted her to watch over Shayna, and she didn't want him to think she'd shirked that responsibility for her own convenience.

With her hair still in a high topknot, damp tendrils sticking to her neck, she dressed in an oversized T-shirt and soft leggings, shoved her feet into her fuzzy slippers, and found the necessary bedding for Brogan. Pillow, sheet, and quilt in hand, she left the bedroom just as Cort let Brogan in through the kitchen door.

He'd gone out that way to keep from disturbing Shayna. He, too, looked freshly showered. He carried a duffel bag and had more supplies for Shayna in a tote bag. Under his other arm, he carried his own pillow and a quilt.

They smiled at each other.

"I was just about to make up the couch for you."

"I can sleep on the floor. Like you said, the couch is a little short." He glanced at Cort. "I have a sleeping bag in the car, but I couldn't carry it all in one trip."

"Want me to grab it?" Cort asked.

He shook his head. "I'll just put this down—and then walk you and Marlow out."

There was some quiet communication going on between the men, but Pixie didn't understand it.

Brogan started out of the kitchen, but paused when he spotted Marlow sitting there on the sofa, staring down at Shayna. Pixie joined him, and then Cort.

It was a heartwarming image. Marlow's deceased husband had twice now surprised her with children from other women, and yet the expression on her face was soft with affection. "There can't be another woman like her anywhere," Pixie whispered.

Because it all made her weepy with gratitude, she got moving again and carried the extra bedding into the enclosed porch. Brogan followed. He set everything down on the couch, but caught Pixie before she could leave.

Cupping her face in his hands, he said, "You're wrong, you know."

"About what?"

He smiled, kissed her forehead, then the bridge of her nose, and then . . .

Pixie held her breath—until he hugged her.

"You're every bit as wonderful. Don't forget that, okay?"

Outside, Cort helped Marlow into the truck and closed the door, then joined Brogan at the back of his SUV.

Brogan handed him a slip of paper. "My number, in case you should need it. If you see Ruth, or hear anything about her, I'd prefer you tell me, not Pixie."

Cort pocketed the note. "You plan to keep things from her?"

His even tone gave nothing away, but Brogan disabused him of that notion anyway. "No. I want her to trust me, and I can't do that if I shut her out."

"Agreed. But you want to protect her."

"It might be better if I have time to make plans with Ruth, without Pixie getting too involved. Not saying I'll take off. I won't—unless it's necessary, and I'd tell Pixie first. I meant what I said about wanting Shayna to have family."

The glow of the porch light didn't reach the back of his car, so he couldn't read Cort's expression. Actually, he didn't need to. He sensed that Cort was about to impose his will. As the owner of the lake house, and one of Pixie's closest friends, he had rights, and he was the type of man who wouldn't retreat.

"Good decision," Cort said. "Because now that she's been introduced, Shayna has family, whether you deem it so or not."

It was a challenge, plain and simple, but damned if it didn't make Brogan grin. "Excellent."

Cort released a smile, too. "Go easy with Pixie. She can handle herself, but right now, I'm not sure either of you know what you want."

As he hitched the strap of the sleeping bag over his shoulder and locked the car, Brogan watched Cort walk away. He was wrong—at least where Brogan was concerned. He knew exactly what he wanted.

With fireflies all around him, he started back around the house to the kitchen entrance.

Pixie opened the door just as he reached it, proving she'd been watching for him. There were questions in her eyes and uncertainty in her smile, but she opened the door and welcomed him.

Yeah, he knew what he wanted, all right.

Just as he knew he had no right to it. That kind of happiness wasn't for him. He hadn't expected it. Had known it was out of reach.

And then he'd met Pixie Nolan, and everything he'd ever known was somehow different now.

Chapter 11

Three days passed, and Pixie was surprised at how seamlessly the new arrangement worked. Brogan truly seemed no worse off for sleeping on the floor. In fact, he seemed comfortable there.

Not that she snuck into the room to peek at him or anything, but the first morning she'd awakened before him, and when she'd glanced—strictly to check that he and Shayna were doing all right—she'd found him still tucked into his sleeping bag, those impressive arms folded behind his head as he stared up at the ceiling. His biceps were . . . Well, she had a difficult time looking away.

Apparently, the man slept shirtless, even though the nights were cool.

Did he have on any kind of pants? Or shorts?

Or did he sleep in his underwear?

Her mouth had gone a little dry while her blood seemed to heat and hurry through her veins.

Soft music played from a small device to help drown out unfamiliar noises. The first rays of dawn filtered through the many windows. Despite the lingering shadows, Pixie saw part of his trident tattoo, as well as several scars, including the top edge of the long slash that cut over his ribs. Seeing all those injuries reminded her that Brogan had been badly hurt—not just emotionally, but physically, too.

However she could, she wanted to help him heal.

Before she could tiptoe away, he'd said in a soft but gravelly voice, "Good morning, Pixie."

That sleep-rough tone sank into her, and then he lifted himself to one forearm, staring at her, and for some insane reason she felt naked. "Morning," she croaked back. For the longest time, they just looked at each other, until mounting tension threatened to snap. What would happen then, she didn't know. "I can put on coffee."

"Thanks."

She'd hurried out and hadn't peeked in on him again, but that exchange started a morning routine that she already cherished.

Whoever woke first would get the coffee started. Once the kids woke up, there was little time for quiet conversation, but before they did—the morning was theirs. Drowsy, intimate chats at the kitchen table were the perfect way to get a day off to a good start. Neither of them was a caffeine junkie, so a cup each was all they needed, and often all they had time for.

Another new routine she loved was Andy's excitement when he woke up and remembered their guests. He'd sleepily open his eyes, cuddle with her a moment, let her change his diaper, then suddenly recall that Brogan and Shayna were in the house, and he'd race out of the room. At first, she had to remind him to be quiet, in case Shayna was still sleeping. He was quick to learn, maybe because he adored the baby so much.

Now, on the fourth morning, he warned her, "Shh"; then he dramatically snuck into the kitchen—every movement exaggerated—to find Brogan grinning at him. As Andy did each morning, he ran into Brogan's arms, where he was scooped up and hugged . . . much as a father might have hugged his own son.

Except that Andy didn't have a father.

It put tears in her eyes. Every. Single. Time. The way Andy clung to the big man. The gentle expression on Brogan's face as skinny arms squeezed his neck and a wet kiss was pressed to his jaw. She couldn't imagine anything more moving.

Over Andy's head, Brogan's gaze met hers. His mouth lifted in a crooked smile that, to Pixie, held not just affection but more.

Wiggling loose, Andy said, "My baby," and ran over to Shayna, who was propped up in her infant high chair.

"He never seems to tire of her," Brogan noted.

Very true. When the baby cried, Andy crumpled, too. If she slept, he'd lie down to watch her, and often doze off.

In no time at all, he'd become Brogan's helper, running to get a diaper for Shayna, anxious to help hold her bottle. When he sat on the couch next to Brogan and they let him "hold" Shayna, his big blue eyes positively glowed.

Oh-so-gently, he would kiss Shayna's head, and occasionally whisper, "My baby," in a way that wrenched her heart.

Those touching moments were the highlights. There had also been a lot of confusion.

Showers were difficult, with Brogan jogging up to the lake house and insisting on taking Shayna with him. At least those first two days.

On the third day, she convinced him that she was more than capable of handling both kids for an hour. Reluctantly, Brogan had agreed and then returned in thirty minutes.

The next day, he'd insisted on returning the favor by watching both kids while she showered and dressed.

"This is working out, isn't it?"

Brogan flashed her a grin while making waffles. "It's easier than I expected."

Unspoken was the fact that life would be better still if they knew where Ruth was.

Brogan had tried calling Erin right away, but her office explained that she was on the second week of a two-week vacation. The good news was, she'd be back in the office at the end of this week, and they'd let her know right away that he needed to speak with her.

Better news was that no one had seen her since the awful scene she'd caused in the driveway. Pixie hoped that she'd managed to drive out of town without Herman seeing her. Brogan worried that she was still hanging around, ready to cause trouble.

"I'm off today," she offered casually. "If there's anything you need to do, we could—"

"I'd like to see Benny." With waffles and bacon served, he joined her at the table. "I had promised to visit him, but then with Ruth showing up . . ."

"I understand."

"Ellen sent me a message this morning. Said Benny is still talking about me." He stared down at his plate as if confounded.

"You don't want to go?"

"Actually . . . I do." His tone and expression both showed his surprise. He shook his head. "I haven't interacted much with kids his age, but Ellen said he's asked a few times. She said she explained to him that I'm on vacation and probably busy—only I'm not. Busy, I mean."

Pixie hid her smile. "Not too busy to see a grateful mother and her son? Of course you aren't. I'm glad you're going."

This time, his gaze settled on her. "She said you're welcome to come along."

Surprised, Pixie barely caught Andy's hand before he got syrup in his hair. "I'm invited, too? I mean, I'd love to see her again, but I don't want to intrude. I thought I'd watch the kids."

"They'd probably like an outing, don't you think? I saw the

grocery list you have going, so afterward we could stop at the store, and then maybe take a walk on the beach."

There was absolutely no reason to get so flustered, but Pixie felt her cheeks heating and knew she wore a blush. "Okay, that sounds great. I don't need to buy any perishables, so walking at the beach will work. Thanks."

It might have been her imagination, but there was a subtle easing of Brogan's shoulders.

The rest of the morning went smoothly enough, and shortly before lunchtime, they were ready to leave.

Anywhere you went with two kids, it took some packing. With both replenished diaper bags, two strollers in the cargo area, and a few toys between the car seats, they left for the drive.

"I'm not sure we'll get to visit the beach," Pixie said with a worried look at the sky. "It looks like it's going to rain." Through the gathering dark clouds, the sun was no more than a hazy, blurred glow. A strong breeze added a chill to the spring air.

"Another time then. I hope the storm holds off long enough for us to visit Benny, though. Ellen said he's looking forward to it."

"It's nice of you to see him."

He hitched a shoulder. "I thought about giving Brian a call, to see if he knows that Ruth had been here."

Sensing it was something he didn't want to do, she asked, "When was the last time you spoke to him?"

He slowed as a rabbit hopped into the road, then came to a stop waiting for it to move. When it finally turned back to the clover, Brogan eased past, his gaze constantly scanning the woods. Finally, he said, "Remember I told you about how Connie came to see me and they blew up about it?"

"Yes."

"That was the last time. Not counting the night I came for Shayna, but there wasn't much talking then."

Touching him was easier now, so she put her hand on his forearm. Not sure if he'd want to share, she asked, "What did he say to you?"

"That he had one kid, a daughter, and as far as he was concerned, I didn't exist."

Such deliberate cruelty astounded her. "Don't call him," she said, unable to keep the anger out of her words.

"Ruth might already be back with him." His hands flexed on the wheel. "Or she might have been telling the truth."

Doubtful. Pixie didn't think people like Ruthie and Brian knew the truth. "About what?"

"Brian could be seriously sick, even dying. It's more likely a lie, but if he is ailing, she might want to be with him."

And if Ruthie wasn't here, there'd be no reason for Brogan to stay with her. "Would you mind if I make a suggestion?"

"I'd like to hear your thoughts."

Flattered, Pixie wondered if he'd change his mind once he heard her idea. "Marlow was a higher-up in an influential business. She handled a lot of negotiations, and she still has clout."

"I don't like where this is heading." He shot her a look, but quickly returned his attention to the road. "I can handle this situation myself. It's not like talking to Brian will be a big deal. I'll just let him know that Ruth crossed a line, and if it happens again, the police will come calling."

"Let's discuss it with Marlow first, okay? I'm sure she'll have some ideas on how best to handle it. In fact, I could invite them down for dinner tonight."

"It's your house—you can invite anyone you want."

Softly, she said, "I'd like you to be there, too."

After another lengthy silence, Brogan said, "I'm not good at this."

"This?"

"Sharing. I mean, with you it's easy. Has been from the start."

He couldn't know how that pleased her.

"But Cort and Marlow? I don't like airing my problems. I prefer to deal with stuff on my own."

"You're not on your own, not anymore." Pixie glanced into the back seat. Both kids were so quiet, she guessed they were napping. She and Brogan had actually timed the trip for it, so they'd be well rested when they arrived. "But you have Shayna now," she unnecessarily reminded him, then added, "And that means you're connected to Andy."

"And with Andy comes you."

She liked the way he said that, with a hint of a smile that told her he didn't mind. "And with me, you get Marlow and Cort." Actually, he got Bramble, because this place was now home to them in all the very best ways. Before his time here ended, she was certain he'd feel the same.

"Sounds like I'm outnumbered."

She grinned with him. "That isn't so bad, is it?"

"Different, but not bad."

Soon, Pixie hoped, he'd start to like it. As she'd learned, having more people in your life was a very good thing.

Benny was healing nicely, but wow, he was excited to see Brogan again. While Ellen entertained Pixie, Andy, and Shayna in the living room, Benny peppered Brogan with dozens of questions. At one point, he asked if he could let his friends know that Brogan was there.

Brogan had agreed with a shrug and soon there were five boys hanging out. Brogan managed to entertain them all.

"Do you think I could, you know, get a pic with you?" Benny asked. "For show-and-tell at school?"

The other boys cheered the idea, all talking at once about how cool that would be.

"Sure." Brogan glanced toward the kitchen, catching Pixie's eye. "I think we could manage that."

Pixie grinned. "I'm happy to take it for you."

Ellen handed over her phone, saying quietly, "Benny doesn't have a phone of his own, but some of his friends do. I try to limit the time he spends on devices."

"Good for you," Pixie said just as quietly. "Parenting is hard, and I don't look forward to Andy wanting all the newest devices. It feels like he changes so much from day to day."

"Just wait until he goes off to school," Ellen said. "Oh, my God, I cried all day, worrying that Benny would feel alone or scared."

Pinched with her own worries, Pixie asked, "Did he?"

"No." Even now, relief showed in her smile. "When I picked him up, he was thrilled to see me, but also excited and telling me a dozen things at once. He couldn't wait to go back."

Pixie hoped the same would be true for Andy. "They're waiting for me. I guess I should take that photo." She looked at where Andy sat on the floor nearby, playing with different-colored spoons Ellen had given to him.

With Shayna in her arms, Ellen said, "He's fine where he is. I'll keep an eye on them both."

"Okay, thanks." It was unusual for Pixie to feel such an affinity with another woman, but she liked Ellen a lot.

She darted into the living room. "Are we ready?"

Brogan went to stand behind the couch, where Benny sat with friends, but he leaned forward.

Benny shot a look at his buddies, who were also crowding in. Seeing the possessiveness in the boy's eyes, she suggested, "How about a group photo, and then one of just Benny and Brogan?"

"Great idea," Brogan said. "Come on, boys, squeeze in for this one, but be careful of our wounded hero here. Remember his stitches."

Benny grinned hugely. "They don't hurt much. They're just itchy."

For the photo, Brogan opened his arms along the back of the couch to encompass all of the kids; as they cheered, fists in the air, he even grinned.

"Got it," Pixie said. "Next shot now."

Tactfully, Brogan got the other boys out of the way, then posed Benny to show off the stitches on his forearm and forehead, while Brogan pointed at him and looked impressed. Benny thought it was hilarious and mugged for the camera.

Touched by how easily Brogan interacted with the boys, Pixie headed back to the kitchen. Then she heard one of the boys ask, "Will you tell us about being a SEAL?"

Another boy said, "My dad says SEALs are the toughest men in the world. Even tougher than superheroes."

Not to be outdone, another chimed in, "You're the real heroes, huh?"

She glanced back to see Brogan's disconcerted face.

He finally said, "I worked with some real heroes, that's true. You know why they joined up?"

"Why?" the boys asked in unison.

"Because they loved all of you."

"But they don't know us," one boy said.

"Not personally, no. But they know you're here, and they want you to have a good life."

While she paused at the kitchen doorway, drawn to Brogan's words, she saw him settle on the couch next to Benny. The other boys clustered around them, one practically on Brogan's lap, one hanging over the back of the couch, and two sitting on the coffee table in front of him.

"They did their part," Brogan said. "You know what your part is?"

They all shook their heads.

"You do the best you can in school, at home, and in all your activities. You don't have to be *the* best—as long as you're doing all you can. You stand up for your brothers."

One redheaded boy with freckles said, "I don't have no brothers."

"They're all your brothers. *All of them.* If you see them doing something they shouldn't, you tell them so. If someone else is mean to them, you stand up and defend them. You treat everyone fairly." Brogan gave that quick thought, then said, "Brothers *and* sisters."

The boys glanced at each other, then groaned.

Mouth twitching, Brogan added, "And always try to be polite."

A blond boy said, "My grandma says I'm real polite."

Brogan offered him a high five. "Excellent."

It was a fact—she was fast falling in love with Brogan. How could she not? But what was the point when he didn't want that type of commitment, and she wasn't ready for intimacy?

"He'd make an excellent teacher," Ellen said. "The boys are hanging on his every word."

Putting the phone back on the table, Pixie nodded. "He's a natural. I noticed it as soon as he met Andy."

Just then, Andy decided to use a wooden spoon to drum against the side of the stove, creating an awful racket. Shayna, who had been sitting on Ellen's lap gurgling at her, let out a startled cry.

Pixie said, "Andy, don't do that! It's too noisy."

He'd already jumped up and rushed to Shayna's side, saying, "Shh, shh," and kissing her head.

Ellen laughed. "*Shh* is right. I think you took Shayna by surprise."

Andy explained, "My baby."

"He's claimed her," Pixie needlessly explained.

"That's so sweet." Ellen smoothed down Andy's hair, watched it spring right back up, and gave him a one-arm hug. "You'll make a good big brother."

Arrested by the idea that news had somehow gotten out, Pixie stared at her. She knew Marlow and Cort wouldn't have said a word, but if Ruthie . . .

Ellen continued her observation. "Benny has a little cousin that he thinks of as a brother, even though Elijah is only five." She glanced up, then went still when she saw Pixie's face. "Are you okay?"

"Oh, yes." Trying to cover for her incorrect assumption, Pixie stifled a fake yawn. "I just didn't get much sleep last night."

"Did your little guy keep you awake?"

It was more like a very big guy had kept her awake daydreaming. "I guess I was just restless. The start of the tourist season is always busy at the shop."

"That's right! You do the amazing designs at Marlow's Whimsy. I've been in there a few times. I love everything you have."

"My friend Marlow owns the shop. I only do some of the designs, but it's a fun place."

Brogan's laughter had both women pausing. Andy went to the doorway to investigate. When Brogan called to him, he gave his little-boy laugh and charged forward.

Pixie watched as Brogan lifted him and, very seriously, introduced him to each boy. Shy, Andy tucked his face against Brogan's chest, but he wore a big grin and repeatedly peeked at the boys.

Ellen leaned forward to whisper, "He's staying close to you, right?"

It was a struggle, but Pixie managed to hold back her blush. "Cort is renting his lake house to him." She didn't admit that they were currently living in the same house.

"I think I've seen that property. It's back in the cove, right?"

"Yes. Cort and Marlow are in the biggest house; then the next house is Cort's rental property, which Brogan has leased for the summer." He did still use it occasionally to do laundry or shower. "And then I'm in the last house."

"You two seem to be hitting it off. Do you think there's any chance he'll relocate here?"

Pixie was quick to shake her head. "I know you come to Bramble to visit the lake, but the town is actually pretty strict about expanding. No new houses and definitely no new retail spaces. That's why Marlow had to set up her shop in Lankton." That was where Ellen lived. To be sure she hadn't offered any insult, Pixie added, "Marlow and I both love the town, and thankfully, it's not that far from Bramble."

"A short drive," Ellen agreed. "Shame he won't be moving here for good. He's a good influence. Can you imagine if he became a teacher? Or if he taught water safety or something?" She shared another grin. "Firefly Lake would get even busier."

Pixie agreed with that. "Very true."

After readjusting Shayna, who was starting to doze off, Ellen said, "I don't mean to pry, and I apologize if I step on your toes or anything."

Again, Pixie froze.

"There was a woman at the grocery store yesterday."

She almost groaned, already knowing what she'd hear. "The store here?"

"Yes, about fifteen minutes from my house. She was talking to a man, a guy older than her, saying some nasty things about Brogan."

"What things?"

"That he wasn't a hero, that he walked around all high and

mighty, but everyone knew the truth. She claimed he'd taken the baby from her."

"Good God."

"She was loud, Pixie, making sure others heard her, though mostly everyone tried to avoid her. I was behind her in the aisle. She made a point of saying his name. It really bothered me because Benny was with me. He didn't need to hear someone talking like that."

No, he didn't.

"As you can imagine, he has a real case of hero worship right now."

One glance in the living room and Pixie could see why. Brogan now had Andy up on his shoulders, his hands holding him securely while he continued to talk with the boys. They were quiet enough that she couldn't catch the topic of the conversation, but the boys were listening intently. Andy bounced a few times, but Brogan didn't seem to mind. When Andy leaned over and tugged on Brogan's shirt, the sleeve of his T-shirt lifted and the kids could see his tattoo.

They all went wide-eyed.

Brogan answered their questions about the tattoo while helping to settle Andy more securely. Pixie's heart seemed to shift, to swell. Andy was so happy with this new experience, his face lit up with glee. "He's a good man, Ellen." The words sounded inadequate. "He's added so many new dimensions to Andy's life." Knowing she was in trouble, that she already cared more than she should, Pixie sighed.

Ellen agreed, with her own sigh. "He's too nice for anyone to believe what she was saying."

"Can you describe the woman?"

She did—and it was Ruthie.

Hiding her anger wasn't easy, and Pixie was unsure how much she should say to her new friend, but she had to say *something.* "I hope you won't spread this around, but that awful woman is his stepmother, and she's here to make unreasonable demands."

Ellen looked down at Shayna, who was now asleep, her little rosebud mouth occasionally puckering. "Does she really want to take the baby from him?"

"I don't think she cares at all about Shayna. She just sees her as leverage with Brogan."

"Well, I hope he keeps her. It's obvious to me how much he loves her, and I can't imagine a better father."

"No one is taking that little girl from him." Keeping her explanation as brief as possible, Pixie gave a rundown of the facts—that Ruthie had no relationship to Brogan and that his sister had legally named him as Shayna's guardian. "Will you let me know if you see Ruthie again? I think Brogan will have to call the police. If you want the truth, she seems dangerous to me."

"To me, too," Ellen agreed. Cautiously, she said, "She also seemed drunk."

Not surprising. "Did she drive to the store?"

"I don't know, but I hope not. There's no way she should have been behind the wheel of a car. I can't know for sure, but she seemed to be with that man, so I'm guessing she arrived and left with him."

Oh, no. Was Brogan's father hanging around, too? "Can you describe him?" She'd be able to share the details with Brogan and maybe he could identify the guy.

"I'd say he was easily twenty years older than her. Heavyset, with unkempt gray hair. I'd never seen him before, but then Lankton isn't as small as Bramble, and I can't claim to know everyone."

"Thanks. I'll let Brogan know.

"Jansen could probably help."

"Jansen?"

Feigning sudden interest in one of Shayna's curls, Ellen avoided eye contact. "Officer Jansen Flynn. He talked with Benny and me at the hospital after the accident, and since then he's checked on us a few times."

Recognizing the signs, Pixie unleashed a slow smile. "Is he handsome?"

"Well . . ."

"Come on, Ellen. Is he?"

With a husky laugh, she purred, *"Very."* Excitement brought Ellen closer. Now instead of looking away, she reached out to clasp Pixie's hand. "I can't tell my regular girlfriends because they'll immediately start a campaign. Since none of them are married, they're always trying to get me to hook up, but as a single mom, you know how it is."

Really, Pixie didn't have a clue, but she nodded.

"Jansen has really dark hair and eyes, and he's great with Benny. He gave him a special badge they have for kids, and he asked if he could take us to dinner sometime."

"Will you go?"

She bit her lip. "I want to. Usually, I dodge interested men, but the difference is that Jansen includes Benny. He doesn't just expect me to get a sitter, you know? Between school and my work, I'm absent enough from his life."

Pixie felt for this lively woman who carried such a big load. "I think having a date every now and then wouldn't be so awful."

"I guess, but I'm not ready for one-on-one. That always seems to include expectations, you know? Dinner with Benny along is less pressure. And Jansen is fine with it. The first time he checked on us, it was official business. The next time he called, he said it was unofficial, and he just wanted to see how we were doing. He's been up front with me."

"I like him already," Pixie said.

"After that awful scare with Benny, I don't mind telling you I was shaken. I could barely sleep because I kept thinking about what could have happened, how I might have lost . . ." Her lips quivered before she firmed them. "I don't think I want to let Benny out of my sight for a while. That's unrealistic, of course. He has school and his friends."

"I understand. You're his mother and you love him. You had to have been terrified." Fortunately, Brogan had been there.

Ellen took a moment to collect herself, and when she spoke again, her voice was softer. "Jansen understands, too. He's been really supportive."

Just like Brogan. Again, Pixie glanced at him. Andy was now leaning over him, his cheek against the top of Brogan's head, his arms hanging loose. She thought he might be ready for another nap.

"I feel really lucky to have met him."

"Who?" Pixie asked.

Grinning, Ellen said, "Well, Brogan, of course, because he saved my boy. But I mean Jansen."

Ellen's happiness was contagious. "I'm sure he's the lucky one."

"He'd be a good person for Brogan to talk to about his stepmother."

"Not a bad idea. I'll mention it to him." Pixie quietly pushed back her chair. "With both kids now napping, I think we should get going."

Ellen cuddled Shayna one last time. "She smells so sweet. I've missed holding an infant."

"Me too. Holding her is nice, isn't it? She's so tiny, and Andy is such a tank."

"He's a gorgeous little boy." Her gaze went from Shayna to

Pixie. "With their nearly identical blond hair and blue eyes, they could both be yours."

Lingering one moment more, Pixie admitted, "I wouldn't mind that at all. I already love her so much."

From behind her, Brogan said, "I feel the same way about this little guy."

Startled, she turned in time to see him duck down as he stepped into the kitchen, careful not to bonk Andy's head on the archway.

With her face feeling scorched, Pixie tried to brazen it out with a light laugh and a nod. "I think he's asleep."

"He's snoring in my ear," Brogan said, "so I'm sure you're right."

Ellen gave her a knowing look.

Brogan just smiled as he maneuvered Andy's limp weight until he was resting against Brogan's chest. "I'll carry him if you take Shayna."

Andy looked so peaceful with his cheek smooshed against Brogan's chest, she didn't want to disturb him. "All right."

Ellen eased Shayna into Pixie's arms. "That was a treat for me, seeing the babies. I hope you'll come again. I know Benny had a great time."

"So did I," Brogan said. "He told me Officer Flynn has been visiting as well?"

Nodding, Ellen said, "Between you and Jansen, Benny has some great role models."

Tipping his head, Brogan gave Ellen a look of sincerity. "I'd say his mom is the best role model."

With a hand to her heart, Ellen nearly melted. "Thank you."

"He's a good boy. Smart and funny, and really curious about life. You're doing a great job."

Her eyes watered, and she gave a shaky laugh. "That means a lot."

Yes, it did. Pixie got all kinds of encouragement from Marlow and Cort, but hearing it from others always reaffirmed that—so far—she was doing okay. She hoped Ellen received similar encouragement from her friends, but if they were all single, they might not be too focused on parenting.

For that reason, she backed up Brogan. "You're working, parenting, keeping house—and inviting over guests. I agree, you're impressive."

"I invited you over to boost Benny, but you're giving me such a boost, too." Impulsively, she leaned in to give Pixie a hug, careful not to disturb Shayna. Then with a smile up at Brogan, she did the same to him.

He was able to free one arm and loosely return the embrace. "Keep in touch, okay?"

Ellen nodded. "This has been a wonderful visit." To Pixie, she added, "Think about what I said, okay?"

"I will." She pretended not to see the searching glance Brogan gave her, but once they were in the car with both kids sleeping, she knew it was time.

The weather had been accommodating enough to wait until they were on the main road back to Bramble before it started to sprinkle. His wipers came on automatically, swishing back and forth as the sky darkened and the humidity swelled. So far, the rain wasn't too heavy, but weather in Kentucky was always unpredictable.

Pixie shifted to face him. "Ruthie is still around."

Other than his hands tightening on the wheel, he didn't show any reaction to the news. "Ellen met her?"

"No. She just saw her in the grocery store."

"How does she know it was Ruth?"

Watching the enjoyment of the day vanish from his face broke Pixie's heart. How many times had Brogan been able to genuinely embrace a good time before shadows set in? Not nearly often enough, she was sure.

Lips suddenly dry and her stomach knotting, Pixie vowed to herself that somehow, someday, she would ensure that he started to see life in a whole new way. The way he deserved.

"Ruthie said enough things to give herself away. She said your name and mentioned Shayna."

With his disgust evident, he said, "Of course she did."

"Ellen thought she was drunk, and she was with an older man."

Predictably, his posture became more alert.

She didn't want him bracing for the worst, hated that he felt he had to. Touching him was necessary, so she opened her hand over his shoulder, the same one that held his trident tattoo. There was no give to his flesh. It was as if he'd been carved from warm stone.

Through the soft cotton of his shirt, she felt his heat, the slight flex of steel muscles. It fascinated her. *He* fascinated her.

"Pixie," he said, his tone strangled.

When she looked at his face, she realized she was affecting him. She, Pixie Nolan, the mouse no one had wanted, was eliciting a reaction from this remarkable man simply by touching his shoulder.

For one of the very first times in her life, she felt powerful—powerful enough to help him. Maybe enough to shield him.

Or at least offer him a distraction.

When he pulled up to a stop sign and turned piercing gray eyes on her, her courage shriveled.

Okay, never mind. Feeling silly, she withdrew her hand, but Brogan caught it, lowered it to his thigh, and held it flat. "What's going on, Pixie?"

Well, she couldn't tell him her thoughts, so she shared a variation of them. Glancing around, she realized they were alone on the road. The windows were starting to fog a little and the rain came down more steadily.

"I can describe the man to you, but I was worried he could be your father."

"Doubtful, but that's not why you were stroking me."

Had she stroked him? And why did that sound so . . . sexual? "I was offering comfort."

For a heart-stopping moment, those silvery eyes held hers. "Huh." He flipped on the defroster and cautiously drove forward. "Felt like something altogether different."

Chapter 12

Brogan hadn't meant to spook Pixie with his observation, and it definitely wasn't a complaint. Yet she'd gone so quiet—and pink—that he felt like an ass.

"So we're clear here, I like when you touch me." He heard her quick inhalation. "Were you holding your breath?"

"Maybe?" She released it in a long sigh. "You confuse me, and then I confuse myself."

Welcome to the party. He'd come to Bramble with one goal in mind, finding family for Shayna. All his life, he'd been careful to limit the things he wanted. He always made sure something was attainable before he even considered going after it. Then he judged whether or not it was worth the effort.

Getting out of his mother's house, finding independence, had been more than worth joining the military. He hadn't gone that route to find a family, but he'd found one just the same. Not a mother and father—the military wasn't about coddling anyone. But brothers? Men he knew would have his back? Yes, he'd gotten them, and in so many ways, they'd been the best part of him.

Until Shayna. That tiny girl had added dimensions to his life that he'd never thought possible. She made his heart capable of feeling things he hadn't known existed.

And Pixie was doing the same now. All those same profound, stirring emotions, but with Pixie there were other elements. Hotter and deeper. He craved more.

He craved her special brand of magic.

He just plain craved *her*.

"Let's deal with this, one thing at a time." He glanced at her and saw the blush still on her face. It took all he possessed not to smile. Right now, Pixie wore the innocent wonder of a woman noticing a man for the very first time.

She shifted the tiniest bit. "Okay. One thing at a time."

"Did Ellen describe the man to you?"

"Yes." After sharing what she knew, she asked, "Does that sound like your father?"

"I haven't seen Brian in so long, it's hard to say. I remember him as a big, good-looking guy. He'd be in his mid-fifties though, and from Ellen's description, I'm guessing the guy she saw is older."

"I guess that's better then?"

Did she think he wanted a reunion with a man who'd done nothing but despise his existence? "It makes things less complicated. If Brian is somewhere else, eventually Ruth will return to him." If they were both here, there'd be a possibility they'd settle somewhere nearby, and he definitely didn't want to chance running into them.

When he pulled into the grocery store lot, Pixie sat forward and asked, "What are you doing?"

"I'm going to run in and get our stuff—if you don't mind waiting here with the kids?"

Worried, she reached out and clasped his forearm. "I don't mind, but are you sure that's a good idea? The rain is really coming down now."

When he leaned forward, her eyes widened until he half-smiled and reached into the back seat to retrieve a rain slicker.

"I won't melt, and I'll be quick. Just promise me you'll stay in the car with the doors locked until I get back."

"I don't plan to play in the rain."

The indignation after her blush made not smiling impossible. God, he wanted to kiss her. To lean forward and touch his mouth to hers. A fleeting kiss that he knew would feel so good.

But he didn't.

"Good to know." Because he had to touch her, he brushed his thumb over her cheek—and watched her eyes flare again. Instead of retreating, he tucked back her hair and gave her a simple truth. "Just so you know, you make everything easier."

Her lips parted, she hesitated, then managed a nod. "You do, too."

Brogan knew better. He'd brought nothing but complications to her life. "You don't ever have to sugarcoat things for me, Pixie."

She surprised him by cupping a hand to his neck as if to restrain him. Brows pinching together with sincerity, she insisted, "I'm not."

Brogan lifted a brow. Did she even realize how freely she touched him? Pixie liked to connect—emotionally, but physically, too. And yet she'd been alone since before Andy's birth. Incredible.

Especially since she was warming up to *him*.

Mistaking his look for mocking disagreement, she said, "It's true! I know there are some difficulties, but we'll get through them, right?"

We'll get through them . . . as in a couple?

"You have been a help, more than you realize. But it's also been so much fun. For Andy and me."

This time, it was her thumb stroking his throat, and the innocent touch found a direct path to all pertinent parts of his body, making every nerve sizzle alive.

"I never knew anything was missing from his life until I saw how much he . . ." The words tapered off.

"How much he what?"

Softly, with extra meaning, she whispered, "He loves spending time with you."

If Pixie loved spending time with him, too, then Brogan would count himself lucky. In his thirty-one years, never before had he felt that way. Luck was not something that visited him very often.

"It's the most fun I've ever had," he shared. "But nothing was missing from Andy's life. I know, because he has you for a mother."

Another flush warmed her skin, this time—he thought—from pleasure. "If that was true, it was before he had you and Shayna. Now, I'm afraid, he'd know exactly what he was missing."

Brogan touched his forehead to hers. "This is a mighty heavy conversation for the grocery store parking lot. So, how about we hit the pause button for now? I'd rather get in and out before the kids wake up."

She looked out the windows at the rain-washed parking lot with only a few shoppers scrambling to get to their cars. "What if Ruthie is in there?"

"She's not the boogeyman, honey. Ruth can't be everywhere at once."

"But she could be here."

Being overprotected like a kid wasn't a comfortable feeling. "If she is, I'll ignore her. Now sit tight until I get back. I'll have my phone on me if you need me." He shrugged the slicker on over his head, gave a quick glance at both sleeping babies, then got out and closed his door as quietly as possible. Rain lashed his face as he jogged into the store. There was no avoiding the puddles that had formed everywhere.

And yet, he was smiling.

The magic of Pixie Nolan was real. For her, he'd make things right, whether that meant going or—hopefully, with a few prayers and some luck—getting to stay.

Ruth was not around to cause any problems. On a day like this, he imagined she liked to stay inside. She didn't strike him as a woman who'd brave nasty weather.

He ran into others he'd met, and they all greeted him with smiles and small talk. It wasn't what Brogan was used to, and he hoped he balanced his desire to hurry with enough polite exchanges to keep anyone from considering him rude.

It wouldn't matter so much, except that he now felt that anything he said or did reflected on Pixie, too. He didn't want anyone to think she'd keep company with a rude ass.

In record time, he found the different items they each needed: more diapers and formula for him, some food items, baby food and fresh fruit for Pixie, as well as some junk food. He didn't begrudge her that. How could he when he'd indulged in a few cookies with her each morning over coffee? That reminded him, he needed to take a turn making dinner for her. Not that he was a great cook, but when the weather lightened up, he could grill steaks. He added them to the cart, along with some baking potatoes.

By the time he was headed back to the car, the storm had eased to a mere sprinkle again, and the sun was struggling to shine through the clouds. Golden rays reflected off the pavement, putting a good dose of steam in the air.

An elderly woman in front of him struggled with her cart around a big pothole, so he shifted his bags into one hand and hurried over to help her. That took longer than he'd expected, when she assumed he'd escort her to her car, which he did. Once there, she opened the trunk of an older-model Buick and offered him two dollars to get everything inside.

A grin got the better of him as he said, "Thank you, ma'am, but I'm glad to help." He set his bags in her cart to free up his hands, then moved her bags into the trunk, including a huge bag of dog food. "Will you be able to get that inside?"

"I have a young man who lives next door. He'll get it into the house for me."

"You're all right to drive in this weather?"

Over her cat-eye glasses, she frowned at him. "I've been driving longer than you've lived."

"Yes, ma'am." He didn't doubt that, since she appeared to be in her eighties. "I just know some people are nervous in storms."

"I'm not one of them. If I don't take care of things, they don't get done. Except for heavy lifting, but that's why I pay the young man next door."

Personally, Brogan thought the "young man" ought to help her without pay. "All right, then. I'll put the cart away for you, okay?"

"Thank you." She glanced back and said with a teasing glint in her eyes, "Drive carefully now. Don't let the weather spook you."

Brogan laughed out loud. "No, ma'am." He watched as she cautiously pulled away, going at a snail's pace, which was maybe a good thing, until she left the lot and disappeared along the main road.

When he looked toward his own car, he saw Pixie smiling happily at him through the rain-streaked window. He quickly stowed the cart in a corral and strode to his SUV. Peeking in, he saw both kids were still sleeping, but it was doubtful he'd be able to get the bags into the back without waking them.

Pixie waved him to her side of the car and opened the door as he reached her. Very quietly, she said, "Just put them on the floor by my feet. With any luck, the kids will sleep until we get home, so they'll both get their afternoon naps in."

As silently as possible, he put the plastic bags on the floor.

Her feet were small enough that she still had room, though it couldn't be comfortable.

"Without you," she said, "I couldn't have gotten my groceries. Or I'd have had to take Andy out in the storm."

"I hope you wouldn't do that."

"It's happened before, once when he had an ear infection. I'd just left the pediatrician's office and had to stop to get his prescription filled at the pharmacy. It was cold and windy, and when we came back out, it was storming. It was a miserable day, believe me."

He frowned, closed the door with a quiet *snick*, and went to the driver's side. Andy shifted when the engine started, but settled back to sleep, once they started moving. "I hate that you had to do that."

"It wasn't fun. Later, Cort told me I absolutely should have called him, which made no sense. Why should he run out in bad weather? The car seat was in my car, so it wasn't like he could have driven us. One way or another, I had to take Andy out in the rain to get home."

Yeah, that would be a problem. He glanced in the rearview mirror at Andy's seat, which was different from Shayna's, and decided he'd order one—just in case anything like that happened. If all went well, he'd be here for months yet. For each and every one of those days, he hoped to spend time with Pixie.

"Of course," Pixie continued, "Marlow went out the next day and bought a car seat."

Well, now, he didn't mind having something in common with the indomitable Marlow.

A smile curved Pixie's mouth. "Sometimes I think she loves Andy almost as much as I do."

Almost, but not quite, because Brogan didn't think anyone could love that boy more than Pixie did. "I'm glad you've had her and Cort."

"I wish you'd had someone like them, too."

He hadn't really planned to talk about his brothers, but he found himself doing just that. For the next few minutes, he shared information about the men he'd called family.

"They all sound wonderful."

That wasn't a description Brogan would have used, but it fit. "They were the best of men."

She sat quietly a moment, then asked, "When you were wounded . . . ?"

His jaw clenched reflexively. In the next second, he forced himself to relax. Pixie had shared so much with him, he wanted to return the favor. "During an ambush, the four of us got separated from the others." His heart started thumping hard, as it always did when he replayed those events. He couldn't share details, so he said simply, "We were hit with heavy artillery, pinned down." His skin went hot, then alternately cold—until he felt Pixie's small hand on him again.

She slid her fingertips beneath the sleeve of his shirt, over his biceps. "You must have been in awful pain."

As if the weather agreed, the rain started in earnest again, this time with bold flashes of lightning and a rumble of thunder that stirred the kids awake.

He absolutely could not talk about this while driving in a storm, so he wrapped up the conversation. "The physical pain was nothing compared to seeing what had happened to the others." For months, he'd wished that he had died, too.

But not now.

Now he was glad to be alive, to be here for Shayna—and to know Pixie and Andy. He was just about to tell her that, when he saw two vehicles off the road, one more mangled than the other.

Reading his expression, she said, "Brogan . . ."

He nodded ahead.

She looked forward and gasped. "Is that the same Buick that was at the grocery store?"

Seemed so, along with a Ford truck that had to be thirty years old. Brogan quickly pulled over, dreading what he might find. An image flashed in his mind of the elderly woman eyeing him over her glasses while playfully chiding him. "Call 911, and lock the doors, okay?"

"Brogan." She grabbed his arm. "I see fire."

The next flash of lightning brought a furious crack of thunder that rattled the SUV. "Make that call, babe." As he rushed out into the rain, he heard Shayna wake with a wail. Again, he thanked God that he was with Pixie.

There might not be anything he could do, but at least he could try to help.

Shayna's cries woke Andy, and before the phone call was answered, both kids were making a racket. Thankfully, the dispatcher who answered was rock steady and took the info as she rattled it off.

For once, her small size was an asset as she climbed over the center console to get in the back seat with the babies. "Shh, shh, sweeties, it's okay. Andy, I'm right here, honey." He reached for her, but she didn't dare take either of them out of their car seats. Brogan had pulled over in a safe spot, but if one wreck could happen, so could another. To be safe, she even put on the center seat belt.

She kissed Andy's head, gave him the edge of his blanket to hold, and found his cup of juice. "Here you go, sweetheart. Shush now, I'm here."

His sniffles faded as he guzzled his juice.

She dug through Brogan's diaper bag and found the insulated carrier that held one of Shayna's bottles. After shaking it, she put the nipple to Shayna's mouth. For a few seconds that didn't work, and her continued cries made Pixie want to cry as well. Finally, Shayna latched on, hiccupping around some sloppy sucking that sent formula down her chin.

While holding the bottle, Pixie managed to find a bib and tucked it around her neck. To be sure the infant was comfortable, she ran the fingers of her free hand around and under all the car seat straps. Nothing appeared to be pinching, and her diaper didn't seem overly wet.

With both babies watching her, their noses red and their lashes spiked with tears, she finally worked up the nerve to look at the wreck. The back side door of the Buick stood open; and a moment later, Brogan awkwardly emerged . . . helping out the older woman. She was favoring her right arm and had a cut on her forehead.

It was like déjà vu, seeing him in hero mode again. Rain lashed them both, though Brogan did his best to shield the woman. The scant traffic had mostly come to a complete standstill. One woman stepped out of her van, gesturing them forward as she slid open the side door. Brogan led the woman there.

Flames surged at the front of the truck, spurring Brogan to leave her in the care of the passerby as he rushed back.

Never in Pixie's life had she been so worried. In so many movies, she'd seen cars explode, but, thank God, Cort had told her that wasn't something that happened—at least not very often. But the flames were growing higher despite the downpour. Gray smoke billowed out around the hood.

Andy sniffled loudly. "Mam."

His quavering voice nearly did her in. "I'm right here, sweetheart. Mam is here. It's just rain. Look out your window at all the rain."

He didn't. His gaze remained on her face, and she knew he was picking up on her fear. She forced a smile, then leaned down to kiss his forehead, his nose, and his chin. "Did you have a good nap?"

"Fend?"

"Brogan will be right back, I promise." But what if he wasn't? She drew her own shaky breath, then made a decision and called Marlow. It was a very short conversation, because Pixie's explanation was limited with little ears listening in. Thankfully, Marlow understood what she didn't say.

"I don't think we'll need you, but I wanted you to know."

Marlow said, "And you wanted someone to talk to. I get it. Cort is already on his way."

Relieved, Pixie briefly closed her eyes. "Thank you."

When Andy asked again, with tears in his voice, "Fend?" Marlow heard him.

"Put it on speaker and I'll talk to him."

"Okay, Low," she teased, using Andy's name for her, so grateful to have a friend right now.

Andy was thrilled to talk to Marlow, and she soon had him giggling, while Pixie stroked Shayna's hair and kept watch on the scene before her.

The lightning worried her, illuminating the area like a flash spotlight. She saw Brogan trying to get into the truck, but due to the way the front end had bent—or maybe because of the age of the truck—neither door would open. To Pixie's fretful gaze, he looked worried as he jogged to the side of the road, selected a rock, and returned to break the window.

Brogan reached through the window, then helped a young man crawl out through the opening. He looked in worse shape than the older woman. The guy didn't budge when Brogan tried to urge him away from the burning truck. Slumped against Brogan, he coughed and talked, pointing at the truck. When Brogan gave a nod, Pixie sat forward.

What now?

She had her answer a second later as a young dog stuck its head out the window. His ears were back with fear. For some reason, that choked her up even more.

Brogan cautiously stroked the dog's head; then, when the

young man managed to stand on his own, Brogan reached in and lifted out the dog. He held it close, shielding it from the rain and talking softly.

It was official. Pixie was 100 percent, completely, genuinely, *desperately*, in love. No matter what happened next, her heart would never be the same.

A fire engine roared onto the scene, making Andy's conversation impossible. Pixie reclaimed the phone, and with a promise to update Marlow soon, she ended the call. Both Andy and Shayna stared in fascination out the windows at the flashing lights that reflected off every wet surface.

The fire engine might have pulled up alongside the wreck, but other cars had stopped and blocked the way. On the positive side, they helped to shield Brogan from being hit by any other skidding vehicles.

Police were now on the scene, too, including the officer who had shown up when Benny almost drowned. Other men took over with the two injured parties, and someone who appeared to know the young man showed up, hugged him, and took the dog from Brogan.

Wearily, Brogan started back toward Pixie.

Until the older woman hailed him.

He walked to her, staying to the side so he wouldn't impede the EMT now checking her forehead. The woman waved off the helpers and put her hand to Brogan's jaw. She wore a small smile as she said a few things, to which he nodded.

It was such a touching scene, Pixie just knew she was going to start sobbing.

By the time Brogan got back to the SUV, he was soaked through to the skin. He opened the driver's door, but then stood there, undecided.

Pixie quickly turned his slicker inside out and leaned forward to put it over his seat. "Come on, Brogan. Get out of the rain. The car seats will dry."

With a nod, he silently got in. Just as he closed the door, Cort tapped on it.

Brogan flashed her an indulgent look that said, "I should have known," and rolled down the window.

Wearing a black rain poncho with a big hood, Cort stood there as if impervious to the weather. "Can't stop playing hero, I see."

Shaking his head, Brogan said, "Not on purpose."

"Guess it has a way of finding some people." He grinned. "That's Dee Pearson, by the way. She's been around Bramble forever. She's retired now, but she used to be a music teacher. Still gives private piano lessons. Everyone in town loves her."

"I could have guessed she was a teacher. She has a way about her."

Cort looked at the mess and blocked traffic. "I know the young guy, too. Gunther Prader. Was he hurt?"

"Banged up. Clunked his head pretty good. He was mostly worried about Ms. Pearson and his dog."

"He's a good guy. Works hard as a mechanic and has a young family at home. Any idea what happened?"

"My guess is those threadbare tires combined with the rain and slick roads. I'm just glad it wasn't worse."

"Especially with the fire," Pixie said.

"I think his engine overheated. He said he'd meant to put in coolant, but worked overtime all week."

Cort's mouth tightened with obvious worry. "Dangerous. Someone could have been killed."

Pixie had been thinking the same thing.

"He said he took the dog along today because his wife is sick with a cold." Brogan struggled a moment, then admitted, "I got his address. I want to check in on him, see what I can do."

"Good idea."

"That's what Ms. Pearson said. She claims I have to come by her house first so she can send a meal over to the family."

"Even better. Marlow and I will also come up with some way to help. I remember what it was like to be his age, trying to figure it out."

"Me too."

"You should take the kids home now." Cort bent down to see Pixie. "I'll update Marlow for you. Just go home and get dry."

"Thank you."

Brogan glanced at her in the back seat. "Are you going to ride back there?"

"I think so." She wasn't about to crawl over the seat with both Brogan and Cort watching. "The kids don't understand what's going on, and if the thunder gets noisy again . . ."

He nodded. To Cort, he said, "Can you make sure it's clear for me to back up and turn around so I can take a side street out of this mess? Too many people are out of their cars now."

It took a few minutes' maneuvering, with so many drivers stopped to gawk, as well as police cars and a fire engine on the road. Once they were clear of the wreck, Brogan drove extra cautiously. By the time they got home, the kids were cranky, the storm was raging, everyone was hungry, and Brogan was withdrawn.

Pixie was lost in her own thoughts.

What did she do with a hero she loved—a man she wanted to keep—when she had so many insecurities, and he didn't want involvement?

Poor Brogan.

He'd planned to keep his head down, to avoid engaging with people, and yet it kept happening to him because, as Cort had said, those situations seemed to be a magnet to certain people. Pixie had the thought that in any trying time, Brogan would be a man who stepped up and did whatever was necessary.

Being a hero was in his DNA. Despite the life he'd lived, or perhaps because of it, he wanted, needed, to help others—to give them the assistance he hadn't received.

It was still pouring when they got home, and they all got wet dashing inside, though the kids were at least protected under blankets. Brogan went back out for the groceries. He'd just stepped inside when the lights flickered, but thankfully, they came right back on.

Since Brogan was soaked through, she insisted that he shower first and get into dry clothes straightaway.

He wanted to argue, that much was obvious from his surly demeanor, but as Pixie told him, he couldn't hold Shayna with his clothes plastered to him.

Leaving Brogan to drip in the foyer, she said, "Just let me grab a few towels and some things from the bedroom, and then you can go in." With Shayna and Andy both fussing, she darted into the room, grabbed clean, dry pajamas for Andy, a big sweatshirt and leggings for herself, and several towels.

As she hurried back, she heard Andy demanding his cup and a muffled reply from Brogan.

She stepped into the room in time to see Brogan peeling a wet T-shirt off over his head. He'd already removed his shoes and socks, and now he stood there dressed only in wet jeans.

Those, too, clung to him.

Pixie stalled. For one of the few times in her life, she didn't hear Andy's complaints. Her entire focus was on Brogan.

When he saw her, he ran a hand over his short hair. "I'm leaving a puddle on the floor."

Spurred by the gentle reminder, Pixie drifted closer. "Oh, sorry." She offered him the towel, then had to take a second to catch her breath as he ran the terry cloth over his chest and shoulders.

"Mam."

Immediately, she turned to Andy. "Hold on, honey." She dropped the clothes on the couch and raced into the kitchen to get his cup. Back in the living room, she shook out a big, soft blanket and got both kids dried off.

Pixie gave Andy his cup, then went about changing Shayna's diaper. She didn't hear Brogan's approach until his big, bare feet came into view. *Even his feet are sexy.* Pixie shook her head and told herself to concentrate. She had a lot to accomplish in the next fifteen minutes. "Do you have anything to change into?"

"Sleep pants."

"Good. I can put your clothes in the wash as soon as you're done showering."

"I'll take care of my clothes." His hand opened on the back of her head, his fingers cupped, and then combed into her hair. "I'm . . ."

Pixie finished Shayna's diaper and lifted the baby so she rested against her shoulder before looking up at Brogan, waiting.

"I'm not used to any of this. I don't mean to be ungrateful."

"You're never that." Understanding exactly what he meant, she added, "I'm not used to it, either, but I keep thinking that being with you in a storm is better than being without you in the sunshine."

His eyes went heavy; his thumb brushed her cheek. "You're soft all over, Pixie—your hair, your skin, the way you care for people, and the things you say." He slowly inhaled and stepped away.

"Fend," Andy said, reaching up for him.

Just that easily, the spell was broken. Brogan grinned. "As soon as I finish my shower, I'll give you plenty of hugs, buddy." He cupped Andy's head, much as he had Pixie's.

With that, he stepped into the enclosed porch, grabbed a bag, and headed for the shower. "Five minutes, tops," he promised as he passed.

Pixie started to tell him not to rush, but he'd already closed the door.

Their relationship was quickly changing, and each day he appeared to trust her a little more. It was risky, but she allowed herself to hope: for him, for more . . . for possibly a future. She hadn't exaggerated when she'd shared her feelings. Any day with Brogan was better than a day without him.

Now she just needed to convince him.

CHAPTER 13

Of all the twists and turns his life could have taken, Brogan had never seen this one coming. The week following the storm was nothing short of wild. It started with how differently Pixie acted toward him.

Proprietary. With more open affection. It was as if she'd come to a decision, and regardless of what he thought about it, she was going to proceed in the way she considered best.

She wanted to pamper him.

Brogan had been largely independent most of his life. Even as a young kid, he'd taken care of himself. His mother had supplied a roof over his head, and usually there was enough food, as long as he prepared it for himself. She'd never bothered herself with his injuries, his grades, his friends, or what time he got home.

Being doted on wasn't something he wanted. Or did he?

Brogan had to admit—on rare occasions—it was nice to have Pixie taking care of him. Like the night of the storm. He'd rushed through his shower, only to find her in the kitchen with the kids, the groceries put away, the puddles in the foyer cleaned up, and a sandwich and tea at the table waiting for him. Both kids had smiled at him. Pixie had asked if he wanted anything else.

Yeah, he wanted all kinds of things, most of them right in front of him.

Warily, he'd thanked her, and after they'd eaten, he tried to repay her kindness by watching the kids and tidying the kitchen while she took her own shower. At that point, the kids were in better moods and there wasn't much mess, so it didn't feel equal at all.

Over the next few days, she found multiple reasons to do things for him. And to touch him. He liked her touches the best. Any connection with Pixie seemed meaningful, and the way she looked at him, with admiration in her eyes, made him feel like a better man.

It wasn't something he'd experienced before, at least not from a woman. With her, anything seemed possible. And maybe it was.

The next day, they visited Dee Pearson together to see how she was after the accident. She had far too many bruises on her thin, fragile skin, but her spirit was intact. As peppy as ever, she still enjoyed razzing Brogan.

"I think you jinxed me, young man," she said as she led them into her formal living room, using a cane for added support. "If you hadn't told me to drive carefully, none of that would have happened."

"I'll take full blame if it makes you feel better," he replied.

"It always makes me feel better to blame someone else." She gestured for them to sit, then eyed the way Pixie held Shayna while Andy clung to Brogan's neck.

It makes sense for me, Brogan told himself, *to carry the bigger kid.* He knew Pixie managed well enough on her own, but he liked holding Andy.

As he sat, Andy tried to scamper off, but Brogan lifted him so his shoes wouldn't be on Dee's couch. Honest to God, her furniture looked as if it had never been used. And the upholstery was a pale pink. He felt uncomfortable just sitting there, as if he might dirty it somehow.

"He's a fast one, isn't he?" Dee said. "At that age, everything is a learning experience." She went into her dining room, opened the bottom of a china cabinet, and got out a set of wooden nesting dolls that looked like animals. A bear, a fox, an owl . . . Brogan wasn't sure of the rest. "Would you like to see these, my boy?"

Andy looked at her shyly.

"Come on then." She set the individual dolls on the cushion of a side chair. "That's about the right height for you."

Brogan looked at Pixie for direction.

She nodded, but said, "Very gently, Andy. We don't want to break them."

Dee showed him how they could be stored inside each other, patted his head, and then slowly made her way to her own seat. "That old set is indestructible. I've had it forever."

With his arms now empty, Brogan sat forward. "How are you feeling?"

"Fine and dandy."

"Yet using a cane."

"Nothing gets by you, does it?" She gave him a mock glare. "So I'm a little sore. At my age, if I paid attention to every ache or pain, I'd never make it out of bed."

"Fair enough." Amused, he glanced around. "Where's your dog?"

"Sleeping right there. He doesn't hear well anymore."

He and Pixie looked to where she pointed, just behind the dining-room table, and sure enough, a large gray dog was sprawled over a dog bed, overflowing it in every direction.

Brogan grinned. "What type of dog is he?"

"The type that puts up with old ladies." Looking over her glasses, she said, "I got him from the shelter. The best dogs come from there, you know. After you get settled in, you should visit and pick out a fifth member for your family. All kids, even babies, deserve a dog."

Fifth member for your family . . . Since Pixie didn't seem inclined to correct Dee, Brogan let that one go. He liked animals, but he'd never been in a position to have one. He could almost visualize Andy with a big affectionate pup.

Or perhaps an older, calmer dog. Not that he could adopt a pet for Andy. Pixie was his mother, and much as Brogan wished it otherwise, he was not the boy's dad.

Over the next hour of their visit, while they sipped iced tea and ate cookies, Dee asked about Shayna, about Brogan being a SEAL—because apparently everyone in the area now knew—and she thanked him for helping her.

"Is there anything I can do for you today? I wouldn't mind at all," Brogan offered.

Pixie chimed in, saying, "We'd be happy to run errands for you. And Brogan is good at heavy lifting."

"I'm sure he's good at a great many things." Dee winked. "With this young family, though, I'm sure you've both got your hands full."

There was no mistaking her meaning, and Brogan had to grin.

"There is one thing. You said you'd be seeing the young man who lost control of his truck?"

"We're going there next," Pixie explained.

"I made a casserole this morning for him and his family, and I have cupcakes. Everything is wrapped up and ready to go, if you wouldn't mind taking it to them."

Pixie nodded. "We'd be happy to."

Brogan hadn't known there were people like this. People who greeted you in their home, thanked you profusely for doing nothing, and offered gifts to those who had harmed them. Granted, Gunther hadn't meant to crash his truck. He hadn't been drinking or speeding or driving recklessly. He was just a young man who'd been unable to pay for new tires.

"You're something else, Ms. Pearson."

"Call me Dee. We're friends now." She smiled at them both. "What a handsome couple you make." She gestured at the kids. "All that blond hair and those blue eyes. No one will know if they got it from their mama or their daddy."

Brogan said, "Well . . ." as he tried to figure out how to get Dee on the right track, but Pixie merely laughed.

He didn't think it'd be long before Pixie started telling people the kids were actually half siblings. She now seemed pleased when someone mentioned their resemblance to each other.

Dee leaned toward Pixie and whispered loudly, "He's a good catch."

"I agree," Pixie said.

Slyly, proving she knew what she was doing, Dee said, "Of course, any man would be thrilled to have you, too, young lady, as pretty as you are."

That's when Brogan felt it was necessary to make a strategic retreat. "If you're sure there isn't anything else you need, we should get going."

Dee began struggling out of her chair, until Brogan stepped forward to help her. In the kitchen, she had him write down his number just in case anything came up. "You won't mind if I call you?"

"Of course not," he promised. "I'll try to help however I can."

"Don't worry. I won't forget that you have those little ones to look after." She got out the casserole, which had heating instructions taped to the top of the plastic wrap covering it. The cupcakes were ready to go. "I made this for you, too."

He eyed the covered dish. "What is it?"

"An apple pie. That's my specialty. I enjoy puttering in the kitchen, but I can only make so much for myself."

No one had ever given him anything before. Definitely, no one had ever baked him a pie. "Thank you, Dee. Apple pie is my favorite."

"Perfect."

He carried the dishes out to the SUV first, then came back in for Pixie, Shayna, and Andy. In the usual course of his day, he wasn't a demonstrative person, at least not with anyone other than Shayna. But he couldn't leave without bending down and giving Dee a careful hug.

She embraced him back, then whispered softly, "Thank you."

He was still thinking about her kindness fifteen minutes later when they arrived at Gunther's house.

It was a very small but well-kept ranch sitting on a couple of acres. Trees, a stocked pond, a large garden—to Brogan, it looked like paradise. Gunther's wife, Lily, who had a red nose from her cold, joined Pixie and the kids on the back patio, but she kept her distance because she didn't want them to catch anything.

Gunther, his five-year old son, Toby, and the dog walked the property with Brogan. The kid talked a mile a minute, telling Brogan how he and his dad were building a fort in one of the bigger trees, and how they liked to fish in the evening. Pretty soon, Toby said, they were going to put in a dock and get a small paddleboat.

Gunther shook his head. "None of that right away. Just a few dreams we have."

Brogan stroked the dog, which bounded around as if greeting an old friend. "It sounds nice. All of it." They arrived at a detached garage, where the truck had been towed.

Not surprisingly, it was out of commission. Gunther was using his wife's small car, but he didn't like to leave her without transportation.

"Me, a mechanic, driving on bald tires and with low coolant.

You'd think I'd know better. It's just . . ." Frustrated, Gunther let his words trail off.

"You've got a lot on your plate. No one is perfect. That storm came out of nowhere." Brogan felt as if he was tossing out clichéd statements, but he meant every word. Seeing how well Gunther kept his property, he knew the young man took pride in what he owned, and he wasn't a slacker. "Will you be able to replace the truck?"

"I have my eye on one. The owner had promised to hold it for me a bit longer until I can come up with the rest of the money. Then Cort Easton—he said you know him?"

"I do. I'm renting his lake house."

Gunther nodded. "He said he had a few odd jobs for me, and if I agreed to do them, he'd front me the rest of the money."

Nice move on Cort's part. "Sounds like a deal."

"Yeah." His son picked up a rock to throw, and Gunther said, "Not in that direction, Toby. Never where it might hit the house or a person."

Brogan was pretty sure Toby couldn't have thrown the rock far enough to do either, but it did seem like a good lesson.

"Pitch it toward the field. Remember how I showed you. That's right. Overhand." After Toby let the stone fly, Gunther patted his shoulder. "There you go. Good job."

Yeah, throwing rocks with a kid. That seemed like a very "dad" thing to do. It couldn't be envy Brogan was feeling, especially since he'd rarely bothered to think of his AWOL father. Besides, there hadn't been any fields where he'd grown up. Just other apartment complexes. The only nearby park had been a hangout for the druggies and gangs. He thought of Andy, though, and knew he'd like to practice throwing rocks with him.

Would he still be around when Andy was old enough? Brogan decided he'd do his best to make that happen.

Brogan stepped forward. "Toby, can you show me how to

throw it?" For the next few minutes, while Gunther stood there grinning, Brogan "practiced" tossing the rocks the exact way Toby instructed.

When he wanted a minute alone with Gunther, he said to Toby, "I think Pixie has a gift for you."

"She does? What is it?"

Brogan laughed. "You'll need to ask Pixie."

When Toby turned toward the others, Gunther stopped him. "Nicely, Toby. Don't go demanding anything."

"I won't, Dad." He took off at a run.

Both men watched him, until Gunther turned to Brogan. "Your wife didn't need to do that."

My wife. A bolt of lightning wouldn't have stunned him more. First Dee's not-so-subtle hints, and now that statement from Gunther. Brogan stared at him while his entire being wished it was true, wished that he could claim Pixie as his own. Of course, that didn't make sense. He'd just told Gunther that he was renting the lake house.

Pulling himself together, Brogan gave a wry smile. "Thanks, but I have no claim on Pixie."

"No?"

"Not that I'd mind." In fact, he'd love it. "Remember, I'm just here for the summer." Then he added, "But I'm trying to figure out a way to stay longer. I'm told it's not easy to move to Bramble."

"True enough," Gunther said. "The mayor is real picky about expanding the population. We like keeping the town small. We have our own laws—Home Rule governing, it's called. State powers can't tell us how to live."

Brogan had never heard of such a thing. "Interesting."

"Some exceptions have been made lately."

"Oh?"

"Cort married Marlow. Marlow brought in Pixie. They were both outsiders, but when Cort said he'd move away if they couldn't stay, no one wanted that. He's our local hero, you know."

"I'd heard something along those lines." One morning over coffee, Pixie had told him how the whole town had pulled together behind Marlow. Having met her, Brogan could understand that.

Gunther grinned. "If you want to stay, you could marry a local."

Automatically, his gaze sought out Pixie. She was busy chatting with Toby. The boy held a toy boat that was usually sold as a souvenir at Marlow's Whimsy. He certainly seemed pleased with it.

When Brogan realized he was staring, he shifted gears. "I wanted to ask you how you're doing. That was a nasty hit to your head. I think you were unconscious for a minute or two."

"Guess it knocked me out when I hit the steering wheel. No concussion, though. Just a nasty bruise." Gunther lifted aside a hank of hair that covered his forehead.

Brogan whistled at the black-and-purple goose egg. "That had to hurt like hell. Still have a headache?"

"Not too bad." He finger combed his hair back over it. "I keep it covered because it upsets Lily. She said she keeps thinking that I could have died if you hadn't stopped."

"Someone would have called 911."

"No one else did, though. Everyone was just watching their driving, eyes on the road because of the storm. Not sure they even noticed me and Dee in the gully. If that fire had spread . . ." He let his words trail off a moment, then forcibly continued. "My door was jammed. No way would I have gotten it open, and after the smack to my head, I'm not sure I had it in me to climb out the window on my own."

"I'm glad I could help," Brogan said, and he meant it. "No other injuries?"

Gunther flexed his arm. "I guess I pulled a muscle, but it's not bad, either."

"You have to keep icing the injuries, okay? That lump on your head, and your arm."

"Sure, Doc." He grinned again; then his gaze moved to Brogan's shoulder. "It's true you're a SEAL?"

Brogan nodded, but added, "Retired." In very few words, he explained about Connie's death and how he was Shayna's guardian now. He did not mention his injuries or time in the hospital.

They talked a bit more, and Toby showed them his boat. Andy wanted to see the pond, so Brogan carried him there and kept a close eye on him while Toby showed him a big frog. Wildflowers were blooming around the shoreline, adding color. Silvery minnows swam by.

The sun was high, and they'd been there over an hour when Brogan decided it was time to go. "I'm sure Pixie put sunscreen on Andy, but Shayna will need a bottle soon, and then it'll be time for her nap." He put Andy on his shoulders and carried him back to the house, with Gunther, Toby, and the dog at his side. As they approached the women, he saw Shayna laughing on Pixie's lap. Whatever silliness Pixie was saying to the baby, she liked it.

Just as Dee had done, Gunther insisted that he and Pixie come back again.

Lily said, "I'd love to cook you dinner, once I'm over this cold." She put a hand to her stomach. "I never get sick—except for when I'm pregnant."

Gunther grinned. "I think we're having another boy. She got sick a lot with Toby, too."

Thrilled for her, Pixie said, "How wonderful! Congratulations."

"Thank you. We're pretty happy about it." She turned to

Brogan. "I don't know what I'd do without Gunther. I can't thank you enough for helping him."

"I'm glad I was there." He shifted Andy around to his chest and picked up the diaper bag. "You want to tell them bye-bye, Andy?"

In reply, Andy pointed to Shayna and announced, "My baby," ending the visit with a nice laugh.

Brogan felt that he was learning the town, not just visiting it. He felt . . . included. This could be home in a way nowhere else had been, except the military.

Before Shayna had been given into his care, he'd only been half living. He realized that now. *Thank you, Connie. For not giving up on me. For trusting me.*

It was too late to tell her he was sorry, that he loved her and was proud she was his sister. He'd blown that chance.

With a glance at Pixie, he vowed he wouldn't blow another.

The next day, during a visit with Cort and Marlow, Pixie suggested that Brogan call his father to see whether Ruthie had returned to him.

Marlow said it couldn't hurt, but then Brogan waffled. He hadn't talked to Brian in a long time—and he wasn't sure he wanted to now.

As long as Ruth didn't show up, she was a problem he'd prefer to ignore. Except it wasn't just him anymore. It was Pixie, Andy, and Shayna, too. He couldn't protect them around the clock. Eventually, he knew Ruth would cause another scene.

No one expected him to call Brian on the spot, and thankfully, everyone was distracted when Pixie showed them the silhouette she'd drawn of the kids looking out at Firefly Lake.

While Marlow and Pixie made plans for utilizing the design on new apparel, totes, and bags, Cort invited him down to the lake to fish for a few minutes. Andy wanted to go, too, and Brogan was happy to take him, so Pixie hurriedly applied more sunscreen, got him a hat, and put on his old sneakers. Brogan had to grin at the sight of him. "What? No sunglasses?"

"Oh, wait! Yes, he has some." She darted off again and returned with a cute pair that had an attached strap to keep them in place.

"There you go," Cort said. "You look the part."

Marlow had insisted on holding Shayna and was currently talking nonsense to her, making silly faces, and trying to get her to grin.

He was still getting used to that, to having other people in Shayna's life. Like creating a friendship with Dee and Gunther, it felt nice.

Cort got a golf cart out of Pixie's attached storage space—like a miniature garage—and they slowly rode up to his house. Andy loved it, and Brogan appreciated the special seat that kept Andy safe and secure.

At Cort's house, they got out fishing rods, including one for Andy.

Brogan asked, "Do you have a life vest for him?"

"What do you think?"

"It worries me after Benny got hurt." He watched Cort get out a vest that was shaped like a fish fin. It took him a second to get Andy in it, because the kid was excited and really wanted to look at the rubber worms in his own little tackle box.

It struck Brogan that Cort and Marlow really were family for Andy. They treated him like a nephew. Before watching Cort with the little boy, that hadn't truly sunk in.

"I might as well warn you," Cort said, "Robin started a petition to get new safety rules set for all kids, whether on the dock at her restaurant or the public beach. We've never lost one of our own, and that accident with Benny was too close."

"It's a good idea." Someone should have done it long before now, in Brogan's opinion.

"She's set on your heading it up."

Brogan froze in the middle of examining the rod. He'd never fished before, so he hoped Cort didn't expect him to know what he was doing. "What do you mean? Head up what?"

"Initially, a program on water safety. She wants you to teach it."

"I'm not a lifeguard."

"You're a SEAL."

"Right. I'm military. I don't compete in swimming meets. I don't even know traditional strokes." He laughed at the idea. Every swimmer he'd ever seen was extra lean and hard—not bulky and covered in scars. "I'm trained for combat."

"You're trained to survive," Cort said while fastening the many clips on Andy's vest. "That's good enough. Plus, you know safety and survival. Wouldn't hurt to share a little of that knowledge."

"I'm not a teacher."

"I disagree. Every time I'm around you, I see you teaching something to Andy or Shayna. It comes naturally to you, and you do it in an easy way. That's not a knack everyone has."

At that very moment, Andy swung up his small rod, barely missing Brogan's face. He said, "Whoa, hold up there, bud." Kneeling down, he showed Andy how to hold the rod. "Keep it out in front of you, okay? You don't want to smack me or your uncle Cort."

Cort straightened with a smile. "Case in point."

Bemused, Brogan came back to his feet. "I hope you're a teacher as well, because I've never fished a day in my life."

"No way."

"First time I've ever held a fishing rod. No idea what I'm doing."

"Will you be squeamish about putting bait on the hook?"

"Guess that depends on the bait."

Cort laughed out loud. He opened a small fridge in his garage and got out a small foam container. As they started down the hill, a big fish splashed as if in welcome and two geese glided by, honking noisily.

The green water looked cold, disturbed by an undercurrent that kept it washing against the rocky shoreline in a melodic rhythm.

Brogan drew a deep breath and relaxed. It was his last easy breath for an hour. The second he cast out, he got a nibble, and it was a helluva lot more exciting than he'd expected. He had his hands full with the fish, listening to Cort, and keeping Andy from going headfirst into the lake.

After a time, Cort said, "It's peaceful, right?"

More than Brogan had imagined was possible. "Yeah."

"I used to fish here nearly every morning, at least until Marlow rented the cottage. Then she'd come down to the dock in cute shorts to watch the sunrise. She'd sit there drinking her coffee until I'd forget about the fish."

It was an amusing image, a Marine getting sidelined by a pretty woman. Amusing, but not surprising. "Got to you, huh?"

"From day one."

That's how he felt about Pixie.

Andy laid aside his fishing pole and wanted to see the rubber worms. Cort had made sure the ones in Andy's tackle box were without hooks. They still had to watch him so he didn't try to eat the things, but mostly he just wanted to squish them in his hands, then stretch them out.

Brogan got curious enough that he squatted down beside Andy and tested the worms, too.

Cort said, "I should take you both to the bait shop. There's a guy on the lake who makes custom lures. I could look at them for hours."

Brogan's curiosity was piqued. "They sell live bait, too?"

"Sure. Worms, minnows, crayfish, crickets . . . I get stuff there, but sometimes I just walk along the road and turn over rocks. Plenty of bait available." He grinned. "Once, I ran out of bait and caught a spider. Marlow was not happy. She made me scrub my hands and arms up to my elbows before I could touch her."

Brogan laughed. "I don't know too many people who are fond of spiders."

"A fisherman will use whatever he has to." Cort spent a few minutes casting out before he continued. "With Marlow, I was surprised. Generally, she's not afraid of anything."

"Especially hard work?"

Cort snorted. "I haven't known many people who'd take on what she does. Pixie doesn't realize it, but she's a blessing to Marlow."

He didn't doubt it; she was a huge blessing to him, too. "Do you mean in some specific way?"

"In all ways, but when Marlow first came here, she was looking for acceptance." He flashed a look at Cort, then took a quick glance at Andy, too. The toddler had lain back and was now putting all the colorful lure worms on his stomach.

Brogan guessed there was no accounting for what entertained a toddler.

"Marlow had this idea of getting back to her roots, and that meant opening up her shop and running it with the same professionalism that she'd applied to the corporate world, but on a much smaller and more personal scale. First, though, she accepted a job at the Dry Frog Tavern."

"Hell of a name."

"Right? It catches your interest, though. Marlow was hooked. I think she took the job as something of a dare, to prove to Herman and me that she could do it."

"And she could?"

"She makes it look easy, when I know it's not." When Cort got a bite, he grew quiet, concentrating on moving his rod this way and that, teasing the fish—until a few minutes later, he reeled in a big bass.

Brogan was fascinated. He observed how Cort unhooked the bass, careful of the sharp fins. "That's a big one."

"Big enough to be dinner."

Andy cheered, "F'sh, f'sh!"

"You want to pet this one, Andy?"

Not only did he rush over to gently pet it, but before Cort could pull back, Andy bent down and gave it a loud, firm kiss.

Both men froze, then looked at each other before cracking up. Brogan swooped Andy into his arms and quickly wiped his mouth. "Maybe we shouldn't tell Mam about that."

Still laughing, Cort said, "Andy will do his best to share, but let's hope his explanation isn't clear enough for either woman to figure out."

Since they were still chuckling, Andy clapped his hands and laughed, too.

After Cort got the fish in a basket, he returned to his story. "Back when I first moved my mother here, I didn't know how much I'd enjoy fishing. I just knew I wanted my mother somewhere safe."

Brogan had no idea what that meant, and he didn't ask. Cort was usually pretty quiet, so he figured the other man would tell him when he was ready.

"My dad was the type who liked to talk with his fists. It's a long story, and I won't go into it all, but you can imagine that I was still pretty young when I tried to defend her."

"Your dad turned on you?"

"He was an abusive drunk. He could have bloodied us both and he wouldn't have cared. Mom took off with me, we got by, and when I was old enough, I joined the Marines. Unfortunately, while I was away, he found her."

Cort's tone of voice, quiet and flat, conveyed the fury he still felt.

"It was bad?"

"Bad enough that the hospital contacted me and I got emergency leave."

Hell of a situation for a man to be in. Caught between serving his country and saving his mother. For the first time, Brogan thought that maybe he'd gotten off easy. As least while he'd served, he hadn't worried about anyone. Until Connie's death, he hadn't known he had anyone to worry about.

"I had to get Mom settled somewhere, so I bought this house and the lake house you're renting. I figured whenever I was home, Mom and I could have our privacy. As soon as she recovered enough, she got a job with Herman, and liked it as much as Marlow does. With me away so often, Herman really stepped up to help her. Other locals did, too."

It sounded as if Cort was as confused by it all as Brogan was.

"I bought this place because Bramble is so small and remote. I figured Mom would be safe here. Until I got to know the town, I didn't know there were places like this."

"Or people like these," Brogan said in agreement, thinking of Pixie's protective coworker, Renee; Benny and his awesome mom, Ellen; Dee, who'd been so generous to a stranger; and Gunther and Lily, such openly loving parents. Any one of them was a marvel, but together? All from the same place? It defied belief, and yet it was true.

"Exactly. These people looked out for Mom when I couldn't, and when I was home, they treated me like family—the biggest, best family I'd ever had."

"More so than the military?" Brogan felt disloyal for even asking.

"Different, for sure." Cort gave a crooked grin. "Warmer. This is home now, and I can't imagine living anywhere else. Mom was really happy here for her last years."

"She's gone now?"

Cort nodded. "I was up for reenlistment when we found out about her lung cancer. Much as I loved serving, I needed to be here with her."

He'd had a mother he could love more than the Marines. The notion gave Brogan a lot to think about because that was how he'd felt about Shayna from the moment he found out she needed him.

It was how he now felt about Pixie.

"Herman and I are close. He's been more of a father to me than my own ever was."

Damn, he and Cort had a lot in common.

Yet they had some huge differences, too. The main one being that Cort had stood by his mother, and Brogan had bailed on Connie.

"I don't think Marlow knew she was looking for acceptance. She just wanted to be herself instead of the person she'd become during an unhappy marriage."

"People here love her."

"Big-time," Cort confirmed. "Serving one drink or burger at a time, she won over the entire town. Herman is especially close to her. She dressed down, let her hair loose, got back to her roots, and found her forever place—where she was liked for being herself, not a hyped-up model of business success or wealth."

Acceptance. Brogan had felt it, too, and it was powerfully addictive.

Thirty minutes later, when Andy rubbed his face against Brogan's shoulder and let out a yawn, he figured it was time to head home. "I have a napper on my hands," Brogan said quietly.

Cort glanced at him, then smiled as Andy nodded off and went boneless. He took the rod from Brogan. "What did you think of fishing?"

"I didn't catch anything, but I wouldn't mind trying again."

"It's a little easier when you're not holding a toddler."

Brogan turned so his cheek pressed the top of Andy's head. His sunglasses were now crooked and his hat was off to the side. "I don't mind holding him." The second he spoke, he laughed at himself. "I'd never even thought about holding an infant or a toddler until I met Shayna and Andy."

"Didn't know what you were missing, huh?"

"I had no clue." Opening a hand on Andy's back, Brogan looked out over the water. Sunlight glinted off the surface, and the air smelled so fresh. "I could get used to this."

"Consider yourself invited anytime. I have more than enough gear. Andy is always welcome, too."

Though he'd never given fishing a thought before today, Brogan already anticipated the next time.

Chapter 14

The following night, after the kids were in bed, Pixie emerged from her bedroom, her hair damp, her face scrubbed clean, dressed in a big sleep shirt and cotton shorts that left her beautiful legs on display.

"Tonight's the night," she said with determination, almost stopping his heart.

He was primed in a way he'd never experienced before.

Every day seemed better than the one before it, and now this?

Alert to every smile, he watched her go into the kitchen and return with two bottles of water. She curled up on the couch next to him, touched his arm, and said, "Call your father. If Ruthie has gone home, we can both stop worrying about her."

"I'm not all that worried," he lied. The problem was that if Ruth was gone, he'd have no reason to stay so close to Pixie. He had no right to keep infringing on her, but he wanted to be here. Near her morning and night. Waking up and knowing they'd have coffee together. Giving Andy hugs good night.

Watching as Pixie cuddled Shayna and the kids interacted.

No right—and yet it felt like the kind of home he'd always imagined, the type of home he'd assumed would always be out of his reach.

Pixie picked up his phone from the end table and handed it to him. "Then call for me, because I worry enough for both of us."

That bothered him. "I would never let her hurt you."

Her expression went soft in that way she had, and she hugged him. "I worry for you, Brogan. Don't bother telling me not to, because that'd be like telling the grass not to grow."

Resisting her was no longer an option, so he held her close, telling himself that for her, he'd do anything. In truth, he'd needed the push. Before Pixie, he'd had an "I don't give a damn" edge. Now, he badly wanted to protect what he had with her.

And so, with the phone on speaker, he tried calling the last number he'd had for Brian.

There was no answer.

Pixie looked more disappointed than he was. Hell, for him, it felt like a reprieve. Talking to Brian was bound to be ugly, and that ugliness had no place in his current peace.

But again, he wanted to do what was right for Pixie.

"Erin might have come back from vacation," he suggested.

"She's not due back until tomorrow."

"To the office. I'll try her at home." He hadn't wanted to interrupt Erin's vacation, but now that he was ready to make the call to Brian, he wanted it over with. A glance at the time on his phone showed it shouldn't be too late to call.

When Erin answered on the first ring, he knew he was right.

"Hi, Erin, it's Brogan."

"Brogan! Hello. What's up? Shayna's okay?"

"Yes, she's doing great, actually. I'm sorry to bother you at home."

"Hey, I told you to call anytime, and I meant it. Never hesitate, okay?"

"I know you just got back from vacation."

"Actually, it was a staycation. I just needed some time away from the office." With suspicion, she asked, "Did you call there? They were told to let me know, no matter what."

Wow. When Erin said for me to call anytime, apparently she meant it. Of course, she'd loved Connie, so it made sense that she'd prioritize anything to do with Shayna. "I did call the office earlier, but I didn't give them any details." He paused for only a second, then explained, "I've rented a lake house in Bramble. I'm set to be here for another three months."

"Whoa," she whispered. "Hold on. Let me get to a comfortable seat."

Brogan had to smile. He'd liked Erin Benning from the moment he'd met her. Her love and concern for Shayna had been as obvious as her grief for Connie. "I should probably tell you that you're on speaker."

"Okay. So, who else is there?" Then in a dawning whisper, she asked, "Is it Pixie Nolan?"

Pixie grinned. "It is. Hello, Ms. Benning. It's so nice to meet you."

"Gawd," she said with exaggerated relief. "You don't sound pissed, so I'm going to assume you're okay with Brogan and Shayna being there?"

"I'm thrilled that they're here. Brogan did the right thing. Siblings should be together."

There was a new, raspy tone in Erin's voice when she spoke again, almost as if she held back tears. "Connie always said that you would understand. She would tell me that as a mom, she looked at things differently, and she was sure you would, too. She insisted that Brogan would be the perfect guardian and that you would never blame a child for what her father did."

Those stark words dug into Brogan. No, Pixie wasn't like that—but Ruth sure was. Her hatred toward him had been palpable even from Brogan's earliest years. He could still remember her screaming at his mom, telling her she was trash . . . and so was her bastard kid.

Being with Pixie now only emphasized the differences between the two women and their individual capacities for love and acceptance.

"I wish I'd known Connie," Pixie said. "She sounds like a remarkable woman. I'm sure we would have been friends."

"She was," Erin assured her. "If she hadn't died so unexpectedly, she might be the one there now, getting to know you."

Pixie's gaze caught Brogan's, and he knew exactly what she was thinking, because to his shame, he was thinking it, too. If things had been different, he wouldn't have met her. He'd still trade places with Connie if he could, but he was damned grateful that he didn't have to, that he'd have a chance to build a better life, with Pixie in it.

"I'm so sorry for your loss, Ms. Benning."

"Since we're all playing nice," Erin said, "please just call me Erin. I loved Connie like a sister, and I adore Shayna. I hope we can stay in touch."

Pixie grinned. "Please do."

As far as Brogan was concerned, Shayna couldn't have too many strong, positive role models. "I'll make sure Pixie has your number, too."

"I want either of you to feel free to reach out to me at any time."

Brogan was glad he'd called after all. "Thank you. I appreciate that." He got right to it. "Did Connie leave a number for her father?"

There was stunned silence before Erin replied, "Yes, of course, but Connie didn't want him in Shayna's life, so I strongly advise you not to reach out to him."

"Normally, I wouldn't," he said. "I don't want anything to do with him. The problem is that Ruth showed up in Bramble."

"The hell she did!"

"She's awful," Pixie added. "She put in a few appearances,

then seemed to disappear until a friend said Ruthie was at the grocery store talking about Brogan and slandering him."

"The nerve of that bitch!"

Knowing how Pixie felt about cursing, he was glad the kids were already in bed. "I don't like having her around just waiting to cause more trouble," Brogan said, "so I might have to deal with Brian just to get some things settled."

With a deep sigh, Erin said, "Not long after you took guardianship of Shayna, Ruth showed up here, too. She demanded payment for the short time she'd kept her own granddaughter."

Brogan stiffened. "I hope you refused her."

"I told her to go to hell, actually. Not very professional of me, but I was acting as Connie's friend, not her lawyer."

"Good."

"The thing is, she said she found some of Connie's papers at the house."

Brogan closed his eyes. Not once had he considered that possibility. "There were more papers?"

"It's possible, Brogan. I'm sorry." Erin sighed her frustration. "Sometimes when Connie was lonely or disappointed, or if she was just looking at Shayna and worrying about her future, she'd write long notes. After she died and I went through her house, I found some under a couch cushion, one stuck on the refrigerator with a magnet, and another on her nightstand. I didn't search through all her things because that wouldn't have been right, but as she'd told me to do, I gathered up everything that was noticeable, as well as her important papers from her desk drawer."

"There were probably others," Brogan mused aloud.

"I'm guessing there were. Connie was obsessed with the idea of Shayna having family."

"Because she knew what it was to be alone."

Hurriedly, Erin said, "She always considered you her brother. I know things weren't great between the two of you—"

"My fault." God, if he could have that time to do over . . .

"No," Erin denied. "Connie rightfully blamed her parents. She was so proud of you, Brogan. You were her hero."

Everything in him seemed to clamp down painfully. "I'm no one's hero."

"Bull. You're Shayna's hero, and don't you forget it. Keep her away from Brian and Ruth. Do whatever you have to, okay?"

"They'll never touch her." Now that he'd seen what a good life Shayna could have, he wasn't about to let her settle for anything else. "That reminds me. I'll need an updated will, right?"

"Absolutely."

"Could you put it together for me? Everything Connie had plus my own accounts. It should all go to Shayna."

"Sure. I'll need you to fill out some paperwork, but I can get that out to you soon. The thing is, Shayna will still need a contingency guardian. Otherwise, if something happened to you, she could go back to Ruth and Brian."

"Never."

"Then you need to think about who you'd want for her guardian."

Pixie nudged him, smiled, and raised her hand.

In that moment, he knew he loved her. God, he loved her so much it almost hurt.

"Brogan?" Erin said. "Did I lose you?"

"No." He put his arm around Pixie and held her close to his side. "Pixie will be the guardian."

"Excellent! I don't mind saying, that's exactly what I hoped for, and I know it's what Connie would have wanted, too." There was some jostling, and then Erin said, "Here's Brian's number. Are you ready?"

"Sure."

She read it off, and Brogan frowned. "That's the number I have, but no one is answering."

"Odd. I'll be in the office tomorrow bright and early. Let me look into things, okay? Give me a day, maybe two, and I'll get back to you."

"All right, thank you."

"Brogan? Thank *you*. Not every man out there would step up for a niece he'd never met, especially when he was estranged from his sister. You've proven you're every bit as wonderful as Connie claimed."

He dropped his head with a gruff laugh. Why wouldn't anyone believe him? He was not wonderful, and he wasn't hero material. He knew the truth even if no one else did.

Erin said, "If your email is the same, I'll send you the info I need to get your paperwork ready. I'll also send a form for a contingency guardian. Fill that out and get it back to me, and you'll be covered for now." She added with some gravity, "Connie believed in taking every precaution."

"Then I will, too."

"One last thing, Brogan. You need to figure out what you're going to do with Connie's house."

He bit back a groan. "I know."

"She didn't want her parents there," Erin insisted. "She was clear about that. The house is legally yours and Shayna's, but the longer you let them trespass, the more difficult it'll be to evict them."

"It's next on my list to do." Right after cementing his relationship with Pixie, which, okay, was fairly new to the top of his list, but it was there now and it mattered. A lot.

"You need to ask them to leave. Of course, that won't work, so then you'll have to begin a legal eviction."

"What does that entail?" Brogan asked. "I signed a lease to be here for four months, and I don't like the idea of driving back and forth to Illinois."

"Actually, I can handle it if you want. In fact, I'd *love* to take care of it. It's a matter of filing an unlawful detainer action and representing you in court."

"That's not your legal specialty, is it?"

"No, but I'll do it for Connie. Trust me, I never liked the way her parents treated her."

Pixie smoothed her hand up and down his arm. "It's a good solution."

He'd be free to concentrate on Shayna—and Pixie. "All right. Go for it. And seriously, Erin, thank you. For everything."

After they hung up, Brogan sat back against the couch, wondering when Ruth would pop up next. "Thanks for giving me a push. I'm glad I made the call."

Pixie curled into his side and put her arm around him.

They were in the position of a couple familiar with each other, used to embracing and getting comfortable together.

Brogan was far from comfortable as he carefully gathered Pixie closer and pressed a kiss to her hair. In fact, he felt strung tight with conflicting emotions—and a torturous type of lust because it wasn't just sexual. It was some powerful combination of physical, emotional, and sexual need.

She smelled like sunshine and flowers, and she felt perfect in his arms.

He wanted more, of course. From her and with her. In every way imaginable.

Wearing a smile and looking far too innocent, Pixie looked at him. "This feels like progress, right?"

Unsure whether she meant Erin's next move, or the fact that he could feel her heart beating, he nodded. "Sure."

"I'm not sleepy yet. You?"

No, he was far from sleepy. "What did you have in mind?"

"A movie. You've rarely had time to just relax, and I almost never have time to watch TV. What do you think?"

At that moment, he'd have been happy to do whatever she asked. "Sure."

"Great. Settle back and get comfortable while I find something." She started to move away from him.

Brogan didn't let go. "I'm comfortable." Without changing their positions, he reached out and snagged the remote. Careful to keep the volume low, he scrolled through the movie channels. "Got a preference?"

"No gory horror. Otherwise, it doesn't matter." She pulled a throw off the back of the couch to cover her legs.

Pausing on *Die Hard*, Brogan glanced at her and caught her grin. "Perfect."

Yes, that summed it up. Being here with Pixie, holding her while watching a movie . . . The only thing that could be more perfect would be having her naked, in a bed—or the couch. Hell, the floor would work for him.

For now, this was more than enough. Far more than he'd expected.

Likely more than he'd ever deserved.

Hours later, after the movie had ended and Brogan had bade her good night, Pixie still couldn't get to sleep. Something was bothering her, niggling at the back of her mind. It wasn't Brogan himself. She'd enjoyed the cozy time with him while they were both relaxed, his guard down and her reserve shelved. They'd settled together as if they were a long-term couple.

Before Brogan, she couldn't have imagined herself slumping against a man, his arm around her as she breathed in his scent. With Brogan, it was . . . easy.

Yet she knew there was a problem. It had something to do with Erin, or rather, something to do with what Erin had said.

Pixie went over the entire conversation in her mind. And then it came to her.

Throwing back the covers, she didn't hesitate to leave the bed, didn't think of the time or the possibility that Brogan was sleeping, as she should have been.

She quietly peeked at Andy, saw he was undisturbed, and then slipped from the room and snuck through the kitchen.

With only the moonlight and a deep familiarity guiding her, she crept across the living room until she stood near the doorway to the enclosed porch.

No, Brogan wasn't sleeping. He stood at the window, his shirt removed, his feet bare, and his hands in the pockets of his jeans as he stared out at the starry night. The blue glow of moonlight bathed his body, making his bare shoulders look even wider. Her gaze moved over him.

Earlier, she'd rested against that hard body, felt his warmth and the tension that had slowly eased away. Yes, she'd shamelessly pressed her advantage, acting as if it was commonplace for her to curl up so familiarly at his side. She was glad she had, since they'd stayed that way throughout the movie.

She might have denied it before, but she couldn't deny it now. She wanted him. Every inch of him. Everything he had to give—the man he used to be and the man he was now. In many ways, it already felt like he was hers, though in reality she had no claim . . . and that made her breathe a small sigh.

Despite the soft sounds coming from a white-noise machine, Brogan must have heard her.

Silently, he turned to her. His face was shadowed, so she couldn't see his eyes, but she felt his gaze and knew he was looking her over, from her loose hair to her oversized shirt, down her legs to her bare feet.

"Sorry." Pixie felt heat creeping over her skin. It wasn't embarrassment. In fact, she couldn't put a name to it because she'd never felt anything so powerful before. It left her nerve endings tingling. Something tightened low in her midriff. Something not unpleasant. Just the opposite, in fact. She thought she might be on the precipice of something so pleasurable that it frightened her. "I need to tell you something," she said in a faint whisper.

Wordlessly, he left the room, stepping around the basket in which Shayna slept, the furniture, and his duffel bag.

At first, he just stared down at her, ramping up all those strange sensations until she thought she might splinter apart.

It wasn't in her plan, was definitely not the reason she'd left her bed, yet nothing else seemed more important than kissing him. Here, now. She went up on her tiptoes, slid her hand up his chest and around his neck, and then put her mouth to his with a soft, hungry groan. That first touch was pure hot sensation.

Years. Years it had been since she'd experienced this fiery rush of want and need. Or maybe she never had, at least not so strongly. Whatever she'd once felt for Dylan had long faded behind the pain of playing the fool, the difficulty of her pregnancy, and then the utter joy of her baby boy.

"Brogan," she whispered, and moved her mouth over his again.

Brogan went very still . . . for three seconds only. Releasing a deep groan, he took over, lifting her flush to his body as he tilted his head to roughly deepen the hungry kiss.

Honest to God, she forgot why she'd wanted to see him. Or maybe in reality, *this* was what she'd wanted. They were immersed in shadow, but she didn't need light, even preferred the darkness.

Pulling back, Brogan said, "I shouldn't be doing this." He kissed her again, his hot breath on her face, his large hands moving over her as if hoping to touch all of her at once. "Tell me no, Pixie—or tell me it's okay."

"Kiss me."

He shifted his attention to her throat, branding her skin with his open mouth, the graze of his teeth, and the stroke of his tongue. He left a damp, hot trail along her shoulder, where it was exposed by the wide neckline of the big shirt.

Desperate, Pixie grabbed his hand and tugged him over to the couch, then silently urged him to sit.

He sprawled into the seat, arms at his sides, his knees angled out, his attention riveted on her.

Barely able to see him, Pixie caught the hem of her shirt, whisked it off, and let it drop to the floor. In case he had better night vision than her, she quickly stripped off her shorts and then straddled his lap. He started to say something, so she silenced him with another kiss.

With a harsh sound of anticipation, he tangled his fingers in her hair and tugged her back. “Tell me this is a yes.”

“It’s a yes, *please*.” No way could she deny herself any longer. “I need you, Brogan.”

While the admission made her more frantic, it seemed to gentle him. His hands moved over her hair and shoulders in long, slow pets. He stroked down her spine, tucked her close, and carefully turned so her back rested on the soft couch cushions.

Coming down over her, he whispered, “You’re sure, honey?”

Insecurity reared up, scaring her. “You’re not?”

“Pixie,” he scolded affectionately, nuzzling his lips to hers. “I’ve wanted you from the second I first saw you. Every day has been worse because getting to know you only made the need sharper.” His forehead touched hers. “I’ve tried to keep my priorities straight, to remember that I’m an intrusion into your life.”

She would have denied that, but he didn’t give her a chance.

“You totally took me by surprise. I’ve never met anyone like you. I’ve never wanted a woman more than you. You have to know that. I’m used to wanting, though, so if you need more time, I can wait.”

“Well, I can’t wait.” Until she said it, she didn’t realize how true it was. "I want you right now. *You*, Brogan. No one but you." She kissed him with desperation and with love. So much love.

"This can't change things," he said as he stood and stripped off his jeans.

Hardly able to believe what she was doing, and anxious not to waste the moment, Pixie lifted her hips and skimmed off her panties. "Meaning?"

"You can't kick me out of your life tomorrow." Settling over her again, skin to skin, their legs tangling, their heartbeats meshing, he said, "I want to be a part of your life."

Thrilled to hear it, Pixie whispered, "You already are."

That must have been enough for him, because there were no more words, just endless deep kissing, warm explorations, and more intimacy than she'd ever experienced. She felt the hard muscles under warm skin, and she felt the rough ridges of scars, especially on his right hip.

Soon she'd kiss all the places where he'd been hurt. And hopefully, his heart would welcome her. Loving Brogan meant wanting him fiercely, while also needing to defend him, to make his harsh life more comfortable. To show him acceptance and affection.

Just as he was showing her. Most of her uncertainty seemed silly now. That had a lot to do with the way Brogan branded himself onto every inch of her body. No, he couldn't see her, but just as she'd felt his scars, she knew he could feel her imperfections.

Clearly, he didn't mind.

She didn't say the words out loud, but they were there, circling her heart, filling her head, stealing her soul. *I love you, Brogan Rafferty.*

"You're mine now," he whispered.

Smiling, she accepted his claim by replying, "And I'll never let you go."

* * *

An hour later, scrunched up on the couch together, with Pixie's breathing finally soft and even, Brogan faced reality. "You should tell me to get lost." She *should*—but he prayed she wouldn't.

Pixie stirred against him, stretching with a small sound of contentment before twisting and shifting, almost sending him over the side and to the floor before she got settled atop him. Brogan knew if he was gifted a hundred years with this one special woman, it wouldn't be enough to sate him.

Her small, cool hand cupped the side of his face. "You told me you didn't want anything to change."

"I don't." He turned his head to press a kiss on her palm. "Here, in this moment with you, is the most perfect my life has ever been. The kids are both secure and well loved. Bramble feels like the most wonderful little town." Mostly because Pixie and Andy were there. "And you, Pixie. You're like . . ." He shook his head, short of words that would correctly convey her importance to him. When he finally figured out what to say, it came out raspy, thick with emotion. "You're everything good that I never imagined in my life. I want this life, with you in it." He wanted it so badly, it shook him.

"That sounds perfect to me."

Idly resting both hands on her silky bottom, he said, "You deserve better than me."

He felt her consternation, then her annoyance. "I don't know what person could be better than you. I wish you would realize it."

"Christ, Pixie." He tipped his head back and closed his eyes. "I'm so freaking flawed, I don't even like myself."

"I like you enough for both of us. Besides, I'm flawed, too, and there are times I don't like myself, either." She rested her cheek against his chest. "You don't know what it took for me to do this—to get naked with a man, I mean. To have sex. It helps that it's dark because my body . . ." Her words faltered.

"Your body is beautiful." He swept his hands over her subtle curves. "So sexy." He kissed her shoulder. "You're irresistible."

"You can't see me," she teased. "I wouldn't change a thing, because I love Andy so much, but carrying him, birthing him, and being sick for so long left their marks."

He smiled despite the seriousness of the moment. He locked his arms around her so she couldn't move, then whispered in her ear, "Honey, I can see just fine." Predictably, she tried to lurch away. "Shh. You just told me how great I am, so trust me when I say your body is right out of my dreams, so small and sweet, and curved in all the right places." As she eased, he stroked his fingers over her skin. "You're so soft."

"I . . . I have scars."

Silly Pixie. "I have worse scars."

She shoved herself up to glare at him, saying sternly, "Your scars are a part of you, Brogan. They show your bravery."

What bullshit. "Anyone can get hurt."

"Not everyone can be a SEAL. Not everyone can deliberately put themselves in dangerous situations. Not everyone can be as resilient as you've been."

"Resilient?" Her unique perspective always threw him. "How do you figure that?"

"Look at everything you've been through. Everything you've lost—but you're here, rocking the whole dad thing."

Though he hoped that was true, he laughed. "Rocking it, huh?"

"Best dad ever, in my opinion. Anyone can father a child, but some people aren't ready to take on the role of provider and protector. Not everyone knows how to love and nurture."

"You think I do?"

"I see it every time you look at Shayna, when you hold her and care for her."

"My little Sugar is pretty easy to love." *And so are you.*

Pixie's warm sigh teased his lips. "You'll probably deny it, but you've been through hell."

No, he couldn't deny it, because at times the reminders consumed him.

"I hate the pain you must have suffered from your most recent injuries, but I love that you're the type of man who faced all that, and you're still caring enough to take on raising an innocent baby girl. You're man enough to love her. Man enough," she whispered, pressing a soft kiss to his mouth, "to come to Bramble and face down more possible hostility so that Shayna could know her brother." She took his face in her hands and gave him a smile. "You're enough, Brogan. For anyone."

Those words sank into him, and in a way offered healing. Like a balm, her sentiment soothed the ragged edges of his guilt and emotional pain. "All of that can be said for you, too, Pixie."

"I'm enough," she agreed, though to him she didn't sound convinced. "But I'd never have made it without Marlow and Cort. That's a fact."

He countered with, "I'd never have made it without Shayna. I didn't want to make it." Her startled gasp almost made him regret the words, yet they were too important to be left unsaid. "She gave me a reason to go on. I'm ashamed to admit it"—especially since she had such a high opinion of him—"but before Erin contacted me to tell me what had happened, I wasn't trying to heal. I ignored the doctors' instructions; I told the physical therapist to fuck off. I lay in that narrow hospital bed, welcoming the pain, wallowing in my misery, and wishing for death."

He hadn't felt like enough, not for anyone.

Sounding heartbroken for him, Pixie whispered, "Brogan, *no.*"

"Yes. I didn't save Sugar. She saved me."

"I'm so sorry." The tears in her voice revealed her distress.

"Don't be." The last thing he'd ever want to do was hurt her or make her feel bad in any way. "I was on a self-indulgent pity trip. It was like I'd lost everything when my brothers died, and then I found out about Connie. While I'd been feeling sorry for myself, she'd been dying—all alone." Reflexively, his arms hugged her tighter. "I bet her last thought was for Shayna."

"Maybe. But she trusted that you'd do whatever was necessary to give Shayna the love and care she needed. I'm sure that gave her comfort."

His fingertips drifted up and down her spine, relishing that she was here with him, that she not only understood him, but saw the best in him. "I hope that's true, but whether it is or not, I'll always do my best for Shayna. I owe it to her, to Connie—and to myself."

Pixie kissed his mouth, then each cheekbone, the bridge of his nose, and his chin.

He smiled. "What are you doing?"

"Kissing you, because you're amazing." When he smirked, she insisted, "You *are*. Despite everything you'd gone through, the injuries, the grief, you still got it together when you needed to."

"I should have gotten to Shayna sooner."

"Give yourself a break. These injuries"—she kissed a shrapnel scar, then one that was worse, and the unsightly slash over his ribs—"they had to still be painful, and I know you were suffering from the loss of your friends. It takes a strong man, a heroic man, to be able to go on."

With a roll of his eyes, he tucked her close to him. "I appreciate the sentiment, Pixie. I really do, even if it's not true. I'm just me, doing the best I can—the same as you, the same as Marlow and Cort, or Gunther and Dee. Everyone has their own strength. If they're using that strength, doing what they can, then they're no different from me."

"I can't agree, but if it bothers you, I'll try to remember not to call you a hero."

Since he might have won that one, he tucked his chin down and said, "I want to tell you something, but I don't want pity."

"I would never pity you. I care about you, and I can sympathize with the things you've gone through and still know you're a . . ." Catching herself, she gave him a quick grin and amended, "Not a hero, okay? I'll say you're an amazing man. An incredible man. A man who just showed me that sex can be better than I ever imagined. How's that?"

"I'll take the sex compliment." Right now, that one felt most important because if she liked being with him, he might be able to expand their relationship. For his part, he already craved more of her.

"I know you better than you think." She punctuated her words with a kiss. "Because you're mine."

Now, *that* he especially liked. "I've never had anyone to call my own. My father was never really mine, so I had no reason to want to keep him. My mother was restless and unmoored, and since she didn't totally claim me, there was no reason to claim her."

Thoughts going inward, he recalled his brothers, each face, their distinct personalities, all of them so different and unique. "I had my brothers . . . but they were killed." As always, that boulder settled on his chest, making breathing difficult. Grief squeezed his throat until he thought he would choke on it.

And then Pixie stroked his jaw. "I'm sure you still think of them often."

Though his eyes were dry, he felt as if he had to rub them anyway, so he scrubbed both hands over his face—and brought himself under control.

"I could have had Connie, but I let her go. I won't make that mistake with Shayna. I don't know what type of parent I'll be, whether I'll be able to handle the daily tasks as well as you do, or the times of near disaster as well as Ellen did. But

I know I'll do my best, and I know myself to be competent. I learn quickly."

"I've never doubted it," Pixie said quietly, her hands still on him, barely moving in gestures of comfort.

It felt so good, like warm flannel on a cold day, or an icy drink in the suffocating heat.

Didn't she realize how stunning she was, not just in looks, with her heart-shaped face, big blue eyes, and soft lips, but in the way she embraced life and the people she cared about? The love she put out into the world?

He knew.

"Pixie . . ." It was a fragile moment, and he didn't want to push too fast.

"You can tell me anything, Brogan."

Okay, fine. He'd see if that was true. "It's not just Shayna I want to keep and protect. It's you, and that's dangerous."

"Caring about someone isn't dangerous," she countered. A touch of happiness lifted the corners of her mouth, giving her the gentlest smile. "I care about you, too. A lot."

In such a short time, his entire life had changed. He'd thought to retire after a long career in the military. He'd never considered being a parent, and he'd never expected to fall in love.

"You're still troubled," she said, as if reading his mind. "You can tell me anything, you know. Everything. I want to know it all. The upbringing you had, your struggles, and your accomplishments in the military." Her gaze searched his. "The losses you've suffered and the injuries you've had."

She wanted to know every ugly aspect of his life. There were plenty, and he wasn't proud of them. Just the opposite. It often shamed him to know he'd meant so little to the world.

But Pixie cared. He mattered to Shayna. And Andy had already stolen his heart. These were his people, the ones he wanted in his life. He loved each of them.

Maybe this was a mistake. It wasn't right to burden her, yet for the first time in his life, he wanted to share. It was the only way he'd be able to make her understand how important she was to him. Still, he gave her one last opportunity to skip the drama. "You have to be getting tired."

"No, sir. I'm wide awake and enjoying quiet conversation—and nudity—with a remarkable man who burst into my life and showed me everything I was missing."

He gave a gruff laugh. "So you were missing me, huh?"

In a heartbeat, she grew serious. "Oh, Brogan, I was. So much."

Skimming a kiss over her shoulder, he whispered, "I think I was missing you, too."

Her smile trembled. "Tell me about your mom, about being a kid, and how you got so strong."

Brogan gave up the battle. Pixie was his own unique form of comfort, and he wanted more.

"When I was ten or eleven, somewhere in there, I got home late."

"How late?"

"I don't know. It was dark, though. Mom didn't keep tabs on me, as long as I didn't cause trouble."

He saw the way Pixie braced herself. "What did she say when you came in?"

"She wasn't around. That wasn't unusual," he hurried to explain, "but it was unusual to find part of a bucket of fried chicken on the counter. I hadn't eaten since breakfast, so I dug in."

Trying and failing to hide her thoughts, Pixie said, "I can almost picture that."

As a kid, it hadn't seemed strange to him to run the streets without supervision. Yeah, it was a wonder he'd survived. "I've always had a big appetite, and I guess I wasn't thinking about anyone but myself because I ate four pieces." He could still recall the taste of the chicken that day. Cold and greasy, but such a treat.

"I bet you were a big kid."

"I guess so." He thought of himself at that age. He couldn't remember ever feeling small, just insignificant. "Mom came in, and, man, she blew a gasket because I'd only left a wing. I guess she'd just run out to get beer, and she'd planned on returning to eat the chicken herself. That's why it wasn't put away. I remember her asking me what the hell I thought I was doing, eating it all."

Eyes widening at the turn in the story, Pixie pressed a lingering kiss to his chest, right over the spot where his heart beat a steady rhythm.

"Man, I got flippant and said I was hungry. I said the chicken was there and she wasn't, and I didn't know if she'd be back that night or the next."

"Dear God," Pixie whispered. "That happened? And you were only ten?"

It had happened often. His mother was as unpredictable as the weather. In lieu of an answer, Brogan shrugged. "Mom lost it." He recalled so vividly how she'd carried on. It had been a turning point for him, a day of stark reality. "She threw the empty bucket at me, and then she threw the bones."

"Brogan!"

"She didn't hurt me," he soothed. Not physically. Emotionally, he'd been devastated by the things she'd said. As much to himself, as to Pixie, he explained, "She was only making her point."

"No, she wasn't. She was being deliberately cruel and violent, so don't you dare make excuses for her."

"I guess your reaction means you know I'd never, not under any circumstances, do something like that to a child?"

"Of course you wouldn't! You're not like that."

"Shh. You'll wake the kids." No, he wasn't at all like either of his parents—and her knowing it mattered a lot. Some of her words had stuck with him, forever embedded in his brain. "Mom said I was lucky to have a place to come back to, that she and my father hadn't wanted me, but at least she'd kept me."

At least I kept you. That's more than your goddamned father did.

He would never forget that statement. It had changed everything. He'd gone to bed that night vowing that he'd take control of his life, that he'd make something of himself and prove to both his mother and his father that he was worthwhile.

Being pragmatic at an early age had prepared Brogan for hard lessons. "Mom had to do everything on her own. Because of me, her life was difficult." She'd never failed to remind him of that. "Neither of them had wanted me, but Mom was right. At least she'd given me a place to live. I had a mattress to sleep on, and heat in the winter and a fan in the summer. There was always food to eat." He gave a smile. "Just not her food."

"It's not funny," Pixie said with tears in her voice. She gave him another fierce hug.

Maybe not, but it had been a valuable lesson. "I decided fast food wasn't for me, not unless I worked, made money, and bought it myself. Or if she offered to share, which she did occasionally."

"I'm very glad you're here with me now, where you are definitely wanted."

He shifted them around until she was on her back and he was over her, one large hand cupping her face. "That's exactly what I was trying to say to you. I went my whole life without realizing how nice that is." Her blue eyes were full of emotion, and he loved it. He loved her. "I like this feeling a lot, Pixie. I swear to you, I will do my best to take care of you. To make you feel as good as you make me feel."

She swallowed heavily and sniffled. "I swear I'll always do my best to take care of you, too."

Frozen in time, they stared at each other, their gazes locked until slowly, very slowly, Brogan's mouth began to curl. "You're amazing." He nuzzled her lips, playfully at first and then with more sensual intent. "Pixie Nolan, with the beautiful spirit, the sexy body, and the sweetest way with words I've ever heard."

"I can't get over that you like my body." Before he could protest, she said, "At the moment, with you kissing me, it doesn't even matter. You matter. *We* matter."

Like a family.

To Brogan, it felt as if they'd just exchanged vows. For now, that was enough for him.

Chapter 15

The next morning, before the kids were awake, Pixie again snuck from the bedroom through the kitchen. She hadn't done much sleeping in her own bed. She and Brogan had dozed on the couch, but he was far too large for both of them to sleep there comfortably. When they heard Shayna wake up, he insisted she should go on to bed.

She'd wanted to stay, to get a bottle for Shayna, or change her diaper, or do anything to lend him a hand. He'd touched her chin, kissed her softly, and said, "I've got this. Andy will be up in a few hours. You need some sleep."

Reluctantly, she'd gone to her room, wishing with her entire heart that they could sleep the rest of the morning together. Still, the moment she'd gotten under her covers, she'd faded into a deep sleep.

The second she'd awakened, she remembered why she'd gone to him last night in the first place. Instead of conversation, she'd gotten so much more. It was difficult to sigh and smile at the same time, but she managed.

Andy was still sound asleep, curled up on his side in his footed pajamas, his chubby little cheeks smooshed and his lips open. Looking at him always filled her with tearful gratitude. He was her own little miracle, born on her birthday.

He was the greatest birthday present she'd ever received.

She'd understood what Brogan meant when he'd said Shayna had saved him, because Andy had done the same for her. Not that her life had been anywhere near as difficult as Brogan's. Not at all. But during the worst of her illness, when she'd hurt all over and weakness had seemed to permeate her every muscle, even her bones, she knew she would have given up and just faded away—except that she already loved Andy.

From the moment she'd found out she was carrying him, she'd known the most indescribable love, the kind of love that made anything and everything possible, even survival under horrible health issues.

Easing from the room, she went through the kitchen and into the living room. Stopping to listen, she detected no sounds, but a moment later, Brogan came from the enclosed porch. He wore his jeans, unbuttoned and unzipped, and carried a shirt and socks. His hair was too short to get messy, but it was somewhat smashed on one side, like velvet nap brushed the wrong way.

She smiled at the sight of him. "Good morning."

He strode right up to her, kissed her mouth, and ran his hand over her disheveled hair.

Unlike him, her hair was badly tangled. "I didn't even think to brush it."

"You're too beautiful for words."

Loving him more by the second, she said, "Maybe coffee will kick-start us both."

Around a yawn, he nodded. On their way back into the kitchen, he said, "Shayna's back asleep. Andy?"

"Still sleeping, too." In a cabinet beside the sink, she got down the coffee and a filter for the basket.

Brogan looped his arms around her from behind. "Right now, I'd like nothing more than to strip you naked again, this time in the morning sunlight."

That sounded both amazing and terrifying. Despite what he'd said, she still had reservations about the changes in her body. "Um . . ."

"I need you to know how gorgeous you are, that every inch of you is perfection."

Now she *really* needed the coffee. "These days," she whispered, "my hips are a little wider."

Brogan growled near her ear. "Your hips . . . mmm."

Her lips twitched. "I used to have a flat stomach, but not anymore."

"You have a woman's body." He opened his mouth on the side of her neck and grazed his teeth over her sensitive skin.

Talking wasn't easy. "I have a few stretch marks."

"Here," he said, cupping his hands over her breasts. "I know."

Her breathing grew heavier.

"You birthed a baby, Pixie. How incredible is that? Your body went through a lot of work and then you breastfed your son."

"I couldn't afford formula anyway, but I had already decided to breastfeed him."

He released her breasts to cross his arms around her and give her a warm hug. "Every inch of your body makes me hot—your beautiful face, your soft hair, the way you smile . . . Your sexy hips, stomach, and breasts are icing on the cake."

"The marks really didn't bother you?"

"Get real. I see you and I want you. I barely noticed them. Besides, nothing about you could ever bother me—unless you told me to get lost."

"I would never!"

"I'm glad." He brushed his nose over her hair and mused quietly, "Everything feels different today, at least to me."

"To me, too."

Where did they go from here?

"I woke up with you on my mind, already wanting you again," Brogan said. "But I think we have some things to discuss, and the kids will be awake soon."

Both relieved and disappointed, Pixie filled the carafe. "Was Shayna up long last night?"

"Long enough for me to change her diaper, give her a bottle, and hold her for a bit. My little Sugar loves to snuggle during the night."

"I think that was more toward morning," Pixie teased, enjoying the feel of him close to her back. "But yes, she loves snuggling with you. She always rubs her face into your neck."

"Which is why I shave every day, whether I feel like it or not." He ran a hand over his raspy morning whiskers. "She's a delicate little thing."

A small light over the sink barely illuminated the room, but shortly there would be sunlight pouring in. "Last night, when I came out—there was something I wanted to tell you."

"What is it?" he asked, his lips skimming along her shoulder.

Knowing this wouldn't be a pleasant subject for him, Pixie started the coffeepot and then turned in his arms to face him. "How Ruthie knew where you were . . ."

Concern brought his brows together. "What Erin said made sense. She loved Connie the way you love Marlow. If she says Connie likely left other papers, she probably did."

What he said struck her. *What would I do if I lost Marlow?*

Marlow was such a big part of her life. In many ways, the best part of her. The thought of losing her sent a shaft of sympathy for Erin through her.

She leaned into Brogan. "That's the thing, though. If Ruthie found things Connie had written, then it's possible she discovered more than just your location here in Bramble."

"Such as?"

Clearly, he hadn't gotten much sleep. The problems were piling up on him, and then they'd spent the night—or most of it—together. Pixie worried that he might leave just to find some peace and quiet. He'd take Shayna, of course—she didn't doubt that—and the idea was equally unbearable.

She loved them both.

Last night reassured her that she was making progress. She believed he wanted to stay.

But would he?

"Promise me you won't do anything until we've had a chance to sort it out."

"Sort what out?" New concern showed in his expression. "How can I make a promise when I don't know what I'm dealing with?"

"Well, you could try trusting me."

His worry lifted and he drew her in close. "I've trusted you from the moment I read the notes Connie left about you. Meeting you just made it more personal."

With her face against his warm, solid chest, his indescribable, addictive scent filling her head, Pixie asked, "Do you mean that?"

Brushing his mouth against her temple, he said, "I swear it to you. And because you trust Marlow and Cort so much, I'm inclined to feel the same about them. I know good people when I meet them."

Perfect . . . she couldn't ask for more than that. Drawing away from him, she looked up and said, "If Ruthie knew you were here, she might know about Andy and Shayna's wealthy grandparents, too."

After a moment, he stepped away with a groan. "Shit. If I don't deal with her, she'll turn to them. That's all I need."

"Eventually, they'll need to know about Shayna."

"Sugar isn't a secret. I'll proudly show her to anyone. I wanted to do it one person at a time, though."

"I understand," Pixie said, because she did. The coffee was ready, so she poured them each a cup, and they took seats at the table.

"After the things you've told me about them, I'm not even sure they'll be interested in meeting Shayna."

"Oh, they'll be interested." Pixie wasn't sure how they'd react, though. Remembering how staunchly they'd defended Dylan, as if their son could do no wrong—as if he hadn't cheated on Marlow, hadn't gotten Pixie pregnant while married to another woman—made her believe they'd be devastated by the news.

Then again, this shouldn't be anything new to them. They'd already had to face the fact that Dylan wasn't the paragon they'd envisioned.

Brogan sat back in the chair. "Ruth will try to extort money from them."

"They'll destroy her if she does."

"Or," he said, disgust heavy in his tone, "they'll give in to her blackmail to keep their son's name untarnished."

A little late for that, she thought. "Would you like me to tell them?"

"No." He sat forward again. "I'll take care of it."

Pixie considered him, but she could see from his expression that he wouldn't shirk what he considered his responsibility, so she nodded.

Then he surprised her by saying, "I'd like it if you were there, too. They know you, and I think you care about them."

Yes, in her own fashion, she did. How could she not when they were Andy's grandparents?

"That is, if you want to be a part of it. No pressure." He huffed out a breath. "Damn it, I don't know the right move here."

"Then let me help by saying I appreciate that you'd include

me, and yes, I'd like to be with you when you call." She briefly squeezed his hand. "I'll get the phone number for you."

He caught her hand before she stood. "Let's wait until the kids are up. I'll call late morning."

As if he was eager to start the ball rolling, Andy called out to her, and seconds later, they heard Shayna. With a shared smile, they headed in different directions, each to change diapers.

After breakfast, Brogan took the kids for a walk while she showered and got ready for work. It was so much easier with Andy occupied. She'd love to work out a routine with Brogan—for the long term. She loved him, she knew he cared for her, and they each cherished the kids.

Pixie couldn't imagine anything more perfect . . . unless it was that special commitment, the one she hadn't dared to hope for after all her disappointment with Dylan.

She finished with minutes to spare and was back at the table, messaging with Marlow and sharing her thoughts, when Brogan returned.

When he'd left, he'd had Shayna in her carrier and Andy in the stroller, but now Shayna was in the stroller and Andy was helping to push her.

Pixie grinned at her son's proud face. "Are you helping?"

He squinted his eyes shut and gave her a huge grin. "Wokin' my baby."

"Yes, you are." She laughed and scooped him up so Brogan could lift Shayna out. "That had to be some tricky maneuvering."

"Little bit," Brogan said. "He's a determined kid. Once he decided he wanted a turn pushing the stroller, there was no talking him out of it. Fortunately, Shayna didn't mind. Andy also showed her his nose, one of his eyes, and a foot."

As she laughed again, Andy touched his own face and announced, "Noz, noz, noz."

"Yes! Where are your teeth?"

He touched his fingers to them, then wanted to touch hers, too. And then Brogan's.

Brogan dried Andy's fingers first, then dutifully opened his mouth so Andy could say, "Tif."

"Such a smart little boy," he praised. "Seriously, dude, you're like genius level. I had no idea."

Pixie laughed at that. "It's something he's only recently learned, and still gets parts mixed up sometimes."

"Kids learn at different levels, I know, but I can't help thinking he's ahead of the pack."

As a proud mom, Pixie wouldn't disagree.

"One thing," Brogan said, his tone joking. "I had to explain that he couldn't poke Shayna's eye—after he poked mine."

Since he said it with a grin, Pixie wasn't too worried. "Did he hurt her?"

"Nope. He means to be gentle . . ."

"But he's still a toddler." She gave Brogan a hug. "Thank you for being patient with him. He'll learn, but until then, we need to watch them closely when they're together."

"He's Shayna's brother," Brogan said simply. "He'll be a better brother than I was, and that's because of you." He kissed her. "You don't know how much this"—he gestured at the kids—"means to me."

"I do, because it means a lot to me, too." She wanted to interact like this forever.

When his phone dinged, they reluctantly stepped apart.

Brogan glanced at the screen and said, "It's Erin."

Pixie took Shayna from him so he could answer. Together, they all went to the living room. Pixie got out toys for the kids while Brogan sat on the sofa.

She listened to his side of the conversation and knew from his expression that it wasn't a pleasant call. Not hostile, but maybe not great news. She hoped Ruthie hadn't caused more problems, but then she heard Brogan repeat the name of a hospital as he wrote down notes.

In ten minutes, she'd need to leave for work, but first she wanted to know what had happened.

Finally, he disconnected.

Cautiously, Pixie asked, "Bad news?"

He let out a long breath. "Not great. Erin found out from a caretaker that Brian is in the ICU with liver failure."

Pixie's first thought was disbelief that Ruthie was here, hassling Brogan, instead of staying with her husband.

"They think he'll survive," Brogan said, "but the next few days will be critical. He has a lot of complications that are going to make daily life rough, especially if he doesn't stop drinking."

Pixie moved to sit beside him, wishing for a way to ease the conflicting emotions he had to be feeling.

With Connie gone and Ruthie playing the part of a badger in Bramble, Brian was left utterly alone. He'd never been a dad to Brogan, and now he might die without ever once reaching out to his son. "I'm so sorry."

Brogan shook his head. "Thanks. I know I should care, but I don't. Not like a son should care for his father. It's more . . . I don't know. Pity for a man I barely know and usually resented."

"With good reason," she said, unwilling to let him feel a single moment of guilt. "What will you do?"

His gaze moved to the kids. Andy was babbling to Shayna again. The funny part was the way he pretended Shayna understood him. She'd grin and he'd nod his head and then show her something as if she'd asked to see it—one of his stuffed animals, a chunky truck that he rolled closer to her, even his hand. Oh, they had a fine conversation about his hand. It was so silly, and so sweet.

"Despite anything else that's going on, they make me happy," Brogan said. "And so do you." After leaning over to kiss her, he said, "I'd call the hospital myself, but Erin advised against it. For one thing, they won't give out Brian's info to someone just because they claim to be related; and for another, she said I could get caught up in his debt without meaning to if I identified myself as his son. One thing is certain, I need to figure out where Ruth is."

"How are you going to do that?"

"I'll talk to Officer Flynn, see if he has any ideas." The smile he gave her lacked his usual energy. "I'll figure it out. You need to get going or you'll be late."

This was one of the few mornings Pixie didn't want to go to work. "Right." She told Andy it was time to go.

He must have been in a similar mood, because he ran to Brogan. Assuming he wanted a hug, Brogan picked him up, but Andy wrapped his arms around the big man like a little monkey and didn't want to let go.

Judging by the way Brogan closed his eyes to savor the hug, he didn't want to let go, either.

"Would you and Shayna like to come to the shop with us?"

Brogan huffed a short laugh. "We'd be in the way, but thank you." He gave her suggestion a quick thought, then said, "You know, I wouldn't mind watching this one, though."

Pixie blinked at him. "You want to keep both kids?"

"Bad idea? I get it. You're almost never away from Andy."

"It's not that." Accepting that she'd be a few minutes late, Pixie moved close again. "I trust you, so please don't think that's it."

He nodded. "Right. I'm still fumbling along with Shayna. Two kids might be a bit much."

"For a regular guy, maybe," she quipped right back. "For you? I don't have a single doubt you could handle it—just as I would handle it, if necessary. But it's not necessary, not right now, especially with so much up in the air."

"You mean Ruth?"

"Can you imagine if she showed up and you had both kids to protect?"

His mouth twisted to the side. "You have a point."

"Brogan?" Pixie put her hand to his jaw. He hadn't taken time yet to shave, and he took her breath away. "Even in the worst of circumstances, I know both Shayna and Andy would be safe with you."

Those piercing gray eyes of his searched her gaze, and he finally nodded. "Thank you." He dropped a kiss on Andy's head and then pried him loose. "Listen, buddy, go on with Mam, and when you get back, we'll take another walk, okay?"

"Wok!" He tried to wiggle down.

"Andy Nolan," Pixie said, lifting him into her arms. "When we get home, you can walk. For now, let's go see Renee."

Stubbornly, he pointed at Shayna. "My baby."

"You'll see her when we get home." Home—with Brogan and Shayna, because they were now family. "Let's go so you don't make Mam late."

"Oh, oh," Andy said, and excitedly pointed at Shayna again. She did a baby feat of rolling twice and coming up against the playpen.

"Wow," Brogan said, hurrying over to pick her up. "That's impressive, Sugar." He turned toward the door and picked up Andy's diaper bag. "We'll walk you out."

Once there, Brogan kissed her again, helped Shayna to wave goodbye to Andy, and then promised Pixie he'd have dinner ready when she got home.

To Pixie, it felt like an eventful start to their new relationship, and possibly a beginning to the "forever" she wanted.

* * *

Pixie would be home in a few hours. Brogan had made good use of his time by making a list of available job positions that were both in his field and near enough for him to continue a relationship with Pixie. He'd also checked out various ads for homes or property in the area. Nothing on the lake—Bramble was strict about letting in strangers—but there were a few listings near Marlow's Whimsy.

When Shayna wasn't napping, he was playing with her, helping her to sit up, though of course she wasn't able to do that without support. Still, her every milestone filled him with pride. As he approached her with a bottle, she recognized it and got excited.

"Little glutton," he teased. Holding her was still a great pleasure for him. He knew one day she'd be using a sippy cup like Andy, but for now, this was their time, with her in the crook of his arm, usually one of her tiny hands gripping his finger.

She dozed off between burps, so Brogan went back to his long to-do list.

He filled out all the information Erin needed and returned it to her. It was important to ensure that Shayna would have love and care if anything ever happened to him. After Connie's sudden death, he knew tomorrow was never guaranteed.

But now, with Pixie in his life, he wanted all the tomorrows he could get.

Lastly, he researched everything he could about his father's situation, both medical and financial. From what Erin could uncover, neither Brian nor Ruth had worked for some time. Brian had lost his business ten years ago. Connie had covered some of that in her papers, citing alcoholism as a major problem, but also a tendency to try to cheat others. More than once, Brian had been beaten for swindling the wrong person.

Brogan came to a few conclusions and had already discussed them with Erin.

The thing was, he wanted to discuss them with Pixie, too.

If things went the way he hoped, they'd be together from now on. Not that he wanted to rush her. She had to come into the relationship at her own pace. Just because he knew his own feelings, that didn't mean she felt the same.

With her job, her son, and her friends, Pixie had a lot on the line. She didn't know that Brogan had job prospects in security, that he had a healthy bank account, or that he planned to buy a permanent residence nearby. And neither of them knew when Ruth might roll up to cause more strife.

He was just about to start the dinner prep, but his phone buzzed. Taking it from his pocket, he glanced at the screen and saw it was Cort. With a swipe of his thumb, he answered. "Hey, Cort."

"You're home, right?"

Home. He glanced around at the beautiful cottage Pixie lived in—a cottage owned by Cort. "I'm at Pixie's place."

"That's exactly what I meant," Cort said, sounding amused at Brogan's careful wording. "Any chance I could get a helping hand?"

"Sure." Whatever it was, he was glad to help any way he could. "What is it?"

"I think you've met Wade, Gloria, and Bobbi, right?"

"Pixie introduced me to Gloria and Bobbi. I haven't met Wade, yet."

"Their home isn't far from you. I'm headed there now. Apparently, one of their largest trees was damaged in that last storm. An hour or so ago, the damn thing fell on the house."

"Anyone hurt?"

"Thankfully, no, but it was close. I know you have Shayna with you, but they've babysat Andy before, and it's not like we'll be far away. Just in the yard and on the roof. What do you say? Pixie told me she'd head that way as soon as she got off work. Marlow still has a few hours to put in."

Gloria had been the woman watching Andy the night Brogan arrived—the first time he'd met Pixie. He figured if she trusted the siblings, he should, too. "I'll need to get some things together for Shayna, but I should be able to head out within ten minutes. Why don't you text me the address?"

"Perfect, thanks. I have my chain saw, and Wade has another one, but we'll need to board up two windows, too."

"They don't have insurance?"

"They do. An adjuster is coming out tomorrow, but they need the place secured now. See you soon."

Within the ten minutes promised, Brogan was out the door with a sleepy Shayna buckled into her car seat. He hated disturbing her nap, but there would always be times when it couldn't be helped.

When he got to the address and saw the damage, he considered it a miracle no one had been injured. There didn't appear to be structural damage to the main house, but the overhang on the front porch was crushed, with two windows shattered and the front door knocked in. The branches of the large oak half-covered the roof and the driveway. Clearing away the mess would take some time. It was the type of physical activity he needed, and a good distraction from the many decisions he had to make.

Pixie peered out the window at the darkened sky. The sun had still been bright when she'd first arrived a few hours ago, but it had since set behind the trees. Cort and Brogan had been working nearly nonstop, only taking one break to eat sandwiches. Because they wanted to finish up today, they were now using outdoor security lights.

At first, Wade had tried to help cut, but neither of the younger men wanted him on the roof at his age. They'd put him to work clearing away some of the smaller branches, but they kept checking on him, too. They were both relieved when he gave up and came inside. As large, capable men, Brogan and Cort worked well together.

They were both remarkable.

Gloria was currently feeding Andy, and Bobbi was rocking Shayna. The kids had been great, but it was past time to get them home. After she'd declined Brogan's offer this morning, would he agree to her taking them home with her? Doubtful. That was something they'd need to work out, because there would always be times when one of them needed to take over with both kids. Plenty of parents did it, so she was certain they could handle it, too.

With fireflies twinkling around the yard, Pixie wondered how much longer the men would be.

They'd already secured the front door and boarded up the two broken windows. The driveway was cleared so Wade could get his truck out of the garage. The car that Gloria and Bobbi shared was parked at the curb.

It was a good thing that Cort had recently finished a remodel to the downstairs of the house; so, if necessary, the siblings could make it their main living space until the front of the house was properly repaired.

Headlights appeared on the road, then slowed and turned into a neighbor's driveway.

Bobbi came up alongside Pixie, grumbling, "There's that interloper again."

"Interloper?" Pixie asked.

Wade joined them. "I don't know what's going on over there, but that house has been vacant since Burton moved to a retirement home near his daughter. His son is planning to make some repairs and then sell it, but it's been empty for a few weeks, and now some woman is living there. I'm thinking she must be a relative or something."

Silent alarms went off in Pixie's head. "What does she look like?"

"No idea," Wade said. "She keeps to herself, coming and going mostly in the dark, although she catches a ride with old Floyd sometimes."

"Old Floyd?"

"He lives in Lankton," Gloria said from the kitchen. "Comes out here to fish and visit friends. I've seen him over there, too."

"He's stayed all night a time or two," Bobbi said.

"Man's got to be older than me," Wade countered. "Get your mind out of the gutter."

While the siblings squabbled, Pixie tried to catch sight of the mystery woman, but the kitchen window wasn't angled right. Pixie had a driving need to see who was staying in the empty house, so she hurried out the back door, called up to the men, "Don't drop anything on me," and then raced past before either of them could acknowledge her.

She didn't slow her pace as she hurried to the other house. Driven by sudden intuition, she rounded the front toward the garage—and came face-to-face with Ruthie.

She stood inside the garage in the dark, but the moonlight was sufficient for Pixie to see her surprise.

Neither of them said anything for the longest time, but inside Pixie, rage built.

She looked past Ruthie at the other car parked there. It was the same one Ruthie had been driving when she'd followed Pixie home. So this was how the woman had vanished. She'd moved into a vacant house and was using someone else's car!

"What are you doing here?" Ruthie demanded. "You don't live here."

Pixie folded her arms over her chest. "Neither do you."

"I can go wherever I want," Ruthie stated with a scowl.

Calm personified, Pixie looked into her eyes. "No, you can't." She took a step forward. "Are you renting this house?"

"What I do is none of your damn business."

Coolly, she stated, "I'm making it my business."

"So am I," Cort said as he came up behind her.

"And me." Wade joined them.

Gloria sidled in next to him. "Same."

Pixie turned and found Brogan in the midst of them all, his expression enigmatic, his attention locked on Ruthie.

Pixie hadn't heard any of them approach. "The kids?"

"They're with Bobbi," Cort said.

Brogan stepped up alongside Pixie, but he didn't take his gaze from Ruth. "Did you know Brian is in the ICU?"

"Of course I know. I'm his wife." Her attitude cavalier, she said, "He's been in there before. They work him over, fix him up, and then he comes back home. If he still has a home, that is."

Ignoring that last shot, Brogan asked, "Do you understand that if he keeps drinking, he's going to die?"

"Now you pretend to care, just because you have your fancy friends around you?"

Wade snickered, elbowed Gloria, and said, "I didn't know we were fancy."

Putting his arm around Pixie, Brogan said, "I called Officer Jansen Flynn. He's on his way."

Ruth's eyes flared. "Why would you involve a cop?"

"Because this house was vacant," Wade said. "You're trespassing."

"And," Marlow said, striding up the driveway, "I told you to leave and never return. Yet here you are." She smiled her serene corporate smile. "Big, big mistake."

"You can't start threatening me! This isn't your property."

"It isn't yours, either," Marlow said.

When she started forward, Cort put a hand on her shoulder. "Brogan can handle it."

Unconvinced, Marlow looked at Pixie, and then gave Brogan a longer look. Whatever she saw, she conceded with a small nod and took her place beside Cort.

To face his stepmother, Brogan stepped apart from the others. "I want you out of my life, Ruth." She started to protest, but Brogan spoke over her. "Brian may not live. Even if he does pull through this time, and you continue the same way, he won't last long. You have two choices. Go home to him, take two months to figure out your shit, and then get out of Connie's house."

"Two months?" she screeched. "You bastard, you—"

"Or," Brogan said, his voice firm, "I can tell Erin to start eviction proceedings in the morning. Brian is going to be in extended care for a while either way, so it's up to you."

To Pixie's mind, his offer was more than generous.

Sneering, Ruth said, "Or I can tell you to go to hell! Maybe Shayna's grandma and grandpa will feel a little more generous."

Marlow laughed. "Aren't you the grandma? Oh, wait, you mean my in-laws? I already spoke to them. Believe me, they want nothing to do with you. In fact, they're now determined to bring the full force of the law against you."

Ruth's jaw dropped, and then she seemed to shrivel.

For the first time since meeting her, Pixie saw the woman's vulnerability. Knowing Brogan would see it, too, Pixie got close to him again, slipped her hand into his, and leaned into his side.

She badly wanted to get him alone, yet that wouldn't happen anytime soon.

What followed was mass confusion. Ruth started shouting loudly enough to bring out other neighbors, even though the houses weren't spaced close together. Gloria meandered off to explain to them what was going on.

Officer Flynn arrived, and after asking a lot of questions, he arrested Ruthie and put her in the back of his car. Wade got hold of old Floyd, who admitted he didn't know how Ruthie had gotten in. He'd quickly figured out that she was bad news and hadn't been back to see her.

Once the officer drove away, Brogan faced Marlow. "You actually spoke to Mr. and Mrs. Heddings?"

"Don't be angry," Marlow said. "Sandra called me, as she sometimes does, and the conversation came about naturally."

Lifting his brows, Brogan asked, "How exactly did that happen?"

"She asked how we were doing, and then she asked about Pixie and Andy, what they were up to these days, and one thing led to another."

Cort, standing beside Marlow, gave a slight smile. "She refrains from asking about me."

Pixie covered her mouth to hide her amusement.

Brogan didn't bother doing the same. Grinning, he said, "I guess I can understand that."

"Well, I can't," Marlow complained. "He's my husband now."

"And he fills the role of Andy's uncle." It bugged Pixie that Sandra still held on to old resentments, but at the moment, that didn't seem quite so important. "How did she take the news of Shayna?"

"Better than I could have hoped. She actually seemed intrigued about having a granddaughter."

"For Sandra Heddings," Cort said, "being intrigued equates to massive enthusiasm."

Nodding, Brogan looked around the area. "I guess we should finish up. It's getting late."

His relaxed attitude concerned Pixie, but she wasn't about to press him on it now. "I'll go in and check on the kids."

"Better still," Marlow suggested, "why don't you and the kids head home? I'll follow and lend a hand. The men can finish up here, and then hopefully we can all get some rest." She yawned. "I'm glad we both have the day off tomorrow."

Pixie didn't want to leave Brogan, but when he asked, "Would you mind?" she happily agreed.

It was another sign of trust, another step in the right direction.

Moving forward with Brogan was what mattered most.

Framing his face in her hands, she went on tiptoe to kiss him. "Take your time, but know that the kids and I will be at home waiting for you."

Chapter 16

It was another hour and a half before Brogan came in. Both kids had been fed, bathed, changed into their pajamas, and were still wide awake.

With a shout of excitement, Andy raced to Brogan and was scooped up for an enthusiastic hug. "I could get used to this, buddy."

Brogan removed his boots while still holding Andy, then carried him to the blanket where Shayna, on her stomach, grinned and pedaled her legs at seeing him.

Somehow Brogan managed to hold both kids for a few minutes, showing affection to both. Andy was especially "talkative," and Brogan nodded and looked surprised at all the right times.

"This amazes me," Brogan said, putting his nose to Shayna's head and breathing in her clean scent. "You got them both bathed?"

"It was easier than you'd think," she answered. Her son's once-set schedule had been altered multiple times recently, but Pixie was too happy to have Brogan and Shayna in her life to object.

He looked down at the kids for a moment. "I never meant to add to your workload."

"Hey, I have you in my life, and I consider Shayna part of my family. Having you both here has livened things up."

Smiling, he kissed each kid on the top of the head, then set them aside. "I'm in desperate need of a shower."

"It's all yours," Pixie said.

He gave her a look. "Don't tell me you got the kids bathed and managed a shower for yourself?"

"Consider me superwoman." She grinned. "I closed them in the bathroom with me and kept constant watch. I didn't get to wash my hair, but it'll be fine until tomorrow."

Wearing a look of admiration and tenderness, he reached over and brushed his thumb along her cheek. "You're amazing."

And I'm yours. Pixie turned her face to kiss his palm. "At least Ruthie is out of the picture."

"For now." He stood. "I'll make it quick."

"No need. We're fine." Pixie stretched out on her stomach near Shayna and looked at Andy's book with him.

It was time for her and Brogan to figure out their future. She decided she'd start tackling that tonight. Marlow had suggested that she tell Brogan how she felt. Since it hadn't been so long ago that Marlow had fallen in love with Cort, Pixie figured her advice counted for a lot. Of course, she always thought Marlow made great points. Her friend was a smart, savvy woman.

In a mere fifteen minutes, Brogan had finished. He wore a clean white T-shirt and sweatpants, which hung loose on his hips. Barefoot, he paused in the kitchen to warm up a bottle for Shayna.

"It's past her bedtime," he said as he rejoined Pixie in the living room.

"Andy's too. He's struggling to keep his eyes open."

"Sorry." Brogan kissed her, then helped her to her feet. "Honestly, you look beat as well."

"A little." Neither of them had gotten much rest the night before. Pixie hugged him and whispered, "I wouldn't change a thing. I need you to know that." Before Andy completely conked out, she lifted him and headed for the bedroom.

Brogan said, "Soon, we need to talk."

"I know," she said over her shoulder. "I'm looking forward to it."

The house was silent by the time Pixie left her bedroom. Brogan had put away the toys and refolded the blanket, but a living-room light was still on, and beyond that was a dim light coming from the enclosed porch. When she followed it, she saw Shayna asleep in her basket and Brogan dozing on the floor beside her.

He didn't have his sleeping bag out. One arm was folded up behind him to support his head. Smiling, Pixie looked at him. Things would have to change. She loved this cottage, but it only had one bedroom, and they couldn't all four sleep in it together.

At the same time, she didn't want him returning to the lake house. She knew Brogan now, so she knew that was his intent. He likely figured that with Ruthie out of the way, he should give Pixie back her space.

It saddened her that he didn't yet know what a remarkable person he was or understand how utterly easy it was to love him with her whole heart.

Intent on telling him, she shifted closer.

The second she moved, Brogan opened his eyes.

He looked so tired, yet there was a new serenity in his gray eyes. "Hey," he whispered.

Going to her knees next to him, she smiled. "I love you."

His eyes flared, then heated. In the next second, Pixie found herself gathered into his arms as he effortlessly stood and carried her to the couch in the living room.

He stood her before him, cupped her face in his hands, and asked, "You love me?"

"So much, I couldn't keep it inside."

His gaze searched hers, and he whispered, "Are you sure?"

She heard the yearning and the disbelief. "For the longest time, I couldn't imagine ever trusting another man, not in an intimate way. Not with my feelings."

"I understand."

Barely tempering her smile, she said, "No, Brogan, you don't. I had worked so hard for my independence, to regain some of my pride and self-worth. I'd forgotten what it meant to be a woman. A mom, yes. I think—I hope—I had that down."

"You're an amazing mom."

She kissed him for that nice compliment and whispered, "Then I met you, and suddenly I was thinking about being a woman, too. You're gorgeous—so, naturally, that stirred things up."

His crooked grin came slowly. "What things?"

"Let's just say I was suddenly aware of body parts that I hadn't paid much attention to."

"Like here?" He curved a hand around her breast. "And here?" He skimmed his lips along her throat. While he was doing that, effectively distracting her, he placed his hand on her inner thigh. Meeting her gaze, he pressed his palm to her and asked, "Here?"

Pixie could barely breathe. "All that, yes."

He kissed her for a long time, until she was dazed and trying to get his shirt off him, before he lifted his mouth and said, "God, I love you, too, Pixie."

Yay. "We'll work it out, okay? All of it. Any problems. Talking to Andy's grandparents, sleeping arrangements—"

"Living arrangements," he said tentatively. "With Ruth out of the way, I need to move back to the lake house, at least for sleeping. I know it's cramped here—not that I'm complaining, but for you—"

"I go where you go."

Two beats passed before he wrapped her in his arms, his face tucked down to her neck, his breath a little ragged. "I'll get things worked out. Job, housing, all that, because I want to be with you, too—you and Andy. I've already looked at some job prospects in the area, and there are houses near Lankton, where you work. I know you'd prefer to be on the lake, but—"

"Things have a way of working out here in Bramble. You'll see. Until then, we'll take it one day at a time."

"You're being generous," he said as he slowly released her. "The thing is, I have to pay my own way. I always have and I will always want to."

"You've already paid for a summer lease on the lake house."

"Yes, but I also want you to have choices."

Stubbornly, she said, "I choose you."

His smile this time was pure sunshine. "You have no idea how good that makes me feel."

It suddenly occurred to her that she was rushing him. His life had been in turmoil for so long—first because of life-threatening injuries, then the loss of his sister, taking guardianship of his niece, and the constant harassment from Ruthie. He'd come to Bramble, as she had, as Marlow had—as so many had—to find some peace and quiet so he could collect his thoughts and find his footing.

And here she was, pressuring him to commit himself.

"I'm sorry." Pixie sat back against the couch with a heavy sigh. "I'm usually not so forceful." But she'd felt so sure of herself and what they had together. It killed her to say it, but she got out the words. "If you want to go back to the lake house, I get it. We'll still see each other." *Just not as much.* "I'm sure you'd enjoy sleeping in a bed for a change."

Brogan slowly took the seat next to her. He also leaned back and then reached for her hand. Together, with each of them staring at nothing, they sat there.

After a moment, he said, "Just so we're clear, I don't need a bed. I'm comfortable enough on the floor. My issue is that I barged into your life, and you haven't had time to sort out how you really feel."

Pixie drew herself up to glare at him. "I know you're not suggesting that I'm so weak I don't understand my own feelings."

"No." His smile warmed even more and he oh-so-cautiously drew her down to his chest. "I would never underestimate you."

"Well . . . good."

"I thought you might like a breather, though, a chance to get back to your routine. We've been moving pretty fast, and it has to be a bit overwhelming."

To counter that statement, she demanded, "Are *you* overwhelmed?"

"A little." When she started to sit up, he locked his arms around her. "In all my plans to come here, to introduce Shayna and get your agreement for the kids to know each other, I never anticipated you. Your impact on me. The way your smiles do me in. How damned pretty you are. And friendly. And talented."

"Stop," she said, half-laughing, a little embarrassed, and even more turned on.

"I never considered that I'd take one look at you and start imagining impossible things. Things I gave up on years ago."

"They're all possible," Pixie softly promised. *As long as we're together.*

"I want you to be sure." His lips touched her temple, and in a raw voice, he said, "You have to be sure."

Because he couldn't take another disappointment, another

rejection. Oh, he'd be fine. He'd get by—just as he always had. But she wanted more for him, for them. So much more.

"Then we can do things your way," she grudgingly agreed. *For now.*

"I'll be at the lake house," he promised. "When you have free time, we can spend it together—as often as you want."

"I want coffee together in the morning," she insisted. "I want Andy to hug you good night, and I want to kiss Shayna good night."

"Done and done."

She shifted around to see him. "I want to know about any jobs you check out, and how your father is doing."

"Of course."

Pixie drew a breath. "And I want sex."

Those steely gray eyes of his smoldered. "Anytime."

As long as he was so agreeable, she added, "I want sleepovers on the weekend."

"Sleepovers?"

"Yes. I need a sleeping bag. We'll camp out right here on the living-room floor." If he could sleep on the floor, she could, too, especially if it meant being curled up with him. "I'll leave Andy's door ajar, and you'll be able to hear Shayna."

"And we'll be together." He did some tricky SEAL maneuver, and she was suddenly on her back with him over her. "I'll get your sleeping bag for you." Brushing his mouth over hers, he said, "I love you, Pixie. Always. Somehow I'm going to make this work."

July rolled in with a heat wave that could melt the fish in the lake. It reminded him of summers in northern Africa, but no longer in such a bad way. The memory of the covert op that went wrong didn't put his chest in a vise. It would never be a comfortable memory, definitely not a happy one—but there were happy moments mixed in. Goofy conversations with his brothers, bad jokes that made the rounds, pranks, and, occasionally, times when they'd truly been able to help innocent people.

Brogan figured it was all about balance. These days, the great memories far outweighed the bad, and he gathered more of them every time he was with Pixie.

They made that perfect little family unit he'd always considered unattainable, at least for him.

Not anymore.

Pixie was a greedy little thing, insisting on every second she could have with him, and God Almighty, he loved it so much. Loved *her* so much. The nights when he slept alone at the lake house grew fewer and further between. They'd fallen into such a natural rhythm together, it was honestly easier to stay at the cottage and sleep on the floor.

Pixie considered it an adventure, but that's because she usually slept more on him than beside him.

He'd interviewed for several jobs, but there was one in particular that excited him. It was consulting for a security firm behind the scenes as an intelligence analyst. Best of all, he could usually work from home.

The money was decent, the benefits—added to his VA benefits and disability pay—would be more than enough, so he'd accepted.

That was another new experience: discussing decisions with someone who got excited for him. Pixie had been thrilled with his plans, and she'd promised that she could help out with Shayna on the days he needed to be away, just as he now helped with Andy when she put in extra hours.

Today he let Andy play in a kiddie pool in the yard while he dipped in Shayna's toes. She happily kicked and squealed each time her feet touched the chilly water, and that kept Andy laughing.

He'd covered both kids in sunscreen and used a large beach umbrella to shade them. It was still broiling hot.

When his phone buzzed, he put Shayna on the big quilt in the shade and then sat in the lawn chair facing the pool so he could keep an eye on both of them.

He checked the screen and answered. "Hey, Erin."

"Sorry to call, Brogan."

Her tone told him it wouldn't be great news. "Is it Brian?" His father hadn't done much recovering. One complication after another, with an already-overtaxed system, had worked against him.

"I'm sorry, but he passed away."

"When?"

"A few hours ago."

Just then, Andy splashed toward Shayna. "Sorry, Erin, hang on one sec." He set aside the phone and went to explain to Andy. "We gotta be easy, bud, remember? I'll bring Shayna over to get her toes wet again as soon as I finish my call, okay?"

"My baby."

He grinned despite himself. "Your baby *sister* doesn't want water to hit her face, okay? It might make her cry."

Immediately concerned, Andy turned to look at her. "No, no, no," he said in a soft voice, shaking his finger at her.

Brogan kissed his head. "You are such a stellar big brother." He offered his fist. With a grin, Andy brought up his own small fist to tap it.

Returning to the phone, he said to Erin, "Sorry. I'm watching the kids."

"You're . . . okay?"

"I am." He was better than okay. "I'm sorry for Brian, but he was literally a stranger to me." He thought to ask, "How's Ruth taking it? Any idea?"

"That's the other reason I'm calling. She's gone. Took off.

It's been two weeks since anyone has seen or heard from her. The state will be burying your father, it seems."

Damn. Ruth couldn't even stick around for the funeral? "She hasn't seen Brian at all?"

"The hospital had been trying to reach her, but her phone number was reassigned. She's gone, Brogan. I checked, but she's taken all of her stuff from the house." Cautiously, she suggested, "Since you gave me power of attorney, I'd like to change the locks to make sure she doesn't pop back up, then hire a crew to clean the house so we can put it on the market. You okay with that?"

Just then, Pixie pulled into the driveway. Seeing her, Andy quickly stepped out of the pool, ready for a mad dash toward the driveway. "Sorry," Brogan said again to Erin as he dropped the phone to catch Andy before he got too far.

Shayna had wiggled enough that she was almost in the grass, so Brogan grabbed her, too, and then greeted Pixie with wiggling kids in his arms. Not a bad thing at all. In fact, these days he felt like the luckiest man alive.

"Hey," Pixie said, already out of her car and hurrying to lend him a hand. Her shirt stuck to her chest and wisps of her hair clung to her temples.

"You look wilted, babe. Everything okay?"

"The air-conditioning in the shop died. There aren't enough fans in Bramble to make a difference." She took Shayna from him. "Great idea on the pool, but Andy's soaked, so he's all yours." After saying that, she leaned forward to give her son a hug and a kiss, then went on tiptoe to kiss Brogan, too. "Mmm, you smell good. I'm melting and you look delicious."

Yes, *this*. The kids, the yard, the fresh air—the woman he loved kissing him when she got home. Or when he got home.

Honestly, life couldn't get any better.

"I've got Erin on a call. Mind taking over for just a minute?"

She set aside her purse. "Of course not."

He put Andy back in the pool, then reminded him, "No splashing Mam, okay? She isn't in her swimsuit."

With an impish expression, Andy immediately splashed anyway. "Legs only, Andy! Legs only," Pixie said while laughing; then she added, "Actually, that feels amazing."

He returned to the phone. "Sorry again, Erin. You know how it is with little ones."

"No," she said, stretching out the word. "Actually, I don't, but after hearing all that, I want to."

"You'd love it," he assured her. "They're amazing. Have I told you that Shayna is sitting up on her own now? She's even trying to crawl." Two months had made a huge difference in her development. Now she needed an actual baby bed, even when "camping out" with Pixie and Andy. "I'm anxious to see what she'll do next, and at the same time I don't want her to change." The thought of her walking, possibly getting into mischief, scared him. He laughed at himself. "Pixie told me that she's always felt the same about Andy."

"Crawling," Erin said in disbelief, and then with determination, she asked, "Do you think I could visit?" She rushed on, saying, "The last time I saw Shayna, she was basically still a newborn. It took me a little while to get over losing Connie. I was so used to seeing her here at the office, to shopping with her and sharing stories about my dates—especially the disappointing ones. My family is great, but Connie was like a sister, a best friend, and a confidant rolled into one."

"I know," Brogan said softly. "Connie included you in a lot of her notes. She loved you, too." He realized he'd not only let down Connie, he'd been unfair to Erin. "I'm sorry that on top of grieving, you had to catch me up to speed, and then handle all the legalities, too."

"No, that was my pleasure. Besides, I'm a person who always needs something to do. If I hadn't become obsessed with tracking you down and gaining your cooperation . . . I don't know, Brogan. I might have just fallen apart." She huffed out a sad laugh. "I know Shayna has changed a lot, and I'm intrigued by the idea of her brother."

Another amazing role model for Shayna? Count me in. "A visit would be great. Pixie would love to meet you in person, and I guarantee the kids are worth the trip." His lease on the lake house would be up after Labor Day weekend, but he hoped to have a permanent residence worked out by then. Regardless, he'd always make room for Erin in Shayna's life. "You're welcome to the area anytime. Unfortunately, neither house has a lot of room for overnight guests, and I don't know if I'll be settled in a new place by then."

With a smile in her voice, she said, "I'd be happy to get a room nearby."

"Butler, the mayor, owns an inn. I can hook you up."

"Listen to you, friends with the mayor."

Brogan cracked a grin. "It's not like that. This town is so small I could jog from one end to the other without getting winded. Everyone knows everyone." He wasn't an official part of Bramble, but he was accepted, even liked. Before Pixie, he wouldn't have welcomed such friendship. Now he relished it.

Hopefully, it'd work in his favor when he put forth his plans.

"Butler had a really outdated security system on the place. The building is old, and it's only busy on the weekends, so he hadn't bothered with it in years. I helped him update everything so it wouldn't cost him too much. He's been calling me 'son' ever since."

Erin snickered. "I take it that's an honor?"

"From Butler? Yes."

There was a slight pause before Erin spoke again. "You sound good, Brogan. I'm happy for you. I know Connie would be so pleased."

He still suffered a lot of guilt for cutting Connie out of his life, but Erin and Pixie reassured him often that Connie had understood. He prayed that was true. His guilt over surviving when his brothers hadn't . . . That had been out of his control, and now that life was so perfect, he was glad to be here. "Thank you."

"About the house?"

At one time, he'd considered living in it to keep Connie's memory fresh for Shayna. Then he'd found Brian and Ruth there, and later he'd met Pixie. Bramble was her home; so as much as possible, he'd make it home for Shayna and himself, too. "Feel free to do whatever needs to be done. I appreciate it."

"Perfect. I have vacation time coming up. I'll get the ball rolling here. Then I'll let you know when to expect me."

After a few more exchanges, they ended the call. Brogan turned back to his family—his *family*—almost choking on emotions too big to name.

Pixie had removed her sandals and sat in the lawn chair with her feet in the pool, dipping Shayna's toes much as he had. The difference now was that Andy, with his mother supervising, did a lot less splashing and spent equal time kissing Shayna and Pixie.

Brogan's heart was full as he approached them with a smile.

Pixie looked up at him. "Everything okay?"

He explained about the call, about Brian passing and Ruth disappearing. "It sounds like she took off right after her court stuff finished up."

With Shayna held close, Pixie stood and leaned into him. "How do you feel about that?"

"I'm fine," he promised, because he was.

She sighed, then tipped up her face. "Good, because I'd like to eat at the Dry Frog tonight."

"Marlow working?" Pixie often liked to grab a burger there to chat with her friend. Cort usually showed up, too. It always amazed him how Marlow could wait tables, carry on conversations, and still control the entire room. Knowing her better now, he easily understood Pixie's admiration.

"She's off tonight, but she and Cort will meet us there."

Nothing new in that, yet something about the way she fought a smile made Brogan suspicious. "So, what's up?"

"Oh, just a little special occasion for the locals." She passed Shayna back to him. "How's that sound?"

Definitely, she was up to something. Didn't matter. "Sure, sounds good." If it made Pixie happy, it made him happy, too.

"Perfect. Watch the kids a few more minutes while I shower and change?"

After another kiss, he said, "Sure, but they'll need to be changed, too."

"We'll do that together. Give me ten minutes." She grabbed her purse and headed inside.

That's how everything went, he realized. Teamwork. Always an easy plan.

An hour later, Brogan found himself in the middle of the entire town, or so it seemed. The tavern was packed with every local he'd ever met, and many he hadn't, though most of them looked familiar. One person after another greeted him. The way they all watched him ramped up his suspicions even more.

Butler grinned widely at him. It was unnerving, especially when the robust man insisted that he and Pixie should sit up front at a table placed in the center of the room.

These were Pixie's friends, people she cared about.

A town full of good, humble, and caring people. He wanted to make it his home, too, but he also had great respect for rules—at least, that is, rules that made sense.

When Butler went to the front of the room and "unveiled" an eight-by-ten framed photo of him in uniform, Brogan realized he was being honored. For what, he had no idea, but Pixie sure looked happy about it.

"Smile," she said, nudging him with her shoulder.

"Where did you get the pic?"

"Cort found it." Her beautiful face lit up with a smile while he suffered in the spotlight.

He twisted to see Cort at the table behind him. He and Marlow were together, watching Shayna and Andy in high chairs. Wade, Bobbi, and Gloria were with them.

Shayna hadn't stopped smiling at Gloria from the moment the woman sat down and started a game of peekaboo from behind her hands. Andy had loudly claimed his little sister by saying, "My baby."

The buzzing conversation in the room grew quiet when Butler started listing Brogan's "good deeds and acts of heroism"—*As if I'd done anything heroic*—and proclaiming that the town would honor him by putting his photo next to Cort's on the wall of the tavern. Okay, Brogan was military, and Cort was military, so that wasn't so bad, but still he felt his neck getting hot.

Chairs screeched on the floor as everyone stood and applauded. Cort lifted his glass of cola in a toast. Andy loved the fanfare.

Brogan, not so much.

Butler loudly cleared his throat. "Before we proceed—"

Proceed with what? Brogan wondered.

"—we have a few special guests."

Leaning close to Pixie, Brogan whispered, "What now?"

"Shh," she replied, still with that teasing smile.

Dee Pearson made her way to the front of the room, with Gunther Prader beside her.

Brogan barely bit back his groan. He scanned the crowded room and saw Gunther's wife, Lily, and son, Toby. Toby waved at him; so, naturally, Brogan had to wave back.

Given how she could embellish a simple act, Dee should have been a storyteller instead of a music teacher. The way she told it, Brogan had saved her from certain death during a horrendous storm. She went on to tell everyone that he still visited her to help with her heavy groceries, like big bags of dog food, canned goods, and lawn supplies. She shared every small gift he'd ever brought to her: flowers, treats for her dog, and a new cake pan she had mentioned wanting.

More applause exploded around the room.

Brogan seriously wanted to sink lower in his seat, but hey, a SEAL didn't do that, so he sat tall and dipped his head in gratitude.

Gunther started in next, also claiming that without Brogan's help, he would have died in a truck fire. He shared how Brogan had rescued his dog from the truck, earning an "aww" from everyone. Then he boasted—*As if it was a big deal*—that Brogan and Pixie had come to visit his family a few times now, always offering to lend a hand.

When the applause died down this time, Brogan hoped that was the end of it. He was starting to get hungry, damn it.

Instead, Ellen and Benny took the floor. Ellen stood behind her son with her hands on his shoulders and let Benny do most of the talking. Brogan had to admit, hearing the tale from the kid's perspective, it really had been a miracle that he'd gotten to Benny in time. Ellen shed some quiet tears while Benny showed off the scars on his forehead and forearm.

Ellen finished up by saying that thanks to Brogan's quick reactions and ability, she still had her son. She said she'd never again let him on the dock without a life preserver.

Brogan gave a firm nod of satisfaction. In his opinion, every kid who was near the water should be wearing one. Accidents happened all the time, and that one really could have ended in disaster.

Of course, Robin, owner of the Docker restaurant, came up next and announced to everyone that he'd helped her to come up with a safety protocol, which she'd posted near the docks.

And she even shared that he'd donated a dozen life preservers, which she'd customized with the restaurant's logo.

Pixie hadn't known about that one, so she turned to him in surprise. Covered by more clapping, Brogan whispered, "I did that while you were working. Didn't think to tell you about it."

"More like you were being modest, but that's okay." She gave him a quick kiss.

When the room quieted again, Cort walked up to the front.

This time, Brogan didn't bother hiding his groan. "There might be one more thing I haven't told you."

"I know," she said. "But Cort shared—and I love the idea."

Cort faced everyone. "Last year, when Marlow moved here, I petitioned to change the rules."

Everyone was back on their feet instantly, the cheers louder than ever.

Marlow joined Cort, all smiles, and announced, "Bramble is the best town ever!"

The noise became deafening. Concerned, Brogan checked on Shayna, but she was taking her cues from Andy, and Andy was loving it. Eyes wide, his little Sugar flailed her arms and squealed loudly.

Cort easily regained the room. "Pixie and Andy are officially part of the town; so, naturally, Brogan would like to be part of Bramble, too. However, he respects our rules and knows we're not allowing new construction on houses, so he's been looking in Lankton."

Everyone fell quiet. Brogan wasn't quite sure what that meant.

"He asked me about buying the lake house, which he's renting right now, so that he, Pixie, and the kids could still visit Bramble often."

More silence. Brogan felt uneasy now, but Pixie was still smiling.

"Marlow and I discussed it, and since Brogan's offer was fair, we'd like to accept—but with a little condition."

Wow. Okay. Brogan felt better now. As long as no one in the town complained about adding a few more visitors, he could go forward with his plans.

Pixie leaned close. "It's a wonderful idea. Thank you."

"I know how you love being close to Marlow."

Butler cleared his throat. "Cort discussed his plans with the board, and we agreed it's a fine idea. We put it to the town, and the town has also agreed." He unrolled a large sheet of paper and came over to place it on the table where Brogan and Pixie sat.

It was a floor plan. Brogan didn't understand.

"This is the lake house," Cort explained, pointing to an outline in red. "This will be an addition."

Wow! Overwhelmed, Brogan briefly studied the plans. One entire side of the house would be opened up to add two more bedrooms, with a bathroom between them. Office space was also added, and the way it was drawn, the room had two desks—meaning he and Pixie would share. Interior walls were shifted to expand the kitchen and sitting room.

They'd still be on the lake, Pixie would be even closer to her family, and there was room enough to raise two kids.

Never in his life had he received a gift—except Shayna. And then Pixie and Andy. And now this? He ran a hand over the back of his neck. "I don't know what to say."

"There's a caveat," Butler said, his tone lofty enough to tell one and all that he was in mayor-mode. "We have a lot of tradesmen in the area. Cort will be the contractor, and you'll need to hire local guys and buy the supplies in Bramble."

He'd been planning on buying a whole different house—so, of course, Brogan agreed.

"Everyone offered to pitch in their time," Cort informed him.

"I'll pay them," Brogan immediately insisted. Accepting an act of friendship or a helping hand was one thing, but for a job that size, people deserved wages.

With a slight smile, Cort said, "I told them you would."

Even after a deep breath, Brogan couldn't take it in.

Pixie took his hand. "Breathe. And try to smile."

He'd gone from being a loner, a man without family, to having the best family and friends, with roots in an incredible town. "I need a minute."

Cort clapped him on the shoulder. "Butler has one more thing to say."

Brogan pushed back his chair and stood.

Clearing his throat, Butler said, "This town could use a safety instructor. One day volunteered each month. A few hours in the afternoon with the school kids, then an evening here at the tavern for the adults."

"I'd be honored."

Cheers erupted.

Raising his hands, Butler said, "Bramble officially has two heroes. Let's get this photo on the wall."

Herman, owner of the tavern, surged forward with a hammer and nail. Once that was done, everyone looked at Brogan.

He wasn't big on speeches, so he kept it super short. "I'm honored. Each and every one of you has given me something I've never had before." He tugged Pixie up beside him, holding her close. "Roots. A real home." That suffocating weight was back on his chest, but this time in a good way. He felt full . . . of happiness. "You've given me a community."

For the next fifteen minutes, he shook hands and accepted hugs from so many people, he couldn't even see Pixie, much less Andy or Shayna, but he knew they were there. He could feel them, and he trusted the others to watch over them until the room finally settled down again.

That happened when Marlow shouted, "Let's eat!"

Fortunately, food had a way of getting people back to their seats in a hurry.

There was some rearranging as Marlow and Cort, with the kids, joined their table. They shared pizza and colas, laughs, and plans.

He was a part of them, of their group, and that was something he'd never take for granted.

While Marlow gave Shayna a bottle, and Cort fed some soft vegetables to Andy, Brogan put his mouth to Pixie's ear. "Will you marry me?"

Startled, she leaned back to stare at him, her beautiful eyes wide and happy. "When?"

"Now," he said softly. "Or a month from now. A year. I don't care. Actually, I do. I'd make it tonight if it was up to me, but I love you so much, I'm willing to wait as long as it takes."

Pixie covered her mouth. Then she grabbed his face and kissed him. A short kiss because she quickly leaned across the table to say to Marlow and Cort, "We're getting married."

Marlow smiled. "When?"

It amused him that both women had asked the exact same question.

Pixie gave them all a beautiful smile. "Very soon."

That night, after getting the kids settled in their beds, she and Brogan stepped out back to admire the fireflies blinking all along the shoreline. The moon cast a glow on the surface of the water, and other than the chirping of crickets and the occasional melodic croaking of frogs, the air was quiet and still.

A new sense of peace had settled over Brogan. Pixie understood. After Dylan had died, she'd been so vulnerable, completely alone with no one to turn to.

Brogan had lived with that feeling all his life.

Never again, she vowed. She stepped in front of him and wrapped her arms around his neck. "Hey."

"Hmm?"

"I like the idea of marrying right away."

"Good." His hand coasted up and down her back. "How soon is right away?"

"Well, there's no wait time for a marriage license in Kentucky. We could apply tomorrow and be married in the afternoon."

She'd barely finished before he was kissing her.

When she could, Pixie laughed and said, "Or we could talk to Erin, see when she'll be visiting, and include her."

"If she'll be here soon."

She loved his impatience because she felt it, too. "I don't need a fancy dress or ceremony. The very idea makes me itchy. Though I suppose I should let Andy's grandparents know, so . . . why don't we plan on two weeks?"

"I've waited a lifetime for you. I can wait fourteen more days." He tilted up her chin. "You've given me so much, everything I always thought was impossible."

"You gave me a lot, too."

"Incredible sex?"

Laughing, she swatted his chest. "That definitely counts, but in the process, you gave me back my self-esteem, my sexiness."

He growled against her throat. "You were always sexy. Never doubt it."

"You also gave me a daughter." Pixie rested against him. "I thought I could never have another child, and now I have a whole family."

"There's something magical about this town," Brogan said. "I felt it as soon as I drove in."

There was something magical about him. He'd brought love back into her life, and now they'd live together in their own lake house, near her closest friends—together. Her life had taken some twists and turns, but to end up here, with Brogan, Andy, and Shayna, she'd gladly go through it all again.

He put his arm around her. "Let's go in. Tomorrow we have wedding plans to make."

Have you read the first Firefly Summer novel?

THE GUEST COTTAGE

In this uplifting series debut, forgiveness and unlikely friendship blossom in the haven of a quiet lakeside town when two very different women bond over one man's betrayals.

Marlow Heddings is starting over. She's carried the outrage of her husband Dylan's affair with a younger woman—and the expectations of his family's powerful Chicago holding company—long enough. Now, after another devastating twist of fate, she's unapologetically moving on.

Arriving in tiny Bramble, Kentucky, Marlow revels in her freedom, swapping her executive suits for sundresses . . . and scouting places to open her dream boutique. Best of all is her new residence, an adorable cottage with gorgeous lake views—and a breathtaking landlord, former Marine Cort Easton. Soon they're sharing dockside morning coffee and nighttime firefly gazing. Marlow's new life feels like a dream.

Then Pixie Nolan arrives on her doorstep. With a shocking secret.

To Marlow's astonishment, Dylan's "other woman" is a desperate girl of twenty, destitute, exhausted, and disowned by her family. Defying her manipulative in-laws' demands, and surprising even herself, Marlow vows to lay down roots in Bramble and help Pixie get on her feet. Then they'll part ways. But empathy has a way of forging bonds. As Marlow grows close to the hardworking, devoted young woman, she becomes something of a big sister to Pixie.

Now, with each sunrise, Marlow awakens to the life she was truly meant to live, one filled with deepening connections, supportive friendship . . . and even a second chance at love.